FRAGMENTS THAT REMAIN

FRAGMENTS That Remain

a novel by
STEVEN CORBIN

Boston: Alyson Publications, Inc.

Published by Alyson Publications, Inc.,
40 Plympton St., Boston, Mass. 02118.
First edition: June 1993

Typeset and printed in the United States of America.
This book is printed on acid-free, recycled paper.

3 5 4 2

ISBN 1-55583-218-0

Library of Congress Cataloging-in-Publication Data
Corbin, Steven, 1953–
    Fragments that remain : a novel / by Steven Corbin. — 1st ed.
        p.   cm.
    ISBN 1-55583-218-0 (cloth) : $19.95
    1. Gay men—United States—Fiction. 2. Actors—United States-
-Fiction. 3. Afro-American gays—Fiction. I. Title.
PS3553.O64394F7 1993
    813'.54—dc20   93-1323
                                                                                 CIP

for
CARLOS PENICHET
1946 — 1990

Acknowledgments

Special thanks to my Band of Angels, who have been sent to love and nourish me unconditionally and who, in one way or another, contributed to my struggle and survival:

Victoria Brownworth, Guy Corbin, Warren Corbin, Cara De-Vito, Larry Ewing, Ross Farley, Bill Flanagan, Winifred "Fred" Hervey, Tonja Jefferson, Dorothy Love, Patrick McCollum, Terry McMillan, Donald O'Hare, Jr., Martin T. O'Hare, Yvonne Corbin-O'Hare, Bill Parks, Douglas Sadownick, Mark Simmons, Sheila Simms, Mitch Walker, and Bobby Watson.

Contents

Sunrise

SKYLAR IS TOSSING AND TURNING when he first smells smoke.

He blinks repeatedly to focus in the darkness. Sniffs the acrid air, noticing clouds of smoke wafting through the cracks of the closed door. The red numbers of the digital clock on his nightstand glow 1:18 a.m.

"Oh my God!" he shouts, tumbling out of bed, groping through darkness and shadows. "Shit!" he whispers, wringing his hand after touching the doorknob, unaware of its intense heat. He runs into the bathroom, clicks on the light, grabs a towel, and thrusts it under the cold-water faucet, inadvertently knocking medicine bottles, toothbrushes, and dental floss out of his way. His body tingles from the rush of heat enveloping the room. He is terrified of opening the door. But far more terrified of leaving it closed.

Loud, crackling flames, the intimidating height of the doorway, leap out and lick at him like spookhouse pranks. He covers his nose and mouth with the damp towel. Through flickering waves of fire and thickening smoke, he sees his invalid father rolled on his side, his back facing Skylar, the wheelchair at the foot of the bed. He lies immobile, lifeless. Skylar can't tell if he's dead, or unconscious.

"Daddy!" Skylar yells, the roar of the flames drowning him out. He must outwit the blaze to rescue his paraplegic father. He stiffens at the inevitability of having to enter the room.

When he spots an opening, he half lunges forward. But pulls back when the dancing flames merge. His forehead drips sweat from heat and anxiety, his black face turning blacker from the dingy clouds. He coughs and chokes violently, his chest inflating, lungs exploding. He paces quickly, on the verge of panic, his mind desperate for a strategy to penetrate the blazing room. His father remains immobile.

He stops pacing. Dizzy from the inhalation of thick fumes, he stands frozen, helpless, incapable of movement. His feet feel one with the floorboards, his alertness waning. Ready to jump through the raging flames devouring the door frame, his rubbery body begins a graceful sway, both arms blocking his face, when the director yells, "Cut!"

■

A loud buzzer sounds. A bullhorn amplifying the director's voice commands cast and crew to break for ten. Silence segues to chatter and laughter. Skylar remains on his mark, the angle of his head submissive. The impatient actor portraying his father leaps out of bed, hissing through clenched teeth. The cinematographer, assistant director, and script girl sigh. The director softly touches Skylar's shoulder. He winces. Pandemonium subsides as everyone empties the set, milling outside the building. It is quiet again and Skylar is alone with the director.

"Is there a problem?" the director asks, his gaze fixed on the cigarette being crushed beneath his toe.

"No," Skylar replies, unable to face him.

"This is the ninth take and you can't walk through the flames." Glancing over his shoulder, he lights another cigarette, which bobs in his mouth as he speaks. "I assure you, the costume is guaranteed fireproof."

"I know."

"And it's not too late for the stuntman to complete the take—"

"No," Skylar replies, more abruptly than he meant to. But he will not be deterred on this. "I insist on doing it ... myself."

"Are you afraid of fire?" He faces Skylar for the first time.

"What does that mean?"

"Just a question. Relax." He pulls deeply on the cigarette, then speaks, the smoke escaping his lips in short bursts. "I've got a schedule, a budget to adhere to—"

"I know, I know." Skylar still avoids eye contact. "Just give me time. I know I can do it." He doesn't care to discuss it any further. "I'll be in my trailer. See you in ten?" He walks away.

The sun blinds him when he steps outside the soundstage. All eyes gang up on him as he heads toward his trailer. No one speaks. They just look, exchange embarrassed glances with each other, and continue their conversations, their eyes trailing the principal actor.

He hears the low murmurs and imagines he's the object of the gossip. He gives less than a shit. For too long, he's waited on Hollywood. Now it can wait on him.

■

Opening his trailer door, he is stopped by the blond reporter from *Rolling Stone*, Brett What's-His-Face. Behind him stands a grinning photographer.

"I'm on assignment for the Skylar Whyte cover story," the reporter says. "I've been waiting since 7:00 this morning," he mews, glancing at his wristwatch. "And it's already after lunch."

"I understand," Skylar says. "But not now." Before the reporter can get another word in, Skylar is inside, the door shut behind him. The last thing he hears is the blond whispering to the photographer, "I bet you those blue eyes are contacts."

Inside, he lies down and, without thinking, begins the breathing exercises he learned in acting classes. Though he won't admit it, he's appalled by his inability to complete the scene. How many takes did John say it was already? It's never taken him that many takes to shoot anything—at least not on his own account. Most times, directors don't really know what the hell they want, though they get it by the third take. But this time it's on him. He could tell John what the problem is. But John's a director, not a therapist. Too long a story. Too little time. Besides, it's nobody's business. He empathizes with the obviously frustrated supporting actor who plays his invalid father. He's such a pro. And thanks to Skylar's mental blocks, the old man must repeatedly lie immobile in a sweltering room, sweating like a pig in the midst of man-made flames. Skylar's inner voice whispers the apologies his lips lack the strength to utter. Art imitating life. Sometimes it comes a wee bit too close.

He's shared many scenes with father characters. The plots and characterizations were usually distant from him or his experience. This film is different. As if painful demons from his past have been resurrected and scattered about the set. While they have their challenges, the scenes before and after the fire are, comparatively, little more than walk-throughs.

It's the damn fire.

Each time he awakens, smells the smoke, glances at the digital clock glowing 1:18 a.m., fact merges with fiction. In character, he slips in and out of motivation — vacillating between what he would actually do, and what he's supposed to do, according to the script. In return for all the grief the man's caused, Skylar could leave his real-life father helpless in a burning room. Put him out of his own misery. In good conscience, he believes he could let the man die. And why not, when he's done nothing but make life miserable for Skylar, his mother and brother? As for the fire itself ... well, that's another story.

He's reminded of his boyhood prayers. Beginning with: Now I lay me down to sleep. Ending with: Please, God, take my father away from our house. Don't let him hit my mother again or curse her and make her cry. It was comforting that, despite his helplessness, there was always prayer. As the eldest child, unable to come to his mother's aid in domestic quarrels, he struck a deal with God. Take my father away from us, he prayed, and I'll never become an actor.

Like the time Skylar had turned seven. His mother had thrown a party. Invited the neighborhood children, Cassandra, Bridget, Lamont, and Kenny-Boy. She had mailed out invitations — a cowboy youngster riding a rocking horse — and followed them up with telephone confirmation from the parents. She had washed and scrubbed the house. She fried chicken, mixed a cherry-flavored punch with fresh lemons, and baked a devil's food cake with chocolate icing, planting seven blue-and-white-striped candles on it. She twisted blue crepe paper into spirals and taped it from wall to wall, the streamers crisscrossing, hanging low in the center of the room. She blew up blue and pink balloons — all the while complaining about her short-windedness — then rubbed them against her body, and stuck them to the wall.

Mixing Ajax and a few drops of water with her fingers, she wrote, "Happy Birthday, Skylar," on the dining room mirror. She tacked a grinning, tail-less donkey to the door, rinsed an empty Nehi for spin-the-bottle, and handed out noisemakers to the children.

Opening gifts, Skylar was standing at the head of the table when his father insisted his meticulously wrapped box be opened last. As Skylar hastily unwrapped it, and the children and their mothers watched with gleeful curiosity, shouting and egging him on to rip open the box, his fingers tearing at the paper this way and that, he noticed his mother wasn't smiling. Maybe she knew. How could she have known?

He wasn't sure how to react when he parted the tissue and pulled out a pink-lace-and-cotton party dress. The room turned silent. Brows furrowed with confusion. He had seen the dress before. Pointing at the mannequin modeling it in Macy's window one recent afternoon, her strawlike blonde hair curled at the shoulders, he'd called it pretty. His mother agreed. His father didn't. He objected to the boy's use of the word "pretty."

Kendall, his younger brother, stared at the dress, fingering the lace, giggling. Skylar's mother cleared the kitchen of children and mothers, and asked them to proceed to the living room for pin-the-tail-on-the-donkey, her left eye twitching. Skylar knew that twitch.

"What the hell you call yourself doin'?" she said, her voice struggling to stay low, a voice that would've roared had the family been alone.

"He liked it, didn't he?" his father said, jabbing at his molars with a toothpick. "He said it was 'pretty.'"

"Can't he say 'pretty'? Christ Almighty. He's only a little boy—"

"Is he?"

There's a knock on Skylar's trailer door. He doesn't respond. Instead, he turns over and folds a pillow around his ears. His agent is whispering through the door, asking if Skylar's indisposed.

"I'm sorry," his agent says. "But I need to speak with you ... It's urgent."

Urgent? Skylar thinks. But he trusts Allen and knows he wouldn't disturb him unless absolutely necessary. He wouldn't even be here on the set, he's thinking, as he jumps up to answer the door.

"Sorry to disturb you like this, Sky," Allen is saying, his darting eyes taking quick inventory of the trailer's interior.

"What's up, man?" Skylar asks.

"Afraid I got some bad news," Allen says, planting himself at the makeup table. "Your mom called the office and—"

"She all right?" Skylar is suddenly alert.

"As well as could be, I imagine," Allen says. "It's your father, actually. He's in the hospital—"

"Oh, that?" Skylar chuckles to himself. "You came all the way out here to no-man's-land to tell me that—"

"It's serious," Allen says, dropping his glance. "Your mom says this time he's dying..."

Skylar

IT'S ONE THING TO BE CALLED a nigger by a stranger.

Quite another when you're sleeping with him.

Skylar is dialing the sixth digit when he decides to hang up. After last night's altercation, Evan'll probably slam the phone down in his ear. It's not as if they don't often fight, or engage in frequent domestic bickering. Just that last night's viciously waged verbal scrap will not be easily forgotten nor forgiven for some time, if at all.

"Medical reports and research claim," Evan had been explaining nonchalantly, as he walked into their Upper West Side townhouse, bringing Skylar into the middle of the story, "that African and Caribbean countries are the prime breeding grounds for AIDS."

"Oh yeah?" Skylar replied calmly, knowing that basically Evan was just trying to start some shit, one of the more obvious stunts he pulls when he's made plans to spend the evening with someone else. Skylar refused to give in that easily. He continued watching a painfully predictable *Hill Street Blues* rerun. Hardly one of his favorite shows. No die-hard *Blues* fan here. Just a timely diversion from whatever neurotic attention Evan wanted to call to himself.

The telephone rang, putting their unfolding feud on hold for the moment. Skylar could tell by the lightning speed of Evan's dive for the telephone that he was expecting a call. Probably his date. But for the past half year or so Evan seemed enamored with, and utterly delighted by, anyone speaking on the other end of the telephone. It could've been the man from HBO, scheduling an appointment to hook up their cable. Yet, Evan crooned and chortled as if he were speaking with Ed McMahon about his having just won the sweepstakes. This was how he addressed everyone these days. Everyone but Skylar.

"Hey!" Evan yelled into the mouthpiece. "Glad you called."

Skylar tried hard to concentrate on the television. But one ear listened to the Crazy Eddie commercial, the other to Evan. He thought of asking him to speak lower, or to use the phone in another room. But he knew Evan was doing it to irritate him. He refused to tug at the bait.

"Did you really?" Evan said, his voice booming. Then he laughed — what Skylar construed to be — that phony, forced laugh. "That sounds fine," Evan said. "I just got in myself, but I'll see you in a bit, okay? Ciao!" He hung up the phone, and his vivaciousness gave way to his brooding former self. The before and after, Skylar called it. Gone from Evan were the smile, the laughter, the sparkle in his eye, the lilt in his voice. How can I not take this personally? Skylar thought. It angered him more than Evan's crack about AIDS originating in Africa. Watching Daniel J. Travanti and Veronica Hamill unleash their passion for each other on the television reminded Skylar of his blissful beginning with Evan. He wondered where it had gone.

"Did you hear what I said earlier, Skylar?"

"No."

Evan read his silence as a refusal to fight, Skylar knew. Evan started opening bureau drawers and banging them shut, looking for a Gianni Versace shirt, so he said.

"Have you seen it, Skylar?"

"Do I look like the maid or the valet?"

Evan persisted with his grand opera of noise. He stomped around the apartment, swore, muttered to himself, and slammed doors from room to room.

"Why do you even watch that program?" Evan said, reappearing in the living room, flustered, his blond hair stringy, spaghetti-like, pasted to his forehead with sweat.

"Why not?"

"You're always criticizing it," Evan said. "Even though you've worked on the show, you're always bellyaching about the network's alleged unfairness to minority actors."

Skylar let that one settle a moment, watching the television lovebirds nearly swallow each other with deep, ravenous kisses. The network went to commercial.

"How many times do I have to tell you?" Skylar said. "I've been formally trained in the theater, only to wind up playing a menagerie of street-savvy punks, ex-cons, rapists, and murderers." Evan had never had one acting lesson in his life. Nor did he have stage experience. Skylar hoped the "formally trained" crack would chill Evan out. Evan hated when Skylar pulled rank; hated the power it had to reduce him.

"Well, if integrity's such a virtue in your career," Evan rebutted, "then why accept the role in the first place?"

"Because I'm not white, or blond, that's why, okay? I don't have as many choices as you. Something you wouldn't understand."

"What do you mean?"

"What do you mean, what do I mean?"

"You know what I mean."

"I'm sure I don't know what the fuck you mean!"

Skylar was getting bored with this. It was becoming a tedious pattern. Recently, they had fought about the Bensonhurst racial incident, where a black youth had been shot and killed. All because Skylar had asked — of someone else on the phone, mind you, not even asking Evan — what could be done about the boil on the ass of America called Bensonhurst? Some months before that, it had been over the so-called "wilding" gang-rape of a white woman by black youths in Central Park. The mere fact that Evan repeated the term "wilding" in their house — a term perpetuated by the New York press to stir further anti-black sentiments of fear, loathing, and distrust — thoroughly pissed Skylar off. Leaving the theater one night, they fought over a Spike Lee film, to the amusement of bystanders waiting in line for the next showing. Evan criticized the inclusion of Malcolm X, whose quote the director juxtaposed on screen as "the last word."

"Fair-weather hypocrite," Evan mumbled, stomping past Skylar into the kitchen.

"Shhh!" Skylar hissed, leaning forward from the sofa to turn up the television volume.

"So, what do you think? Huh?" Evan carried on, relentlessly. "Think AIDS is bred in Africa? After all, you're the self-appointed spokesman for black America, right? So, enlighten us with your opinion."

Skylar remained silent for a long while, hoping Evan — who stood looming above him awaiting a reply — would shut up. "I don't have one. Now, would you be quiet. I'm trying to watch TV—"

"My point is, if that's true, then I could possibly catch AIDS from a black person."

Nothing. Not the African theory. Not the "wilding" crack. Not even the Malcolm X versus Martin Luther King battle they'd waged countless times, had caused Skylar to lose the control he was on the verge of losing at that moment.

"You wanna know where AIDS came from?" he shouted, seemingly leaping off the sofa in a single bound and clicking off the television, all in one fluid movement. "It probably came from the filthy, animalistic, barbaric sexual practices of white boys in bathhouses, public parks, and restrooms. That's where it's bred. Twenty-five-cent peep shows. Glory holes. West Side docks. Shitting on each other. Golden showers. Pissing in each other's mouths. And let us not forget fist-fucking!"

"You're probably more racist," Evan yelled, "than any lyncher from the backwoods of Mississippi I could think of."

"Does that make you feel better about yourself?"

"You're just like them. Malcolm X, Huey Newton. Assholes. And if you sympathize with them, then you're a nigger just like them!"

"What did you call me?"

Skylar reached for the nearest object. It just so happened to be the original Picasso ceramic they purchased together in Barcelona at Evan's insistence. Several thousand dollars splattered against the wall into God knows how many pieces. Evan was out the door. An escape so swift he didn't bother waiting for the elevator. Just screamed, "Crazy Nigger!" as he descended the stairwell, the words, "*Crazy Nigger!*," reverberating through the tiled foyers. He hadn't found the Gianni Versace shirt he had been searching for. Good — let him buy another one! His face and name were so recognized (far more than Skylar's, even though Skylar had worked at his craft longer with a sacrifice that wasn't even part of his lover's vocabulary) that the salesperson would probably give Evan the shirt free for merely gracing the store's aisles with his celebrity.

Leaving the phone booth after hanging up, finding his way back to the lobby, Skylar is replaying last night in his thoughts, while the soothing voice on the intercom calmly pages Doctor So-and-So to report to...

Skylar hates hospitals. In his mind, hospitals epitomize sickness and death. His favorite uncle died in a hospital, tortured by a body suffering from third-degree burns. The doctors said approximately 35 percent of his body was severely, irreparably damaged. If he lived, they confided to his mother, chances were he'd be a vegetable. "Better off dead," his mother said softly enough for only Skylar to hear.

"Excuse me, ma'am?" the doctor spoke up.

"He's lived a full life," she said before turning away, heading toward the chapel to pray for his salvation.

He refuses to see his dying father without his mother. She said she'd meet him here in the lobby by three-thirty. It's almost four o'clock. Traffic being what it is, she'd be lucky to get here by four-thirty. There's a vein throbbing, pulsating within him, a vindictive urge to stand over the old man's bed and gloat, a fantasy of refusing to forgive his father his sins. But Skylar can't bring himself to do this to the man who's half-responsible for giving him life. Nor can he, at this late date, begin to love the man either.

Though his mother professes no more love for the dying man than Skylar does, she remains the go-between. She's the bridge linking Skylar to the estranged male who, over the years, has called himself Skylar's father. With her by his side, he'll feel less uptight, more apt to relinquish the bad blood they harbor for each other. His mother is the mediator. The peace pipe. The conduit without which he can't reach his father at all. Better off dead...

While waiting, he mentally pats himself on the back for thinking thoughts other than those which orbit around the planet that calls itself Evan. Perhaps his love for Evan is beginning a slow evaporation. Yet he feels nagged, harassed, and pulled at by the prevailing question of why they can't enjoy regular, uncolorful, banal arguments, like the regular, uncolorful, banal couple they're not.

I'm so glad you're finally home! I've got a great idea—
Please, not now.
C'mon. It'll only take a minute.
Gimme a large break here!
Okay, okay. You don't have to yell.
You're right. I'm sorry.
Let's start over, shall we? ... How about a movie tonight?
Nah.

Wanna get a bite to eat at—

You go ahead. I'm not up to it.

What's wrong?

Bad day.

That all?

Bad mood.

You poor baby.

I'm not fit for humans tonight.

Would you like a massage? I can order take-out, maybe rent a video. How's that?

I don't deserve you.

Tell me about it.

He picks up a past issue of *People.* On the back of the magazine, his gaze is met by a full-page ad of a posing, expressionless Evan. His brown eyes are hidden behind aviator sunglasses. His right arm cradles a crash helmet. The shirt collar is splayed sufficiently to display the chest hairs, sprouting bushlike. Facial expressionlessness oozes attitude. The left hand clutches a burning cigarette between the middle and index fingers. Worn, faded jeans boast an abundant crotch. Beside his face, the caption reads: Light My Lucky.

Althea

HE WOULD HAVE TO die on me now.

Just when I get to show him what I'm really made of.

She sits in the backseat of a gypsy cab, stuck in congested midtown Manhattan traffic. Determined pedestrians weave in and out of the gridlock. Truck and cab drivers hurl insults, leaning on their horns, shooting one another the finger. The cabbie punches his steering wheel. He apologizes via the rearview mirror to the attractive, executive-type, middle-aged black woman in the back. She nods, accepting the apology, before withdrawing from his complaints of the "friggin' New Yawk humidity" by settling into a nest of her thoughts.

When Althea Hutchinson accepted the one and only marriage proposal of her life, she was ecstatic — an ecstasy laced with apprehension about marrying out of her league. It wasn't the standard fate of a young colored girl of her origin and background to luck out with an engagement to a colored, college-educated CPA. She was the undisputed envy of her friends and neighbors. A bandwagon also joined by each of her six sisters.

"Girl, you gonna have it made."

"Gonna be livin' high style."

"Just like one of them white ladies."

"And he a pretty yaller nigger too, with them green eyes and wavy hair."

Her parents, two Southern-born-and-bred, blue-collar workers with no more than sixth-grade educations, couldn't thank God enough. Everyone entertained nothing but the best of wishes and prayers for the newly engaged couple. To love each other faithfully until death do them part. Have stairstep babies, one commemorating each year of matrimonial bliss. Purchase a home on the outskirts of Brooklyn Heights and erect a white picket fence. Get a dog or two. Play bridge or canasta with the girls one day a week. Volunteer free time with the PTA. Become den mother for the Boy Scout troops her sons belonged to. Everyone wished her this unselfishly, which was more than a mouthful for a nineteen-year-old Negro girl from Harlem in 1951. Everyone, that is, except her in-laws, who felt their son was marrying beneath him.

She was petrified of these people. These light-skinned colored folks with "good" hair, their green and hazel eyes gawking at her like she was a sideshow freak, who spoke pretentious English and used large words when small ones would've done just fine. They were marginally polite to her — as in "Hello" and "Good-bye" — otherwise holding intense conversations and intellectual debates among themselves, which usually passed over her head. She wasn't versed enough in the laudable organizational work of A. Philip Randolph, or the orchestral progressions of Duke Ellington's compositions.

So, planted beside her fiancé in his family's parlor on a Sunday afternoon in Jersey City, while his sister played Toccata and Fugue in D Minor on the piano, she listened closely, soaking up the fresh knowledge, smiling occasionally, hoping someone would smile back. Mostly, only Howard returned her smile. "Be a lady," her mother had reminded her. "Don't give them highfalutin folks no reason to think you is lowlife or that you don't come from no good trainin'. Speak when spoken to. A lady's to be seen, not heard." Those were her mother's words. Her mother's wisdom. And she sat, head erect, hands clasped in white gloves, too dignified to sweat, hoping someone, aside from Howard, would speak to her about something other than the wonderful weather they were having, or the latest European fashion trends as envisioned by Christian Dior.

The clannish way in which the Whytes patronized or ignored her might just as well have made them a bunch of white folks who hadn't quite caught on to the notion of desegregation. She could've been in the midst of the Rockefellers, the Carnegies, or the Kennedys of Hyannis and not found much difference. When her mother-in-law to be — a calculating, Rock of Gibraltar matriarch, devoid of mirth — addressed her directly, she froze.

"Where'd you say you went to school, girl?" Mrs. Whyte said, impatiently, her facial expression letting it show that she'd already made up her mind about Althea. And Althea hadn't said anything earlier about where she'd attended school. Eyes and heads turned in the direction of this dark brown woman who stood out among them because of her complexion. She even heard someone *Shhsh*-ing! the children as they eagerly awaited her reply.

"Well, ma'am, uh, I, um...," she floundered. Take your time, a voice in her head instructed her. Gather your thoughts. Take a deep breath. Speak slowly. "I attended Dunbar High—"

"High school," Mrs. Whyte repeated, in mock amazement, glancing at her family, whose grins were about to burst into laughter. "I'm not talking about high school, child. Where did you go to college?"

"Well," Althea said, looking to Howard, who held her hand. "Actually, I only finished the tenth grade—"

"The tenth grade."

"Yes, ma'am. You see, I'm the middle child in a family of eleven. I had to quit school to help out with, you know, the household and things — stuff like that." She heard someone gasp. Another suppressed a snicker.

"What did your father do?" Mrs. Whyte's eyes narrowed, as if she were having difficulty seeing Althea.

"He was a janitor at Columbia. And my mother, well, she, uh..." She trailed off, noticing that the eyes which had narrowed in judgment had now become slits. "She used to work for Jewish women in midtown—"

"A domestic," Mrs. Whyte interrupted her for the third time. The jagged lines around her eyes revealed the only emotion Althea would ever read in the old woman's face, in all the years she would know her.

"Yes, ma'am," Althea replied, sheepishly. She'd never been ashamed of her mother's vocation. Not until now.

"Well, a snowball would have a better chance in hell," Mrs. Whyte declared, "than I would, cleaning up the filth of some white woman's house."

They probably wouldn't hire you, Althea couldn't help thinking. You ain't dark enough, for one thing. She considered coming to her mother's defense. But manners and diplomacy, her parents had taught her, were the best weapons against folks like these, who walk through life with upturned noses, like they smell something bad. Never stoop to their level. And fear only God. As the chorus of snickering and throat clearing rolled like a wave across the stuffy parlor, Althea excused herself and retreated to the bathroom. She climbed the staircase in high heels as quietly as possible. Couldn't stand the idea of calling more attention to herself than she had already. In the bathroom she locked the door, leaned against it, and closed her eyes. This was going a lot worse than she'd expected.

She turned on the cold-water faucet, began removing her white gloves, and stared at herself in the mirror, picking herself apart. She saw that in their presence, everything about her screamed inferiority. When she'd purchased it two days ago, she'd thought this was about the smartest, most elegant dress she'd owned. And then she saw what the Whyte women were wearing. Her eyes turned red and moist and mascara streaked her cheeks. Already she'd been reduced to tears. Dinner had yet to be served. She was splashing water on her face when she was startled by soft taps on the door.

"Yes?" she said, keeping the tears out of her voice.

"It's me," Howard whispered. "Open up, baby."

She unlocked the door. He entered and locked it again.

"You have to forgive them," he whispered, softly kissing her eyes, her ears, her neck, her cheeks. "They're just overly concerned about who I'm marrying, like any family would be."

Althea didn't think her family would be overly concerned, nor would they behave that way. But she kept it to herself, not wanting to distract him from comforting her. Still, she had something to say. She'd never forgive herself if she didn't.

"Honey," she whispered. "I'm not sure ... if ... you know, if I fit in—"

"It's really nothing, baby, really. My two sisters-in-law endured the same kind of first meeting, but they survived—"

"It's more than that. I don't know any of them names they talk about. I ain't educated like they are." She started getting panicky. "I don't know who Thoreau is, or, um, Langston Hughes, and, uh, what's-his-name, Forkner—"

"Faulkner."

"See, that's what I mean."

He smiled at her. She couldn't tell if he was laughing with her or at her.

"That's what I love about you, Althea. What you're talking about is nothing more than knowledge you could get from books. You can read, can't you?"

"Yeah, but I ain't read a book since—"

"Don't say 'ain't.'"

"Why?"

"It's incorrect grammar, that's why."

She didn't like the sound of that. What difference should it make —"isn't" or "ain't"? But he was right. She couldn't argue with logic.

"I'll teach you everything I know," he said, cradling her cheeks between his scratchy palms. "I prefer a simple woman like you, anyway, without all that sophistication. I need a partner who'll stand behind me, and raise a family. I want someone there when I get home from work. It's tough being colored in an all-white accounting firm, where they'd rather hide me in the broom closet. But it's a new day for the colored man."

That was it. That's what she adored about this man. Her heart paused when she heard colored men talk like that. And this one was hers. Yes, she would take his name. And have his babies.

"Another thing," he said, wiping her tears with his palms. "Having a domestic for a mother, and a janitor for a father, is nothing to be ashamed of."

"I ain't ... I mean, I'm not ashamed." She inhaled a final sniffle, dabbing at her nose with shredded toilet tissue, laughing inside at her frailty. She never divulged the true cause of her tears. It wasn't his mother's condescension or prejudgment of her parents. She could hear, ascending the staircase to the bathroom, his mother soliciting wagers as to the dark girl's virginity.

During the first year of marriage, Howard and Althea moved into a quaint but cramped three-room apartment. Summer of '52. He loved her enough to ignore his family's advice and move from the middle-class Jersey City neighborhood of his youth and cross the Hudson to establish new roots. She was happier and more at peace than she'd ever been in her life, a happiness augmented by the recent news that she was pregnant. For the child inside her, she was bold enough to dream of a universe traditionally denied members of the colored race. She envisioned the world, the infinite sky, for this new being growing inside her. A world she didn't dare dream of for herself.

She spent her daylight hours meticulously carrying out wifely responsibilities. She rid the sparsely furnished apartment of dust particles that had settled since she'd last cleaned the day before. She cooked meals that challenged her culinary limits. Performed feats with pots and pans that would make Betty Crocker herself seem mundane by comparison.

Living in a corner apartment above a pharmacy in Harlem had its pros and cons. Except for the occasional racket of traffic and children's voices, the apartment was peaceful. There was a nice breeze in the summer evenings off the Harlem River. The relatives she wouldn't dream of leaving lived within walking distance in any direction. Her in-laws were conveniently separated from her by a threatening body of water. She knew not to expect any visits from them. And, it was a welcome change worrying about feeding two and a quarter mouths instead of the thirteen she'd been used to.

No more morning alarms screaming in her ear. No clocks to punch for a meager salary. She was a housewife. Howard took good care of her. Surprised her on several occasions with tickets to hear Billie Holiday at the Apollo, or Paul Robeson speaking at a peace rally in Randall Park. Those were the days of an endless string of surprises, whether roses, a Hoover vacuum cleaner, or ringside seats at an Archie Moore bout.

But in time, though he professed to have married her for certain reasons — the reasons he outlined so articulately to her that afternoon in the bathroom — he began to hold those very reasons against her.

If she had it to do all over again, she would tell him to go to hell. Perhaps spit in his face, if she'd known then what she knows now.

"Mama, why don't you leave him?" she could hear a wise-beyond-his-years Skylar asking, barely eleven years old.

"What you mean, leave him? That's your father you talking about. Where you hear talk like that?"

"Friends."

"Oh?"

"When their parents don't get along, one of them leaves. It's usually the mother."

"I see. So, you think I should leave, huh?"

"Yep."

"And go where?"

He shrugged. "I haven't thought about that part."

"Well, maybe you should. Then we'll talk about it, okay?"

She had made a mistake. Aside from giving life to two beautiful boys, the mistake of a lifetime. A mistake her children were still paying for. This is where she draws the line. The suffering shouldn't be theirs. And the guilt she harbors because of it is, she thinks, insurmountable.

The good Lord said to honor thy mother and thy father. A proverb she found herself reiterating to her boys. They were to love Howard, honor him, never speak a harsh word against him. She taught them that with as much conviction as she taught them the Golden Rule and Mother Goose. Yet she knew that Skylar, her oldest, had every justifiable right to deplore the man from whose loins he had issued. He'd earned it. Long and hard. Poor Skylar, she would think. Had she gone through with her father what he endured with his, she's not sure she would've survived. Kendall, the younger, Howard's blatant favorite — now that's another story. Ironic that Skylar's fate shot him to the heavens, while Kendall's pitched him into hell.

She spots her elder son, her darling boy, dozing off in the hospital lobby, an opened *People* magazine spread across his lap. He reminds her of the tenacious five-year-old he once was, begging to stay up past his bedtime, trying to keep awake in the easy chair to witness Santa's slide down the chimney, his head fallen to one side, mouth agape, drooling. She wakes him with a smooch on the forehead which startles him. Groggy, he embraces her longer than he ever has, surrounded by a room full of strangers. When she sits beside him, this child who reminds her of her brother, Aubrey, he takes her hand, intertwines his fingers with hers, and squeezes.

"Looks like his time has finally run out," Skylar whispers. "So, let's—"

Before he can complete his thought, she covers his mouth with her hand, a stern look on her face. He's still your father and my husband, her eyes say. How dare you be so disrespectful, Skylar Edward Whyte? I know I raised you better than that! She didn't stand for that kind of talk before and she won't now. He and Kendall are not to hate their father. Period. She's bursting with enough hatred for the dying man to suffice the next two generations. Skylar reads his mother's facial reprimand with precision and cuts himself off in midsentence.

Together they walk, hand in hand, a coupling of strength. They listen intently as the registration desk nurse directs them to the semiprivate room on the sixteenth floor. "Excuse me, sir," the nurse says impulsively, bright-eyed and perky. "But are you Skylar Whyte, the actor?"

He smiles halfheartedly, making his way toward the elevator, disappearing into the shadows of the whitewashed corridors.

Kendall

"YO, BLOOD, WHAT IT BE LIKE?"

He grunts a response to Junebug, the towering shooting gallery owner, who glances furtively up and down 116th Street before closing the rickety door behind them.

"Yo, my man," Junebug says, speaking to Kendall's back. "Last week, I saw your brother, Skylar, on *Hill Street Blues*. That lucky m'fucka!" Junebug is laughing, coughing up phlegm. "He big-time now, ain't he?"

Kendall grunts again, climbing the rickety staircase, whose deteriorating foundation sways and squeaks as the two men climb up to the second landing.

When he enters the gallery, a dozen or so men are grouped around a table, which is empty except for the three-quart pickle jar that serves as centerpiece. The jar contains a pink mixture of water and human blood. The room is stuffy, reeking of sweat, bad breath, funk from filthy, unkempt bodies. Overhead, a naked Sylvania bulb hangs, shedding feeble light. A few of the men acknowledge his arrival. Others ignore him, lost in the ritual, preoccupied with the spike in their veins, gingerly squeezing the nipple. Dark blood rises in eyedroppers ... Bang! Bang! Then disappears ... Shoot! Shoot!

"Yo, everybody. This here one o' my main men, Kendall." Junebug throws a beefy arm around Kendall's neck. "Not only is he one o' my best customers, but his brother a fuckin' movie star. Dig that!"

"Oh, yeah?" one person says in a raspy voice, without lifting his head, concentrating on the needle sunk in the fold of his arm.

Junebug starts laughing, shaking his head. "Y'all m'fuckas don't even know who his brother is. He the hottest thang since Sidney Po-tee-yay. Y'all need to pull y'all heads outta that cooker for a minute."

Kendall knows these junkies don't give a shit about nobody's movie star. If he and Skylar weren't brothers, Kendall probably wouldn't either. What impresses a junkie is how good the dope is, and judging by the faces sagging, the heads nodding, the vocal chords dropping, there's a handful of impressed dopeheads in this room, which makes Kendall tingle with anticipation.

"How'd you get your hair to dread?" someone asks. Last thing Kendall wants right now is to discuss his dreadlocks.

"Why did you do it?" another disembodied voice rings out.

Because it's a statement of ethnicity and the politically correct way to wear my hair, you stupid-ass mothafucka, Kendall thinks.

"I mean, is it a style or a—"

"It's my response to Jheri curls," Kendall says.

"I been wanting to wear my hair like yours, that Bob Marley kinda shit," the first brother admits. "But my ol' lady say she ain't sleepin' with no nappy-headed Rasta. And if I do it, she say I could kiss her ass good-bye. How you do it, man?"

"Ain't nothing to it, but to do it," Kendall says, indifferently. "Twist your hair into the size dreads you want. Keep on doing it, till the hair gets matted and locks."

Kendall recalls his mother's reaction to his dreadlocks, when he started them.

"Kendall James Whyte!" she exclaimed. "What you doin' to your hair?"

"I'm dreadin' it, Ma."

"Mmm, hmm. And from where I stand, I'm dreadin' it too!" She touched his hair, cautiously, then sniffed it, her mouth twisted as if she tasted something putrid. "When's the last time you washed it?"

"Last week. I can't wash it a lot right now, or they'll come out."

"Worse things have happened. Walking around here, lookin' like Medusa. You need to get those snakes cut off your head, boy."

If it were Skylar, he thinks, she would've been less critical.

One of Junebug's customers, who's been trying, unsuccessfully, to get a hit in his vein, starts swearing about his clogged spike.

"Again?" someone says. "Maybe it ain't clogged, blood. Maybe you just ain't got no m'fuckin' veins left." They roar with laughter, slapping each other high and low fives around the table. The disgruntled customer begins unlacing his shoe. He pulls off a stiff, dirty sock and, with needle in hand, zeroes in on the large vein leading from his big toe. When that doesn't work, he demands another set of works from Junebug.

Kendall is settling down at the table when another brother whose face he's seen in and around the circuit asks, "Who's this movie star you're related to?" He doesn't reply. Busy unfolding the aluminum foil of Chinese rocks he copped from the Ricans on Avenue B, he unbuckles his belt and slides it free of the pant loops. Before he can answer the brother in his own good time, Junebug cashes in on the opportunity.

"Skylar Whyte," Junebug says.

"No shit!" the brother says, surprised. He studies Kendall's features. "Yeah, now I can see the resemblance. So, your younger brother, Skylar—"

"I'm his younger brother. I know I look old, but goddamn, cut me some slack."

Ain't we a bunch of prehistoric dopeheads, or what? Kendall thinks, looking around the room. In the '90s Age of Crack, he feels like a dinosaur, a walking, talking, breathing anachronism, one of a species nearing extinction. But he's never been a cokehead, except to speedball every now and then. Even thinks he's superior to crack smokers, though he's not sure why. He's still developing the theory to substantiate his supremacy as an old-fashioned, all-American, run-of-the-mill dope fiend. Aside from which, cocaine only winds him up for seven- to eight-minute intervals, before the crash. And heroin, dope, smack, boy, horse, witch — whatever you want to call it — wraps a pair of warm, hefty arms around him for hours, rocks him like a baby, sings him a lullaby, and buzzes in his ear like a woman in heat.

He has tied the leather belt around his elbow. He flexes his fist until the purple-green vein rises to his skin's surface. After pouring what can be likened to rodent droppings into the cooker, an Alka-Seltzer bottle top, he wraps a bobby pin around its grooved edge for a handle. He glances at the pickle jar centerpiece, and reminds Junebug that it's about time to change the water. "I don't want nobody's AIDS, man," Kendall says. He prides himself on sharing his needles with no one, and on always using clean water. Junebug complies, gladly, snatching the jar from the table, and heads for the sink.

"Hey, Junebug, you jive-ass. You didn't do that shit for us."

"We been askin' you all afternoon to change that nasty-ass water—"

"For the brother of a movie star who I grew up with in the 'hood," Junebug says, returning with the jar of clean water, "Anythang! Y'all other niggers can kiss my funky, black ass."

Kendall places the needle inside the jar and watches it suck up the water, while Junebug boasts of the *Hill Street Blues* episode he watched last week, explaining the entire plot to his customers. He is reminded of something, cuts himself off in midsentence, excuses himself, and leaves the room.

Kendall squeezes droplets of water into the cooker. The Chinese rocks melt slightly, turning the water muddy brown. Striking a match, he positions the flame beneath the bottle cap until the mixture comes to a sizzling boil. Steam rises from the melted rocks, the nauseating aroma sticking in his throat. He shreds a filter from a Kool cigarette, places it in the cooker, allowing it to soak up the brown liquid. He is tightening the belt around his arm again, flexing his fist, slapping his arm, the spike first popping, then penetrating his skin, when Junebug re-enters the room carrying a handful of typewritten pages.

Kendall's thumb and forefinger squeeze the nipple, the brown liquid entering his blood system with a burning sensation. When the eyedropper empties of liquefied rocks, it is quickly replaced by blood. Muscles relax, vision blurs, head becomes woozy, body turns to putty, as a rush of calm envelops and tames every nerve, bloodshot green eyes rolling, flickering to the back of his head, and waves of warmth roll, wash over him. He is now at peace. He is at one with himself as the heroin reconstructs the fragmented bits of the disintegrated Kendall and makes him whole. He feels that now he may get on with his life.

Stroking his parched mouth and stubbly chin, he boots the blood back into his vein and waits for the dropper to fill up again. Junebug stands over him, waving a handful of typewritten pages. He watches Junebug's lips move, but doesn't hear a word he's saying. He struggles to keep his eyelids from pressing shut, then surrenders, his head sinking into the bosom of euphoria.

Nodding into oblivion, he sees the antique Oriental vase resting upon the mantelpiece, too high for his reach.

He was in his bedroom on a Saturday afternoon, minding his own business, taking inventory of football cards he'd be trading later with Butch down the street. His deck consisted of three Jim Browns, and he needed only one to trade for three others of his choice. Maybe five. He'd feel Butch out, see what he could get away with.

It was pouring rain. Otherwise, Kendall would've been in the streets with his buddies, looking to see what trouble they could get into, like swiping string licorice and stale buttermilk cookies from Miss Leona's Candy Store around the corner. Or ringing Grandma Tilson's doorbell, then hiding each time she came to the door, and she would come every time. Or defacing the walls of the Harlem Boys Club of America with words like "pussy," and sketching, with Magic Markers, enormous penises protruding from curly pubic hairs.

His mother was working her part-time gig at Bessie's Fish Fry. Though his older brother was in the house, he couldn't hear him stirring, which meant Skylar was probably reading one of his stupid books, like *Pride and Prejudice*, or *A Tale of Two Cities*, or some corny crap like that. Skylar was weird. Even Kendall's friends said so. Who could be bothered with reading a book when the teacher didn't say you had to? When instead, you could be stealing model airplanes from the nearby factory that employed a wino as security guard.

He was studying Jim Brown's running statistics, listening to the rain drum heavily upon the skylight. Outside his door, the floor-boards creaked beneath the old rug. He thought the light tapping at his bedroom door was Skylar. Without looking up from his cards, he invited him in. When he glanced at the cracked door, a slice of Daddy's smiling face was squeezed between the door and frame, his hand turning the knob. Daddy sat beside him on the bed and lovingly caressed Kendall's neck.

"You really like football, don't you, son?"

"Yeah. Especially Jim Brown," Kendall replied, studying the photo of Brown posed with a football cradled in his arms. "And tomorrow, it's the Browns against the Giants."

"Your brother doesn't like football like we do."

"No, Skylar's weird. He reads books."

"Sissy," Kendall could've sworn he'd heard his father say.

"Could you use some spending money to buy more football and baseball cards?" Daddy asked. Kendall's eyes lit up the room. Daddy pulled a dollar from his billfold. "I need you to do me a favor, son," Daddy said, handing Kendall the dollar, without completely letting it go. "Will you?"

"Sure." Kendall's eyes crawled across the green paper like it was something to eat. Daddy finally released the dollar, and Kendall stuffed it in his pocket.

"I've got a secret," Daddy said. "You like secrets?"

"Yeah!"

"I can't tell Skylar, because he tells your mother everything. You're the only son I can trust." He paused for such a long time, Kendall couldn't tell if he was finished. "You know that Oriental vase on the mantelpiece?"

"Mama's vase?"

"Yeah, that one. Your grandmother Hutchinson got it from her mother and gave it to us when we got married. Jewish women always give stuff like that to domestics."

He led an unsuspecting Kendall down the staircase, into the parlor where the vase sat. "That's it," Daddy said, pointing. He was whispering now. "I want you to 'accidentally' knock it on the floor."

Kendall didn't understand. For years, they'd been warned to steer clear of that vase, indoctrinated in the value and importance of a family heirloom. Althea drummed into their consciousness the fact that colored people never have heirlooms to give to their children. One day, she said, she would give the vase to one of their wives when they grew up and got married. Kendall shook his head No, fearing he would get a beating.

"No one will know," Daddy reassured him.

"But you know," Kendall explained, gazing at the floor. "Won't you tell?"

Daddy shook his head, No.

"I'm too short, anyway," Kendall persisted. "I can't even reach it."

"If you jump up, you can."

"But—"

"Kendall," Daddy whispered, "I won't be in the room when you do it. That way, I haven't seen a thing. And if I can't see, I can't tell. Understand?"

"I think so."

"That's why it's our secret."

He thought about this long and hard. Projecting his fate into the near future, he foresaw his mother's horrified expression when she discovered it after working her shift, waitressing in the greasy spoon. Personally, he didn't like the vase; he thought it was ugly. But her feelings would be shattered, not unlike the tiny ceramic pieces.

"Why?" Kendall wanted to know.

"It's ugly," Daddy said. "I want to buy your mother a brand-new vase, but she likes this one."

He declined the offer in his thoughts, but feared Daddy's wrath. Besides, Daddy always treated him okay. He broke and bent rules for Kendall when he didn't for Skylar. And, if he refused to do it, Daddy might treat him like he treated Skylar, and Mama. Kendall adored and worshipped his father. Yet he feared Daddy's capricious, sometimes violent behavior. No one knew when he would snap. And when he did, everyone had to run for cover — everyone except Kendall, who never so much as got a reprimand from Daddy for the most despicable behavior.

"No, Daddy," Kendall was saying, shaking his head. "I don't think I want to do it. Ask Skylar."

Daddy regarded him gravely, his eyes narrowing with disappointment. "How many times have I saved your little ass from getting whipped by your mother? Remember when I lied to your mother so you could have your way? Am I right?"

Kendall trembled from the pressure and indecision, while Daddy turned back several pages of their familial history, painting himself as hero and savior. Then he reached into Kendall's pocket to retrieve the dollar he'd given him. Not until then did Kendall decide. A smile slowly worked its way back into Daddy's lips. "Here's your dollar back."

"You sure I won't get a whipping?"

Skylar was blamed for the broken vase.

Kendall's too small to reach the mantelpiece, Althea reasoned, throughout the refrain of Skylar's pleas of innocence. Skylar got a whipping, tears streaming down Althea's face as she raised the belt repeatedly, bringing it down upon his writhing body. Skylar screamed, "No!" as his mother struck him. She interspersed the blows with a laconic warning that sounded chantlike. "Didn't I ... tell you ... not to ... touch that ... damn vase!" — each word punctuated by a follow-up blow.

Through his bedroom wall next door, Kendall listened, guilt swelling within him. He fingered the crumpled dollar bill he no longer wanted. As the muffled screams went on and on, Daddy entered Kendall's bedroom, grinning. He produced another dollar from his wallet, grasped Kendall by the arms, and embraced him.

He comes to, Junebug is grasping Kendall around the elbows, yanking the needle out of his arm. "What the fuck's wrong with you, blood?!" Junebug is shouting. "You know the rules, man. No ODing in the pad, my man. You gon' haveta chill on that. An' I means that shit! Yo, blood," he said, shaking Kendall. "You all right?"

"Yeah," Kendall says, his voice like gravel, an octave lower. He snatches his arms from Junebug's bearlike grip, reluctantly snapping back to consciousness, groping for mental and visual clarity. Junebug is still waving the typewritten pages in his face.

"I want you to give this here to your brother," Junebug claims, thrusting the manuscript in Kendall's face. "This here's a bad-ass movie script I wrote. Skylar could be my Hollywood connection. It ain't what you know, but who you know, right?"

Kendall glares at him skeptically, clicking his tongue, gathering his paraphernalia, thinking, Shit, man, you probably can't even write your own fuckin' name. "Damn," Kendall says. "How long was I nodded out?"

"You gonna see Skylar any time soon?"

"Probably now at the hospital. My old man's sick again, the fuckin' drunk. We don't think he gonna make it this time." He places the works, after having cleaned them, inside the empty Sucrets box, snaps it shut, then stuffs it inside his thick boot sock.

"Don't forget my script, man," Junebug reminds him.

"I won't," Kendall replies, knowing he'll never breathe a word of it to Skylar.

"I hope your brother ain't forgot me, man. You know how niggers get when they make it," Junebug says, his face growing thoughtful, his thoughts reeling back through memories. "Him and my brother, shit, man, they usedta be partners, and he always been like a brother to me, even though m'fuckas be breakin' on him, an' callin' him a fag, an' shit."

"Oh, you lyin'-ass mothafucka, don't gimme that," Kendall snaps. "You was one of them dipshits who called him that. I ain't forgot. I kicked your ass about it one day. And you remember too. Don't play that amnesia shit."

He wishes he were on his way to Tonja's house, instead of the hospital. She was the finest, sweetest, most calming breeze to ever blow into, and fill, his hollow life. And he'd fucked that up royally. Like he's fucked up everything else in his life. Tonja has since become a bank executive, married some yuppie, faggot-ass, bourgie doctor, has two kids, lives in Englewood. Daydreaming, inebriated, and unsteady, Kendall bumps slightly into Moose, a gallery veteran, sitting at the far end of the table, a hypodermic protruding from his jugular vein. "Watch it, mothafucka!" Moose barks. "You tryin' to kill me or somethin', man?"

Howard

REMEMBER, the baby comes first.

Every time he turned around, she was picking up that boy again.

She needed to let him cry sometimes. Babies're supposed to cry. She'd mess around and turn that child into a mama's boy. Worse yet, a sissy.

This time he almost got to the finish. His and Althea's rookie sex life was becoming threatened by too many interruptions. He thought tonight, at least tonight — the eve of their second wedding anniversary — Althea would let the boy scream his lungs ragged until they were finished. Since the baby had come home from Harlem Hospital, he hadn't had a decent piece of ass. Most new fathers found themselves losing sleep, the baby waking all hours of the night. He wished it were that simple. His first son was turning out to be an impediment, sitting like a roadblock in the middle of their sex life.

Tonight, he'd planned their entire evening to be childless. Several times, he'd suggested that Althea find a permanent babysitter. On his salary, they could afford it, which made little difference since Althea had six sisters and a mother who'd jump at the opportunity, so he and his wife could have the night off. But, no. Not Althea. She cared too much for her own good. Maybe for the good of her marriage. As if she didn't trust her only child to be cared for by anyone other than herself. He'd heard her sisters volunteer, many times, to take their nephew while his parents spent time alone.

They were watching the final reel of the movie *Come Back, Little Sheba*. Burt Lancaster was drunk again. He had picked up some young tramp who was wilder than a bucking bronco, pressing her naked foot against his on the accelerator. One of the more action-packed scenes in the whole damn movie. Althea just had to excuse herself like she was going to the ladies' room for the zillionth time.

He knew she was in the lobby, hunched over the receiver in the telephone booth. Just couldn't wait. Even in Skylar's absence, the little bastard continued to dictate her actions and priorities. Sucker wasn't even a year old yet.

At the restaurant, she barely touched her food. She sat there and twirled the spaghetti around her fork so long he thought of force-feeding her.

"Baby," he said softly, touching her hand. "Don't worry, he'll be all right. We'll be home in no time. But now, you should enjoy yourself."

"Mmm-hmm," she replied.

"Are you okay, baby?"

"Mmm-hmm."

She was angry or distracted. In either case, the evening was not turning out as he'd planned. They could've stayed home.

Before he got the chance to tell her about his new promotion — the secret he was keeping for the double celebration — she got up again. Said she was going to the ladies' room. "You're going to piss and shit yourself to death, baby," he told her, laughing, though he didn't think it was funny. He knew where she was going. So, he planned to break the promotion news sooner, when she returned to the table. She came back in a huff, mumbling something about Skylar's fever, his temperature rising alarmingly. Her sister, Gloria Jean, didn't know what to do with him. He was screaming his head off and nothing she did made him stop. Though he proposed the idea of first going home to make love in peace, Althea was leading him by the hand in the opposite direction.

After she got the boy to sleep, he begged her to come to bed, watching her body arched over the crib, lying on his back, one arm folded behind his head, fondling himself.

Soon, he was sweating bullets, giving her everything he had. On the downstroke, grunting, salivating, his lips moist with yearning, drooling on her shoulder. Her eyes were wide open — no expression, less feeling. She couldn't wait for him to finish. He felt like he was doing all the work. She was along for the ride. Why didn't she just yawn, glance at the clock, and ask how much longer he'd be needing her thighs?

He was nearing the finish. She might as well have been a corpse. Dead women must give up better, more thrilling ass than this.

Stupid woman wouldn't know a good fucking if it kicked her squarely in the ass! His body trembled, and rocked, and stiffened, as he edged closer toward the explosion. Skylar started stirring in the crib. Althea tried to raise her body. "Just one more minute," he was panting, pinning her down by the shoulders, making it impossible for her to wriggle free of his grasp. He was looking into her eyes, breathing heavily. She was looking toward the crib. He pulled her face back; tried to kiss her. She struggled so, it felt like he was raping her. Maybe he was.

She managed to wriggle free of him, as Skylar screamed like he was being strangled. She was up and out of bed, and cradled the boy in her arms. No sooner had she picked him up than the crying stopped. She paced the bedroom floor, rocking his little body against hers, his head lying flatly upon her shoulder, nose and lips pressed against her neck. Howard watched them from the bed. These two strangers. He felt like a stand-in. Skylar was her undisputed first love, and had been since he'd come home. He only sufficed if Skylar didn't need her attention.

"Althea," he said hoarsely, his voice piercing the darkness.

"Yes?" she replied, pacing, not giving him her undivided attention.

"What's wrong, baby?"

"I think he's got a bad cold—"

"Us, baby. I'm talking about us."

"Ain't nothing wrong," she said.

"I know there's three of us now, and being the good mother you are, you're spending a lot of time with the baby. I understand that." How could he phrase this delicately? "But since we had him, you don't seem to ... pay any attention to me anymore." He tried to chuckle, suddenly embarrassed by what he'd just admitted, wishing he could snatch the words from the air.

"Is that what you're worried about, Howard?" Althea said, laughing.

"Well, it's true."

"You're jealous of your own firstborn," she said. "Silly man."

"What's so silly about that? Why're you laughing?"

"Because, nothing has changed between us. The baby just demands a lot of my time and attention—"

"But you give him too much attention."

The laughter fled her instantaneously, her lips curling downward into a pout. "You got a lot of nerve," she said. "This child has needs and you don't lift a finger to do nothing for him. He's yours too, you know—"

"I know that—"

"Maybe I'm doing my part and yours."

"Look, baby, I'm not trying to start a fight about it. I just want my wife back."

"She ain't gone nowhere, Howard. When the baby's a little older, things'll return to normal. It's not just me and you anymore, you know." She started pacing again, and he could hear the infant breathing through a congested nose. "Remember, the baby comes first."

He rolled over on his back, turned on the table lamp, and lit a cigarette, cursing quietly under this breath.

Wasn't his fault his mother had two marriages.

Neither was it his fault that he was the only child born of the first marriage. His five younger brothers and sister were products of the second — or as his mother termed it, her "good" marriage. They seemed to get all the attention he so craved. She never touched him. Kissed him only on birthdays — if then. Treated him like slave and servant to the children of her "good" marriage. And, whipped him good if he complained or became remiss in his responsibilities.

His stepfather was worse. Howard thought to himself that he might as well have been invisible, so little notice was taken of him, unless he was in trouble. It didn't matter who he fought or why; his stepfather invariably sided against him. Strolling on Sunday afternoons, to or from church, when the old man introduced the other five as "his" children, Howard stood off to the side.

"This is my oldest. He's in the third grade. Math whiz. And this one's my youngest — stand up straight, William. He's the gifted athlete in the family. And this one here is my..."

He could've been the family dog.

Once, when he and a younger brother got into a fight against two snotty-nosed kids around the block and were brought home by a protesting neighbor, his stepfather opened the door and filled the doorway, fists pressed against his hips, like the genie from the magic lamp.

"This one's not mine," he declared, pointing at Howard. He placed his hands on his son's shoulders. "I'll take care of this little one," he said. "But my wife will discipline the other boy."

The other boy. The old woman, a churchgoing Christian, was shocked. She tried not to show it. But Howard, even as a child, could see the embarrassed look in her face, as if the man had divulged his bedroom secrets. But once he got them inside, he started wailing Howard with a switch he'd broken off a tree and kept at his bedside, a switch Howard assumed was exclusively for him. No one else was ever disciplined with it. His brothers needed only a good talking to. They never got whippings. "That boy of yours again!" the stepfather was saying to his wife. "Can't let him mislead the little ones. He has to set an example."

Howard expected his mother to rise to his defense. When the switch was raised in the air, he knew she would stop it from swooping down on him. Instead, she watched, drying dishes at the kitchen sink. The other children planted themselves on the sofa and watched. Embarrassed and ashamed, he ran to his bedroom and cried himself to sleep. And when his mother called him some hours later, her tone suspiciously sweet and endearing, he thought it was time for an apology. She'd confess how sorry she was, allowing him to be whipped by a man who obviously held him in contempt. She must've lost her mind for a moment, because she loved her little Howie very much and...

When he got to the foot of the stairs, she was putting on white gloves, flexing and wiggling her fingers.

"My husband and I are going out," she said, proudly, yet lacking emotion.

"Can I go—"

"No. We need you to babysit. Your dinner's still warm on the stove."

"You ate dinner without me?"

"If you weren't sleeping away this lovely Sunday afternoon, you could've joined us."

"But nobody woke me up, so—"

"We're going now. Take good care of the children."

They were never "your brothers and sister." They were always "the children." It was never "your father," not even "your stepfather," but always, "my husband."

He watched her admire herself in the beveled, full-length mirror, tilting her veiled hat, fussing with the angle.

"And when we come back," his stepfather warned him, "this house better be like we left it, understand?"

No, he didn't understand.

What had he done? Against whom had he unknowingly committed this unspeakable crime? Watching Althea pace that damn floor, the child snuggled to her breast, he watched his own unfeeling mother, rocking and pampering one of the newborns of her "good" marriage. He couldn't let it happen again, not two in one lifetime, no matter what it took, what it cost, who or what was sacrificed.

"Ouch!" The cigarette had burned down to his fingers. He stubbed it out in the ashtray, clicked off the lamp, turned over, nestled his head into the pillow, and grumbled something unintelligible under his breath, hoping Althea would give that damn lullaby she was singing off-key a rest for the night.

E van

IF YOU LOVE COLORED PEOPLE so much, why don't you go live with them?

Hearing this taunt repeatedly, he'd promised himself that one day he would do just that. He projected himself into the future. Pictured his mom fainting at the sight of her colored daughter-in-law, belly swollen with his seed...

The nerve of Skylar breaking that Picasso ceramic he coveted — and paid for. Isn't it just like a black person to become violent when they're at a loss for an alternate means of negotiation? His mom had warned him. His dad had warned him. He wonders if this is an isolated incident, or if he's turning into his parents.

Skylar is perpetually angry, never satisfied, searching high and low for a racist between every crease and fold. White people aren't the only racists living in America. If he had a dollar for every black person who persecuted him with their eyes ... What is it about him and Skylar that, whatever the day's headlines happen to be, there's always the prospect of it creeping, from the front page of the newspaper, the radio broadcaster's lips, or the TV anchorwoman's desk, into their household, driving itself between them.

Certainly they share personal problems too, like any other couple who've been together too long. Maybe he wouldn't mind so much if, for once, they argued about Skylar leaving his clothes on the floor, or his inability to listen, really listen, to the other side of a dispute, or that he eats red meat, or watches David Letterman in bed while Evan's trying to sleep. This he could tolerate. He's never fought with former lovers about the issues he tangles over with Skylar. Normally, a relationship soured because they got bored with one another, or one was chronically late for dates, or didn't show up at all, or the lover slept around a lot. But week after week, world news had become a widening arena for his and Skylar's conflicts. Now he's beyond patience, feeling he lacks the spit to say the words, "racism" and "bigotry," let alone the strength to argue them.

They had two first fights, he likes to think: one personal, the other having nothing to do with them at all. The first happened because Skylar accused Evan of not introducing him to some of Evan's friends.

"What's the big deal, Skylar?" Evan said. "You'll meet them all in due time."

"Tell me," Skylar said. "When exactly is 'in due time'?"

"Don't worry about it—"

"I'm not worried about it. It's just that we've been dating nearly six months and you've met everybody in my life — my parents, my brother, and most of my friends—"

"And you'll meet mine, too—"

"When? Oh, that's right: 'in due time.'"

"There's no need to be sarcastic, Skylar."

"Evan, we've agreed to be open and honest with each other, right?"

"Yeah."

"Then I must ask you this question. Because it's been on my mind, and I have to be honest. But if it's not true, then I'll forget about it, and never bring it up again, okay?"

"Shoot."

"Am I not meeting some of your friends ... because ... I'm black?"

"Skylar, that's outrageous!"

Actually, it was no more outrageous than the three of Evan's friends, Matthew, Gerard, and Brian, who did frown upon his dating a black guy, whether he was gorgeous or not. Didn't matter that he had blue eyes, or that he was *the* Skylar Whyte, the celebrated actor. Evan was too embarrassed to divulge that information to Skylar. The more he pondered it, the more shame he felt for having friends who thought this way. Then he felt mortified for allowing their attitudes to intimidate him into hiding Skylar in his back pocket whenever he was around them. And these were decent, intelligent, educated, hardworking, successful people.

"How's your black boyfriend?"

"Evan, I didn't know you ate watermelon."

How could he tell Skylar that? If he had, they would've fought something awful. Though Evan would have retorted and challenged him word for word, his heart wouldn't have been in it. He would've agreed with everything Skylar said.

The second time they fought was over a racial incident: a black youth had been killed by a mob of white teenagers. Evan was in no way justifying the boy's death, but he didn't agree with Skylar either.

"People are always so afraid of black people," Skylar said. "Because we're supposedly so violent. And look at this—"

"It's only one isolated situation—"

"Nobody's more violent than white people—"

"Now, wait a minute, Skylar—"

"No, you wait. This country and Europe were founded on white folks' savagery and violence. History bears me out—"

"And black people aren't violent?"

"I'm not saying we're not. But if you shove any given race of people into the conditions blacks suffer, anybody would be violent..."

"Those goddamn niggers, I'll tell you. Violent as the day is long," Dad declared, in a faint Georgian drawl, gulping down a can of Ballantine ale, reclined in his easy chair, watching the replay of last night's Watts riots on Channel Four news.

"Honey, don't cuss in front of the boy," Mom said, pushing through the swivel door, carrying a bowl of steamy mashed potatoes from the kitchen into the dining room, her hands covered in cumbersome, vomit green oven mitts.

Evan sat rigidly in the chair, breathless, as he watched the black-and-white footage of Molotov cocktails being pitched through store windows, leaving behind trails of smoke that lingered in the night air. Hordes of people were looting stores, seizing as much as their arms could hold, some of them laughing like it was a party. Policemen were busting and cracking skulls, backs, and kneecaps with billy clubs, while others fired pistols into the thick crowds. A chorus of sirens, bullhorns, and car radio static roared in the background, as the TV reporter, one hand placed over his ear, narrated the action.

An apparently innocent man was passing by the intersection. He wasn't one of the looters, nor was he hurling bricks and garbage cans at the police squad cars, or through windows. But the policeman grabbed the passerby by the collar, and repeatedly bashed his skull with the nightstick. Through disbelieving eyes, Evan witnessed the man stumble, his knees buckling as he went down, his head hitting the pavement, blood spreading across the sidewalk.

"Yeah, goddamn it!" his father shouted, punching his open palm, the smacking of flesh making Evan wince. "Show them son-of-a-bitchin' niggers—"

"Walter!" his mother protested again, halting in the midst of spooning the potatoes onto the empty plates. "I've asked you not to use that language around the boy—"

"He ain't no goddamn boy, I keep tellin' you." He took another swig of his brew, inhaled a last drag from his Camel cigarette, and stubbed it out in the ashtray. "The boy's almost ten years old. What's wrong with hearing a few cuss words?"

They always have the same fights, Evan was thinking, recalling a similar squabble they'd had in the car last week. Driving through their middle-class neighborhood of South Gate, California, into nearby Watts, he couldn't help noticing the stark disparities and the separateness of the communities that bordered one another. In his neighborhood, everyone was white, blue-collar, where, walking down the street, one might hear the phrasings of the Everly Brothers or Elvis Presley, coming through open windows. Go a mile west, and the manicured lawns and two-story homes became housing projects and apartment buildings, the faces of the inhabitants black, and the music Aretha Franklin, Sam Cooke, and Ike and Tina Turner. Or it spilled into the street from the storefront churches, which banged out the gospel on crashing drums and out-of-tune pianos.

Evan was fascinated by this colorful community, and its people who were so full of life. His drab neighborhood was a black and white existence that blossomed into living color when he crossed the border. He loved watching them dance in church, filled with the Holy Ghost, speaking in tongues, popping tambourines, or just plain shuffling and wiggling on the street to Martha and the Vandellas screeching from a static-filled radio. They didn't seem to have what the people in his neighborhood had. They didn't dress as well as the people he knew. Their houses weren't as clean and presentable as those on his block.

"Why do we live over there, and they live over here?" he asked Dad, who was making a left turn on Central Avenue.

"They, who?"

"The colored people."

"'Cause they don't deserve no better," Dad replied.

"They're not worthy enough to live like us," Mom added.

"Why?"

"'Cause," Dad said.

"Why, Mom?" he persisted; he was getting nowhere with Dad.

"Because, honey, that's the way God planned it."

"Why'd he plan it that way?"

"Now, that's a goddamn 'nough," Dad said, flicking his cigarette butt out the car window.

"Walter, I've asked you not to talk to him like you're around your friends at the bar."

He knew that was Mom's way of getting back at Dad, whose drinking she abhorred.

"Look, woman," Dad said, facing Mom instead of the road, his foot still heavy on the accelerator. "Don't you never raise your goddamn voice to me."

"I just said—"

"Did you hear what I just said?"

"Yes, Walter. How can I not hear you screaming in my ear. I'm sitting right next to you—"

"All right then, goddamn it."

Evan couldn't take another one of their fights. He decided on a diversion.

"Well, I don't care," he said, staring at a group of colored boys singing "That Ol' Black Magic" a cappella on the corner. "I like them. I think they're neat."

"The niggers?" Dad said, wounded and indignant.

"My teacher, Mrs. Conway, says we shouldn't use that word," Evan said.

"If you love colored people so much, why don't you go live with them?"

As it was, he was forbidden to associate with anybody or anything having to do with "niggers." He could not buy nigger music.

He could not sing nigger songs. He could not have nigger friends. He could not watch niggers dance on television. He could not put pictures of niggers on his bedroom wall. Before his official introduction to this implicit household dictum, he'd tripped over the rules purely by accident. Upstairs in his bedroom, rocking with the Four Tops to "Sugar-Pie-Honey-Bunch," he was snapping his fingers, gyrating his waist, as he'd seen the colored kids do on television, wiggling across the carpeted floor when, like a madman, out of nowhere, Dad charged in. He slapped the tonearm off the record, snatched the vinyl from the turntable, and broke it in half over his knee. It all happened so fast, Evan was speechless. He couldn't find his tongue.

"You don't never play no nigger music in this house, boy, you understand?"

"But, Dad—"

"Do you understand?"

"Yessir."

Later that evening, he would be indoctrinated in what he would come to call his parents' Ten Anti-Nigger Commandments. Now he had to smuggle Motown records and *Jet* magazines into the house. He read the magazine in the privacy of his bedroom and listened to the records when his parents were out.

So how was he going to explain Michael?

Tell them the truth, an inner voice advised him.

It was Mrs. Conway's idea. Evan was nearly a straight-A student, with the exception of mathematics, his only weakness. His teacher had suggested some time ago that he seek his parents' assistance. He did so, asking for help that same night. They pretended not to hear him, which made him wonder if they knew their times tables.

When his grades didn't improve the following semester, Mrs. Conway summoned Evan. While speaking with him after class about the failing grade on his last long division exam, she said she had a wonderful idea. Evan could be tutored by Michael Watson, since math was Michael's strength. There wasn't much time during school hours, and because they lived close to each other, Mrs. Conway encouraged them to work together at home. Evan thought it was a great idea. Now he could attain the straight-A report card that, because of math, had eluded him. He'd never talked much with Michael in class or in the playground. Rival brains were not bosom buddies. But Michael was likeable, outgoing, confident. Only one problem:

Michael Watson was colored.

Evan not only proposed they study at his house, but extended the invitation to Michael to stay for dinner. He'd told his parents he'd be bringing home a classmate for tutoring, and asked if it was okay for him to stay for dinner. His mother became so enthusiastic at the request, since they never had company, that she started considering aloud all the possible dishes she could make.

"Honey," she said to Evan. "How about a macaroni-and-cheese casserole? You know how you love my casseroles."

"I don't care, Mom. Whatever you cook."

"Well, what does your friend like? How about a pot roast?"

He'd never expected her to react this way. He didn't have the chance to tell her who the guest was — more specifically, what he was. With all her culinary preparations, he didn't have the heart to do it.

When Evan opened the door and wiped his feet on the welcome mat, and Michael stood behind him, grinning, Mom and Dad froze. If he could've touched Mom with his fingertips, she would've broken into a million pieces. Dad was lighting a Camel. The match flame burned down to his fingers before he dropped it on the floor. "Goddammit!"

"Mom and Dad," Evan said, noticing that their horrified expressions transcended his most nightmarish expectations. Now he wondered if he'd done the wrong thing. "This is my classmate who's going to tutor me in math," he continued, his voice shaky, watching Dad's face and neck turn crimson. Michael walked toward Mom and stuck out his hand.

"Hello, Mrs. Cabot," he said, shaking her hand. She barely touched his fingers. "Thank you for having me to dinner."

"And this is my dad," Evan said, standing next to Dad's recliner, Dad clutching a beer can, staring at Evan as if he were a stranger.

"Nice to meet you, sir." Michael extended his hand.

"Is this some kind of joke, Evan, or what?" Dad never shook Michael's hand.

"No, Dad. What joke?"

"Walter," Mom said from across the room, and flashed Dad a look.

They sat down at the dining room table. Dad couldn't stop staring at Michael. Evan was becoming impatient and embarrassed.

"So, now," Dad said to Michael, "let me get this straight. You here to tutor my son?"

"Yessir."

"In what?"

"Math. He needs help with long division and—"

"What do you know about it? This here long division?"

"Walter," Mom said.

"I'm just asking a question," Dad said, holding up his hand like a stop sign.

"I don't know that much," Michael admitted. "I just know what I've been taught in school so far."

"Where'd you learn to talk so good?" Dad asked.

Michael looked surprised, and hesitated before he replied. "At home ... and in school, I guess."

"He's the smartest boy in the class," Evan said.

"Oh yeah?" Dad said, clearly unimpressed. "And what you plan on doing with it, boy?"

"Walter," Mom said again.

"Well," Michael said, chewing on a slice of roast beef, picking the stringy parts from his teeth. "I plan to go to college—"

"Do you, now?"

"Me too," Evan chimed in, though he'd never before considered college.

"What college you going to?" Dad said, turning his attention to Evan.

"I don't know. But I'm going."

"Who's gonna pay for it?" He sipped his beer, and belched. Mom shot him another look. She hated when he didn't excuse himself.

"You and Mom."

"Oh, no we ain't. You don't need to go to no college, boy."

"Why not?" Evan asked.

"Because me and your mom ain't never went to no college. You don't need to go to none, neither. What good it gon' do you? How much education you need to be assistant plumber with your old man?"

"I don't want to be a plumber," Evan protested.

"Well, what then? Study this, this here math whatchamacallit? So you can go to college with him?" he said, indicating Michael.

"Walter!" Mom said, for the fourth time.

"Goddamn it all to hell," Dad said, rising from the table. "I done lost my appetite. I'll be upstairs, goddammit." He rose and headed for the staircase, while the room choked on silence.

Evan absentmindedly picked at the food with his fork. He wanted to shrink to the size of the green pea on his plate, and seek refuge in the lumpy pile of mashed potatoes. He wondered if Michael, who was staring into space, trying not to look uncomfortable, would tell their classmates what he'd just seen and heard.

"And when your friend leaves," Dad said, halfway up the stairs, "I'm gon' have a word with you, Mr. Smart-Ass. I ain't hardly finished with you yet."

Christmas Eve, 1962

MAMA, DO I HAVE white people's eyes?

White people's what?

The kids at school say I have white—

Baby, you have your eyes. They were given to you by me, your father, and the good Lord above ... Understand?

Skylar didn't understand. Most colored people he knew had brown eyes. His mother's family. Folks in the neighborhood. Kids at school. His father's side of the family had green, gray, and hazel eyes. But not blue.

He was alone in the basement, eagerly awaiting the arrival of his favorite uncle, who'd be spending the holidays with them. Like all children, Skylar loved Christmas, his favorite holiday. Beyond that, it held a special significance. The chances of family squabbles and abuse were slim. Daddy seemed to relax around the holidays, smiling and laughing more frequently. Peace on Earth had a strange way of humbling Daddy. He passed around Good Will Toward Men like the aluminum icicles he handed out to the family to toss onto the tree. Skylar felt, presents or no presents, Christmas tree or no Christmas tree, the uninterrupted peace was gift enough. Even if it only lasted from Christmas Eve to New Year's Day.

Skylar was playacting. A tattered and dirty bed sheet cloaked about his shoulders, a bent curtain rod as rapier in his hand, he waged a vicious battle with a fire-breathing dragon. Take that, you beast! As in the Errol Flynn movies he'd seen, Skylar swashbuckled his way to conquest, cavorting, leaping, kicking, swinging from beams and water pipes, landing in his mother's basket of laundry. "Be careful and don't tear up nothing!" he heard Mama yell down at him from the first floor. "Yes, ma'am!" he yelled back. "I'm being careful." Proudly, he walked across the floor, swaggering, stroking his chin, sizing up his victory, snickering at the slain dragon clutching a mortal wound to the heart, the torch in his nostrils simmering down to a flame. The train of his cloak swishing behind him, he entered the king's court to announce his exploit. He had saved the kingdom and the fair princess. On one knee, he knelt before the throne to be knighted Sir Skylar the Terrible.

Upstairs, the front door opened and shut. He paused, listening to the wood expand, as muffled footsteps thumped across the floor into the kitchen. The voices were low murmurs. He couldn't tell if his uncle had arrived or not. When he didn't hear Mama scream with joy, he knew he hadn't come yet. So, it must've been Daddy. Hiding behind the staircase, he heard the voices a little more clearly.

"Merry Christmas, baby," Daddy said, and kissed Mama.

"Oooh! What's this?" Mama said. Skylar could picture her shaking the gift box, and pressing it against her ear, as she always did when Daddy gave her a present.

"Open it up and find out."

Skylar listened to the floor creak, the pipes hum, bang, pop, hiss, the wind howling outside, pushing against and bending the windows. He heard the tearing of paper, and the box being opened.

"Oh, honey, this is beautiful! Just what I needed! Thanks!" Mama said, her voice higher than usual. He could imagine them kissing.

"So, what time does your brother arrive?" Daddy asked. Daddy hated Mama's brother. If he didn't show up at all, Daddy wouldn't have cared.

"Pretty soon, I guess," Mama said, offering no further information.

"How long is he staying?" Daddy asked.

"Few days, that's all."

In those few days, Mama would be constantly trying to keep the peace between the two men, as she'd always done. Daddy hated his in-laws. The Hutchinsons were nothing more than lowlife niggers, as far as he was concerned. He said it all the time. Sometimes he said Mama wasn't quite up to his standards, so their marriage wasn't equal. Why'd you marry her in the first place? Skylar would think. Sometimes, I wish you hadn't.

Daddy said that while his family was far more educated and well bred, and discussed the more significant matters influencing the world — politics, art, culture, history — Mama's family wasted

their words talking about each other, the people in the neighborhood, how big and goofy Althea Gibson looked on the tennis court,
instead of how brilliantly she beat the pants off that white girl at
Wimbledon. The Whytes expected college degrees from their
children. The Hutchinsons settled for high school diplomas. If that
much. They married, usually at a young age before their adult lives
began, then had babies they couldn't support. Daddy reminded
Skylar how lucky he was.

"It's one thing to be born a Hutchinson," Daddy had said,
opening a can of beer, smiling as if he knew something Skylar
didn't. "But your mama got lucky, boy." He took a sip of the beer.
"She married into my family by becoming the wife of a CPA. Know
what that means?"

"No."

"Means there's hope for you, boy."

He said Skylar was better off than his maternal cousins, who
spoke poor English, and said things like "ain't," "gonna," and "I
seen" — words that weren't allowed in Skylar's house. Nigger talk,
his father called it. "How're you going to expect white folks to like
us, and consider us equal, when we can't even speak the language?"
Just the week before, when Skylar was bold enough to ask if he'd
be getting his five-speed Schwinn bicycle for Christmas, Daddy
repeated that he was lucky to be getting anything at all. Some of his
cousins sure weren't. "That Aunt Evelyn of yours" — meaning
Mama's oldest sister — "she can't even get off her lazy, black ass,
and go to work. Her kids get their Christmas gifts when we're
already into the new year. You want to live like that? You'd rather
eat mayonnaise or syrup sandwiches, or hominy grits and sardines
for dinner? Count your blessings, boy." Jesus, Skylar thought, I
only asked if I was getting a Schwinn this Christmas, that's all.

But what Daddy never complained about was how Skylar's
paternal grandmother treated his oldest son. The Whytes loved
Kendall. Probably because, of the two boys, he favored Daddy
most. Kendall shared Daddy's butterscotch complexion, green
eyes, and had a head full of what they considered "good" wavy
hair. All twelve of Skylar's paternal cousins shared that look. Skylar
was the black sheep. Literally. He'd taken after Mama's side, dark-
skinned, thick-lipped, coarse, kinky hair. Only difference was his
blue eyes.

"Maybe God made you black, with kinky hair, but at least he gave you blue eyes," Grandma Whyte said, rocking in her chair, her long, thinning white hair pulled back in a bun. "Now doesn't that beat all."

His cousins made fun of him, called him Black Sambo. "Skylar stayed in the sun too long and drinks black coffee," they said. Most times, he never complained. He could take his cousins calling him Sambo. If he cried, he did it privately. It was Kendall's joining in that made him cry. Kendall, the lucky one. He was Daddy's favorite. Daddy was in charge. Nothing Mama said or did meant anything. Sometimes, Kendall would lead the chorus of "Black Sambos," and say that Skylar wasn't his real brother. "He can't be since he's so black and ugly. He was left on the doorstep by African gypsies."

Once Mama caught the children in the act. She scolded them. Grandma Whyte caught her scolding the children. As Mama walked away, leading Skylar by the hand — Mama said she couldn't stand being around her mother-in-law too long — Grandma Whyte laughed, and said that his cousins were telling the truth. "Skylar is black, isn't he? And you know, children," she added, "they're the most honest, truth-telling people walking God's earth."

Someone opened the basement door. A crack of light inched across the floor. Skylar hid behind the broken refrigerator.

"Get washed up and ready for dinner, Skylar!" Mama called down to him.

When he reached the top of the stairs, the doorbell rang. A handsome, well-dressed man in a three-piece suit and cashmere coat stood beneath the mistletoe, smiling, his arms overflowing with brightly wrapped gifts, a suitcase resting at his feet.

"Uncle Aubrey!" Skylar yelled, running to the tall, slender man, who dropped the gifts and picked up his favorite nephew. Skylar wrapped his legs around the man's torso. Laid his head upon his shoulder. Uncle Aubrey hugged Mama, who rushed into his arms. Daddy stood off to the side, nodding his head, grunting.

"Merry Christmas!" Uncle Aubrey said. Releasing his sister and nephew, he approached Daddy, his arms open. Daddy backed away, and extended his hand. He never smiled, but smirked, mumbling something that sounded like, "Yeah, yeah, yeah."

"Where's Kendall?" Uncle Aubrey asked.

"Upstairs, trying on his new football spikes," Daddy said softly. He turned and walked upstairs to get Kendall.

When they returned, Uncle Aubrey insisted they open his gifts. Mama got a dress she'd been wanting and talking about for a whole year. A dress Daddy said they couldn't afford. She pressed it against her bosom, and admired herself in the mirror.

"How do it look?" she was asking the men of her family.

"It's so you," Uncle Aubrey said. "You're still my prettiest sister."

"It's too small," Daddy said. "Maybe because you're gaining weight."

Mama rolled her eyes at Daddy, and sucked her tongue. "I ain't gained more than five pounds since you met me. What could I wear with this?" she asked, turning side to side, admiring her figure.

"Maybe," Uncle Aubrey suggested, "you could wear it with something Howard bought you."

Her smile disappeared. "He doesn't buy me clothes ... Open up your gifts, boys. Let's see what Uncle Aubrey bought you."

Kendall got a football with Y.A. Tittle's signature. Skylar got three books: *Catcher in the Rye, Oliver Twist,* and *Tom Sawyer.* He shouted with excitement. "I've already read *Tom Sawyer* in the library, but I'll read it again." Daddy and Kendall looked at each other.

"And this," Uncle Aubrey said to Daddy, "is for you."

"What is it?" Daddy asked. "Another tie?" He opened the box, and pulled out an expensive-looking silk tie with a tiny paisley design. "Just as I thought," Daddy said, closing the thin box, walking into the dining room.

"Don't worry, Aubrey," Mama whispered. "He likes it. He wears everything you give him. Honest."

The roasted turkey was the centerpiece on the dining room table. Mama led grace. Daddy said he wasn't in the mood. They said "Amen," and passed around bowls of mashed potatoes, peas, buttered rolls, and cranberry sauce. Kendall reached in front of Daddy and Uncle Aubrey to get at the bowls, his elbows resting on the white lace tablecloth. Mama reminded him to mind his manners. It was impolite to reach in front of others at a dinner table without excusing himself. "And get those rusty elbows off my tablecloth."

"Leave the boy alone," Daddy said. "It's Christmas and we're only family. Let the boy be a boy."

The room grew quiet. Skylar could hear them chewing and swallowing. Mama watched Daddy and Uncle Aubrey, her eyes jumping from one to the other.

"So, Mr. World Traveler, my baby brother the costume designer," Mama said. "Where you been lately?"

"You know I was recently in London doing a show, right?"

"Yeah," Mama said. "We got your postcard. You have a good time?"

"Wonderful time. London's marvelous. You should go sometime, Thea."

"The British think they're superior to Americans," Daddy said. "Don't they?"

"Not necessarily," Uncle Aubrey said. "Probably, Americans think they're superior to the British—"

"Well, what about the French? I hear the French are rude to—"

"No more than Americans are rude to them."

"Well," Daddy said. "That's what everybody I know says about those people. Everybody but you."

"This is what you hear?" Uncle Aubrey said, his lips poised to sip the wine.

"Yeah, all the time."

"But you've never been there?"

Daddy took a long time answering him. "No, I've never been myself, but—"

"Well, then," Uncle Aubrey said, placing a forkful of candied yams in his mouth. "Your judgments are a bit premature," he said between chews. "Wouldn't you say?"

Mama looked like she was getting nervous, especially since she was eating slowly. She'd barely touched her plate. "How long were you there?" she asked her brother.

"Not nearly long enough," Uncle Aubrey said. "I stayed with friends in the West End—"

"Then what you come back to New York for?"

"I have an interview to do the costumes for a Broadway show called *Golden Boy* ... starring, get this, Sammy Davis, Jr.—"

"What happened to that friend of yours?" Daddy said, interrupting. "What's his name?"

"Lyle, you mean?" Uncle Aubrey guessed, suddenly looking sad. "Oh. Well ... we don't see each other anymore."

"I see," Daddy said. "Does that mean you're going to take a wife instead and make liars of us all?"

Mama gave Daddy a dirty look. Skylar didn't understand what Daddy meant, or why Mama looked at him that way.

"Mama!" Skylar yelled. "Tell Kendall to stop kicking me under the table."

"I didn't mean to," Kendall pleaded. "But if Skylar's leg wasn't so fat, then it might not be in my way."

Skylar felt another kick, and knew Kendall was showing off in front of Daddy and Uncle Aubrey. Half-standing in his chair, he reached across the table and pushed Kendall.

"Daddy!" Kendall shouted.

"You keep your hands to yourself," Daddy told Skylar. "I'm not going to tell you again that you're too big to be picking on your little brother."

"But, Daddy," Skylar said. "We're about the same age—"

"Don't contradict me, boy," Daddy said.

"Sshh!" Mama said. "Y'all hush all this fuss. It's Christmas Eve dinner. You two can be civil to each other for one day, can't you? You want your uncle to see what bad boys you two can be?"

"Skylar," Uncle Aubrey said. "You still want to be a movie star?"

"Yep," Skylar said. "I was—"

"What did you say?" Daddy glared at him.

"I mean, yes," Skylar said, lowering his voice. "Before you came, Uncle Aubrey, I was practicing downstairs. I was Errol Flynn in *Robin Hood*. I practice every day." He felt brave talking about his dreams to his uncle, who encouraged his passion for theatrics. To Daddy, he couldn't raise or even hint at that subject. With his uncle around, he somehow felt safe, protected, as if someone was on his side. Uncle Aubrey made him feel secure — even from Daddy, who was now clearing his throat.

"Do me a favor," Daddy said to Uncle Aubrey. "Don't encourage Skylar about becoming a movie star. Colored people don't become movie stars, and you come here and get him all worked up over something he'll never achieve."

"Oh?" Uncle Aubrey said.

"He needs something more practical," Daddy continued. "Something that'll pay his bills, whether he's famous or not."

Mama had stopped eating altogether. She'd even stopped smiling, watching Daddy set her brother straight.

"Take me, for example," Daddy said. "Now, I'm a CPA—"

"We've heard," Uncle Aubrey said.

"I'm the first colored CPA with my company, I might add—"

"We've heard that, too," Uncle Aubrey said.

"Let me finish. It took a bachelor's degree in accounting, passing the CPA exam, lots of hard work, and determination. A man's gotta be a man. Not some sissy stuff, like a pampered movie star."

Uncle Aubrey waited a good while before he spoke, as if formulating in his mind what he would say next. "If colored people don't become movie stars," he said, patting his lips with his napkin, "then how do you explain Hattie McDaniel, Dorothy Dandridge, Bill Robinson, or ... or, uh, this guy, what's-his-name? Sidney Poitier? They're colored, aren't they? And they're movie stars. Don't shatter the boy's options. Allow him his dreams."

Daddy set down his fork and knife, resting his elbows upon the table, as Mama had told Kendall not to do, no more than ten minutes ago. "Let me remind you," Daddy said. "This is my house. This is my wife, and these are my children. And I don't appreciate you contradicting me in front of them. I'm the man here. If I say he goes to college and becomes a CPA, then that's what he'll do, understand? What do you know about it? You don't have a family. I've never met any woman you call your wife ... hell, I've never even seen you with a woman. In my family, we set pragmatic goals, with reputable, sturdy foundations. We don't allow our young ones to wander aimlessly through life like the rest of these niggers in the neighborhood—"

"Niggers?" Uncle Aubrey's eyebrows arched and his lips wrinkled. "Well, in my family we don't place any expectations on each other. We allow the freedom to express ourselves, just the way we are."

"I guess so," Daddy said, giggling. "Look what you turned out to be. And how about those nieces and nephews of yours — high school dropouts. Half of them on welfare. The other half with broken marriages. See, that's what happens when you allow too much 'freedom.'"

"Anyway, don't worry, Skylar," Uncle Aubrey reassured his nephew, patting the boy's hand. "One day, I'll take you to the movies — even better, to a movie with glamorous, colored stars."

"I think it's time we change the subject," Mama said. "It don't matter, right this minute, while we breaking bread, what the boys grow up to be. Let's take this a day at a time. Let's get through Christmas Eve first."

"You shut up!" Daddy said, pointing his finger at Mama. "What do you know? You're lucky you married into my family. You have no background, not even a high school diploma. Better be glad I picked you up out of the—"

"Don't you talk to my sister like that! Who the hell're you? God?"

"Look, you little punk, this is my house, and I can throw your ass into the street! Who do you think you are? A traipsing globe-trotter who blows into town once in a blue moon, with your designer tweeds, and hotsy-totsy mannerisms. Remember where you are. I don't give a good goddamn what she is to you. That's my wife, this is my home, and I'll say any goddamn thing I please!" Mama was trying to calm Daddy down, settling him back into the chair he was halfway out of. "Now, you don't like that," Daddy said, "there's the door. It swings both ways, and may it hit you in your narrow ass on the way out!"

Skylar's stomach churned. He lowered his gaze to the plate, picking at the food that was getting cold. Just like the other times there had been family arguments at the dinner table, his appetite was gone. He took Mama's and Uncle Aubrey's side, refusing to make eye contact with Daddy. Daddy'd probably say something like, And what the hell're you looking at? before jumping down Skylar's throat. He was tired of fighting. Arguing with Daddy. Scuffling with Kendall. Couldn't they have just one night's peace? Just one?

He watched Kendall calmly watch Daddy. Kendall never got frightened when his father flew into a rage. He longed for the day Kendall got yelled at by Daddy, who had now jumped up from the table. He squawked something at Mama, spit flying like sparks from his lips. Skylar wouldn't listen to the words. He had become an expert at drowning out the arguments by plugging his ears with his fingers, and humming songs he'd learned at school. "The Star Spangled Banner." "America the Beautiful." Anything. After "From sea to shining sea...," Skylar ran out of songs. He unplugged his ears, and tuned back in to the unfolding holiday drama.

"Howard," Mama was saying. "Could you not act a fool for once in your life? Sometimes, people will have opinions that disagree with yours. That ain't no reason to—"

"What'd you call me?" Daddy said.

"A fool. You acting like a fool—"

Daddy reached across the table and slapped her. Her face jerked and turned with the force of the blow. Before she could react, Uncle Aubrey seemed to fly across the table, and the two men were locked into a fistfight. Somehow, Mama pried them apart. Skylar watched, horrified. His stomach plunged. He couldn't eat. Couldn't think, as the Christmas tree lights blinked off and on. Daddy kicked over his chair. "Step outside, Aubrey," Daddy said, panting. "Like a man."

"No!" Mama screamed. "Don't go outside!"

Daddy grabbed his coat and jammed his arms into the sleeves. Then he got hold of the Christmas tree by the trunk and, with a violent yank, toppled it. Glass ornaments smashed on the floor. Colored electric bulbs sparked like flashes of lightning. Mama screamed, "Are you crazy? You could start a fire!"

"Maybe one day I will," Daddy growled over his shoulder. "I'll set this house on fire and burn up all you worthless niggers in it! Later for you and your sissy brother. You're a stupid woman, Althea!" he barked on the way out the door, which slammed behind him, making the entire house shake and rattle.

Then, a long silence. A silence finally broken by Kendall's plea. "Can I have my dessert now?"

Uncle Aubrey helped Mama rescue the Christmas tree. She was sobbing. "I apologize for Howard. I'm sorry he ripped your shirt. He's getting worse. Sometimes, he's good and kind. Then he snaps, when you least expect it. Like tonight. He never acts like this around the holidays. I don't know what I'm going to do," she said, shaking her head. "He constantly rides me and Skylar. Nothing we do is ever good enough—"

"Why don't you leave him?" Uncle Aubrey asked, placing the aluminum star back on the tree's point, wiping her tears. "He doesn't deserve you."

"What else can I do? What kind of work will I find to raise two growing boys? Waiting tables in a greasy spoon doesn't pay enough as it is. I ain't got no choices."

"Oh yes you do," Uncle Aubrey said, comforting her. "You've got to make choices. Create them where they don't exist. Story of my life. Look! How many times a year do I get to see you? Right? I'm here in New York visiting my favorite sister, and we're going to have a good time."

Uncle Aubrey unlocked his suitcase and pulled out a bottle of Jack Daniel's. He poured two glasses and handed Mama one. Skylar, though no one saw him, headed back down to the basement. He'd use this time to perfect his English accent for the next scene he was about to play opposite Maid Marian. Closing the door behind him, he heard the glasses of bourbon click and Mama softly weeping. "It's better that he's gone anyway," Uncle Aubrey was saying. "Now, maybe we can have a Merry Christmas, despite Scrooge. Cheers, Thea!"

Interview

"TELL ME SOMETHING about your father."

"Like what?"

"Something, anything. Was he instrumental in your becoming an actor?"

Why, Skylar is thinking, does the first question of a supposedly lengthy interview have to be about my father? What has he heard already? Skylar is versed in the occasionally wicked, surreptitious nature of the journalist. He wonders if this guy's already gotten the dope, testing Skylar's spontaneity and truthfulness. He thinks quickly, turning the tables in an attempt to gain control.

"In order that I don't repeat information you already have," Skylar says, with the widest smile he can manage, "why don't you tell me what you know. Then I can fill in the blanks."

Brett What's-His-Face, legs crossed, pencil in hand, cassette recorder running, flips back a few pages in his notebook, shakes his head, and admits, "The only thing I have on your father is that he's in the hospital as we speak ... dying, I was told. Is that correct?"

I'll *bet* that's all the information you have on him, Skylar thinks, wishing he could interpret precisely the pensive lines in Brett's face. "Yes, that's true," he says. "He's dying..." His thoughts stray a moment. So far, he's not enjoying this. He never does when it comes to talking to strangers about his family. The *Rolling Stone* readers of America will not root around further on his family's already dirty laundry. "My father made his living in bookkeeping—"

"You mean, he was an accountant?"

"I mean, he made his living in bookkeeping. He's a man of some education, who preferred that his sons—"

"How many brothers do you have?"

"One. Daddy wanted us to go to college and study those things he considered, quote unquote, pragmatic and stable. You know, like any concerned father, I suppose. Law, medicine, accounting, whatever—"

"So, he wasn't happy about your acting ambition?"

"I wouldn't say that. Actually, he was very encouraging."

Skylar's eyes meet Brett's. He's searching Brett's face for a sign: a twitch, a suppressed gasp, an arched eyebrow — any indication of doubt, disbelief, or challenge to what he's just said. There seems to be none.

"Daddy, I guess you could say, got a kick out of the idea that one of his children would become an actor. He had a great deal of respect for blacks who found success in this industry, and I think he kind of liked the idea that I, you know, might one day join the distinguished ranks, so to speak."

"How thrilling is it, Skylar, to be one of Hollywood's most promising black—"

"Why does it always have to be limited to black? Can't I just be lumped together with all my peers, black, white, whatever?"

"Okay. You're right. Let me phrase this differently. How does it feel to be one of Hollywood's most promising movie stars—"

"Excuse me, but I'm not—"

"Not thrilled, or not—"

"I'm not a movie star."

"What do you mean by that?"

"Just what I said."

The photographer catches him off guard, snapping what Skylar assumes will be an uncomfortably candid shot. He wonders what facial expression was captured on the celluloid.

"You see," Skylar says, "there's no such animal as the black movie star. The last real black movie star was Sidney Poitier. You do realize how long ago that was."

Brett is rapidly scratching away on his notepad. A smile is creeping into the corners of his mouth. Skylar assumes this means good print.

"Either you're modest," Brett is saying, still scribbling, without raising his head, "or you're terribly naive. I mean, here you've been nominated Best Actor by the Academy; you won the Golden Globe—"

"So what?" Skylar says more emphatically than intended. He tones down his petulance a few notches. "I'm neither naive nor modest. There's no successful actor who is. Let me put it to you this way. When Liz Taylor farts, it's news. Or, I can better illustrate my point by giving you a handful of names of so-called movie stars, okay? Jane Fonda. Robert Redford. Marlon Brando. Even James Dean, or Marilyn Monroe, and they're dead."

"I'm afraid I'm missing the point here," Brett says.

"Think about those names for a moment," Skylar insists, getting a charge out of interviewing the interviewer. "Whether these people work or not, whether their work is acclaimed, or panned, the American public keeps them alive and current, despite what they may or may not be doing filmically. See? They're celebrated nonetheless."

"So," Brett is saying, "because you're black, you think 'essentially,' you can't be a movie star—"

"No," Skylar says wearily, bored with this movie star bullshit. "But because America thinks so — or thinks not, as the case may be — I mean, look at the careers of Monroe and Dean. They're much bigger now than they ever were. Look around you at the memorabilia, the tributes, what have you. Monroe didn't quite enjoy this when she was alive and working. And that's nothing to sneeze at, considering the woman was the quintessential American sex-symbol movie star — blonde, big tits, and vulnerable. You have a whole new generation of people who weren't even alive when she died. America won't let her die, man. So, you tell me."

"What's the difference between, say, her, Dean, Brando, and Poitier?"

"The difference is obvious. So-called black movie stars burn on a fuel that's finite. They take off and then either die out or simmer down."

"But isn't that true of many white stars as well—"

"Absolutely, but the opposite is never true of blacks. See what I mean?"

"Then how would you explain—"

"If you don't mind," Skylar says, finally, "I'd rather not talk about movie stars. I hate the word 'star' anyway. What does that mean? What does it buy, and what's the cost? I'm just an actor. Plain and simple. I love what I do whether I'm famous for it or not. I'm not trying to be a movie star. I'll settle for just getting better and growing with each role I'm lucky enough to land."

Brett pulls a pack of Marlboros from his shirt pocket and offers one to Skylar, who refuses with a wave of the hand. Brett lights up one for himself. Over his shoulder, Skylar sees the *Entertainment Tonight* crew setting up their lights, cables, and cameras for his subsequent on-location interview. The film crew is several yards away, quietly recording another take, as John, the director, watches from his chair in silence, stroking his chin. Brett uncrosses and recrosses his legs, asking the photographers to get some photos from the opposite angle, to be sure he catches Mr. Whyte's stunning, sea blue eyes.

Skylar hates these interview sessions, and the Catch-22 ramifications of the abnormal probing into his life. But given the circumstances, he doesn't have much of a choice. He needs all the fuel his career will burn. Recognition. Accolades. Exposure. Without them, he might just as well be Joe Blow on the street. Nobody would know who he is. But without some monitoring on his part, he knows the media can ruthlessly make or break him, whether he refuses interviews or is a media darling.

The overzealous appetites journalists can bring to a session, not to mention the imbecilic questions, are enough to frighten him away. Or at least to make him clam up about information he feels comfortable revealing. It's all such a contradiction in terms, he thinks. Willing to stand before a live audience, vulnerable before hundreds of judgmental spectators and opinionated, unkind critics, he holds back in the presence of one brain-picking journalist. As it is, he's a day late beginning this *Rolling Stone* cover story that, he's been told, will take several days to complete.

And there's still *Entertainment Tonight* to contend with. Or is it *PM Magazine*? At least it'll be quicker and lighter, not as time-consuming and prodding as *Rolling Stone*. He's wondering how long it will take before Brett asks about his nonsecret live-in association with Evan Cabot. He imagines Brett is awaiting the precise moment, after peeling away the requisite layers, before diving into areas that can be the most personally unsettling.

"In your acceptance speech for the Golden Globe, you dedicated the award to the memory of your Uncle Aubrey. Why?"

"The seed to act was always inside me, and my uncle ... cultivated it, I guess you could say." Skylar acknowledges the hand signals of the assistant director in the distance, indicating that they're ready for his next scene.

"Was he an actor?"

"No."

"This is your mother's brother or—"

"I'm sorry, Brett, but they're ready for my next shoot." Skylar rises. "We can talk about Uncle Aubrey in the next session—"

"Just one more quick question—"

"Okay, but quick."

"What's it like being the successful brother in a family of two? I understand your brother hasn't been as fortunate. Has it slanted the family portrait, so to speak, in any way that—"

"My brother is doing just fine," he says, quickly coming to Kendall's defense. "We all have problems in one form or another. We all make mistakes. My brother," Skylar says, careful not even to pronounce his name, "has had his share of problems like anybody else, and now he's overcoming them. That's all I'll say about that."

■

Skylar and Althea were sitting at Howard's bedside, impassively watching *The Newlywed Game* on the television monitor. Howard, tubes stuck into his nostrils and veins, was breathing evenly. His eyes were shut, the lids apparently glued together from an excess of mucus. Neither comatose nor awake, he was unaware of anyone's presence. He slept with the serenity of a newborn. His butterscotch complexion was pasty, ashy. His straight, receding, thinning hair lay mangled and matted about his skull like wet, tangled silk. It occurred to Skylar that he'd never seen his father so defenseless. So incapacitated.

Despite all they had been through — the perennial bad times, and the infrequent good — he found himself feeling sorry for the old, broken man. His father was like a tyrannical, former reigning boxing champion too pooped to punch. Skylar wasn't clear as to why he and his mother had been sitting and waiting these past couple of hours. For the old man to wake up? Then what? For Kendall to finally show up, if he was planning to show up at all? Then what?

What was going through Althea's mind?

He watched his mother, catching a faint whiff of her Estée Lauder perfume. Her head was tilted as she gazed up at the television screen. She was conservatively dressed in her navy blue two-piece business suit, an attaché case resting beside her smart, Fifth Avenue pumps. Until now, they had exchanged minimal whispered conversation. They communicated mainly through half grins and eye winks. Earlier, he'd confided in her about the previous night's argument with Evan.

"Evan and I had a terrible fight last night. The worst ever." The words spilled from his mouth before he could catch them. He'd never discussed with Mama his relationship with Evan, good or bad. He was never certain how she felt about his being gay, living with a white man.

"Oh?" she replied, without turning to face him.

"I think Evan likes black people for all the wrong reasons, Mama."

"I'm sure you two will work it out when you get home tonight." She faced him, and while her words sounded perfunctory, Skylar sensed her sincerity. Though he knew how badly she wanted grandchildren.

"He won't be there when I get home," Skylar said. "He left."

"He'll be back," she said, with an edge of confidence and wisdom, as if she'd experienced this, and the answers were stashed away in her attaché case.

"Actually," Skylar said, "I'm even tired of talking about it. Rehashing it. Like beating on a three-legged mule."

Now it ought to be her turn, he thought. What was going through her mind? He wondered if she wasn't just a bit perversely pleased with the slow death of her husband. It was poetic justice. The man with whom she had shared her bed, and thirty-odd years of physical, psychological, and emotional abuse. With Mama, it was hard to tell. Over the years, she had learned to conceal her innermost emotional seesaw. She had lifted herself up by the soles of her shoes, taking destiny into her own hands, and mastered the reins on this wild horse ride called life. She couldn't possibly be threatened any longer by an expiring husband, whether he lived or died. Still, it was hard to tell with Mama.

He noticed her glancing at her watch every ten minutes or so. She looked toward the door for the arrival of Kendall, who, they had thought, would volunteer to stand a 24-hour vigil over his father's bed. For fifteen years, Howard had been Kendall's devoted champion. That was before Kendall got wise. A wisdom he had encountered when it was too late. The damage done. His innocence irrevocable. Now, Kendall was left with the burden of unraveling the knotted rope by which his life hung. Thinking about it, Skylar realized it was all the more reason for Kendall to stay away, to avoid his final shoulder-brushing with gruesome reminders. Arriving at that stroke of insight, Skylar, in his heart of hearts, didn't expect to see Kendall at the hospital at all.

"How're you doing, Mama?" Skylar said, touching her hand.

"I'm all right," she said, managing a tight smile, glancing once again at her watch.

"Can I get you something?"

"No, baby."

"So...," Skylar said, sighing. His mother wasn't in a talkative mood. "How's work?"

"Everything's fine. I hired three secretaries this morning."

"You really like working in personnel—"

"Human resources," she corrected him, then laughed. It lifted his heart to hear her laugh. "I'm only teasing you, Skylar. Yeah, I do love working in personnel, because I like people. Did I tell you Mrs. Manson is leaving—"

"Really? Will you get promoted to manager?"

"I don't know," she said, undoing and then retying the bow on her blouse, crossing her legs, the nylon stockings squeaking. "I sure hope so, but they're interviewing for the position, too."

"Will it bother you, if you don't get it?"

"No. I don't mind being assistant to the manager."

Skylar wasn't sure how to phrase his next question. "So, how's...?"

"George?"

"Yeah."

"Sshh! Your daddy might not be asleep," she whispered.

"He's asleep. He can't hear us. How's George?"

"He's all right, I guess."

"You haven't gone out with him yet?"

"Skylar! Your daddy's still alive. I'm a married woman."

"So what?" Skylar said, knowing it wouldn't persuade her. Mama's values were archaic, reflective of a repressed generation. Studying her, he could see why George, a co-worker and widower, was attracted to her. Life's short, Skylar had reminded her before. And George had been relentlessly pursuing her, asking her to dinner, to the movies, to a Labor Day barbecue to meet his children and grandchildren. Mama was obviously flattered. He'd never heard her talk and behave like a schoolgirl, her voice raised an octave. What was she waiting for?

"Things happen in their own time," Althea said. "Let's talk about you."

"We already have."

"How's this movie you're working on?"

"It's coming along okay."

"You working with anyone I know of?"

"John Fleming is directing. And Lionel Toussaint plays my father."

"Really? Oh, Skylar. I've always loved his movies. He's old now, huh?"

"No older than you," Skylar said, laughing.

"So, you like working with them?"

"Yeah. It's okay."

"Any problems?"

Skylar thought about the nine failed takes of the fire scene, which hadn't plagued him since he left for the hospital. Should he tell her, or not? "No," he said. "No problems at all."

Distracted as they were, Althea and Skylar heard Kendall before they saw him. He was arguing with a nurse who was probably frightened by his physical appearance. Confronted with a man who was disheveled and unshaven, with bloodshot eyes and dusty hair matted in dreadlocks, the nurse obviously had asked about Kendall's business as he wandered through the hospital corridors.

"Sorry, ma'am," Althea apologized, pulling Kendall by the arm, as he screamed at the nurse. "This is my son," she said. Then, to Kendall, "Just hush, Kendall. She's only doing her job."

Kendall kissed his mother's cheek. He glared at the nurse, as if to say, See, bitch! I'm Skylar Whyte's brother. Just goes to show, you never know who you're talking down to. Stoned, he tripped over the cart, then regained his balance. He hugged his brother tightly. Skylar kissed his brother's cheek, then peeled his arms from around his neck. Kendall sat down on the vacant bed, without acknowledging the unconscious man in the opposite bed. If she was calm before, Skylar could see now that emotion was erupting within Althea. She had deplored Kendall's dreadlocks — had advised him on more than one occasion to cut that shit off his head. She turned to her younger son, her eyes full of pity and indignation.

"I see you've shown up," Althea said, "in your all-too-familiar state." Her left eye twitched, a warning of what was to come. "Just had to shoot some of that shit in your arm before you met us here today, didn't you?"

Kendall didn't answer immediately. "I ain't high," he said. "I'm just tired, Mama. Groggy from no sleep."

"I don't know why," Althea said. "You don't work. Haven't had a job since God knows when. What're you tired from?"

With a look, Kendall sought support from Skylar, who said nothing. He began nodding out, his eyes closing suddenly, like a narcoleptic. His head dropped, his stubbly chin kissing his chest, and his body faltered. He whispered, conversing with himself — or "with his demons," Althea would say. As suddenly as he'd slipped into the nod, he slid out of it, and back to consciousness, his eyelids snapping open like rolled-up window shades. He fondled one of his dreadlocks, and asked, "Anything to drink?"

"There's water," Skylar said, pointing to the pitcher on Howard's tray.

"I swear, though," Kendall reiterated, "I ain't high. Honest. I ain't shot no dope in months." He grabbed the pitcher of water and poured himself a glass. Then his hands were all over his body, scratching and rubbing so fiercely Skylar wondered whether it was the quinine cut in the heroin, or possibly parasites feeding on his person.

"Kendall," Althea said, pleading. "I have asked you before, why don't you turn yourself in to a rehabilitation center?"

"Turn myself in sounds criminal," Kendall said.

"Exactly," Althea said. "You have committed the ultimate crime against yourself."

The nurse looked in. "You have ten minutes left," she said.

"We were just about to leave," Althea said, standing, collecting her handbag and attaché case. She turned to Kendall. "If you must destroy yourself, you can at least have the respect not to come around me looking like something the cat just dragged in. Just look

– 71 –

at you! Don't know whether you're coming or going. I wish you could just see yourself, Kendall James Whyte. You're truly a sight."

Kendall turned to Skylar. "I'm sorry, Sky," Kendall said. Since age fifteen — though only when he was high — he'd been apologizing to Skylar for all the times he'd been a bastard to him under Daddy's influence. "I love you, Sky. You're my only brother, man. Please forgive me."

Skylar had already forgiven him a thousand times. He loved his brother too. He was grateful they were able to smooth out the bumps of their once-turbulent relationship. When he was old enough to comprehend, he stopped holding his younger brother accountable for all that had happened between them. But since that time, some fifteen, twenty years ago, Kendall had continued the agonized apologizing, which made Skylar uneasy.

Althea was standing by the door, her hand on the knob, when Skylar placed his arm around his brother's shoulder. Kendall was about to say something when he began to gag. He covered his mouth with his hand, belched loudly, and vomited on the floor, the liquid oozing through his fingers, splashing Skylar's favorite shoes.

Stormy Weather

"MY SON'S NOT GOING anywhere with those two ... freaks!"

"Would you lower your voice. They ain't deaf, you know."

"They're not normal either ... and I've told you before, there's no such word as 'ain't.'"

"You understand what I'm saying. He told you all about it. You already said it was okay."

Skylar was embarrassed for his Uncle Aubrey. Though the conversation had been conducted in the upstairs bedroom, every word tumbled down the staircase, loud and clear. Skylar covered his ears, but the words filtered through his fingers and penetrated his eardrums.

Uncle Aubrey appeared relaxed. His legs crossed, he fanned himself nonchalantly with his fedora, the sheer curtains stirring from the unusually hot June breeze. The oscillating electric fan blew hot air as flies the size of kidney beans buzzed overhead. Uncle Aubrey's friend, George, wasn't as calm. He paced the living room floor, cursing under his breath, apparently annoyed and insulted by the conversation bellowing from upstairs. When he heard the word freaks, he looked at Uncle Aubrey, his mouth shaped in an O, gesticulating with his hands, pointing upstairs with his thumb. Uncle Aubrey grinned. His serenity put Skylar at ease. As it was, Skylar was wondering if he was all dressed up on a Sunday afternoon with no place to go.

Greenwich Village.

Skylar had never seen anything like it. Though a native New Yorker, he hadn't realized until then that he hadn't seen much of this wide and wondrous city. Outside Harlem and midtown, he'd barely explored the diverse neighborhoods. During the subway ride downtown on the A train, the dark tunnel was broken with an opening of yellow light. The conductor's voice announced Waverly

Place. Uncle Aubrey tapped his nephew on the shoulder, and the three of them walked between the sliding doors onto the platform. Up several flights of stairs they climbed, the roaring of underground trains rumbling and shaking the foundations on which they stood. One last flight of stairs and they strolled out onto the sidewalk of Avenue of the Americas.

Skylar couldn't believe his eyes.

He'd never seen such ... strange people. "See those men over there with the beards, earrings, berets, and sunglasses?" Uncle Aubrey explained, with the authority of a tour guide. "They're the last of what's called beatniks." They walked a block or so through the thick, slow-moving crowd, Skylar repeatedly bumping into passersby, his head constantly turning, neck craning, soaking up the sights.

"And this," Uncle Aubrey said, "is the Village. Never in your life will you ever see a place as fantastic as this." The streets teemed with so many people, Skylar imagined that every New Yorker was crammed into this neighborhood. Crowds were gathered at several spots, where opposing political viewpoints were being passionately put forth, as people cheered, clapped, or booed. They were debating civil rights, abortion, capital punishment, and something called Vietnam. Skylar had never heard those strange words before. Hadn't realized, until now, that his country was at war. His uncle pointed out a tall brick building with bars covering the windows. The Women's House of Detention, his uncle called it. A red-haired, freckled white girl in green pedal pushers and white sneakers, licking a strawberry ice cream cone, clutched her mother's skirt and pointed at Skylar. "Mommy, look! He has blue eyes!" Her mother slapped her pointed finger, and scolded her, whispering that it was bad manners to stare and point.

Scattered every few feet on the sidewalks were portrait artists, who sat before their easels capturing the likenesses of their subjects on paper with charcoal, pastels, and watercolors. Skylar was excited. He didn't understand why, but he was. A street poet recited verses aloud from a book. "He's reading Kerouac," Uncle Aubrey said. "One of my favorites." They stopped to listen. Skylar's attention strayed, his eyes studying a family of Negroes draped in dazzling African garb. The woman's hair was not straightened, long, flowing, and shiny with relaxer, like his mother's. Their hairstyles were identical. Coarse, bushy, thick.

"What's that?" Skylar asked his uncle.

"They're called Afros."

Skylar thought it looked horrendous. The little girl beside them, whose hair was a miniature version of that of the two adults, also wore a dashiki, beads, and sandals. The woman's ears were clipped with large wire hoops. Strings of multicolored beads looped, swung, and clicked about her neck. Skylar wasn't sure he liked it. But it was fascinating just the same.

They headed down Eighth Street, turned into MacDougal, and entered a park called Washington Square. The swaying trees danced to the clashing musical pulsations. Negro men played conga drums and bongos, while a chorus sang a South African chant, dancing as if possessed by ancient spirits. "They're singing that Miriam Makeba folk song she did on *The Ed Sullivan Show*," George said to Uncle Aubrey. At the fountain, before the structure resembling the Arc de Triomphe, another group sat in Indian squats. A long-haired man in sunglasses who called himself David Peel was backed by his band, the Lower East Side, as he sang risque songs entitled "I Do My Balling in the Bathroom" and "Up Against the Wall, Motherfucker."

Uncle Aubrey and George laughed at the songs' lyrics, but Skylar felt left out, missing the inside joke. It frustrated him not knowing what balling meant. A hat was passed around among the spectators, collecting donations. Skylar's eyes followed the strange-smelling cigarette, which strangers passed back and forth and drew deep puffs from, holding their breath and speaking as though they were suffocating, their eyes red and glassy. There were dancers, jugglers, mimes, men doing two-bit magic acts, a young mezzo-soprano standing on a milk crate and singing opera. A circus. Not quite Barnum & Bailey at Madison Square Garden, but strange, and wonderful. Skylar never felt this much at home in his native Harlem.

"Now," Uncle Aubrey announced, affectionately wrapping an arm around Skylar's shoulder, "we're going over to the East Village. You like it so far, Sky?"

"Yes," Skylar said. "A lot."

"People here are free," his uncle said. "You can be what you want and nobody cares."

They had crossed Second Avenue and St. Mark's Place before entering a run-down theater called the Bijou. What a weird name,

Skylar thought, nibbling his Nathan's hot dog, sipping an Orange Julius. Uncle Aubrey let him do as he pleased. Quite different from being out with Daddy, who always reminded him: Don't do this — You can't do that — Stand over here where I can see you. Skylar wished Uncle Aubrey was his father. If for no other reason than, Uncle Aubrey never used the word *don't*. It didn't seem to be part of his vocabulary.

In the darkness of the theater, Skylar sat with a large container of buttered popcorn and Bon Bons in his lap. With Daddy, he was allowed one small box of popcorn which he had to share with Kendall. Strains of orchestral music floated from the orchestra pit to the ceiling as the stage curtains parted slowly. Weren't many people in the theater, and it was as if they had it to themselves.

Skylar couldn't believe what he was watching.

This Greenwich Village was bubbling over with surprises, one after another. His eyes bugged out of his head, watching a large white screen filled with faces as black as his. Skylar loved the movies. He'd seen what he believed to be hundreds of them. But this was different, new, unfamiliar. He'd never seen a movie with an all-colored cast of actors, singers, musicians, and dancers. When his family went to the drive-in, his parents brought along blankets. They anticipated the children falling asleep halfway through the picture, so the blanket was to keep them warm. Kendall fell asleep, invariably. Most times, Skylar would watch until the end, but he, too, fell asleep if the movie didn't hold his interest.

Compelling movies like *Imitation of Life* and *Psycho* had held his attention throughout. They were indelibly imprinted in his memory. The former, because he couldn't figure out why a white girl was calling a Negro woman Mama. The latter, due to the mentally disturbed man who dressed like, and spoke in the voice of, his dead mother. Skylar was forbidden to watch the shower scene. His mother held up the blanket across the length of the front seat, like a curtain. If he saw it, he would have nightmares, she explained. He construed that to mean it was the best part. Though he missed it, he liked the movie anyway. It was scarier than even Vincent Price's *House on Haunted Hill*.

This movie with the all-colored cast would keep him awake, he knew. He heard wet, smacking noises. When he turned, he could've sworn he saw Uncle Aubrey kissing George. And though the theatre was dark — he was almost certain, but could've been mistaken — it looked as if the two men were holding hands. Skylar decided he didn't like Uncle Aubrey's friend George.

Then it happened. On-screen, a beautiful woman, the complexion of his father and brother, the most breathtaking woman he'd ever seen, sang an unforgettable song. She was leaning against a window, her head tilted back, cocked gracefully to the side, bangs covering her forehead. Elegant and sultry, her hands enhanced the strange beauty of her sorrow with fluid, airy movements. Outside her window, rain poured and winds blew over her and her gauzy dress. It reminded Skylar of the living room curtains at home being blown by the summer breeze.

Skylar was mesmerized. An engaging melody poured like liquid gold from the divinely sculptured lips of this exquisite woman.

"That's Lena Horne," Uncle Aubrey leaned over and whispered, his chair creaking. Skylar heard but didn't hear, much too captivated by the novelty of it all. She sang of love, of her heart being broken by love. She moaned about there being no sun up in the sky. She swooned about the rainy weather, since she and her man ain't been together. When he heard her sing "ain't" in the lyric, he recalled Daddy scolding Mama, not three hours earlier, for using the same word. Daddy should see this lady, Skylar thought. Nothing she said, or sang, could possibly be wrong, grammatically or otherwise. When the song finished, Skylar exhaled. He hadn't realized he was holding his breath throughout each arresting verse.

The movie ended, screen going blank, curtains closing, house lights coming up. "See, didn't I tell you?" Uncle Aubrey said to him. "Your daddy said there's no such thing as a colored movie star. Now, you've just seen a whole movie full of them. Sky, you can be anything you want to be. You're a beautiful, bright, promising child. Let no one stand in your way of what you want to do ... not even your father. Understand?"

Skylar nodded his head. He understood all too well. Daddy never said things like that to him. He said them, instead, to Kendall, who entertained aspirations of NFL stardom.

Skylar became somber. He thought the day had ended, that this wonderful Sunday afternoon out on the town in Greenwich Village with his favorite Uncle Aubrey and his friend George was over. When Uncle Aubrey mentioned that they had one more stop before boarding the A train back uptown, he was happy again. But he didn't understand Uncle Aubrey's warning of, "Promise me you won't tell your parents I brought you here. Not even your mother, okay?" Skylar agreed, unsure of what he was agreeing to.

They were in front of a building that flashed a yellow neon sign. GOLD BUG. Opening the door, they descended a long staircase into pitch darkness. Skylar was a little frightened, and held onto his uncle's sleeve. An old, crusty man, with facial pockmarks, sat in a booth collecting money, handing out tickets, like the ticket-taker at the Bijou. He stamped their hands with a mark detectable under a fluorescent light which meant, Skylar assumed, they were members of a secret club. Judy Garland was on the jukebox belting, "Sing Hallelujah, Come On Get Happy!" and several young and middle-aged men snapped their fingers, or bobbed their heads to the rhythm.

This place was strange. Dark, murky, not a woman in the joint. Uncle Aubrey's warning flashed back into his head. But as yet, he could see nothing to tell his parents about, even if he wanted to. Uncle Aubrey ordered two Jack Daniel's for George and himself, a Roy Rogers for Skylar. The bartender with the plucked eyebrows acted sissyish and pinched Skylar's cheek.

"You're the youngest customer we've ever had here at the Bug," he said. "And by far the cutest."

Skylar didn't like him. He smiled too much. And behaved more like a woman than a man. Skylar grew uncomfortable, fidgeting on the bar stool, spinning quarters and nickels on the counter. The men started dancing — with each other, mind you. Skylar didn't know what to make of this. Girls were allowed to dance with each other. Hold hands. Even kiss. That was socially acceptable and tolerable. But not boys. If the kids uptown saw him doing this, he'd be called a faggot. Come to think of it, that's what they called him anyway. And they'd never seen him dance with anybody. After two sips of his soda, he doubled over, complaining, faking a stomachache. His uncle assured him they'd be leaving soon. "I promised your mama I'd have you back by dark, and I'm not in the mood to fight with that father of yours again today," Uncle Aubrey said, sipping his Jack Daniel's. "We fight so much, I should be getting paid for it." That being the case, Skylar thought, I should be rich.

When they finished with late-afternoon cocktails and were headed back toward the direction of the Sixth Avenue subway, Skylar decided that he was displeased. He didn't like George. Hated that place where the men danced together. Uncle Aubrey was talking to him, probing him about his observations of the entire day. Uncle Aubrey could tell, by Skylar's grunts and one-word replies, that the child was troubled about something.

"What's wrong, Sky? Tell your Uncle Aubrey."

Skylar wanted to speak his mind. But when glancing at George, he changed it. Uncle Aubrey excused himself, taking Skylar to the side in private conference.

"I don't want you to take me to that place again," he said, his big blue eyes glowing in the setting afternoon sun.

"Why?" Uncle Aubrey asked.

"Because ... just because," Skylar said, shrugging his shoulders.

An early-evening storm was hovering. Warm drops of precipitation splashed on the sidewalk, the air heavy with the smell of the Atlantic Ocean. Uncle Aubrey, turning up his collar and lapels, stooped to look his nephew straight in the eye.

"Sky," he said, "everybody in the world isn't the same. Some of us are ... different."

"Different how?" Skylar said.

Uncle Aubrey took his hand. "You know I love you, right? You're my favorite nephew, and I have two dozen if I have one, right? I would never tell you anything wrong. What I'm trying to say is ... everybody's not meant to ... grow up, get married, and have children."

"Is that why Daddy always calls you a ... freak?" Skylar said, deliberately being a smart-ass.

"I guess," Uncle Aubrey said. "But that's because I'm different. Those men we just left in the bar are also different. But we're still the same as any other human being. What we do, and how we live our lives, is not shameful. We have feelings like anybody else and we take pride in our difference. You may not understand now. But I'd be very pleased if you remember what I've said..."

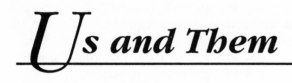Us and Them

SO, GOT A NEW FRIEND, HUH?

I didn't know niggers could be friends.

What's the matter? Our skin too white for you to play with?

Nigger lover.

Ain't we good enough for you anymore?

No, they weren't. If they could have such terrible attitudes about colored people, then maybe he was too good for them.

Ever since Mrs. Conway had paired them for tutoring purposes, it seemed everyone, except Evan and Michael, was displeased with the arrangement. His junior high school classmates treated him differently now. They accused him of being a traitor.

"It was Mrs. Conway's idea, you guys," Evan pleaded, when a handful of his friends cornered him outside the gymnasium. "He's tutoring me."

"That doesn't mean you have to be his friend," Tommy Wharton said, whistling through his chipped front tooth.

"You're making us all look bad, Evan," Chip Jaworski added, pushing up his sliding eyeglasses.

"I told you," Evan said again, his gym sneakers tied together and slung across his shoulders. "He's just tutoring me, you guys. Honest."

"Yeah," someone mumbled, as they dispersed and walked away from him. "That ain't all he's doing to you."

After school, Evan waited for Michael. He was trying to think of a new place where they could meet at three o'clock before studying together. Not that he was ashamed of being seen with Michael — he was actually proud. Michael was such an exemplary student and, Evan was finding out, a good friend. He just couldn't endure the harassment. If he passed by a certain group of guys snickering in the corridor, they were likely to break into a colored song, any colored song, before bursting into a chorus of howls and hisses.

Even the girls, who were usually neutral about everything except boys, boycotted him. Before Michael, he could hardly keep them out of his face. Every other week, a different girl had requested his telephone number. Or they dropped love notes or letters in his locker, or slipped them inside his books or his jacket pocket. Or Mary Ann Frazier urgently needed to speak with him because Francine Stassi, her very best friend in the whole wide world, had a terrible crush on him and was just wondering if he was going steady with anybody.

Now the girls avoided him. They said nothing when he passed by them in the hall. No longer did they smile, giggle, or blush from behind thick, blue linen loose-leaf notebooks. The moment he thought of a private place where he and Michael could meet, Michael was walking through the school gate, waving, smiling. He must not be getting the cold treatment, Evan thought.

"What's wrong?" Michael asked.

"Everything," Evan said.

"Like what?"

"The kids at school—"

"That?" Michael wrapped an arm around Evan's neck. "You shouldn't let that stuff bother you."

"Well, you would if it happened to you," Evan said, unwrapping Michael's arm from around his neck.

"And what makes you think I don't get teased?" Michael said, stopping to face Evan.

"Because," Evan said, "nobody's treating you like—"

"How do you know that?"

"Well, are they?"

"Maybe."

"You mean Chip Jaworski and Tommy Wharton are—"

"More like Denzel Jefferson and Cardell Flowers."

They walked a block in silence, the late-November sun about to go down behind the Santa Monica Mountains, mixing with the smog for a breathtaking, champagne pink sunset. Evan hoped Mrs. Conway was happy. She had brought all this on. It was her fault. Yes, he'd benefited from Michael's tutoring. The kid knew his stuff. There was nothing he couldn't multiply or divide, no matter how many numbers, or how irregular the fraction.

And Evan's grades had improved. He was now a member of the National Honor Society and he felt he owed it to Michael. Mom and Dad never opened their mouths when they saw the usual C+ in mathematics preempted by an A. It didn't matter to them. But it mattered to Evan. He was going to college, no matter what Dad said. After Michael brought it up that night at dinner, the idea became more attractive as Evan thought about it. He considered going away to school, a school where students didn't care who he was friends with.

"Why didn't you tell me your friends were giving you a bad time, too?" Evan asked.

Michael shrugged and released a sigh. "It's no big deal," he said. "Those guys're just jerks."

Evan was bothered that Michael wasn't bothered. Why couldn't he adopt that attitude? Why was he so worried about what his friends thought?

"What do they say to you?" Evan inquired.

"What?" Michael seemed distracted.

"You know," Evan said. "What kinds of things do they say?"

"Why?" Michael asked.

"I'm curious."

"They call me ... Oreo."

"Oreo?"

"Black on the outside, white on..."

Evan started laughing. It was the first time he'd laughed all day.

"What's so funny about that?" Michael said.

"I don't know. It just is. What else do they say?"

"They say I try to act and talk white, and that I think I'm too good for them and—"

"That's what my friends say about me!"

Evan couldn't comprehend the logic behind that. So what, if he made a friend who wasn't white? Why should they think he felt superior to them? Besides, he and Michael had a lot in common, some of which they discovered the first night of tutoring.

Dad had gone upstairs and hadn't come back down for the remainder of the evening — not until Michael left. Mom was washing and drying dishes, burning tangerine peels on the stove burners for fragrance, and humming a tuneless tune, watching them, it seemed, through one eye, the other focused on the sink. She hummed nothing in particular when her mind was occupied with something else. That told Evan that she was watching every move he and Michael made, monitoring every word they said. Having watched television, they settled down to the books. Michael was demonstrating an example of multiple division when, absent-mindedly, he began whistling a tune that sounded familiar to Evan.

"What's that?" Evan said.

"It's the number of times this number can go into this—"

"The song you're whistling."

"That? Sam and Dave—"

"You like Sam and Dave?" Evan nearly shouted, remembering where he was.

"Yeah! You too?"

Evan lowered his voice as Mom's humming became more direc-tionless. "I have some records upstairs," Evan whispered. "And I got that one, too."

"Why're you whispering?" Michael said.

"Well, because," Evan whispered, furtively glancing over his shoulder. "Because my mom doesn't like loud music."

"You should come to my house, then."

"Can I? When?"

As Evan walked into Michael's home, the oven was on, filling the small, three-bedroom stucco house with a soothing heat. But there was another kind of warmth in the air. Of all his friends, Evan had never met anyone's parents who smiled when they met him and heartily shook his hand, as if they meant it. Michael's mom, cheeks full and round, a gap in the center of her smile, wiped her hands on the apron and placed breaded chicken breasts into a pan.

Evan looked around the clean, well-kept living room at the plastic-covered sofa, the armchairs, the coffee table and matching end tables with fluffy doilies, the mantelpiece over the fireplace supporting sepia-toned family portraits, the black-and-white tele-vision resting on the gold stand, the white lace curtains that were beginning to yellow, the throw rugs spread here and there on the floor ... In other words, from what he could see, their house looked a lot like his. That was yet another thing his parents had lied to him about, the way they claimed colored people lived. Like a Polaroid, his mind's eye snapped pictures of this living room. He wanted to be prepared, detail for detail at his fingertips, when Mom said,

What did I tell you? You satisfied? They live like, and have the manners of, filthy pigs, right?

"We're pleased you could join us for dinner," Michael's mom said, pulling up a chair for Evan to sit in. "Please sit down, honey. We've heard so much about you."

"How good is your chess game?" a voice bellowed from behind. Michael's dad, his feet sliding across the floor in slippers, his t-shirt barely covering his potbelly, reached out and shook Evan's hand so firmly, it hurt for a moment.

"I'm not that good at chess, sir," Evan explained. "Why don't you play Michael? He's pretty good."

"I need somebody else to beat for a change," he said, chuckling. He opened the refrigerator door and retrieved something, and his wife playfully slapped his hand.

"Now, don't show off 'cause Evan's here," she said, winking at Evan. "Dinner's ready in ten minutes. And I done told you about your nibbling. Nibble here, nibble there. You worse than that rabbit Michael used to have."

"But I'm hungry," he pleaded.

"Just march your hungry self right back into the living room where you came from until I call you," she said, grinning. "And not a minute before."

How pleased Evan would have been had his parents been as polite and attentive and humorous to Michael that first night. Now that he thought about it, he could count the times he'd seen Mom or Dad laugh and tease each other. Everything about this household looked right. Smelled right. Felt right.

"Mama," Michael said. "We'll be in my bedroom playing records if you need me."

"Oh no you won't either."

Evan turned toward the voice. Standing before a bedroom doorway was the prettiest girl he'd ever seen. Janet Lyden and Francine Stassi thought they were hot stuff. They didn't stand a chance against this girl.

"Oh yes we are," Michael said to the girl.

"Daddy," she whined. "Michael's going to play records and I'm ready to study."

"Well, baby girl," Michael's dad said, "Mike got company. And he just wanna show his friend a nice time. Could you study later?"

The girl eyed Evan up and down, her face expressionless. "I guess," she said, clicking her tongue.

"This is my ugly sister, Marla," Michael said to Evan. Ugly? Evan thought. Not from here, she's not.

"Pleased to meet you," he said, and nodded. Marla didn't say anything. She just looked.

As they walked past her into his bedroom, she said, "He's cute, Michael."

"I know," Michael said.

"What do you mean, you know?" she asked.

"That's why you agreed so quickly to study later," Michael said, entering his bedroom, and kicked the door shut.

A candy store of vinyl is what it was. Michael had every record Evan had and more. They bounced from the Four Tops to Jackie Wilson to the Supremes to James Brown to the Temptations. Michael taught Evan a few dances: the Watusi, the Shing-a-ling, the Monkey. It was the first time Evan was dancing with a live colored person. Normally, he danced along with them, separated by a television screen. They were having such a good time Evan had forgotten why he was there.

After dinner and studies, the boys spun more of Michael's 45s on the record player. After which, they accepted Michael's dad's invitation to a family game of Scrabble.

"Ain't got nobody to beat in chess," his dad said.

"You never beat me," his mom said.

"You can't even play," his dad said.

Evan didn't want to go home. He could've stayed there forever in the warm house, with the warm people, the pretty girl, the endless stack of 45s they were allowed to play as loud as they wanted. Why, he thought, were his parents and friends so afraid of and hateful toward these people? They had to be some of the best he'd met. He called home to have his seven o'clock curfew extended.

"Hello?"

"Mom, it's me."

"You coming home now?"

"That's why I'm calling. Could I stay a little longer—"

"No! That's out of the question."

"Why?"

"Because I said so, that's why."

"But I'm having a good time."

"Be lucky your dad let you go to begin with." She covered the mouthpiece with her hand and mumbled something to Dad. "How was the food? What did they feed you?"

He didn't know how to answer this without Michael's family overhearing. "It was great."

"But what? What was it, I'm asking."

His mind relived and retasted Michael's mother's incredibly tender, breaded chicken breasts that melted on his tongue, the potatoes *au gratin* oozing with cheese — as if she knew how much Evan loved sharp cheddar — and the firmest, most buttery broccoli he'd ever tasted. Mom's seven-course annual Christmas dinner never tasted as good as that. "Nothing," he said. "Just regular stuff."

■

They were crossing Firestone Boulevard when Michael detoured from their usual route home.

"Why're we going this way?" Evan asked.

"I want to show you something."

"What?"

"You'll see."

"See what?"

"Guess what, Evan? I can shoot."

"Shoot?"

"Yeah, you know, with girls."

"Really?"

"Yep."

"How do you know?"

"Because this morning before I woke up, I was having a dream, right? And in the dream, I was doing it to Charlaine Munson, this girl who lives on my block. And it felt good down there—"

"Down where?"

"In my dick. I never had that feeling before. Anyway, it felt so good, I was doing it to her harder and harder." A grin parted his lips. "Before I knew it, I woke up, and my underwear was all sticky."

"From what?"

"You know what. And when I woke up, I was sleeping on my stomach. I never sleep on my stomach."

"Wow! How did it feel?"

"Great, Evan. Can you, I mean, have you yet?"

"No," Evan said, his head drooping.

"I'm a man now," Michael said, his chest stuck out a bit more than Evan remembered it.

They walked across a wide-open junior high school running track and climbed the fence. Evan followed Michael into the shadows of the freeway underpass, where it smelled of urine and beer, and sparkled when the setting sun reflected off jagged pieces of glass. Michael wasted no time unzipping his trousers, pulling them down to his knees. With his thumbs, he yanked down the elastic waist of his briefs and humped the air. "See?"

"You got hair down there already?" Evan said, astonished.

"I told you. After this morning, I'm a man," Michael said. "I'm going to get all the pussy now."

Evan studied the brown, limp penis, the firm, heart-shaped scrotum, and the curly hair growing on them both. He knew this was supposed to happen when boys became men. As yet, he'd only found a single strand of hair on himself.

"You don't have hair yet, Evan?"

"Yeah," Evan said, trying to sound convincing. "I do."

"Let's see," Michael said.

Timidly, Evan opened his zipper without pulling down his pants.

"Where?" Michael said.

"See?" Evan said, pointing.

"I don't see anything," Michael said. "You want to touch mine?"

"Sure," Evan said, knowing that if his friends knew he was doing this ... and yet, they all did it too. They were always in the locker room comparing prick sizes. He touched Michael's pubic hair. He felt himself. Then he felt Michael again, his forefinger slipping to the base of Michael's penis.

"Pretty neat, huh?" Michael said.

"Yeah." Evan must've looked or sounded disappointed.

"Don't worry, Evan," Michael said, pulling up his trousers and zipping them shut. "It'll happen to you too. One day, you'll be a man like me. C'mon, let's go study."

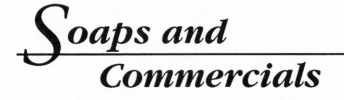

Soaps and Commercials

AREN'T YOU GLAD YOU use Dial? Don't you wish everybody did?

"Hell, no!" Althea shouted at the television screen, as she did to all TV commercials that ground her nerves into dust. Every time she turned around, the television was selling her another damn product — products she had no money or use for. White women were afforded such luxuries as dishwashers and self-cleaning ovens.

"Hey, you know, Howard," a friend of Howard's had said one night, during dinner with the family. "Ain't no telling what the white man'll come up with next. Now they got this new thing called a dishwasher. Can you believe that? A machine that'll wash your dishes. You should get one for the missus here."

"I already have one," Howard said, pointing to Althea. "Came pretty damn cheap, too."

Fab, all-temperature Cheer, cold-water All, new improved Tide, the white knight of Ajax Ammonia, Mr. Clean, Crest toothpaste, approved by the American Dental Association ... Good Lord! All she wanted was to watch the update of *As the World Turns*. If only she could trade her problems as Harlem housewife, mother of two, for the life of Miss Suburbia Rich Bitch, whose primary concern was which gown to purchase from Bergdorf's for her daughter's fairy-tale wedding.

She was picking up a pair of Howard's funky-smelling argyle socks, Kendall's dirt- and grass-stained football jersey, Skylar's knee-worn dungarees, when her eyes strayed to the headlines of the *Amsterdam News* on the coffee table. Dr. King was down there in Selma, Alabama. Police let ferocious German shepherds loose on the reverend and the marchers. If that wasn't enough, they sprayed them down with water hoses as if they were yard dogs. They even sprayed that colored woman old enough to be my mother! Lord have mercy! Why is it people hate colored folks so much?

She was dusting the end tables, humming Dr. King's anthem, "We Shall Overcome." She picked up the family portrait. The one they posed for in Central Park at the Labor Day picnic with Howard's job. She studied it closely, noticing something she'd never seen before. Howard's arms were wrapped around Kendall, hers around Skylar. Butterscotch on one side, chocolate on the other. Now, ain't that tellin'? she thought. She adored her two boys; even her husband — what love there was left for Howard.

If she did nothing else in life, she wanted to be the best mother she could possibly be. She treated her boys equally. She'd never loved any two people so assiduously. But it was difficult with Kendall. Howard was God to him, which made it difficult for anybody else to reach him, make him obey, convince him that his mother's words held as much weight as his father's. From the time he was two, she hadn't spanked him. Barely yelled at him. Lord knows he needed it. If she said anything, Howard climbed all over her. Whatever she told Kendall, discreet or not, would find its way back to Howard's ears.

Then there was the confrontation. Got so she felt an invisible line divided their household. Like she and Skylar were Us and Howard and Kendall were Them. Civil war was no way to run a family. She wanted to raise her boys equally, groom each son to be the gentleman she thought she'd married. Was a woman's duty, since women gave birth to all the men in the world, to mold and shape them, so they'd be better husbands for their future wives than the kind of men who would inflict upon their women the hell she was enduring.

Was difficult pinpointing where Skylar went wrong with Howard. He had never done anything to provoke it that she could recall. If he had, it still didn't warrant a life sentence to mental and emotional abuse. Furthermore, there was nothing sissified about that boy. Skylar was just softer, more sensitive than other boys. Most boys, hardheads that they were, could've benefited from their feelings. That was the problem with men to begin with.

Like the night when Skylar was no more four months old. He'd been so ill, she'd worried herself sick. Didn't seem to bother Howard, who had his mind set on the movie, dinner, and dancing.

She could understand he was doing what he thought best. After all, it was their second anniversary. Bless his heart. But what was best was staying at home with their sick child. They could go to the movies anytime. It was their collective duty — not her mother's or her sister, Gloria Jean's — to nurse him through his nasty fever.

Althea's mother had had eleven children of her own and was in no position, or frame of mind, to care for someone else's. Althea helped raise and nurture the bottom half of her younger siblings. Responsibility was overwhelming for her mother alone. Althea and her older sisters each adopted one of the little ones. Caring for a baby brother or sister, while barely a child herself, prepared her for the undivided attention she paid Skylar. She didn't mean to give the impression that everyone was inept when it came to her child. She just preferred to do it herself. It was her way. She knew it was getting on Howard's nerves, the way he sighed, sucked his tongue, his patience thinning. But then, he wasn't much help with taking care of babies either. Just loved to make them. Then his part was finished. Like most men. The Lord should create something else for women to marry.

Here she was fussing with her firstborn, administering his medicine, greasing his little pained body with castor oil, cleaning his nose by blowing into his mouth. He screamed so, she thought his lungs might burst. The phlegm from his nose splattered on her cheek. She rocked him in the cradle, using his stuffed dolls as puppets to amuse him. She sang lullabies, stroking his back with her tired, aching fingers. And there was Howard, off to the side, propped up in the bed, watching her as if he were timing how long she'd be busy with Skylar, playing with himself under the sheets like he didn't have a bit of sense left in his head. Men. All they think about are three things. Pussy. More pussy. A whole lot of pussy.

Didn't he see why she couldn't relax and watch the movie? Didn't he know there was something more pressing on her mind? Why wasn't he as alarmed as she was? Men see what they want to see. That's the name of the game. She had gotten up four, six, eight times to go to the telephone in the lobby. When she got back, all he could say was that she had missed the best part, some stupid part where Burt Lancaster got killed with some young hussy. And her child is home with a babysitter, coming down with God knows what. You'd think he'd ask about the welfare of his own son. His firstborn. But, no. He was worried about getting to the restaurant on time, about their reservations possibly being canceled, talking about his job, the rise of the colored man, chest all puffed out, full of himself.

Didn't he think about anything or anybody else? If she heard one more time about his being a CPA, the first colored the company hired, she was going to glue his lips shut in his sleep. If he was enjoying such prosperity as "a colored CPA," why were they struggling and wrestling with household bills? Living damn near paycheck to paycheck. Just what was he doing with his money anyway? Even after she talked with her sister, Gloria Jean, from the restaurant, and insisted they leave at once, he still had his mind on fucking. Ain't that just like a man. Here the child is screaming his head off, Gloria Jean scared to death, not knowing what to do with him, and Howard's trying to drag her off for a quickie. Sure would be nice if God could punish men; let them be pregnable. Then see how they like it.

By now she was furious. So livid with her husband's behavior, she decided not to speak to him. She couldn't. If she opened her mouth, she knew she'd say the wrong thing. So she kept her thoughts to herself. She was crying inside. She was in the middle of a tug-of-war between the needy child screaming in one corner and her resentful, jealous husband in the other.

When she nestled next to him in bed, after she got Skylar to sleep, she decided she wouldn't take part in the act. He could have her body. But not her participation. It was her way of saying, You won't do your part in raising this child, I won't do mine in bed. He dove into her. With each pounding thrust, she couldn't tell if the man was sex-starved or if he was punishing her for spousal neglect. But she'd fix his little ass. Howard liked to kiss when he exploded inside her. His favorite part. She felt next to nothing; she did it to please him. Wasn't like she was sharing that explosion. Intercourse usually left her exhausted and sore. This time she decided not to let him kiss her. She hadn't talked to him all night, and he hadn't gotten the hint, or didn't care to. He was grunting in her ear like an excited pig, eyes rolling to the back of his head. She knew the precise moment. They'd been doing it every other night since the ring was slipped on her finger. Would've been every night if she'd let him have his way.

She turned her face toward Skylar's crib. Howard's rough hand grabbed her by the jaw, and pulled her face back to his. She didn't want to be there. In the most essential way, she wasn't. As if her spirit had got up, climbed out of bed, walked across the floor, leaned against the wall, and watched this fool pumping away at a woman who didn't want to be bothered. He was making love to a shell. Then Skylar started screaming. She was out of that bed in one movement. With the weight of a grown man pressed against her, she didn't recall how she did it. She felt Howard's eyes burning through her. Skylar was crying. She was too, inside. Howard was cursing her under his breath. She drowned out those filthy words by singing a lullaby to her son.

Weeks later, she feigned headaches when Howard pressed suggestively against her. Having been put off several times with that excuse, he surprised her one night.

"Still got that headache?" he asked, his hands concealing something behind his back.

"Yep!" she said. "Been keeping this migraine since I don't know when. I should see a doctor about it..."

He pressed a tiny wrapped gift into her hand. She was surprised and delighted by his thoughtfulness.

"For me?" she was saying, realizing he hadn't bought her a thing since their anniversary. She sat up in bed, nervously untangling the ribbon.

"Anacin?" she asked, perplexed, and perturbed. Another one of his sick, gift-wrapped jokes.

"You have a migraine, right?" he said.

"Yeah, but—"

"But nothing," he cut her off. "Take two and keep them here on your nightstand. That way, Presto! No more headaches."

White women come apart at the seams over a run in a stocking, she was thinking, bent over the ironing board, starching and pressing Howard's white shirt, shaking her head at the final act in her soap, wishing she could trade places with those white women and give them something to really cry about. Colored women put up with so much. And in return, get so little. Her own problems should be so insignificant, fretting over her husband's inability to remember their wedding anniversary, worrying about whether the children had cavities, or which guest room the widowed mother-in-law would sleep in when her flight arrived from Capri. She was shaking her head at the nonsense of it all, when there was a knock on the door. Now, who could that be, dropping by this time of the day? she thought. Glancing at the clock, she turned the doorknob.

"Gloria Jean!" Althea said.

"Hi, Thea."

Althea made two cups of Maxwell House coffee and they sat at the kitchen table.

"How's Mama doing?" Althea said.

"She doing fine," Gloria Jean said. "Daddy been home a lot from work 'cause he sick, and he getting on Mama's last nerve, but other than that..."

"How's James? Anybody seen him lately?"

"That ol' hardheaded brother of ours, he make me sick sometime ... You know, Pearline owe me some money. I should get it from her. She just got paid ... Did I tell you Aubrey called the other night from Los Angeles?"

"What's he—"

"Annie Mae had a baby girl. She say she tired of girls."

"You all right, Gloria Jean?" Althea said, listening to her sister jump from one subject to the next.

"Yeah, why?"

"'Cause you acting kind of—"

"Am I? I'm sorry. Nerves, I guess." She turned and glanced out the window. "What was I talking about?" she said, returning her attention to Althea.

"I don't know. You was talking about three or four things at once. You said something about when Aubrey called the other night. What did he say?" Gloria Jean wasn't looking at her.

"Gloria Jean!" Althea said, becoming annoyed.

"What? I'm sorry. What did you say, Thea? My mind wandered."

"You sure you all right?"

"Sure, I'm fine, honey, really. Maybe not as good as you. You the one with the successful husband, and two gorgeous boys. You ain't gotta get up at five in the morning to fight snow and traffic to get to work, where you don't wanna be in the first place. I swear, I hope to be like you one day, girl. You got it made."

Althea could've set the record straight for her. Could've separated myth from reality, giving her baby sister the real low-down. But why discourage the innocent and naive. Gloria Jean was romantically involved with a former petty criminal. She'd find out for herself soon enough. Marriage had a way of doing that to folks.

"All of us wanna be like you, Thea," Gloria Jean said, sipping her coffee. "Evelyn, Margie, Loretta, Mildred, LaVern, me — all your sisters. You the lucky one. Your in-laws are light-skinned and got good hair. One of your boys got green eyes, the other one got blue. The Lord is truly blessing you, girl. What you do that I didn't do? Nobody else in the family had that big wedding, like y'all was royalty, or something. Then you lived in one apartment, and your husband bought you a two-story home. And if you don't mind my saying so, Howard got to be one of the prettiest niggers I ever seen. I swear, I want a life like yours. But..."

Suddenly, Gloria Jean started crying. Between sobs, Althea couldn't tell what she was saying. She got a bottle of Howard's whiskey and poured Gloria Jean a glass. She stroked her back and neck, sat down, and held her hand.

"Tell me what's wrong," Althea said.

Between sips, Gloria Jean summed up her problems in one syllable: "Floyd." She sniffled, then looked out the window again, her forefinger absently tracing the rim of her cup.

"When he got outta the Tombs—"

"What was he in there for?"

"Breaking and entering. But, Thea, he's really a good man, really. He ain't no thief. Anyway, he did six months and said he was going to marry me when he got out. Every time I went to visit him in prison, he told me that. When he got out, I never got an engagement ring. And my heart was set on having this here big wedding ... like yours. But every time I bring it up, he get quiet. Sometimes, he get an attitude. 'Tha's all you damn women ever think about, marriage,' he said to me." She mimicked his growling, bass voice, which made Althea laugh. "Now, I think he got another woman. Ain't that something? I'm finding phone numbers in his pocket left and right. My girlfriends seen him out with other women in after-hours bars. Somebody else said he got a child by some other girl in the projects—"

"Did you ask him about it?"

"Yeah."

"And?"

"He denied it, what else? But I can tell he's slipping away from me. If I'd known before, I wouldn't have done it."

"Done what?"

"You know."

"You mean, you—"

"Thea, can I borrow some money?"

"For what?"

"I gotta get rid of it. I know it's wrong, but what am I gonna do with a child whose daddy don't want me? I know God's gon' punish me for killing what's inside me..." Her voice trailed off as she swallowed back tears. "A girlfriend of mine know a woman who could do it; she work right here in Harlem. I hear she's safe. Ain't nobody ever died before. But she charge a lot. Could you lend me the money?"

"How much?"

"Two hundred dollars."

"Jesus, Gloria Jean. How long do it take?"

"Half hour, I think."

"Who's this woman? What's her name?"

"Some lady named Verlean. Nobody know her last name."

"You sure it's safe?"

"Yes."

"And nobody ever died?"

"No."

Althea juggled these answers in her head, knowing Howard would break her face if he thought she was secretly withdrawing funds from their savings account. She'd have to put the money back. Quickly. Especially since the savings withdrawal would be double the amount Gloria just quoted her. For Althea's body had been telling her recently that something was growing inside her as well. She tortured herself, agonizing over decisions. She couldn't have any more babies. Couldn't chance Howard's mistreatment of another child. Or worse, shaping that child into his loyal ally, turning her son or daughter against her.

She couldn't live like that. Kendall was more than enough. She hadn't told anyone. What Howard don't know won't hurt him, was her thinking. For weeks, she'd been wondering what to do about it.

And here comes her baby sister with an answer as plain as the tears on her cheeks. She hadn't considered getting rid of it until Gloria Jean paid her this visit. She remembered caring for Gloria Jean as a baby, and now that baby was grown up and trying to get rid of her own. She couldn't bring another human being into that house of turmoil. Handing it over directly to the Lord was, for her, the lesser of two evils. She would then humble herself, ask His forgiveness, and pray that Howard never found out.

Nowadays, he was blaming her for having left his family in middle-class Jersey City for tenement-infested Harlem. She had "coerced" him into abandoning his family. His children weren't as close to the Whytes as they were to the Hutchinsons. They were picking up all the Hutchinsons' bad habits, bad English, bad influences. He said he couldn't pry her away from those worthless niggers with a crowbar. Having another child, she thought, might "force" him to move the family to Jersey for sure. Lord knows he wouldn't leave by himself.

Just then, Howard walked in for lunch. Althea had lost her sense of time, not realizing it was almost twelve-thirty. Gloria Jean quickly wiped her tears. First thing Howard noticed was his bottle of whiskey on the kitchen table.

"What're you doing here?" he asked Gloria Jean, the first words out of his mouth.

"Just visiting," she said. "I was on my way out."

"Best idea I've heard all day," he said, picking up the bottle of whiskey and examining the remaining contents. "Just can't wait until the noonday sun before you start guzzling it away, can you? Boy, I tell you, niggers and flies..."

Separate Ways

"SKY, LOOK, UH ... UM, I uh, well ... I've decided ... to move out."

Skylar absorbs the words, like a sponge soaks up water, dimly aware of the rain drumming on the skylight as he contemplates a response. He had figured it would come to this. On occasion, he had suggested it himself, thinking it best that Evan leave, that they were not "sharing the same space" compatibly anymore. He'd even held the door open for Evan to split. Evan never did. He ranted about being kicked out of his half of the property. Now Skylar thinks all it takes is the smashing of a Picasso ceramic against the wall for Evan to pack his bags. Talk about lousy timing. It would have to happen now, when Skylar really doesn't want him to go.

"Do what you have to do," Skylar says, shrugging his shoulders, watching lightning flash outside the window, momentarily illuminating Evan's sullen expression in the dark room. Before Evan stopped by, Skylar had been dozing off on the sofa, half watching a documentary about parrots. The narrator claimed that the birds live fifty years or more, and maintain one mate for a lifetime. Why, Skylar thought, can't Evan and I be parrots?

Skylar waits for the proper dramatic pause to pass between them. "Why the sudden decision? Why now?"

"I won't live in a violent environment where I feel my life is threatened," Evan says, his breaths coming harder and faster, his lower lip quivering. "Maybe you were raised in that type of environment and function from that desperation, and—"

"Oh, Evan, come off that," Skylar interrupts him. "I don't believe that—you don't even believe that yourself. Before last night, you'd never seen me violent."

"Yeah, but knowing your temper, and how emotional you are, I've always expected it to come to this."

"Because I'm black, and from Harlem, right? And to you, blacks and violence are synonymous, aren't they?"

"There you go again," Evan says, exasperated. He walks away hastily, then stops suddenly, turning to face Skylar. "Why you consider me racist, yet sleep with me for years, is beyond me."

"Evan, we've been through this before. It's not that I think you're a racist ... well, not an aggressive one, anyway, but ... Evan, you're not as liberal and unbiased and unbigoted as you think, either. You always say you're above racism, but the truth is ... you're not."

Evan grabs a Samsonite from his walk-in closet and begins packing. Skylar can tell by the way he's stuffing and tossing expensive clothes into the suitcase, he's really pissed off by what Skylar just said.

"If I were racist," Evan says, pausing from the packing, facing Skylar, half chuckling to soothe the pain, "then why would I sleep with black people?"

"That's my point!" Skylar says, rising from the sofa, following behind Evan, who is walking from the closet to the open suitcase on the bed. Skylar is standing in his way, making it awkward for Evan to pass. "Just because you fuck us, you think you're extraordinary, exceptional. And since you fuck us — no, I take that back — since you fuck us, ex-clu-sive-ly, you're an expert on blacks somehow, in a patronizing way—"

"Sky, Sky," Evan says, his voice calmer, softer, more controlled than Skylar's. "It's too late for all that now, don't you think? What's the problem? You wanted me to leave. So, I'm leaving, okay?"

"Evan," Skylar says, unable to look at him, about to chance a final plea without making it sound like one. "You know my father's dying ... I'm in the middle of this film and ... it's just a difficult time for me right now."

"But I thought," Evan says, stuffing laundered shirts into the Samsonite, "that you hated your father. Why the sudden change of heart? And what's the big deal about making a film? You're a hotshot movie star with an Oscar nomination and a Golden Globe. You can handle it. You don't need me, that's for sure. I mean, you're the one with all the 'formal training,' and 'stage experience,' right? What do you need me for? Me, who's never been on stage, and who's never had an acting lesson in my life?"

You fucking white boy! Skylar can't help thinking. Restraint stops him from saying it, though he thinks he should. Especially after being called a nigger last night.

He should've known, before becoming emotionally involved, how far Evan's liberalism stretched.

They were invited to an Upper East Side industry party with a guest list that was mostly black. Skylar remembers that party falling on the same day that he had received a fan letter forwarded to him by the studio. It was written by a black woman in Youngstown, Ohio, who went on about how much she'd loved Skylar and his movie, and how ticked off she was when he lost the Oscar to "that little funny-looking white boy." She told him how physically attractive she found him. She liked the fact that he didn't have a Jheri curl, that his blue eyes weren't contacts. And, "most importantly," she stressed, she'd never seen his picture in any newspaper or magazine with a white woman on his arm. Not only did she approve the latter from a sociopolitical perspective, but personally, it gave her hope, as she wanted to meet him.

Until that point in the letter, Skylar had found the writer's remarks flattering, amusing, honest, and to the point, not unlike most of his fan mail from black women. But when he got to the eighth paragraph, the smile and internal laughter died and his swollen head deflated. "There's only one thing I heard about you that I didn't like," she wrote. "The rumor that you're homosexual." She claimed she didn't think it was true. He was too masculine, his voice too deep, to be a faggot. He reminded her of one of her brothers, who was as straight as they come. And she understood that Skylar was busy, but requested that he please write her back and tell her it wasn't true.

He wanted to write her back, all right.

He carried that letter in his head to the Upper East Side party with Evan, who was tight-lipped and uneasy. They were in the taxi, crossing the middle of Central Park, the taxi driver studying the two good-looking, well-dressed men in the backseat. Skylar noticed Evan was quiet and more tense than usual.

"What's the matter?" Skylar said.

"Nothing."

"Yes there is. What is it?"

"I just get like this when I go to parties where I don't know anybody."

"But you do. You know me, and at least ten other people."

"Do I?"

"Yeah, you'll see." Skylar smiled. Evan's expression remained unchanged. "Now what's the matter?"

"I don't know..."

"Yes you do."

"I'm a little uncomfortable."

"About what?"

"Promise you won't get mad?"

"Promise."

"I've never been in a room full of black people..."

"And?"

"I'm nervous, I guess."

"About what?"

"I don't know."

"These are upper-middle-class blacks, you know—"

"I know—"

"Not a bunch of cutthroats."

"See, that's why I didn't want to tell you. You're offended now, aren't you?"

"All I can say is, after tonight, you'll know what my entire life has been like."

The taxi let them off at the corner of Third Avenue. They entered a turn-of-the-century apartment building and were greeted by a doorman, who took their names and coats and directed them to the elevator. Seated on the velvet benches inside the elevator, Skylar looked into the panoramic mirrors and straightened his necktie. The doors opened and they entered a loftlike penthouse, where Skylar noticed that most of the people were, like himself, dressed in elegant black. Black on black, he called it. He turned to Evan, who looked as if he'd just entered a thug-infested cul-de-sac in Bedford-Stuyvesant.

"Relax," Skylar said. "Nobody's going to mug you."

First person Skylar noticed was his friend Brandyn, an attorney in the motion picture business. Standing beside her was her husband, Jeff, a pediatrician, whom Skylar had always found utterly boring, homophobic, and terminally heterosexual. Skylar felt Jeff resented his relationship with Brandyn. When Skylar met her a couple of years earlier in Los Angeles, she had assumed, not unlike most people, that he was straight.

"I've got a girlfriend I'd like you to meet," Brandyn had said, suggestively, stirring her cocktail with a pinky. "I think you two would hit it off."

"Hit it off how?" Skylar had asked.

"Don't play naive with me, Skylar—"

"I'm not naive. I'm gay."

He got a charge out of saying that to people who least expected it. Wasn't for shock value, necessarily. He was just offended by being mistaken for heterosexual.

"You are?" Brandyn said, obviously shocked, trying unsuccessfully to conceal it. And, not unlike other "eagerly liberal" folks he'd met over the years, she immediately coughed up a string of names of other gay friends she had, like a proud mother pulling from her pocketbook a charm bracelet from which the birthstones of her children dangled.

He couldn't help pushing this a bit further.

"So, you want to match me up with somebody?" he said.

"Yeah, sure. You're a good catch. Why not?"

"You have any male friends looking for a mate?"

"I'm sure I do."

"Are they gay?"

"Yes."

"Good. I like that in a man."

He touched Evan's arm, and they made their way toward Brandyn.

"Hi," they all said, then pecked cheeks, European-style. Jeff was icy and distant, as usual. Thinking about it, Skylar couldn't recall ever having seen him so much as crack a smile.

"Evan, this is Jeff," Skylar said. "Jeff, you know Evan."

"We've met," Jeff said. He placed one arm behind his back, took a sip from his drink, and turned away, a body language that said, ever so loudly, he would take no part in any of this.

"So, how's it been going, Skylar?" Brandyn said. She was so beautiful, so bright, so cultured, so sensitive. What the hell was she doing with Jeff? If Skylar had been straight, he'd have married her.

"Things're going fine, Bran. It's funny running into you, because just the other day, I was thinking about Michelle. I don't know why she popped into my head. Do you still see her?"

"Yes," Brandyn said. "As a matter of fact, next weekend we're all getting together for a picnic. She and her husband, Jarret; Felicia and Jason; Bobby and Brenda—"

"And I wasn't invited?" Skylar was half-kidding, half-serious.

"Oh, Skylar," she said, looking suddenly embarrassed. "I didn't think you'd be interested. This is for married couples—"

"Aren't we a married couple?" Skylar said, indicating Evan and himself.

At which point, Jeff said to Brandyn, "I'll be back in a few minutes. I'm going to get another drink." He walked away, and Skylar wondered why he had stood there with them as long as he had.

"So, anyway," Brandyn continued. "Are you working in New York now?"

"Why weren't Evan and I invited?"

"Oh, Skylar, because you're..."

"Queers, right?"

"Skylar, give me a break. This is Brandyn you're talking to. You know I have lots of gay friends."

And none of them are on the guest list for your exclusive, hetero picnic, are they? Skylar thought. The most liberal, least homophobic people didn't place a gay relationship on the same level with a straight one. Aside from the obvious differences, many of the dynamics were incredibly similar, far more than straights were willing to admit. But somehow one was legitimate, the other wasn't. Some part of his relationship with Evan was forever being denied and discredited and attacked by someone. And they weren't always straight people.

In the past, he and Evan had gotten the most disparaging stares and challenges from the gay community. They were dancing one night at a black bar when Evan had to go to the bathroom. Someone tapped Skylar on the shoulder.

"You trying to insult us?" the person said.

"What?" Skylar said. "How?"

"Parading your white boy. We're offended by it."

"Why?"

"We're tired of white boys taking our men, that's why."

This explained why they'd been getting dirty looks that Skylar and Evan thought, and hoped, they had been imagining.

Wasn't too different at certain white bars either. Evan found some of the people were chilly toward him — even the bartender, who took his sweet time waiting on Evan, and before serving Skylar, demanded to see his "black friend's I.D." Skylar had already been hassled at the door for the same reason. Though he was convinced they knew he wasn't a minor, they hoped he had forgotten his driver's license so they could refuse him entrance. Skylar felt he and Evan were throwbacks to the '60s and its taboo on interracial dating.

"Are you okay, Evan?" Skylar asked, as they said good-bye to Brandyn and milled about the penthouse, mixing with other guests.

"I'm all right," Evan said, which Skylar found unconvincing.

"I can't believe you're intimidated."

"I said I'm okay, didn't I?"

"Evan," Skylar said, stopping to wave to someone across the room, someone he didn't want to talk to. "Don't force me to remind you about your friends."

"What friends?"

"The ones you'd never let me meet. The ones who didn't show up for your birthday party, though I'd planned it for just the three of them—"

"What's the point of this?"

"You're the one with the racist friends, Evan, not I."

"I resent you calling my friends racist. Brian, Matthew, and Gerard aren't racist—"

"And I'm Chaka Khan."

One of the things Skylar hated about himself was his sensitivity to racism. America had made him that way. His forebears had not sailed into New York harbor, saluting, rejoicing and fainting at the sight of Lady Liberty in the narrows, her tarnished torch raised, as they docked at Ellis Island. His ancestors had come as livestock. Not immigrants fleeing religious persecution, seeking the New World. Irish, Italian, German, what have you, the bigotry they endured was short-lived before they assimilated into mainstream society. Some even changed ethnic surnames, and shed identities and values. Blacks weren't offered these transitions into the melting pot. They had to contend with complexions that made it impossible for them to blend and disappear. But having fought every major war — the Revolution, the Civil War, World Wars I and II, Korea, Vietnam, the

Persian Gulf — they'd still fallen short of equality. Ellis Island immigrants weren't even around for the Revolution and the Civil War.

Patriotism.

Skylar would give his left nut — or maybe would have ten years earlier — to know what it was like. Uncle Sam. Hail to the Chief. America, love it or leave it. He envied Evan and any other die-hard patriot. Americans intoxicated themselves on the delusion that they didn't see color. He had believed that, starving to know what it was like to love a country or a flag so much you'd be willing to die for it. But when he'd dropped his guard, forgetting his color, shoving aside the black race's plight, he'd always be reminded of it. He was gorgeous. But black. Highly intelligent, well educated. But black. Extremely talented and promising. But black. He'd lost several acting jobs that way. Nobody read better for those parts. He'd acted dust around those white boys, transforming cold readings into warm, sometimes hot ones. But they invariably got the job, unless the part called for a black.

He didn't know what it felt like to despise and fear the Russians. An Eisenhower baby, he recalled the heightened cold war of the late '50s, early '60s. Fallout shelters. I Like Ike. Better Dead Than Red. But Communist Soviets were not his enemies. Racist white Americans were. From where he stood, the U.S. and U.S.S.R. were both six of one ... Which was why they were world powers. Archenemies. They shared similar traits too close for comfort. Avarice, insatiable thirst for power, the arrogance to annihilate a society in order to preserve one's own. United States and Soviet Union. US, SU Mirror images. Like twin sisters showing up at the senior prom in the same dress, their bitchy rivalry was such. Bette Davis and Miriam Hopkins in *Old Acquaintance.* They were both white, both omnipotent, both fueling hatred based upon fear, ignorance, and bigotry.

But political ploy or not, the Russians had received Paul Robeson in their country with a deference he'd never experienced in his native America. Skylar imagined that if America really didn't see color, and could marginally confront truth, then Robeson — all-American, Golden Boy, Renaissance Man — could've and should've been president. As could have W.E.B. Du Bois, or Frederick Douglass, for that matter.

Skylar had grown impatient with trusting white people who would turn around and stab him in the back with one hand while they greeted him with the other, smiling all the while. White folks were good for a smile. They'd burn crosses on your lawn, kill innocent black girls in church bombings, and smile their asses off in your face. Not raised by his parents to reciprocate bigotry — though they had versed their children in the ways of white America — he'd learned to hate on his own, from his own experiences, a reaction to white action, a response to a stimuli that produced an outer, impenetrable shell. Hate them before they hate you, had become his modus vivendi. And everybody hated black people. Whites hated blacks. Latinos hated blacks. Asians hated blacks. Even blacks hated blacks.

Closest he ever came to feeling patriotic was listening to Ray Charles or Ella Fitzgerald bluesing and jazzing up "The Star Spangled Banner" at a baseball game in Yankee Stadium.

"Skylar, why don't you eat some fresh vegetables for a change?" Evan said, as they stood at the buffet, fixing plates of food. Evan liked poking fun at Skylar's dietary habits. He called Skylar the Cholesterol Kid.

Skylar scraped the roast beef off his plate and picked up some sliced carrots, celery, broccoli, and cherry tomatoes. Evan got on his nerves with his obsession for protein drinks, vitamins for every letter in the alphabet, tofu, fresh vegetables, unfiltered fruit juices, fiber, cultured yogurt, bran, organic this, organic that.

"I'm definitely not into red meat," Evan had said when they first moved in together.

"I know," Skylar had responded. "You're into black meat."

Evan stands at the door, his hand poised on the knob. "I need the space right now. So do you."

"Don't tell me what I need, Evan."

"You do, Sky. We need to think about us and reevaluate—"

"Is this temporary, or permanent, your leaving?"

"I'm not sure, Sky. That's what I'm trying to find out."

"So, what am I supposed to do, Evan?"

"Look, Sky. I love you. You know that. Nothing changes that. I've never loved anybody or anything more."

"I love you too, Evan. So, what's the problem? Why're you leaving—"

"Our love is becoming painful ... destructive ... counter-productive."

Skylar watches him speechlessly, helplessly. He has nothing else to say. He wants to walk across the living room floor, remove the suitcase from Evan's hand, wrap his arms around him, and plead with him to stay. His father is dying. What a week! Mama said luck, good or bad, comes in threes. He looks at the pieces of the broken Picasso ceramic, scattered across the floor. He likens the ceramic to their relationship. Once classic, original, united, whole. Now destroyed, disintegrated, broken, unmendable, lying on the floor, waiting to be swept up and disposed of. With no trace left. As if it had never existed. Skylar wants to say these things but doesn't. Pride won't let him.

"So, that's it, huh? You just pack your things and split. That's it?"

"All I want is a relationship: a good, constructive sharing of two souls. But Skylar, you're so full of anger — a lot of which I think I understand. But you're too busy trying to change the world. And you're racist, too."

That's the last thing Skylar wants to hear. As it is, he arm-wrestles with his ambiguity, his ambivalence on race. Okay. No. He had no love for white people, generally. They were all racists unless proven otherwise.

Just tonight, at dusk, before Evan stopped by, Skylar had been returning from the neighborhood supermarket on Columbus Avenue. Heading home, a middle-aged white woman had been walking down West Seventy-sixth Street toward Central Park West, a few yards ahead of him. Hearing Skylar's footsteps, she glanced over her shoulder at the well-dressed black man, both his hands occupied with heavy grocery bags, and winced, her face distorted with fear. No, she didn't do that, Skylar thought. Instantly, she crossed the street. Just to fuck with her, so did he. As he reached the sidewalk, she stopped and turned to face him.

"You go ahead," she said. "Since you're in a hurry."

"I'm in no hurry," Skylar said.

"Yes you are, and I'm in your way."

"There's plenty of room on the sidewalk for both of us," he said, outraged that this bitch was going through all these changes, insulting his intelligence. "You don't want me to walk behind you, because I'm black."

"Don't be silly."

"Silly? You think this is the first time this has happened to me? You ought to be ashamed of yourself," he nearly shouted, as people he thought he recognized as neighbors held onto their dog leashes and stared. "Just because I'm black doesn't mean I'm going to mug you, lady."

"Would you please go ahead?" she said, her arm poised, as if she were politely holding a door open for him to enter.

"Bitch!"

If shit like this happened to Evan, he too, would be "full of anger."

"And while you're trying to change the world," Evan continues, "you're taking me through changes I'd rather not go through."

Suddenly Skylar stands. He walks over to Evan and embraces him. Evan drops the suitcase and hugs him back.

"Evan," Skylar says. "It seems like we're just reaching in different directions, doesn't it? I don't want you to leave, but you've got to do what you feel is necessary for your survival. I understand. That's all I'm doing, trying to survive. You know what, Evan? I'm going to share something with you I won't even tell my own mother ... There's a fire scene in this film I'm doing, right? I'm supposed to walk through it to save — get this — to save my father. Simple enough, right?" he says, trying to laugh, but the laughter won't come.

"Except, I can't walk through it. I'm having the nightmares again. I'm afraid of what that means. What that says about me. Evan ... I'm scared."

He can't believe he just said that. Now he knows he's desperate. Times like this, Skylar thinks about lesbians. He envies their relationships: the longevity, the commitment, the dedication, the ability to weather the low points. If he and Evan can't be parrots, why can't they be lesbians?

"I'll be in touch, I promise," Evan says, framing Skylar's face with his hands, tenderly kissing him on the lips. "But right now, it's not working." He turns and bends down to pick up his luggage, then stops, remembering something. "By the way," Evan says, staring at the floor, the toe of his shoe making invisible circles in the carpet, like a stage-frightened child, "I'm really sorry about what I called you. Please forgive me. I really didn't mean it." He picks up the Samsonite, walks down the same foyer through which, the night before, he'd fled for his life.

As quietly as possible, Skylar says, "Evan, I think it's important that you understand I'm not trying to change the world ... I just refuse to let it change me."

Rude Awakening

KENDALL CHARGED INTO THE HOUSE, out of breath. Panting, wiping his forehead of sweat and dirt with his shirt sleeve, he leaned his back against the door. His forehead was scratched, nose bloody, shirt torn.

"Kendall James Whyte!" Althea shouted from the kitchen. "You out there fightin' again?"

"Yes, ma'am."

"Why, Kendall? Why're you always fightin'?"

"I don't know. I didn't start it. It's not my fault."

"I know," Althea said, wiping her hands on the apron. "Never is." She pulled up a kitchen chair. "Sit here and be still." She examined the scratch, the bloody nose, the torn shirt.

"You done it now," Althea said. "Just gone and ripped that good school shirt. Wait till Daddy gets home. He'll whip you good!"

"No, he won't," Kendall said. "Daddy never hits me."

"He will this time. And don't sass me. Now, I want to know why you're fightin' again. Tell me."

Kendall looked at his mother, then glanced at his brother standing in the doorway with a book in his hand. Kendall's gaze dropped to the floor.

"I'm waiting," Althea said. "And you won't get up from that table until you tell me."

"Well," Kendall said, "I was fighting because..."

"Because what?"

"Because somebody said Sky's a faggot. They say he can't fight. I was just—"

"That's enough," Althea had said, placing her hand over his mouth. "Listen to this, and listen good. Your brother is no faggot, understand? That ain't no reason to be fightin' nobody. And the next time you come in here all busted up, it's gonna be me and you. You gonna have to fight me, okay?"

"Uh-uh," Kendall said, shaking his head. "Daddy said you can't hit me."

Althea slapped him across the face. "Now, go on upstairs and wait till Daddy gets home," she demanded, one hand on her hip, the other pointing toward the staircase.

Kendall snarled at her, holding the side of his face. He glared at Mama through loathing eyes.

"And don't you dare look at me in that tone of voice neither," Althea said, then marched him upstairs to his bedroom.

Lying across his bed, legs crossed, arms folded behind his head, he thought of his recent street fights. As far as he could tell, he hadn't lost one of them. Classmates and neighborhood kids agreed. Kendall was a tough, no-shit-taking mother's son. Small for his age. But his fists made up for his size. Of all the fights he'd had, having fought nearly everywhere — school, the street, the movies, the park — school fights were his favorite. Someone — at least the way he remembered it — would challenge him with, "Outside, three o'clock. Me and you, punk." Often, they miscalculated. He was small and had a faggot for a brother. Just how tough could he be? Kendall relished the three o'clock, after-school fights because no one broke them up. He loved the audience. Kids got the chance to see him kick some butt. Then they'd know, for future reference, just how bad he was.

The school principal had broken up one of his fights, though.

Skylar had told him not to fight. It was freezing cold, snow and ice on the ground.

"You shouldn't be taking off your coat in this weather," Skylar warned him.

Kendall fought anyway. He told himself he wouldn't have, but the schoolchildren incited it, egging him on.

"What am I supposed to do, Sky? I can't just chump out. Besides, I'm fighting Tyronne because he called you a faggot."

"Kendall, I don't care."

"I do. You want to fight him instead?"

"Be serious."

"I am."

"You're just fighting Tyronne because any excuse will do."

"Baddest man pass first lick," Marlene Henderson said, placing her hand between the two contenders.

Kendall passed the first lick by hitting her hand. She, in turn, hit the opponent, Tyronne.

"Oooooooh!" the crowd moaned, laughing and slapping each other five.

"Tyronne, man, you gonna take that shit offa li'l-ass Kendall, Mr. Tough Guy?"

Elijah Wigfall found a Popsicle stick on the ground. He placed it on Kendall's shoulder.

"If you knock this off," Elijah explained to Tyronne, "then you knock off Kendall's mama."

"Kendall," Skylar said. "Put your coat on and let's go home. It's cold out here."

"Boooooooo!" the crowd yelled at Skylar.

Tyronne knocked the Popsicle stick off Kendall's shoulder. He and Kendall locked and rolled, John Wayne–style, through the snow and dirty slush. Out of nowhere, a large, silver-haired man thrust his large, freckled hands through the crowd of cheering spectators. With one hand, he pulled Kendall off Tyronne.

"Let me go!" Kendall screamed, wiggling and contorting his body to break loose of the man's firm grip. "You white motherfucker!"

The children, aware of Mr. Benway's sudden appearance, scattered in every direction. Skylar was speechless. He was the older brother and even he didn't use language like that, especially to Mr. Benway, the principal of P.S. 224.

"It's you again, huh, Whyte?" Mr. Benway said, leading Kendall by the collar into the school. Skylar didn't know what to do. What would he tell his parents? With Kendall's parka and loose-leaf in his hand, he waited outside the school gate, shivering, warming his feet by jogging in place, blowing on his hands. When Kendall came out, about fifteen minutes later, he bopped and swaggered toward his brother.

"Slap me five, Sky."

Skylar looked at him as if he were crazy.

"What happened?" Skylar asked.

"Nothing," Kendall said. "The fucker just suspended me, that's all."

"That's all? Kendall, you're gonna get it."

"Nuh-uh, 'cause Daddy said if somebody hits me, hit them back." He copped a boxer's stance and jabbed at the air. "Hey, Sky, man, you see how I dusted off that chump, Tyronne? He ain't shit. His sister Margie can go better than that. He didn't get one punch in, 'cause I kept weavin' on his ass. He won't call you no faggot no more. I'm slick as dick, an' don't take no shit!"

Skylar glanced at him sideways, shaking his head. "Kendall, put your parka on before you catch a cold."

"I'm at the end of my rope with that boy," Mama said, when they got home. "It's all right to fight your brother while you're still kids. That's natural. But Kendall, I don't know. There's something wrong with you, boy—"

"I don't believe," Daddy said, "that Skylar just stood there and let him fight, and get suspended. You're to blame for this, Skylar. You're the oldest, and you should know better—"

"But Daddy!" Skylar protested. "I did tell him not to fight, but he—"

"I don't want to hear it!" Daddy said. "Kendall is your responsibility. If he gets in trouble, I'm going to whip you."

Skylar threw his books down and started up the staircase.

"Come back here, Mister!" Howard said. "Don't you ever walk away when I'm talking to you. Now, pick up those books. Go upstairs and wait for me in your bedroom. I'm going to whip your ass good."

Skylar picked up his books, climbed the staircase gloomily, and slammed his bedroom door.

"Whatchu blamin' Sky for?" Althea said. "He didn't do nothing. You wanna beat somebody, beat that little troublemaker right here. He's the one who needs it, not Sky. He's the one got suspended, not Sky. What kinda damn sense do that make? Lord have mercy!"

For Kendall's two-day suspension, he received a solemn talk from his father. Skylar got a whipping.

"If the kids weren't calling Skylar a faggot," Howard said, "then Kendall wouldn't have had to fight. Skylar should've fought his own battle. But he was incapable of upholding his honor. Somebody had to protect the family honor. Kendall's just being a man. Doing what a man's got to do."

Lying across the bed, Kendall grinned at the recollection of that school suspension. Now, at school, he was treated with respect. Not only did he kick ass, he'd been kicked out of school for it. Neighborhood kids likened his fight with Tyronne to Sonny Liston taking the title from Floyd Patterson. When he was enrolled again the following Monday morning, his teacher called him pugnacious. He didn't understand the word.

"Look it up in the dictionary," the teacher told him.

"I will," he said, sarcastically. He loved smart-mouthing the teacher. "Get back to you about it tomorrow."

"You do that."

The class roared. The teacher hushed them.

"I'll ask my brother what it means," he leaned over and whispered to Buster. "He knows that kinda shit. I don't have time to look up nothing in nobody's Webster."

He wouldn't fight so much, he convinced himself, if people didn't always start it. He never started it. Just finished it. Usually, he was minding his business. Then somebody'd say something he didn't like. He couldn't let them chump him. He had to defend himself. And, if my brother wasn't a ... if the kids didn't call him names, I wouldn't have to fight.

Who did Mama think she was anyway? She was just showing off because Daddy wasn't home, telling him to march upstairs and stay in his room until Daddy got home. She doesn't tell me what to do, he thought. When Daddy finds out what she did, he's gonna kick her ass. She had slapped him in front of Skylar, embarrassing him. She had no right hitting him. Daddy even said so. Ordering him to his room was one thing. But slapping him...

He knew at any moment, since it was Saturday afternoon, Mama would start vacuuming the downstairs den. With the electrical humming so loud, he could slip back outside and she wouldn't notice. All week he'd been waiting for Saturday. He had a game of marbles to play with the boys. Then they were planning to hit the model airplane factory where the security guard was a drunk. Then go down to Central Park and snatch a few white ladies' pocketbooks. And ... Oh, shit! They had games of stickball, and touch football to play this afternoon. Couldn't forget that. He had an entire weekend planned. No way Mama could keep him inside.

What would he tell his friends? My mother said I can't come out to play? Then they'd think he was a sissy, too.

The vacuum switch clicked on. He heard it moaning, as she moved it back and forth across the rug. He cracked his door open and looked toward his brother's bedroom door, which was closed. He removed his black Converse hightops. In his stockinged feet, he tiptoed down the stairs. They creaked so, he took a step at a time.

They were playing stickball in the street. Kendall was up at bat. He'd already struck out twice. It was up to him to get a hit. Bases were loaded. With severed mop stick in his grip, he concentrated intensely upon the pitch.

"Knock the shit out of that ball!" his teammates yelled.

"Send it flying into the Bronx!"

The pitcher pitched. The girls on the sidewalk gasped. He watched it coming toward him, getting bigger by the second, and he swung with everything he had. Plop! He kissed the ball with the stick. It didn't exactly sail into the Bronx. Instead, it bounced off a second-floor window, cracking the bottom half, which shattered. Shards of glass went showering onto the sidewalk. The game stopped. On the sidewalk, the girls giggled, covering their mouths with their hands.

"Oh shit!" one of his teammates uttered.

They all knew whose window it was. And Bubba Tyson was nobody to be messed with. What was it, two o'clock in the afternoon? He was probably still in bed.

Within seconds, a shade on that second-story window flew up. The window was raised. Bubba leaned halfway out and shook his fist at the children below.

"Who broke my window?" he yelled.

No one said anything. A few of the children looked at Kendall. Others looked at the ground, or each other.

"Oh, don't nobody know, huh?" Bubba said, slamming the window down, pulling the shade back in place. A number of children fled to their apartments. They chose not to witness a display of Bubba's nasty temper. Mostly Kendall's teammates, his close friends, stayed, as did a handful of onlookers thirsty for a street-side spectacle.

Bubba bounded down the stairs onto the sidewalk, a greasy do-rag wrapped around his head, fastening his shirt as he jumped.

He had red, beady eyes, facial keloids, a top lip that always looked swollen, and his face and teeth looked as if he hadn't cleaned them in weeks. He walked directly over to Kendall, who held the stick in his hand.

"Check this out, my man," Bubba said to Kendall. "I'm gonna ask you nice and I'm only gonna ask you once. You broke my window?"

"Maybe," Kendall said, puffing his chest out. He looked at his friends and winked.

"Whatchu mean, 'maybe'?" Bubba grabbed Kendall by the collar.

"Get your fuckin' black hands off me."

"And what if I don't? Whatchu gonna do? Kick my ass, or somethin'?"

"Let me go! You big, black, ugly motherfucker!"

Bubba slapped him across the face. "That's fo' breaking my window, sucker." He slapped him again from the other side. "An', tha's fo' shootin' yo' mouth off, you li'l snotty-nose punk. Now, whatchu gonna do?"

Kendall's ears were ringing. Instantaneously, he understood the saying "seeing stars." He had to compose himself, hold back the tears stinging the rims of his eyes. He couldn't cry in front of his boys.

"I'm gonna tell my daddy on you," he said. "You just wait. He's gonna kick your ass, you black mother—"

"Go get that yalla-ass wife-beater! Everybody know he a punk, beatin' up on women an' shit. You his son, an' you a punk just like him. And when you bring him, you li'l snot-nose bastard, tell him to bring my money, 'cause y'all gonna pay fo' my window. I mean that shit. Go on, go 'head, go get him. I be waitin' right here fo' his ass!"

Kendall looked at his friends who had been snickering, but now they stopped. No one came to his aid. Bubba had said his piece, and now it was on Kendall — as were the eyes of everyone on the street. Some people had come out to see what the ruckus was about. Tenants raised their windows, parted curtains, hung out over ledges, and watched the afternoon street theater.

When Kendall stomped through the door, he was surprised to hear his father's voice in the kitchen. Kendall hadn't seen him return. Howard had been working at the office, as he usually did on Saturday mornings. Kendall walked into the kitchen where his parents stood.

"You're in trouble!" Althea said. "I told you to stay in your room and you deliberately disobeyed—"

"Daddy," Kendall said, ignoring Mama, cutting her off. "That black nigger Bubba across the street slapped me twice ... for nothing."

He displayed the evidence: two large red hands imprinted on both cheeks. His father examined his face.

"Althea," Howard said. "Get an ice pack. All of you stay here, while I go and find out what the hell happened."

But when Howard walked into the street, Kendall followed, Althea following Kendall, Skylar following Althea. Bubba, smoking a cigarette, watched Howard coming across the street, and stood up from the car fender he was sitting on. He flicked the cigarette into the gutter, and stuck his face in Howard's face.

"What seems to be the problem here?" Howard asked.

"That li'l smart-mouth kid of yours broke my window, tha's what seems to be the problem here," Bubba said, mimicking Howard. "You know, somebody need to put they foot up his ass!"

"Now, now," Howard said. "Did you slap him?"

"Yeah, I slapped the li'l m'fucka. I just told you he broke my window and started mouthin' off. And, you gonna pay for it."

"Now, I don't have a problem with that, but I don't want you putting your hands on my son anymore."

"Go ahead, Daddy!" Kendall yelled from the curb, Althea holding his shoulders, keeping him from running to his father's side. "Hit that black African nigger!"

"Whatchu mean, don't hit your son? M'fucka, I'll hit you! How you like that?" Bubba said, putting up his dukes, copping a boxer's pose. "You wants some too, punk? C'mon, c'mon, everybody on the block is here. Let's see how bad you is. Kick my ass like you beat up your wife, chump." He pushed Howard in the chest. "Yeah, c'mon, gimme a reason to take you out, sucker. You think you is better than everybody 'round here anyway. I ain't never liked yo' yalla ass from jump street, nohow. All that proper shit you be talkin', it don't mean shit on this turf. 'Round here, you gots to kick ass to stay alive. Dig? Now, c'mon, show me yo' manhood. C'mon, give it up."

"Don't, Howard!" Althea yelled from the sidewalk. "Oh, my Lord!"

Bubba pushed Howard again. He punched him once, Howard's face jerking to the side. Bubba moved around him, jigging and skipping, with the finesse of Muhammad Ali. He slugged Howard in the chest. Howard grabbed himself, and doubled over. Althea ran into the street, Kendall hanging onto her dress. She turned Howard around by the shoulders, and led him back toward the house.

"We'll pay for your window," Althea said to Bubba. "But you keep your goddamn hands to yourself! I ain't scared of you!"

As Howard, Althea, Skylar, and Kendall headed back to their house, Bubba laughed, lit another cigarette, and spit on the ground.

"See! His woman had to come save his ass," Bubba said to the crowd. "He beat her ass, and she save his. Ain't that a bitch." He spit on the ground again. "In the joint, we got a name fo' m'fuckas like him: Pussy! That's what he is, a clit. Betcha he won't jump in my face no mo'. Punk-ass m'fucka."

Kendall ran to his bedroom, barely hearing Althea's warning that she would deal with him later. "If you had kept your little bad ass in the room, like I told you to in the first place, none of this would've happened!"

He slammed his bedroom door shut. Took out his baseball and football cards, ripped some of them, and flung them across the room. He threw a football spike into the closet, ripped the calendar with the athletes' photographs from the wall, jumped into bed, buried his head under the pillow.

Daddy had been chumped.

And if that wasn't bad enough, he was chumped in front of everybody on the block, including Kendall's friends. He'd never hear the end of it from them. He was always bragging about how tough his father was. His father took no shit. And was scared of nobody. Daddy wouldn't let anyone hurt him, not even his mother. "Is that protection, or what?" he had said to his friends. But there, in broad daylight, on the street, in the presence of everyone who mattered, Daddy had let him down. Not only had Bubba slapped Kendall twice, but he'd punched Daddy in the chest and face. Bubba "broke" all over Daddy. And what did Daddy do? He looked like a sweet bitch out there, getting her butt kicked by her husband.

Bubba and Daddy, standing in the middle of the street, looked like Daddy and Mama. What could Kendall say to his friends? How could he explain it? If Daddy couldn't protect him from Bubba, who could he protect him from? Maybe Mama could whip his tail after all. She was the one who took control of the matter. Even she had bad-mouthed Bubba. She wasn't scared of him. Daddy was sweet-talking him, like he was asking for a loan from the bank. Ass-kissing!

That night, while Kendall prayed on his knees, his father came into his room. Kendall hadn't seen him since the incident.

"What happened, Daddy?"

"Let that be a lesson for you, Kendall."

"What?"

"Bubba's not like us. We're better than him. He's lowlife trash. Spent most of his life in juvenile detention homes, city jails, state prisons. He's a killing machine, ignorant, niggerish, without a brain in his head. His fists are his brains. He would've killed your daddy, if I gave him what he wanted. You don't want Daddy to get killed, do you?"

"No!"

"Well then, that's what I mean," Howard said. "I'm not planning to tangle with a killing machine like that. Only way to deal with the Bubbas of the world is to exterminate them like the vermin they are. If I killed him, then I'd go to jail for life. You want that to happen?"

"No, Daddy ... but—"

"But what?"

"Would you protect me if somebody else slapped me?"

"I sure would. Don't worry. Daddy won't let anybody really hurt you. How's your face feel?"

"It's okay," Kendall said. "Did he hurt you?"

"Nah. He hits like a woman. Didn't even feel it. Soon as he hit me, I shook it off. Now, you be a good boy, and get some sleep."

Now Kendall knew what to tell his friends. He now had explanations and justifications at his fingertips. His daddy was no chump. He just didn't want to have to kill Bubba in front of the whole block. Too many eyewitnesses. Daddy would be sent to the Tombs, that place where Aunt Gloria Jean's boyfriend used to be before he got out.

He had turned off the light, stuck the Bazooka bubble gum on his bedpost, and placed the Cleveland Browns helmet next to his pillow. His door opened again. The light from the hall crept into the darkness. Althea stood at the door, shaking her head at him.

"I don't know what I'm gonna do with you, Kendall James," she said, walking over and sitting on the edge of his bed. "You will be punished for this. But I wanna know, did you learn anything from all this here mess? Huh, Kendall James? You hear me talking to you, boy?"

"Yes, ma'am. I learned my lesson."

"And what lesson is that?"

"I should do what I'm told," he said, telling her what she wanted to hear.

"Good," she said, standing up to leave. "Now maybe you understand that your daddy ain't God after all. Now is he?"

Summer Nights

INVISIBLE CRICKETS WHIRRED outside the window. Dogs barked faintly from neighborhood yards in the distance. Mosquitoes buzzed in the darkness. Pic repellent burned like incense, the lit end glowing in the dark, the smoky, evergreen odor filling the room, all but deterring the bloodsucking insects. The festive voices of grown-ups sitting on the front porch rang through Skylar's open bedroom window. He tossed and turned, the sweat making his body stick to the sheets.

Outside, the grown-ups — his parents and Mama's family — sat on the porch, cooling off in the late-night humidity. The air so still, he could hear ice clinking in glasses, parched throats guzzling cans of cold Ballantine ale, the inhaling and exhaling of unfiltered cigarette smoke, dirty jokes passing among them, jokes told only in the absence of children. "Three nuns walk into a bar..." Someone, probably Aunt LaVern, brought a record player that was connected, by extension cords, to an indoor outlet. They were listening to a frumpy, toothless, deep-voiced Moms Mabley declare, "Dat's da ugliest damn baby I done eber seen!" And each time she insulted a lover and then smoothed it over with, "Lub dat man!" the adults roared with laughter. Skylar himself had to laugh, though he wasn't sure what he was laughing at.

Miss Vivian, who lived down the street, was returning home from one of her numerous dates.

"Yoo-hoo! Hey girl!" Aunt Loretta yelled across the street. "C'mon have a drink with us."

"No thank you, girl," Miss Vivian yelled back. "I'm tired, chile."

"Oh, c'mon," Aunt Evelyn urged her. "One drink. It's too damn hot to sleep anyway."

"What the hell," Miss Vivian said.

Listening through his upstairs bedroom window, Skylar figured that Miss Vivian wouldn't refuse the drink. Daddy had said she'd drink panther piss if that's all the bar was serving. Skylar could imagine her in a billowy, low-cut, summer print dress, like Marilyn Monroe's, with an open neckline, bulging tits, spike heels clicking and scraping on the concrete pavement, hair pulled back in a French roll, the men, including his father, salivating over her. He could see, in the darkness of his bedroom, the men parting, like stage curtains, to give Miss Vivian a seat. The women in the neighborhood talked about her the way they would a dog. Yet they enjoyed her company because she kept a party rolling. Always good for a laugh. Moms Mabley was over. Someone changed the record and played Ray Charles's "Georgia On My Mind." With Miss Vivian around, he thought, who needed Moms Mabley?

"I would give y'all a coupla dollars for this here drink," Miss Vivian said. "But I'm so poor, I can't pay attention."

Adult laughter rose from the porch.

"Vivian, girl," Nanna said. "You is too much, chile!"

"Tell us 'bout this new man you got," Aunt Mildred said.

"What new man?" Miss Vivian said.

"The one with that brand-new '63 Cadillac," Mama said. "The one who just dropped you off."

"Him?" Miss Vivian said. "Shiiiiit! He ain't gettin' up off no cash. I told that fool tonight, don't play with the pieces unless you plan on keepin' the whole damn puzzle." Again, they broke into a round of laughter that Miss Vivian allowed to play out before she continued. "That's right, honey. I'm sick and tired of niggers window-shopping on my time. Know what I mean? Either they buyin' the merchandise or they can keep on walkin'!"

Skylar heard the front door open and shut. Light footsteps creaked on the carpeted staircase, headed toward his brother's room. Kendall's door opened and shut. Moments later, someone turned Skylar's doorknob. He pretended to be asleep, quickly turning toward the wall, closing his eyes. His room was briefly washed in light, then returned to darkness. Two strong, masculine hands picked him up, and the person sat on the edge of the bed and cradled him like a baby. The arms rocked him gently. A pair of chapped lips kissed his cheek and forehead, the whiskey breath making his nostrils flare. Then the person carefully placed him back in bed, pulled a sheet over his nearly naked body, considered the heat and humidity, pulled the sheet off, turned to leave, and bumped into the dresser bureau, half stumbling out of the room. Who was that? He knew it wasn't Mama. Just as the door closed, he stole a glance. He didn't see the face, but he caught a fleeting glimpse of Daddy's hand closing the door behind him.

What a weird thing for Daddy to do. Actually, it was no stranger than Daddy's reaction to Halloween.

Every year, he acted so impatient with the ghoulish holiday, Skylar thought Daddy was afraid of the witch, ghost, and skeleton costumes of the trick-or-treaters. When it came to choosing his and Kendall's costumes, Daddy wanted no part of it. He let Mama take them shopping and trick-or-treating.

"It's those damn kids again," Daddy would say, as the children rang their doorbell for goodies.

"Trick or treat!" the children would shout.

"Let me know when it's over," Daddy would say, disgusted, making his way up the staircase.

"What's wrong with him?" he and Kendall asked each other, before asking Mama.

"I don't know," Mama said. "He always acts like this on Halloween."

Suddenly, Skylar was aware of Mr. and Mrs. Crocker across the alley in the neighboring apartment as they started fighting. This time it seemed to be about their daughter Lillian, a homely girl known to the boys as Li'l Bit. Known for giving up a li'l bit to anyone who asked. On the way home from school one day, Skylar had watched a train being pulled on her behind the bushes near the playground, as one of the boys, his pants pulled down to his ankles, yanked on an invisible cord, and said, "Chooooo! Chooooo!" For a dollar, it was said, she'd show her nasty. A bargain indeed, since her nasty was covered with hair, like a woman's.

"It's all your damn fault she pregnant!" Mrs. Crocker shouted, as Skylar leaned on his elbow and peered out the window of his darkened room.

"My fault?" Mr. Crocker shouted back. "Must be my fault she only thirteen, too! Woman, I should whip yo' ass!"

"Try it!"

He slapped her. She slammed him in the face with a frying pan. They fell to the floor, scuffling like boys in a schoolyard. Skylar kept watching and listening. The laughing voices on the porch turned silent. Pots and pans rattled and fell, flesh pounded and slapped flesh, glass broke, Lillian screamed, as if she were being choked. Ray Charles sang something about moonlight through the pines...

"Them Crockers is at it again. Ain't got no pride," Mama said. "They don't care who sees them fighting, or hears what they say."

Lillian was backed in the corner, her hands clamped over her mouth. Of all the domestic sideshows on the block — there were the McFaddens, the Hightowers, the Jeffersons, the Lovejoys, and of course, the Whytes — Skylar enjoyed the Crockers the most. They fought openly, like Mama said. They never closed their windows or shades, or muffled their words, which rang through the night for anyone who cared to listen.

"That noise from the Crocker apartment gonna wake up my boys for sure," Mama complained.

"They were sound asleep a moment ago," Daddy said. "I just peeked in on both of them after I went to the bathroom."

"They better stop all that fuss," Nanna insisted. "My gran'babies is tryin' to sleep."

Skylar smiled. How he loved Nanna, his favorite grandmother.

Nanna loved the theater. At one time, she had had hopes of her youngest son, Aubrey, becoming an actor. With a sixth-grade education, she'd read a script that her grandson with the blue eyes was rehearsing for a school play. He knew she couldn't read, because Daddy laughed about it all the time at home. She was faking it; he knew it and loved her for that. Nanna's eyes scanned the words on the page, assuming he didn't know. And he would recite the lines, thinking she probably didn't know the place on the page. Just the same, she would applaud, and sometimes shout, "Bravo!" Once, she shredded a vase of wilting Mother's Day roses and tossed the petals at his feet.

"Folks likes to throw roses at the end of a sho'-nuff performance," Nanna said. Then she would sit him down at her kitchen table and fill his stomach with everything it could hold. There were fresh biscuits from scratch, sprinkled with flour on top. Her bubbling rice pudding was always bursting with cinnamon and so many raisins that it looked to Skylar like raisin pudding.

She enjoyed knitting. And was forever knitting booties and a blanket for somebody's child, either in the family or on the block.

Babies're always being born, he'd think, his Nanna completing at least the thirtieth pair of booties he'd seen. While she knitted, she asked him to read to her.

"I likes readin' an' stuff lak that," she said. "Jus' wish I coulda had me some more learnin'."

And without flinching, she'd brag to anyone who'd listen, neighbors, family, the mailman, the butcher, about what beautiful "dikshun" that grandson of hers had. Her little Boy Wonder. And they'd all heard it more times than they cared to.

"He gonna grow up an' really be somethin'. Y'all watch an' see. He gonna put the Hutchinsons on the map!"

Poppa's love was quiet, undemonstrative. Skylar loved watching his grandfather silently going about his business when he spent the weekends with them, something Mama usually had to fight Daddy for, since he didn't want his son spending too much time with the Hutchinsons.

Poppa was tall, his skin eggplant purple, his receding gray, wavy hair always covered in a stocking cap when he got out of bed in the morning. In a yellowing t-shirt, his trousers supported by buttoned suspenders, he'd drag his feet in his slippers. Skylar could always tell where Poppa was in the house by the sound of his slippers. First thing every morning, Poppa got up and emptied his and Nanna's bedpans. Still living in the four-story brownstone where Mama had grown up, they'd become too old to climb the stairs to the fourth-floor bathroom. Instead, bedpans rested on either side of their bed. Skylar looked in the pans several mornings as Poppa made his way to empty them in the toilet. They never did number two in the pans, only number one.

Then Poppa would shave, using a thick brush to lather his face with a menthol-scented cream, moving the razor blade in upward strokes from his neck to his sideburns. He'd slap a palmful of Old Spice upon his face and rub what was left into his hands. The sweet, spicy aroma ignited the entire house, lingering for hours. He wouldn't say much, but each day he managed a "Good mo'nin', Hutchinson" before bending down and sticking out his jutting cheekboned face for a kiss from each grandchild. When they planted a smooch on his cheek, he'd reply with "Hmmmmm yankum!" The children loved that. Skylar's lips would brush against prickly whiskers of the cheek Poppa had just shaved. When Poppa hugged him back, his face felt like fine sandpaper.

At Nanna's and Poppa's house, Skylar could cash in empty soda bottles at Ruby's Candy Store for pocket change. Two cents for the 12- and 16-ounce bottles, a nickel for the family-size. Daddy forbade him and Kendall to return empties. Daddy said they had too much pride for that. No empty bottles! No shining shoes!

After clearing the sink of breakfast dishes, the squeaky-clean kitchen sparkling like a cover photograph from *Good Housekeeping*, Nanna would place the hot comb on a burner and part her hair in the mirror, greasing her scalp with Dixie Peach. Skylar watched as, section by section, she'd magically transform the kinky, nappy edges into flowing straight locks that shone. He marveled at the sizzling sound of the comb making contact with the scalp, the burst of smoke rising from the steel teeth, the hair relaxing into a shine, a smell of burnt hair and grease hanging in the air. When done, she'd gather a handful of fallen hair, place it in an ashtray, and burn it. He usually asked if he could strike the match. "Sho!" she'd say. He'd seen Mama do this at home.

"Nanna?"

"What, baby?"

"How come you burn your hair in the ashtray, instead of just throwing it away?"

She laughed, her smile so wide he could see her dark gums.

"That's so folks can't put no roots on ya," she said.

So, that's why Daddy called Mama's hair-burning ignorant and superstitious.

Last weekend, while Nanna cornrowed the hair of two grand-daughters as Skylar watched from the kitchen table, his chin resting upon the flat surface, he got an idea.

"Nanna?"

"Yes, baby?"

"Would you like me to read *Huckleberry Finn* later on this morning?"

"I sho would," she said, turning to her granddaughters. "Y'all wanna hear ya cousin read later—"

"Nope!" Maureen said.

"We gonna jump double-dutch," Robyn said.

"I see," Nanna said.

"Then we're goin' roller-skating and swimming."

"Well, Sky," Nanna said. "Don't seem like nobody have a 'peciation for these things, like me and you, huh?" She chuckled, braiding one cornrow with another in Robyn's hair. "I guess we is by ourselves on this one, baby."

She chuckled again, in a way that made Skylar want to hug and kiss her, nestle his head in her neck and bosom, which always smelled of lye soap, perspiration, and whatever meal she'd cooked that day. He thought that morning her neck would smell of thick slabs of crisp bacon, fried Spam, scrambled eggs, and buckwheat pancakes.

"One time, I saw Paul Robeson do *The Emperor Jones* right here in Harlem," Nanna started bragging.

Paul who? He'd never heard the name. Nanna spoke of that man as if they'd discussed him in the past.

"That man is one grand sight," she had said, her eyes and voice drifting in a way that made Skylar think she was reliving it. "He ever'thang a colored man's supposed to be: smart, proud, dignified. I was lucky to get the tickets. My madam, Mrs. Rosenfeld, got sick on the night of the show. So, she give the tickets to me, an' me and Poppa saw it together. Good thang it was at the Lafayette Theatre in Harlem. Colored people wasn't allowed in theaters on Broadway in them days. One day," she said, patting Skylar on the head, "you gon' grow up an' be jus' lak him. I jus' knows it. I talks about it with the Lawd ever'day. Mr. Robeson done pave the way — ain't that how they says it? He done pave the way for other colored performers like you. Because of him, you ain't gonna have it so rough. Lawd knows, these white folks done give him a harder time than the Depression."

Skylar, in his mind, made it his business to find out who this Paul Robitsun guy was.

Skylar must've fallen asleep.

Miss Vivian, it seemed, had gone home. Of all of the voices downstairs on the porch, he couldn't hear hers. And Ray Charles was still singing "Georgia." Why didn't they play something else? The racket surrounding Lillian Crocker's pregnancy across the alley had stopped and the lights were out. Having fallen asleep, he'd missed the final round. He wondered who the winner was.

The missus was known to give her spouse, lick for lick, punch for punch, a run for his money.

"Althea, it's getting late," Daddy said. "Why don't you go to bed now?"

"I don't want to," Mama said. "Why don't you?"

"It's pretty late, that's all," Daddy said. "You don't have to show off in front of your family."

"Why not?" Mama said. "You always show off in front of yours."

"You know, Howard," Nanna said. "I remember when you an' Thea first met, befo' y'all was married, an' she was so worried 'bout impressin' yo' family. F' weeks, she saved her money, an' we went an' bought her that beautiful dress she'd been wantin' since I don't know when. I had a coupla dollars lef' over that week, an' gave it to her, so she could get her hair done, too. All she worried 'bout was if they was gonna like her. Then yo' family turn 'round, an' treat her like dirt. I know ... I know. This done happen 'bout ten years ago now, an' it's taken me this long to say this to you, but I done had a coupla drinks, an' I got somethin' to say."

Skylar's ears perked up. He'd never known Nanna to drink. But he'd noticed that after grown-ups started drinking liquor, a whole lot of truth came out.

"Now, maybe my baby didn't get all A's in school, like you did," Nanna said. "An' maybe she can't wear them there fancy dresses like the womens in yo' family—"

"Mama, don't—," Althea pleaded.

"No, I gots to say this—"

"Mama—"

"An' she don't live as high as they do, but I wants you to know that I — rather, me an' Jesse — we done raised a good girl. She a good wife, an' a good mother. She a good daughter, too, ain't never give me so much as a day's worth a trouble. An' what yo' family did to her that day ain't right. God as my witness. Thea made me promise a long time ago—"

"Okay, Mama, you've said enough," Althea said. "That's ten-year-old water under the bridge—"

"Thea done made me promise not to never say nothin' t' you 'bout it. An' I promised her, an' I pray she forgive me, 'cause Lawd knows I don't lie to my chirren, an' I don't break no promises neither, but God as my witness, what yo' family did ain't right.

Now, that's all I been wantin' to say, an' I'm through with it. I'll never bring it up again."

Skylar was surprised Daddy hadn't said anything. Probably because he was outnumbered. The silence gave way to murmuring, and somebody was giggling.

Uncle James started talking, his voice louder than everyone else's. Skylar could tell he was nearly drunk.

"...Kennedy what? Kennedy wouldn't be doing shit about civil rights if it wasn't for King," Uncle James said. "And that punk-ass brother of his, the attorney general, thinks that politically the time ain't right for the march on Washington next week. Not politically expedient for this administration, or some bullshit like that."

"That's not true," Daddy disagreed. "I believe in the good faith of the Kennedy boys. Number one, JFK's young and progressive, kind of like Thomas Jefferson." Skylar could tell by the slurring of his words, Daddy was just this side of drunk, too. "Number two, as the first Catholic elected to office, he, himself, is a minority to some degree. I think he cares deeply about the plight of Negroes. I'd be willing to bet you, Jimmy, that Kennedy supports the march next week, and he would—"

"Don't matter," Uncle James said. "'Cause King's gonna march any goddamn way. He don't need approval or support from the White House."

"If your prognostications are as erroneous as your grammar," Daddy said, "we're all in trouble."

"Ah, motherfucker," Uncle James said. "You know what the fuck I'm saying, man. Ain't no white folks around here. Just us. I talk any way I want!"

The porch got quiet again. "But that's some First Lady, though," Aunt Mildred said, playing peacemaker, like she always did.

"Yeah, that Jackie's one sharp, good-lookin' somethin'," Aunt Evelyn said.

"They make such a beautiful couple, don't they?" Aunt Gloria Jean said.

"And he's so handsome," Mama said. "That's how he got my vote."

"You know what yo' problem is, Howard," Uncle James said. "You think you too goddamn good for your own kind. Who the hell you think you talkin' to, a chile?"

"I think I done heard enough," Nanna said. "Now, James, y'all jus' be quiet. Y'all get to drinkin' in this heat, an' wanna start cuttin' up. Take that mess on from 'round here. It's late an' folks is 'sleep."

"No!" Uncle James persisted. "I ain't never liked this man. You can't never have a conversation with him without him trying to tell you how to talk. What kinda shit is that? Yalla-ass nigger, I know how to talk."

"It's obvious," Daddy said, "that people like you feel threatened around people like me. I know what I'm talking about. I analyze it intellectually, cerebrally, if you will. You deal with everything emotionally, Jimmy. That's the problem with Negroes now. Always has been. Too goddamn emotional. But I'll tell you this, dealing with it viscerally only makes for—"

"Come down off the ivory tower shit, man," Uncle James said. "You know, I hates motherfuckers who use big words when little ones is enough. The last time I—"

"Okay, that's it!" Mama said. Skylar could hear her folding the lounge chair, picking up bottles, glasses, beer cans, bags of pretzels, potato chips. "I think this party has ended. Goodness! It's almost two-thirty."

What followed was the folding of chairs, the cleaning up of whatever mess they'd made, voices attempting to hush Uncle James, who was now shouting. Smacking noises told Skylar that the women — Mama, Nanna, and his aunts — were kissing each other good night. He heard the front door open downstairs, Mama trying to hush Daddy, whose voice now boomed inside the house. Ray Charles sang about No peace he could find ... Skylar rolled over on his stomach, wrapped the pillow around his ears. He could still hear Uncle James having the last word. "An' another thing, mother-fucker! You hit my sister one more time, an' I swear 'fo' God, I'll..."

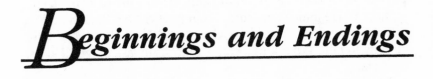Beginnings and Endings

LYING AWAKE, PROPPED UP in his hospital bed against double pillows, Howard studies Skylar asleep in the chair. He's not sure how long Skylar's been here; he had been asleep when his son arrived. He watches Skylar's head hang, slightly bobbing. He wants to wake him but fears that if he does, he'll have nothing to say. Been years since he and Skylar have been left alone with each other. What would he say to his firstborn son, with all the time in the world to say it? With death breathing down his neck, he thinks he should say something. He owes Skylar that. If only the words of remorse and pleas for forgiveness could be thawed from his frozen heart and find their way to the edge of his stubborn lips.

Sitting at the foot of the bed, keeping him company, is Marshall, the little boy with leukemia who visits him daily. Together, they watch Marshall's favorites, Bugs Bunny and Elmer Fudd, on the television monitor. Howard wonders how long it's been since he's watched cartoons with his own boys.

Where did he go awry?

In his lifetime, he's seen a lot. The desegregation of schools. The first black major-league baseball player. Men walking on the moon. The assassination of one president, the impeachment of another. But he'd never seen anyone dote on a child like Althea doted on Skylar. Everything changed when that boy came home. To this day, Althea would deny it. She had said things between them would get back to normal when Skylar got older. But they never did. That baby became her singular concern. Everything was Skylar. Skylar's hungry. Skylar needs this. Skylar might not like that. You know what Skylar did today? He'd never, in his life, hated a baby. And he shuddered to know what God thought of him, since that baby was his. How could he have possibly felt that way? It kept him awake nights. Kept him mumbling idiotically to himself at work. Kept his lips glued to the rim of a shot glass filled with whiskey.

You're jealous of your own firstborn...

Was he? Had he revealed it that much? Could a grown man actually be jealous of a baby? He wanted to hurt Althea back for discerning his naked feelings. He'd felt so exposed, so ashamed, so humiliated by that remark.

He had faith that circumstances would change once Skylar was walking and talking. As a toddler, the first word he spoke was "Mama." The second word he spoke was "Mama." Everything was Mama, which Howard found unusual and unhealthy, since most boys were father worshippers. Not that damn Skylar. When he saw Howard, he'd run to Althea. If Howard held him, he'd burst into tears, though he'd been just fine moments before. When Althea left Skylar alone with Howard in the room, Skylar yelled himself red until she returned. Howard hadn't known how much more he could take. He couldn't even sneak up on the little bastard and kiss him on the cheek.

"You two act as if I'm not here," Howard had said, half watching the television, feet crisscrossed, propped up on a hammock, the sports section of the newspaper spread across his lap.

"I don't know what you talking about," Althea said, playing patty-cake with Skylar, who stood in her lap, jumping, giggling, clapping, and drooling. Not once did she face Howard. Not once did her eyes leave Skylar.

"I'm the boy's father, and he doesn't like me."

"You need to stop being so mad at him all the time," she said, rubbing her nose against Skylar's. "Babies can sense that, you know."

"Sense what? You've turned the boy against me—"

"Don't start that again—"

"You did. He only knows and wants you—"

"You haven't been much of a father—"

"You won't let me!"

Skylar became as much Howard's obsession as Althea's.

He saw him everywhere. Commuting to work on the subway, he saw, in the seat near the sliding doors, Skylar nursing at Althea's breast. In the office, on top of the filing cabinet, Skylar played patty-cake with Althea, dribbling and gurgling. At the luncheonette, sitting on the short-order cook's hot, greasy griddle, Skylar splashed his bathwater, as Althea baby-talked to him.

He needed to talk to somebody about this. But who? He didn't have any real friends. There was no one at work he confided in. He wasn't close to any of his brothers or his sister. His mother was out of the question. A psychiatrist? He didn't say he was crazy. He just had a ... problem? The only person he could talk to about it, he already had. And she hadn't listened.

Althea had such influence over the boy, he'd ceased being a boy. Maybe she'd always wanted a daughter, though she'd never mentioned it to Howard. She allowed Skylar to behave with the delicacy of a girl. She permitted him to express his emotions like a girl. She let him use words that belonged in the mouth of a girl. When Skylar described the pink lace dress in Macy's window as pretty, Howard knew at that moment that things had gone too far. Last thing he would do was raise a faggot.

He'd bought the dress — what was it, Skylar's seventh or eighth birthday? — to teach Skylar, and maybe Althea, a lesson. This way, he figured, if Skylar ever used that sissyish word again, he'd remember the humiliation he'd suffered in front of the neighborhood children. Okay, so he overdid it a little. But he believed he was protecting Skylar from himself, and his mother. He was preventing him from growing up to be a ... Well, it sure didn't do much damn good, did it?

In his day, a man was a man, a woman a woman. There was little room to mistake one for the other. A man's hair was short, a woman's long. A man wore pants, a woman didn't. A woman wore earrings, a man didn't. Nowadays, it's all mixed up. Everybody does what the hell they want to do, and then don't want you to attach labels to them.

The day Althea told him she was pregnant again, he'd claimed this one before she finished saying it. She had Skylar. The next one was his.

The pampering and attention he paid Kendall was no more than Skylar got from Althea. He didn't mean for it to go as far as it did. He wanted, essentially, the best the world could provide for both his boys, like any father. Only somehow, things got perversely twisted. He'd channeled his energy into Kendall's dream of sports stardom. Discouraged Skylar from his acting leanings. Skylar wound up with an Oscar nomination. Kendall with zip. And still, he has yet to congratulate the son who was honored at the Academy

Awards earlier this year. There's so much he needs to say to Skylar, especially about the truth of what happened on the night of the fire ... Where does he start? The beginning is always the best place, he thinks.

Althea.

Who would've guessed she'd turn out the way she did. The power of that Women's Liberation mess is not to be underestimated. A formerly uneducated, nonprofessional woman who has become both. How the hell did she do it? What was the source of her motivation and drive? It baffles him, how they've traded positions of power, against his will. Now he is victim.

Cirrhosis of the liver, he thinks, is quite an undignified way to go.

As a toddler, all he had known was his mother. Recently divorced from a man she felt had failed her — a man who had fallen short of providing her the economic status she felt due her — she set out to make a life for herself and her only son, Howard.

His father was a big-time manager for colored performers starring at the Lafayette Theatre. He was a good-looking, light-skinned man with wavy hair who, with his three-piece suits, expensive cigars, and dangling watch chains, could've been the president, sharp as a scissor blade. Things looked bright for them and their only son in 1929. Howard's father represented the likes of Ethel Waters, a trumpet player from New Orleans named Louis Armstrong, and there were prospects that he would soon manage Bill Robinson. Marian had wondered, as a young wife and mother, why she never got to meet any of these people. But, she reasoned, a man's got to do what a man's got to do. And show business in the middle of New York City was no place for a woman and child to be anyway.

The day Howie took his first steps, she was too elated to await her husband's return from work. As it was, he came home well after midnight when they were asleep. She decided to surprise him. She purchased a darling sailor outfit for Howard, dressed herself, and took a taxi to the Lafayette Theatre in Harlem, the vaudeville house she'd heard so much about, but had never seen.

"Yes, may I help you?" the man at the admission door said.

"I'm looking for Howard Miller," she said.

"He really busy right now, ma'am," he replied, in a slow, thick way that she despised. He spoke like all those other dark, stupid, know-nothing niggers.

"I'm his wife, and this is his son, Howard, Jr.," she said, growing impatient with this ... no wonder they were called eight balls.

"He busy right now. I'll have to give him the message."

"What kind of nigger joint is this, anyway?" Her hands were on her hips now, her head jerking with the utterance of each word. "My husband's managing Ethel Waters and Louis Armstrong, and his wife can't even see him about something important..." Her voice trailed off, the rapidly fired words winding down like an engine. The man was laughing so hard in her face that she felt embarrassed, standing there on the sidewalk of 134th Street in front of all those dark people in line, some of whom were laughing with the man.

"What's so funny?" she asked, on the verge of calling him something he would not have liked.

"Howard ain't nobody's manager around here."

"Well, he must be managing the theater or something. I could've gotten it a little mixed up."

"I think you got it a lot mixed up. Howard's only an usher here, miss. But, like I said, I'd be glad to give him your message. What you want me to..."

Before he could finish, she had walked away. She could've stood there and argued with the man. But the realization of what a fool she'd been swooped down upon her. Now she knew why she'd never met these people. Why they never came to the house.

He came home late that night, later than usual. This time, she wasn't asleep.

"Do you know how much you humiliated me today?" she squawked, throwing a shoe at him. She sniffed the air. "And you got the nerve to come home drunk, too!"

"I'm really sorry," he said.

"Are you a manager, or aren't you?"

"No...," he said. "But I didn't mean to lie to you all this time. I thought, by now, that I would be, and that things would be better — and they will be."

A year later she was a divorcée, in pursuit of the man of her fantasy, a young son tugging at her skirt. She envisioned a secure, prosperous life for herself and her son, a life enjoyed mostly by white people. She had the complexion and hair texture to pass for white if she chose to. But her fantasy-man had color. Light-skinned, good hair, but colored just the same. She flatly refused the hand that life was dealing colored women of her generation, the down-trodden, uneducated, unskilled, poverty-stricken proletariat, that nauseating stereotype, cleaning up white people's filth as they accumulated their own, playing Mammy, nursing someone else's white children, no milk salvaged for the nurturing of their own. She never knew any of that. She was from good stock, of high and prestigious standing in the community. Of all the possibilities she imagined for herself, the wife of an usher at the Lafayette Theatre wasn't one of them.

She saw the ideal American family. The good life. A prosperous husband, a son, a daughter, herself as leisurely housewife.

Meantime, Howard, Jr., was her entire existence. Aside from her work as a librarian, she spent every waking hour with him. She indulged him, fed him, washed him, read to him, rocked him to sleep, let him sleep with her when he should've been sleeping alone. Nothing and nobody was of more importance. Whatever decisions she made always centered around him and his well-being. Return-ing to her son at the babysitter's after work was what she lived for. In light of the extent to which she doted on him to the exclusivity of the outside world, she was advised by friends that maybe she in-dulged the boy just a bit too much. They were dangerously close and it could be traumatic for him when he started school. She frowned at this criticism, casting it off as envy. She and her son were light-skinned, with good hair and green eyes, the prettiest colored people on the block, and her neighbors couldn't stand it.

What she felt from time to time was the pain of how much Howard favored his father. She had grown to loathe the man who had deceived her. A shameless, pathetic liar. Though she could lose herself in work and mothering, she was constantly reminded of the Senior through the Junior, so striking was their likeness.

"Looks like Howard, Sr., spit him out."

"Seems like he had that boy by himself. Like you had no part in it."

And it didn't stop there. Howard, Jr., was beginning to draw the same reactions from her that his father did. For one, she tended to overreact when he displeased her.

"Did you break that?" she asked Howard, pointing at the ashtray.

"No," he said, staring at the floor.

"Then who did it? I didn't!"

Howard started crying, alarmed by her anger.

"You're a little liar," she said. "You know that? Just like your no-good father." She picked up the broken pieces and held them in her palm. "I won't stand for two liars in one lifetime, do you hear me?"

She finally found her dream merchant, a restaurateur who took to her immediately. But as warm as he was to her, he was cold to her son. He had plans for her. Howard was in the way. Someone else's child. His treatment of the boy, while he courted the mother, was perfunctory and slighting. Aside from marriage, he wanted his own children. Little Howie could never totally be a part of that. The only thing he would ever give the boy was his name.

By the time Howard was five, his mother had remarried. As she paid more and more attention to her new husband, she paid less and less to him. For her, life was panning out as planned, everything falling flawlessly into place, on schedule. She'd found the perfect, good-looking, light-skinned man — an entrepreneur, who really was an entrepreneur. She "impulsively" dropped by one of the restaurants he claimed he owned. She quit her mundane job as librarian. Set up a lovely home in a comfortable, middle-class Jersey City neighborhood where her new husband was from, so her children could have a front yard to play in. She already had a son. What she wanted now was a daughter. That hefty slice of American pie was on her plate. All she had to do was dig in and eat it. Lick and smack her lips if she wanted to.

During her sixth month of pregnancy with the second child, she took Howard through the neighborhood for his first celebration of Hallow's Eve.

Having dressed him as a pirate, she led her five-year-old by the hand, belly inflated, through the streets of Jersey City, ringing doorbells, shouting, "Trick or treat!" Little Howie was frightened by the costumes of monsters and witches. He'd never seen anything like it. He whined throughout the entire evening, tugging at her skirt so, she almost had to drag him down the street, his feet refusing to walk. He insisted she carry him. And after blocks and blocks of incessant protest, she picked up her five-year-old, who was too frightened to walk. His arms were wrapped so tightly around her neck, she couldn't breathe.

"You're Mommy's big boy," she said. "Why're you so afraid?"

He buried his head in her neck, his teeth nipping her shoulder. Walking several blocks this way, she became exhausted and dizzy. She stopped at a porch and sat to catch her breath. That was when she felt it. Something erupted inside her. She could feel the mass of flesh and water moving, heaving, raging within her. Sparks of pain shot up her back, her thighs trembling as the water broke, dripping down the insides of her legs upon the filthy sidewalk, as if she were peeing on herself. She screamed. Neighbors and strangers came to her aid. They carried her back home, someone — she didn't know who — leading her son by the hand. Immediately, she was rushed to the hospital.

She had miscarried.

The child emerged, stillborn. The fetus, female. How, she wondered, could she have so carefully carried this growing life in her womb, nourishing and caring for it over the past six months, to have it end up as nothing, in a single instant of disaster? For a long time, she would mourn the daughter she would never know.

Howard was blamed for the miscarriage.

Marshall, the boy from the next hospital room, has gone. Resting upon Howard's stomach is a crayon portrait of him, drawn by the seven-year-old who sits with him every day in a terrycloth robe, watching cartoons. Scribbled in large, uneven letters, Marshall has written the words "My Friend."

Though he doesn't deserve it, he'd love to hear his sons call him their friend. Maybe Kendall would. He wonders where Kendall is. To his knowledge, Kendall hasn't been by the hospital to visit him yet.

"And you know Kendall, my youngest," Howard used to say to people who hadn't asked. "He's on his way to play big-time college football for Notre Dame." Kendall had actually been kicked off his high school varsity team by the coach.

"And how's Skylar?" the person might say. "I hear he's a student at Columbia."

"Columbia? Shit," Howard would reply. "What kind of football team do they have?"

He watches a commercial about AIDS that advocates the use of condoms. He sighs. From his deathbed, he worries about AIDS. Kendall could get it because he's a junkie. Skylar could get it because he's a ... Not that his son is actually one of them, but those faggots have created a disease that could kill his sons. He doesn't want his boys to expire that way. It would kill Althea.

Depressed by the commercial, he raises himself up and changes the channel with his remote control. He notices Skylar squirming in the chair, waking from his sleep. Howard lies back down, cocks his head to the side, and feigns sleep. His son yawns, then shakes him gently by the forearm.

"Daddy, are you awake?"

Howard doesn't move. He lies motionless, as his son strokes his matted hair.

"I have to go now," Skylar whispers. "I'll be back tomorrow, if I can, to see how you're doing."

He listens to Skylar walk away, footfalls clicking on the linoleum floor, as he struggles with the tears trying to squeeze through his closed eyes.

MRU

GOT A DATE WITH Dick Johnson tonight!

High school.

Skylar found himself going through a transformation of sorts. Though he was a loner in elementary school, ninth grade found him blooming from introverted outcast into social extrovert. Moving through the rite of passage into young adulthood, he obsessed over a thousand and one anxieties. Instead of welcoming the transition to puberty — hormones exploding, hair sprouting on his chest, legs, groin, armpits, voice deepening — he just as soon would have remained preadolescent. He had as much in common with other boys his age as he'd always had — almost nothing. All they talked about was pussy. Getting laid, having their wood polished, pumping leg, licking bloomer pudding. Skylar couldn't relate.

Sure, he liked girls, ladies, whatever, but not in the same way other boys did. He thought his hormones were retarded, a bit delayed. Maybe that's why he wasn't so excited about dating girls in high school. The sexual craving he did sense within himself he hoped would soon pass. A phase that all boys his age experienced. Soon, he would be hunting down the nearest piece of pussy, and talking about it every chance he got, like everyone else.

He considered jockism. More than being accepted into the university of his choice, or winning an Academy Award, he wanted Daddy's love and approval. Kendall, gifted athlete that he was, got all Daddy's attention and support. Skylar wanted some of it. Having Mama on his side was no longer enough.

How would he accomplish this?

He spent waking daytime hours and sleepless nights worrying about it. Football, he decided, was definitely out. Far too brutal. Macho was a mask he refused to wear. Besides, Kendall was the star halfback in the family. Skylar reasoned that if he couldn't become a quarterback, which would have put him on an equal footing with Kendall, there was no point.

Boxing. That was something his father would respect and admire. All his life, he'd watched what he considered the disgusting spectacle of that so-called artistic sport. Sandwiched between Daddy and Kendall in the living room, he'd pray for the coming and going of the fifteenth round, as Daddy and Kendall ooohed and aaahed with each crashing punch to the jaw, sweat pouring from the opponent's face, the impact of the blow forcing the mouthpiece to pop out and sail across the canvas. The more blood, the more they loved it, the more they screamed. It made him queasy watching some guy with two bloodied, disfigured eyes being pounded to the tune of encouraging grunts and screams from the crowd. No. Hell no. Boxing was out, too. No way he would voluntarily mutilate his pretty face. Not when freshman year was the time he needed it most.

Track. Now, that was a brainstorm.

It involved no bodily contact. No spectacular finesse of any kind. All he needed was two legs. The wind to go the distance. He imagined himself as anchor, the baton being slipped into his sweaty hand, as he hauled ass toward the finish line, popping the tape, the photographers and sports journalists documenting his victory for all to see and remember. Wow! he thought. Track is a way to achieve athletic respect from jocks. And track is the easy way out. No bruises, no scars, no broken bones, no stitches, no punch-drunkenness. Shaking hands with that compromise, he felt relieved. He'd win Daddy's respect if it meant trying out for the Olympics.

Growing up in the neighborhood, he'd already been considered one of the fastest boys on the block. "Man, that Sky Whyte can run his ass off!" the kids said, during races up and down the street, or around a square block. All he needed was speed and training. He already had one, God-given; he'd get the other from a coach.

During tryouts for the frosh cross-country team, he was standing near the bleachers, changing into sweats, when he noticed three guys standing a few yards away near the track, whispering about him. He could tell from the way the lanky one's lips moved, and they all turned his way. One of them was on the ground, stretching, his arms extended to his toes, his forehead touching his knees. He got up, jogged in place, flexed his legs, repeatedly kicking at the air, and they started walking toward Skylar.

"Hi!" the first guy said, pulling a t-shirt over his head. "My name's Alvin." He extended his hand, and Skylar shook it.

"Skylar."

"And this," Alvin said, "is Henry and Charles." They all shook hands.

"You're in my sister's algebra class," Charles said to Skylar.

"Really?" Skylar said. There was something about them he liked. They smiled and seemed friendly. "What's her name?"

"Karen Taylor."

"Karen's your sister? Yeah, you look alike."

"We're glad you're trying out," Alvin said. "We hear you're a pretty fast dude."

"If what we heard is true," Charles said, "we want you as the fourth member of our relay team."

"Come time for the Penn Relays," Henry said, "we gonna turn the mother out!" He snapped his fingers.

After stretching and warm-up exercises, a couple of laps around the track, and a few 110-yard dashes clocked by the coach, Skylar made the team. The four of them rejoiced, as if winning their first relay meet. Before heading home, they celebrated at Lula Belle's Soda Shoppe with ice cream sundaes. Skylar felt like Wally Cleaver, hanging out with the guys at the malt shop with the shoestrings of their track shoes tied together and slung around their necks, gold C's on the chests of hooded sweatshirts, and blots of moisture beneath their armpits. For the first time ever, he felt like one of the boys.

Skylar was surprised that Alvin, Henry, and Charles weren't boasting about tracking down the next piece of pussy. Nor did they discuss last weekend's score between the New York Jets and the Redskins.

"Have you heard that great new song by James Brown?" Charles asked. They were huddled around a small table. The jukebox thumped, the music thick with bass, as teenagers filled the hamburger-and-french-fries-smelling air with chatter and laughter, punctuated by the swishing sound of the soda fountain, and the bell tinkling each time the door opened and slammed shut, a gust of September wind chilling their faces. "It's called, 'Say It Loud, I'm Black and I'm Proud!'"

"Yeah, I heard it on the radio!" Alvin said. "It's outtasite. Imagine what white people must think about that record."

– 141 –

"Everybody's singing about social messages these days," Skylar said, pleased they were discussing music. This was something he could identify with, a conversation he could contribute to — instead of panting and foaming at the mouth over Bertha Mae Henderson's 38D cups and making bets about who, among the four of them, would be the first to fasten their lips on them. "The Beatles probably got that started with 'Sgt. Pepper.'"

"Has anybody seen *Rosemary's Baby*?" Henry asked. "It's the creepiest movie I've ever seen. The whole thing takes place at the Dakota Building on Seventy-second and Central Park West, where all the celebrities live."

"I love the movies. When I grow up, I want to study acting and make movies," Skylar said, shocked at himself for admitting this to three strangers. "I've been practicing since I was about seven years old."

"Wow!" Alvin said.

"Imagine if you became a movie star!"

The guys seemed to be impressed with this. First time Skylar could remember, outside of Aubrey and Nanna, that someone regarded his acting ambitions as impressive. This track stuff, Skylar thought, will be a lot easier than I imagined.

Recently, he'd been missing Uncle Aubrey. It was still difficult accepting his death, though it had been almost four years. A lot had happened in that time, most of which he would like to have shared with his uncle. How could that saint of a man have suffered such a horrible death? His body destroyed by that fire...

In the coming winter months, as cross-country meets became indoor competitions, Skylar and his new friends got close. They called themselves the Four Tops. With them, he could be himself. He didn't have to talk about girls and Joe Namath for acceptance. Growing up in his neighborhood had been everything but that. If not for these guys, he probably would've quit the team months ago.

"That's no damn sport," Daddy said. "So, what you think, because you've joined the track team, that makes you a man?"

His plan had failed. His mission unaccomplished. He realized that if it wasn't brutal, blood-drawing, and vicious, Daddy couldn't use it.

"There are two kinds of sports," Daddy said, forming a V with his fingers. "Men sports, and sissy sports."

"What's the difference?" Skylar asked.

"Football, basketball, boxing, and hockey are men sports," Daddy explained, counting them with his fingers, while Kendall snickered. "Track, tennis, swimming, fencing, those are sissy sports."

"So, you mean, noncontact sports are—"

"Call it what you want, boy," Daddy said. "All I'm saying is that real men don't play tennis or run track."

"What do you think of Skate?" Alvin asked Skylar, one brisk afternoon at Lula Belle's, following practice.

Skylar gazed into three pairs of eyes gazing back at him, awaiting his response with anticipation, it seemed. He felt he was being challenged, and that he'd been brought in right in the middle of a story-in-progress.

"Well," Skylar said, "he's the fastest sprinter we have. Besides, he just won a scholarship at Adelphi University and—"

The other three started laughing. Skylar grew uneasy, feeling he was the punchline of their inside joke.

"That's not what we mean." Charles spoke up. "We mean, what do you really think of him?"

"Well," Skylar said, slowly, noticing they all shared similar grins. "I guess he's all right. I don't really know him that well—"

"Fuck all that!" Henry said. "Don't you think he's cute?"

Now wait a damn minute! Skylar thought. Is this a trap? What the hell's going on here? His heart pounded, his palms moistened. Just when you think you know people ... Why would they ask a question like that? He swung back and forth between telling the truth or a lie, not knowing which answer they were looking for. The wrong response, whatever it might be, could sever his ties with them. And, they were the closest friends he'd ever known. He played it safe.

"Why?" Skylar said. "Do you think he's cute?"

"Yes!" they replied in unison, as if they'd rehearsed.

"Because of him," Alvin added, "I live for the showers."

Skylar watched the three of them laughing, slapping each other five. Except, it wasn't the handshake by which brothers were known to dap and slide palms. Rather, they slapped palms in the air.

"What's that you're doing?" Skylar asked.

"This is how gay people slap five," Charles said.

It was wonderful and strange to Skylar. They even had a secret handshake. The brothers had their dap and gay boys had this. Yes, he liked these guys a lot. He exhaled, relaxed, as if he'd been tightening his muscles, and holding his breath, for the last fourteen years. His friends were smiling. Charles patted him on the arm.

"It's okay, Sky," Charles said. "We always knew you were one of us."

"What do you mean, 'one of you'?" Skylar said, playing dumb.

"Oh, come off it, Whyte," Charles said. "With boys like Skate, Tyronne Wilson, and Ray-Ray Jenkins strolling around Clinton High, who can think about pussy?" They laughed.

"I, personally," Charles added, "have been in love with Skate since I was yea high. My ultimate goal in life is to throw him to my body before he graduates in June. How about you, Sky, isn't there someone you carry a torch for?"

Skylar's first sexual awakening had happened when he was eight years old.

Tyronne Wilson, the same Tyronne for whom Kendall had been suspended from school, had lured him into a basement. Curious, he followed. Leaning against the gas meter, Tyronne unzipped his pants and pulled it out. Skylar stood there, not knowing what to do.

"Let me see yours," Tyronne suggested.

Skylar did the same. Then Tyronne grabbed him around the waist and they rubbed against each other until Tyronne said it was enough. In coming weeks, they would have other such incidents, except they became more challenging, involving a bit of fantasy.

"Feel like wrestling?" Tyronne would say. "And if I beat you, I dick you in the butt. If you beat me, then you can do it to me, fair?"

And they'd tumble on the filthy concrete floor of Tyronne's basement, or through the dirt of an empty football field. Sometimes Tyronne won and sometimes Skylar. There was never any real penetration except the rubbing against each other's buttocks. They never spoke about it, before or after, except to suggest: "Feel like wrestling?" Then they'd pretend nothing had happened. But that was a long time ago. He had been with no one since, male or female. Tyronne, as budding teenager, had since emerged as Mr. Best-Looking himself. Skylar was sure he'd win it in the yearbook's Who's Who, when their senior year rolled around. But Tyronne was like all the other guys in the neighborhood or at school. Girls occupied all of his time and attention. And he had groomed for himself an image and reputation as cockhound.

"Yeah," Skylar said to his friends at the table in the malt shop. "I kind of like Tyronne Wilson."

"You do?" Henry said. "'Cause I heard he plays, if you know what I mean. This guy I know from Brooklyn had him, and it wasn't that long ago, either."

"Really?" Skylar said. "'Cause I had him too — well, that was a long time ago. We were just kids, really."

"Have you ever wondered," Alvin asked, "why you never see us at school dances and house parties?"

"No," Skylar said. "I don't go myself."

"Well," Alvin continued, "since we know you're one of us, we can let you in on a secret."

The four boys huddled closer together, Alvin's voice dropped to a whisper, the Sound of Motown throbbing on the jukebox.

"We know places in the Village," Alvin said, "where only men go."

"What do you mean?" Skylar asked.

"You know what I mean," Alvin said. "One's called the Gold Bug. And there's two other places: the Bon Soir and the Stonewall. You've got to come with us one weekend—"

"But," Skylar interrupted, "we're only fourteen and fifteen years old. Do you guys have phony I.D.?"

"No," Charles spoke up. "You don't need any. They never ask us for any identification and we can drink liquor and dance with men. I tell you, it's fabulous!"

Gold Bug ... Gold Bug ... The words sounded so familiar to Skylar, and he wondered why. That weekend, he found out.

It was the hole-in-the-wall where Uncle Aubrey had taken him during his maiden voyage to the Village. The Gold Bug was basically the same place, as he remembered it, with only minor changes, such as, Judy Garland was no longer a jukebox selection with "Sing Hallelujah, Come On Get Happy!" She'd been preempted by Diana Ross and the Supremes' "Love Child." He was having the time of his life, hole-in-the-wall or not. And he had no curfew. He'd told his parents he was staying at Charles's house in the Bronx. Charles's parents thought he was spending the night with Skylar in Harlem and so on. That night, and every weekend which followed, the four of them club-hopped between the Bug, Bon Soir, and Stonewall, the dark, cavernous sweat-boxes teeming with men, black, white, Puerto Rican. Skylar loved it. What was not to love?

Except, there was one unattractive, risky feature. The red light. Each underground club had a red light. In the event of a police raid, the light would go on, the other lights off, and the music would stop. Then it was every man for himself, the festive mood shifting to panic and pandemonium. And if they weren't quick enough, they would be beaten with billy clubs, kicked in the face, pulled by the hair, and escorted into a waiting paddy wagon. Next stop, Greenwich Village police station. Then it would've been all over. If Daddy ever got a call from the N.Y.P.D. that his son, a minor, had been busted in an adult homosexual bar that served liquor ... But he took that chance. Week after week. There was nothing to stop him. Pandora had already opened her box.

During lunch, study halls, locker-room chitchat, the Four Tops conversed in codes:

Got a date with Dick Johnson tonight!

You lucky fool! Is that right?

He's a good friend of mine. You know Dick—

The Dick Johnson?

What other Dick is there? You know what they say.

A Dick by any other name—

Just ain't the same. Anyway, my friend, Dick, well he knows I love him, and he's got this really big head about it, you know, his—

Does he still wear that turtleneck sweater?

You have met Dick, haven't you?

I believe I have—

The one with the thick vein in his throat—

And sometimes he has to pull his turtleneck sweater back a bit so you can see his face good?

I'm positive you know him, good ol' Dick.

He does sound familiar...

The Four Tops had now become inseparable. In and around school, they drew the cold and skeptical glances of people like Larry Moody, Cheryl Rivers, and Pee Wee Glover.

Somebody told me the Four Tops are actually the Four Fags.

Don't they screw each other at Charles's house, when his folks ain't there?

You mean, at the House That Fags Built?

I thought it was called Fairyland.

I always knew there was something fishy about those four.

The Four Muske-queers.

And, don't they be ridin' around in Charles's brother's Mustang convertible?

Yeah, the Fagmobile.

In the *Clinton Gazette,* the school newspaper, they read about themselves in the gossip column: S.W. loves C.T. loves H.R. loves A.A. loves S.W.

Skylar was embarrassed. He hoped nobody would know he was S.W. There was Sterling Williams. Shirley Wilson. Stanley Whaley. Steven Washington. But judging by the looks and taunts he got in the locker room, the corridors, the cafeteria, everyone seemed to know beyond doubt who S.W. was. He couldn't walk into the auditorium for study period without someone tapping someone else on the arm or shoulder, or leaning over to whisper in their ear, alerting them to the fact that S.W. had just walked in.

"Hi, Skylar," girls would say to him in the corridor, between classes, girls he knew well and always stopped to speak to. Now, they kept walking, real fast, and giggled with their girlfriends.

"What's so funny?" Skylar would ask. The giggling, as they ran away from him, would then turn into a howl.

"Yo, Sky, I got something for you," Josh Perry said, in the locker room, as they changed into shorts, t-shirts, and sneakers for Phys. Ed.

"What you got?" Skylar said.

"I got some bubble gum and some dick," Josh said, smiling. "And I'm all out of bubble gum."

In February, during a record-breaking snowstorm, holed up in Charles's house in the Bronx on a Friday night with nothing to do, nowhere to go, no one to see, they talked about boys, boys, boys. The ones they liked. The ones they'd had. Those they planned to have. After several glasses of Bacardi and Coke, Charles became teary-eyed. Like a jilted lush marooned at a singles' bar, he sang to the record playing on the phonograph, Nancy Wilson's "Face It Girl, It's Over." Hoarse and off-key, he crooned, his voice cracking.

"I'm desperately in love with Skate. He doesn't know I'm alive," Charles whined. "What am I going to do? He's graduating, and June's right around the corner."

"Stop wasting tears, feeling sorry for yourself," Alvin advised, slightly inebriated. "Just call the man up and confess your love, shit!"

A few moments passed as Nancy Wilson, like a drum roll, sang, "I know, I know, I know, I know, I know, I know, I know, it's over!"

"Tell you what: I got an idea!" Alvin said, standing, swaying from the rum. "Let's call up the boys we like. Fuck it! I'm game! At least we'll get it off our chests. Huh? What do you say?"

Skylar volunteered first, thinking it was a great idea, realizing the alcohol had everything to do with his burst of courage. Didn't matter that Tyronne Wilson was in his homeroom class. That he'd have to face him first thing Monday morning. According to his intoxicated rationale, if they'd done it before, they could do it again.

Skylar dialed the number, losing his courage with each digit he dialed, sobering with each subsequent telephone ring, deciding it wasn't such a good idea after all. But Alvin, Henry, and Charles egged him on.

"Let the phone ring."

"No time to back down now."

"Nobody's home," Skylar said, secretly relieved, faking disappointment. "I'll call back another time."

As he said this, hoping his friends would let him off the hook, someone answered.

Click!

"Hello ... uh, hello."

"Yeah..."

"Can I speak to Tyronne?"

"Speaking."

"Yeah," Skylar said sheepishly, clearing his throat, having lost half his voice. "This is Sky Whyte."

"Yeah?"

"...Yeah. Well, uh, I um, I thought I'd give you a call and see how you're doing."

"You see me every day at school, man."

"I know, but ... well, we used to be so close when we were kids—"

"Uh-uh, man, we wasn't never close ... Look man, I'm busy. Whatchu want?"

Nervously, Skylar looked at his buddies, who surrounded him so closely, they smothered him. He felt Alvin's warm, rummy breath blowing down the nape of his neck. The three of them were whispering advice. Skylar covered the mouthpiece with his palm. "Ssshh!" Skylar said.

"Anyway, Tyronne—"

"Hey man, this a joke or what? Who's that whispering?"

"Nobody."

"So, make it quick, man, I'm busy."

"Yeah ... um, well, I thought we could get together sometime, you know, maybe hang out and do something."

"Get together for what? Do something like what?"

Skylar paused a moment. "I don't know." Another pause. "Feel like wrestling?"

"What?! Hey man, you drunk or somethin'?"

"No, I'm not. I just thought that maybe—"

"Thought my ass! I should punch you in the fuckin' face!"

Click! Dial tone.

Alvin, Henry, and Charles started in simultaneously.

"What happened?"

"What did he say?"

"Did he get mad?"

In homeroom Monday morning, Skylar couldn't look Tyronne in the face. Over the weekend, he prayed the snowstorm would close school for the next few weeks, or that Tyronne would be absent, or that he'd transfer to another school, or move out of the state. It started before the teacher took attendance. Boys in the back of the classroom disguised their voices like girls and made loud, smooching noises.

"I love you, Tyronne."

"Oh please, please be my husband."

"I'll give you some face anytime you want."

Another voice behind Skylar said, "Oh, my darling Tyronne. Will you be my lawfully wedded husband? To have, to hold, to love, to cherish, to dick me in the ass every time I get the itch?"

"Be cool, y'all," Tyronne said. "Knock that shit off!"

The class roared. Girls giggled, and shot Skylar dirty looks, glances of reproach. Skylar felt humiliated. He knew he'd done the wrong thing. Got angry with himself for allowing the guys to talk him into such nonsense. And not one of them had called their heartthrobs. His stomach bubbled. His palms sweat. He wanted to do the 110-yard dash out of that classroom, flee into the boys' room, throw up in the toilet, then flush himself down with the vomit and floating cigarette butts.

For weeks following, he couldn't wait from 8:45 until the nine o'clock bell rang. Fifteen minutes of homeroom had become his most difficult class.

He soon learned that humiliation made for character, which was put to the test on the first of May, when, as in each year past, he had to decide whether to attend school or to play hookey with his friends and other gay guys who'd travel to Forty-second Street and watch Barbra Streisand movies all day in Times Square. The first of May at Clinton High was known as Fag Day. Each year, this tradition was upheld by jocks and bullies who decided to beat the shit out of any faggot bold enough to come to school that day. It was open season on homos — or Moes, as they were called. Only the really tough gay guys would go to school ready for a fight. And, each year, there were many.

Playing hookey was as alien to Skylar as heterosexual coitus. Wasn't so much he thought he was tough enough to survive the first of May. It was just easier than hanging around Times Square at the risk of his father finding out. With his luck, he'd bump into Daddy during his lunch hour. So, he'd attend school, wearing the proper attire in the event of a brawl. And brawl he would, discovering there was more punch, stamina, and heart to him than he knew he had. Even the straight boys who hunted them down like ducks through the corridors, the boys' room, and the schoolyard, respected the balls these guys had for showing up in the first place.

"Them scaredy-cat Moes at the movies ain't got no balls," they said. "They hearts be pumpin' Kool-Aid an' shit."

First time Skylar realized faggots and punks weren't necessarily synonymous.

If nothing else, the first of May following his telephone call to Tyronne prepared him for future street fights. There were always straight boys challenging them in the Village while the gay boys jumped double-dutch rope, or danced the Bump, or harmonized on Smokey Robinson tunes in the summer heat outside the Bon Soir. Had he known how adept he was at kicking ass, he might've trained to become a boxer to please Daddy after all.

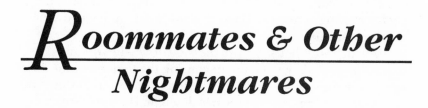

Roommates & Other Nightmares

FIRE ENGINES SOUND CLANGING alarms in Skylar's head.

Sirens whine like alley cats in heat. He tosses and turns, arms and legs swinging, cutting, slicing the air, entangling himself with the sheets.

Althea's pained voice screams from the opposite end of the house. Footsteps gallop down the carpeted foyer toward his bedroom. The door flies open. Clicking on the light, Althea's eyes sweep across his bedroom. Behind her, clouds billow about her nightgown. Skylar is unable to see her feet, which are shrouded in smoke. She appears to be floating. Slow motion governs the graceful, flowing beckoning of her hands. Skylar tries to scream. Nothing comes out. He tries to move. Paralysis prevents him from doing so. Althea turns, floats away, smoke filling her path.

The bedroom walls dissolve to the outdoors where fire engines block off the street. Neighbors and strangers, in Sunday, church-going finery, gleefully watch the burning building. As they chew popcorn, their intense concentration focuses, trancelike, upon the late-night catastrophe. Skylar gropes his way through the thick maze of spectators. He glides around torsos, some slim, some obese. He dives between legs, tugs at the skirts of women who don't seem to be aware of him. Hypnotized, they gaze at the inferno, grinning, chewing popcorn, jaws grinding in unison.

He struggles with syllables that refuse to fall from his mouth. The voice inside him pleads for the whereabouts of his parents, his brother. He tries calling their names. No sounds form in his throat. He is lifted off the ground by a large, portly man, clad in a dark, mortician's suit, who points at the burning house. "That's some fire, little boy," he says to Skylar. "You know the people?" Skylar wants to reply, but he's lost his voice. The man places Skylar upon his broad shoulders for an unobstructed view. Skylar covers his eyes, then muffles his ears, silencing the loud crackling of wood, the roaring of flames, the piercing sirens in the distance. Spotlights probe, moving across the black Harlem sky, a Hollywood motion picture premiere.

He watches his house burn at the east corner, the windows glowing an intense orange, the fire devouring the parlor and the room above it on the second landing, his bedroom, the flames so towering and bright that the street is bathed in daylight. The west corner of the house remains intact, undisturbed, undaunted. His nostrils fill with the stinging pungency of burning wood, the smoke curling, disappearing into the black sky. Searching for Mama, Daddy, and Kendall, he is suddenly back on the ground. The mortician has disappeared.

A pair of paramedics charge out of the smoldering, two-story structure, guiding a stretcher with a white sheet that covers the victim's face. The paramedic steps before him, pulls back the white sheet. Skylar catches a glimpse of Uncle Aubrey's disfigured, charred face...

"Noooooooooo!"

There's a loud pounding on the door.

Skylar awakens, moist with sweat, the book falling from his lap onto the floor, the sirens in his head diminishing. Who the hell could that be? he thinks, panting, glancing at the clock, hoping it's Evan, knowing it's not. He remembers a phone call he'd received that evening from a woman asking for Evan. She'd refused to leave a name or number.

He climbs out of bed, slides his feet into slippers, and wraps a robe around his body. "All right, I'm coming!"

Unlocking the door, he is shocked to see Kendall standing in the vestibule. "Sky, man, sorry to bother you but...," Kendall says, staring at the floor, fingering his dreadlocks. "I need a place to stay for a few days."

Skylar steps back, opening the door, rubbing sleep from his eyes.

"Are you all right?" Kendall says, noticing the sweat on his brother's forehead.

"I'm fine," Skylar says.

Kendall studies him a moment. "You're still having the nightmares?"

"What nightmares?"

Kendall glances at him as if he's crazy, but says nothing. He parks himself on the sofa.

"Why don't you have a place to stay?" Skylar asks, wiping the perspiration from his forehead, knowing Mama wouldn't throw Kendall out into the streets if God told her to.

"I left. It's a hassle living alone with Mama in that house. She has her own work, but she's always fuckin' with me, complaining about my life as an unemployed junkie refusing to seek help. She says she's sick and tired of looking at me in my pitiful state, and I'm tired of listening to it. Living in her house. Playing by her rules. Who needs it? I got a good possibility for a job at the post office come Monday morning. I'ma find myself a crib, even it if means rooming at the Y. Now, I don't wanna get in your way ... or Evan's." He lights a cigarette, the air suddenly heavy with nicotine. "You know I'm sorry for what happened the last time I stayed with y'all."

"That's in the past," Skylar says. "Matter of fact, Evan's gone. He left two days ago ... for a shoot in L.A." Kendall's eyes widen with satisfaction. "You can only stay about a week. Evan will be home by then."

"I'm starving," Kendall says. "I ain't put on the feed-bag in days. What's in the fridge?"

Groggily, Skylar gestures toward the kitchen. Kendall walks into the kitchen, but Skylar stays put in the living room.

"Have you been to the hospital recently?" Skylar asks.

"Nope," Kendall says, his voice muffled, head buried inside the refrigerator. "Not since the last time. Oh, by the way, sorry for throwing up on you that day at the hospital."

"Don't you plan to visit him?"

"Who?"

"Who else?"

"What's this can of Spam doing in the cabinet? All your money and success and you still throwin' down on Spam?" Kendall says.

"It's there for a reason. You're welcome to eat anything else, but not that. Aren't you going to visit him?"

"Yeah, I guess so, next week some time. I'm just chillin' out right now. Getting my head together."

"You really should make a point of it," Skylar says. "Now is a crucial time—"

"Not meaning to break on you," Kendall says. "But how come you're so worried about the old man? I mean, after all he's done to you? To us?"

"I don't know. I guess I'm beginning to feel like Mama. We're still family; he's still our father, and he needs us."

"Yeah," Kendall says. "Like Diana Ross needed the fuckin' Supremes. Maybe it's easier for you to forget, Sky, your being so successful and all. But me, look at me — I'm not so willing to let go."

Skylar waits for the refrigerator door to close, for Kendall to reappear in the living room before he continues. "I haven't let go either," Skylar says. "Not completely, anyway."

"I swear, Sky," Kendall says, biting into a cold chicken leg. "I don't understand you and Mama. For years, he dogged y'all; treated me like a prince. And every time I turn around, both of you are puckered up, kissing his ass. I swear I don't get it. Shit!" He tosses the chicken leg back on the plate. "Now I've lost my appetite."

Skylar is angry, refusing to submit to this recurring, stalemate argument they have. He can't understand his brother's attitude, and Kendall can't fathom his. What else is new? The point's moot. With a five a.m. wakeup call to face the cameras, and no energy left for a fight, he decides to turn in, hoping the nightmare has come and gone for the night. Maybe he'll read another half hour of Toni Morrison. Books remind him of Evan, because Evan never read any. It was another point of dispute between them.

"Good night, Kendall. Turn out the lights when you go to bed." He turns to leave, but stops. "Oh, and by the way, let's reach an understanding now, okay? If I find any of your spikes or drugs in the house, or anything missing, like money, or if I catch any of your friends in my house, out you go. Understood?"

Kendall nods his head, his feet resting on the coffee table, arms folded behind his head.

"Understood," Kendall says. "You won't hear a peep out of me, Sky. You won't even know I'm here, man."

That's what you said last time, Skylar thinks, picking up the novel from the floor, parting the pages, crawling back into bed.

They had been having a party, celebrating the release of Evan's first feature film. Celebrities and highbrows mingled in the Upper West Side townhouse. Caterers, a staff of domestics, photographers, and studio bigwigs were milling about, the guests sipping champagne and stuffing themselves with hors d'oeuvres when the doorbell rang. Skylar was engaged in small talk with the director and members of the cast, when the feisty old Cuban chef tapped him on the shoulder.

"Meestair Cabot's lookeeng forrr ju," he said. "He says eese beddy eemporrrtant."

Skylar excused himself, searching the crowd-filled rooms. When he found Evan, he looked as if he'd been told that his movie would not have a theatrical release after all.

"What's wrong?" Skylar said.

"Listen, we got a problem," Evan said. "Your brother's here..."

"So?" Skylar said.

"So?!" Evan nearly shouted. "He's stoned out of his face and his hair's a fright. Look, Sky, I know he's your brother and I know he's welcome here anytime he wants, but not now, not today. You've got to get rid of him, please."

"What would you like?" Skylar asked. "For me to dress him in a uniform and he can play busboy for us?"

"Look, Sky," Evan said. "I'm not trying to make you defensive about this, but he's got to go. Please don't fight me on this."

"Where is he?" Skylar said, defeated.

"I took him to our bedroom. He's in there."

Skylar found Kendall sitting and nodding in the wing chair, his head bobbing. When he opened his eyes, he tried smiling at his brother. "Could I use the toilet?" Skylar led him to the bathroom as two attractive, elegant women were leaving. They glanced with repulsion at Kendall, before smoothing their lips into a smile for Skylar. They moved out of Kendall's way as if he were diseased.

Inside, Skylar locked the door behind them. His brother knelt on the floor, lifted the toilet seat, and placed two fingers down his throat. Skylar was nauseated but said nothing. Let him get it out, he thought. Better in the bowl than on one of the guests. "I need a place to stay," Kendall said, flushing the toilet. "Daddy, that fuckin' drunk, he threw me out and there's nowhere for me to go. I won't cause any trouble, Sky, I swear. You won't even know I'm here, man."

"Don't worry about it," Skylar said. "You'll stay here with Evan and me. We'd love to have you."

From day one, Skylar sensed that Evan, though he never said it, was irritated by Kendall's mere presence, stoned or sober. Though he was a great help to them around the house, performing chores and running errands, Kendall acted as if the townhouse belonged exclusively to his brother. The two barely spoke to each other, sometimes acknowledging one another in the presence of Skylar, their go-between.

"Did you think she was good in that?" Evan said to Skylar. "I've seen her give better performances in better films than this one."

"I don't think so," Skylar replied. "This film is some of her best work."

"I have to take you to see the work she did in France before—"

"Hey, Skylar!" Kendall interrupted. Skylar knew he'd done it on purpose, feeling left out, vying for his brother's attention, knowing Evan didn't like, but tolerated him. "Remember the time we saw *Psycho*, when we were kids?"

"How could I forget?" Skylar said, noticing that Kendall was deliberately excluding Evan, whose smile had collapsed to a frown, as he pretended to brush lint that wasn't there from his shirt and ignored Kendall.

"But we missed the shower scene," Kendall said. "Mama wouldn't let us watch—"

"An-y-way," Evan said, obviously irritated. "She did, let's see, oh, three, maybe about four ... yeah, I think it was four films in France, before she ever came to America."

"Did she?" Skylar said.

"Yeah," Evan said. "She worked with Truffaut; I think, Rohmer—"

"And Sky," Kendall said, "how about that dude who was talking and acting like his mama—"

"I can't think of the other directors she worked with, Skylar," Evan said. "But somehow, I think she also made a film—"

"That creepy-ass dude, remember?" Kendall said. "What's his name? That weird motherfucker. He scared the shit outta me!"

Skylar didn't know how much longer he could endure this.

"Evan," Skylar said, that night in bed. "Do you have a problem with my brother living with us?"

"Not exactly," Evan said. "But you will admit he's a bit crude, his manner could use some refining, and I wish he wouldn't walk around this place like he owns it. Just look at him. Why doesn't he comb his hair? It looks disgusting."

"Disgusting is a strong word for ethnicity," Skylar said. "You like dreadlocks on other people. What's different about my brother's?"

"I don't know," Evan said. "He just looks dirty."

"Even though he showers every day and washes his hair," Skylar said, "you think he's dirty."

When Evan was gone the next morning, Skylar spoke with Kendall about the personality clash.

"I'm offended by his arrogance," Kendall said. "I mean, I know he's your lover and all, but he's just another white boy as far as I'm concerned. From the time I first knocked on your door, Evan stared me down like I had just taken a shit in his doorway. I already said I was sorry, though I didn't even want to, for crashing Evan's stupid-ass, tired-ass party. If I knew there was a party going on, I would've come later when everybody was gone. Evan complains if I fart. He even gave me a plate, a fork, a glass, a spoon, and a knife for me to use, and nobody else. What the fuck? Am I being quarantined, or what? No matter what I do, Evan doesn't like it. If I'm listening to the stereo, Evan turns it off when he gets home. If I'm watching television or movies on the VCR, Evan says he has a videocassette he wants to watch. He tells me to use this towel, this facecloth, this bar of soap, and not that one. There are things in the house he told me not to touch. Like I'm some fuckin' kid!"

With all the bickering, Skylar was being split down the middle, and it was getting to him. Life was colorful enough without monitoring personality conflicts, playing arbitrator.

"Evan, who the hell do you think you are," Skylar said, "to tell my brother to use certain towels, and designate certain plates and forks for him to eat from?"

"I was just giving him his own personal things to use," Evan said in a monotone, not looking up from his newspaper. "Just trying to make him feel at home, that's all."

"Don't try it, Evan."

After six weeks as a threesome, Skylar realized that Kendall had stopped helping with the chores, and for the most part, was lying around on his ass. He never cleaned up after himself, taking full advantage of the maid who cleaned once a week. Skylar got fed up with arriving home after long, arduous days of twelve, fourteen hours, to find his brother nodded out in the bathroom, or sprawled across the new white sofa with his dirty shoes on, the stereo blasting.

"Kendall," Skylar said, calmly. "This shit's got to stop."

"What shit?"

"This!" Skylar said, ten seconds away from slapping Kendall out of his nod. "This is Evan's house, too, you know. And there's only so much I can say in your defense, when you're being a pain in the ass—"

"What am I doing wrong?"

"This is not a vacation resort. We don't mind you being comfortable, and watching videos, or listening to music, or whatever. But you don't contribute to the household anymore. You did when you first moved in—"

"Why do you let him talk to me that way?" Kendall asked. "I'm your brother. I'm blood. He's not."

"That's your problem, Ken," Skylar said. "Being a brother is your final answer for everything, but it's not that simple. I can't bail you out every time you fuck up. You must respect Evan's wishes as well. And though he hasn't, if he asks you to leave, there's not much I can say or do ... not unless I want to create problems for myself. Just do your part. Don't call attention to yourself. Don't be a pain in the ass. It's very simple, really."

Skylar felt certain that things would get better. Now that they'd all communicated with each other, there was no room for further misunderstanding.

That was before he discovered money missing from the house.

Thoughtlessly, he and Evan shared a habit of leaving large bills around the house, mounds of loose, silver change. Little by little, it was disappearing. Skylar didn't suspect the maid. She had worked for them too long. She might've been ornery and absentminded. But she was no thief.

"Kendall," Skylar said. "Are you stealing my money?"

"Hell no, Sky," Kendall said. "You hurt my feelings just asking. I ain't seen a dollar in so long, I forget what Georgie, baby, even looks like."

Skylar arrived home another evening thinking at first that he was in the wrong apartment. His kitchen table was surrounded by junkies, the likes of which he hadn't seen since he moved from the old neighborhood. With his townhouse turned into a shooting gallery, he was so flustered he couldn't even speak.

"Yo, Sky!" Kendall said, nervous and embarrassed, making a poor attempt to hide the paraphernalia with his hands. "This here is Mookey, Ronald, and Jay Jay," he said, indicating the men seated at the kitchen table. "Y'all, this here is my brother, Skylar, the movie star. See? Didn't I tell y'all mothafuckas he was my brother? And y'all thought I was bullshittin'." The junkies stared at Skylar, riveted, as if he'd announced that this was a drug bust.

"Yo, brother, this is one bad-ass crib!"

"Man, you must be a billionaire."

"This crib is cleaner than the Board of Health!"

"Can I have your autograph? It's not for me, though. It's for my woman."

"Kendall, can I speak to you in private?" Skylar said. They walked into the living room. "You better get rid of them immediately. And, if I ever catch you entertaining your friends here again..." Skylar felt lucky that it was he who walked in on the shooting gallery, and not Evan.

Weeks later, while he was in Boston on a shoot, Evan had come home and found Kendall passed out on the bathroom floor. According to Evan, he had entered the apartment and found the bathroom door closed with the faucet water running. Evan knew it was Kendall; Skylar had left two days earlier. Evan didn't think much of it at first. But the water continued to run. No one stirred inside. He knocked on the door. No reply. He knocked again. Called Kendall's name. No answer. Panic set in, as he tried opening the door, which was locked. He charged the door again and again with his shoulder until the lock gave. The door hardly budged. Kendall's body, sprawled across the black-tiled floor, at first blocked him from entering. Once inside, he picked up the eye-dropper with the attached spike. Drops of water-diluted blood freckled the mint green porcelain sink. Ripped-open glassine bags rested near a cooker and several burnt matches. Examining Kendall's arm, he noticed the fresh puncture.

"Kendall's complexion was pasty," Evan said. "His mouth appeared dry, crust gathering around his lips. There was no sign of life. I didn't know what the fuck to do." Evan called the paramedics, who arrived quickly, carried Kendall's body on the stretcher into the ambulance, and revived him during the ride to the hospital. "It was the most harrowing, most humiliating experience I've ever lived through," Evan said.

Kendall, recuperating in the hospital, offered Skylar his explanation.

"It wasn't a case of life and death, or any bullshit like that. Evan's exaggerating his ass off. Just that the smack was so powerful, I passed out for a while, that's all. I know Evan wants to be hailed as the Big Bad White Boy Hero, saving another nigger junkie from his own destruction. But he didn't do shit, not really. In time, I would've snapped out of it any fuckin' way. And I bet the ambulance got there so fast because it's a white neighborhood. I ain't never seen no ambulance or poh-lice arrive so quick. If I knew Evan was on his way home, I never would've done it there from the get-go. Okay, I fucked up. I'm sorry, Sky. Don't look at me that way, man. What else do you want me to say?"

Skylar didn't want him to say anything. He just had to leave. His time was up, his welcome mat reduced to a few bare threads.

When Skylar awakens with the five o'clock alarm, his ears are attacked by a continuous, high-pitched tone. Another television station has signed off another day of broadcasting. He rolls over, third time this week, nestling into the body that's no longer there. His legs, feet, and arms, of their own volition, their own memory, grope for the warmth of the body that was once theirs to cuddle. They are learning that pillows are a feeble substitute. In the living room, he clicks off the television and watches Kendall snoring, head tilted backward, mouth wide open, legs crisscrossed on the marble-and-glass coffee table. Before getting into the shower, Skylar clears the coffee table of food and dishes, where Kendall had helped himself to a banquet. He's cursing under his breath, knowing history is about to repeat itself. He can just feel it.

Neon Shadows on the Blue Meringue

"DON'T WORRY ABOUT IT," Marla said. "I'll take care of it."

"What do you mean?" Evan said. "Don't I have a say in this? It's half mine too, you know."

"That's true, but it'll affect my life more than yours."

"So, what are you planning to do about it?"

"Get rid of it, what else?"

"That's pretty damn selfish!" Evan said, averting his gaze and focusing on the C-shaped moon, which appeared to him as a wedge of lime in a gin and tonic — a drink he could have used right then. He had called her selfish. He wanted the baby to prove something to his parents. Was he not being selfish, too?

Using his hand as a visor, he guarded his brown eyes against the first burst of blazing Manhattan sun. Suitcase in hand, he stood at the corner of Eighth Avenue and Forty-second Street, taking in an eyeful of the fast-paced metropolis, which looked like a speeded-up film in comparison to the Los Angeles he'd just left. Watching the white whore dressed in tawdry platforms, miniskirt, midriff blouse, and a tattoo that read, "Sweet Meat," being pounded by the fists of her hysterical black pimp, he couldn't believe that no one, not even the police, would come to her aid. Ignoring her cries for help, as everyone else seemed to be doing, he craned his neck and glanced upward at the towering monoliths of steel and glass that reminded him of Stevie Wonder's lyrics in "Living for the City" — Skyscrapers an' ever'thang!

He headed east on Forty-second, watching prostitution and drug deals and God knows what else being negotiated in broad daylight. He needed to find a job, and a place to stay for the night. Wherever it was, it wouldn't be along this turf. He stopped at

Chock Full o' Nuts for coffee, and pondered his strategy for big city survival.

The more he tried to expel Marla from his thoughts, the more indelible she became, her image pressing against his conscience. She had law school to consider, and he understood the obstacles an unplanned child could present. Did he love her? He must have. Why else would he have put himself through the familial, social, and mental trials, openly dating her during senior year in high school. His white friends stopped speaking to him. White girls didn't look his way. Was he using Marla to make a point? Was he trying, with utmost success, to provoke his parents?

"How long you plan on goin' out with that nigger gal?" Dad had said.

"If you call her a nigger gal one more time, I'll—"

"Do you know what people are saying?" Mom said. "We're getting threatening phone calls. Sometimes, they just hang up."

"Why can't you accept the fact," Evan said, "that I'm not like you. I like black people. If you don't, that's fine. But stop trying to make me like you—"

"You're doing this just to shame us, aren't you?" Mom said.

"Of course he is," Dad said. "He'd do anything to embarrass us. You don't plan on marryin' her, do you? An' havin' babies?"

"What's wrong with that?" Evan asked.

"What's wrong with your own kind?" Dad said.

"Everything!" Evan said. "White girls like me for all the wrong reasons. Marla's not like that. She likes me for who I am. Not Mr. Best-Looking, or Mr. Congeniality, or Most Popular. Not because I'm blond."

"Not that it would happen," Mom said. "But what if you did marry her and had children. You'd be making life hard for them, you know. Have you thought about that?"

"Mom, this is the twentieth century. It would be hard for them, because bigots like you would make it hard."

"Our neighbors give us dirty looks these days," Dad said. "And your friends don't call you anymore—"

"I don't care," Evan said, recalling his Mustang that had been "mysteriously" smeared with egg yolk and Coca-Cola, the night he escorted Marla to the school dance. "Screw them!"

"Watch your mouth, Evan!" Mom said.

"You're forcing our hands," Dad said. "We're gonna have to take your car back."

He couldn't wait for next year. He would be living on the other side of town as a freshman in Men's Residence West on the campus of USC.

Why was he putting himself through all this? Was it for Marla? Or was it for...

Michael had grown up to be prettier than his sister. His panther-like physique, biceps, triceps, pectorals glistening with sweat during his and Evan's one-on-ones waged on the basketball court, charged Evan with inexplicable libido.

Michael touched him a lot, constantly patting him on the butt when Evan executed an outstanding maneuver on the basketball court. In the showers, Evan furtively watched Michael's naked beauty, the shower head spraying a waterfall sheen on his body. Evan wanted to apply the bar of soap to Michael's muscled shanks, the ripples in his stomach, the expanding, broad shoulders scarred with stretch marks. He found himself getting aroused, and turned away to conceal his lust. Why was he feeling this way about his best friend! He had been harassed and alienated as a nigger lover—not a queer.

The more time he spent with Marla, the more wistful he became over Michael. The sweet and sexy things he said to Marla, he wanted to say to Michael. He had reason to believe that Michael's feelings were mutual. For months, he rehearsed how he would approach him, what he would say, how he would say it. He got the opportunity in the shower when they were alone.

"You'll never beat me on the court," Michael said, laughing from the neighboring stall, rubbing the soap into his armpit, splashing water into Evan's stall.

"Why not?" Evan said, watching Michael's back muscles flex and contract.

"'Cause you're a white boy," Michael said. "I know you don't think you are. But the basketball court tells all." He laughed.

They were toweling off when Evan's courage assumed a volition of its own. He was becoming erect, as he touched Michael's waist. Michael noticed him becoming aroused, as Evan stared at him. Michael twisted Evan's arm behind his back, and shoved him, face first, against the powder blue tiled bathroom wall, as Evan had seen police do to black people on the streets.

"You lost your fucking mind, or what?" Michael said, a rage glowing in his eyes that frightened Evan. "What the fuck you think you're doing?"

"Nothing," Evan said. He'd never considered that Michael's reaction would be so severe. "Let me go, Mike, you're hurting my arm."

"I'll hurt you more than that," Michael said, releasing Evan's arm, "if you ever try that shit again—"

"Try what?"

"Come off that dumb shit, man. I saw you. Getting a hard-on. I should tell Marla."

"Don't!"

"I won't, Evan. I don't want to hurt my sister's feelings. But I will, if you ever try that shit again."

"But I didn't do anything," Evan pleaded.

In a split second of spontaneous passion, Evan had lost his best friend. There were no more one-on-one competitions on the basketball court. No more sharing of confidences. He could no longer look Michael in the eye. Michael now spoke to him, he imagined, only for Marla's sake. And there was no way of telling if Michael had told her, or anyone else. When he walked across the stage on graduation night to receive his diploma, fellow graduates might have known more than they were letting on.

College taught him that he had marketable looks. As a teenager, he'd been constantly mistaken for a fashion model.

"Haven't I seen you on television, and in magazines?"

"If you're not a model, you should be."

He envisioned himself as a *GQ* cover model, then movie star. He had the looks. Tight, toned body, square jawline, blond hair, cleft chin. He modeled Trojan t-shirts, sweatshirts, and gym shorts for the university bookstore catalogue. He stripped naked, posed for art students, fantasizing his nudity in the centerfold of *Playgirl*, the new women's magazine on the newsstands. Modeling provided him the allowance which Mom and Dad had deprived him of. He saved nearly every cent, knowing that after graduation, he'd purchase himself a one-way ticket.

The week before graduation, he told Marla his plans.

"I'm leaving for New York and you're the only person I've told."

"Didn't you tell your parents?"

"No. I'll drop them a line once I'm there," he said, meaning, when it was too late for them to talk him out of it. He wanted his departure hassle-free, without scenes, without melodrama, without Mom morosely painting a New York replete with muggings, homicides, and Harlem.

"I'm shocked. I don't know what to say." She stared at the pavement, sighing, then lifted her eyes. "I thought we were planning to live together, while I'm in law school?"

Just last week, they had checked out vacancies in Venice Beach and Los Feliz, where their interracial coupling might have survived housing discrimination and social harassment.

"I need a radical change of locale," Evan said. "As in, the other side of the continent."

"No problem," Marla said. "I could study at Columbia or NYU."

"I want a space ... alone."

"What do you mean, 'alone'?"

There was a lingering silence that burned his ears.

"I'm pregnant," Marla nearly whispered.

"You're what?"

"You heard me—"

"How many months?"

"Two, probably."

"Why didn't you tell me this before?"

"I just found out myself."

Now she was telling him this. Or was she lying? He couldn't tell. He's leaving for New York and all of a sudden, she's pregnant, making it difficult for him to abandon her. Just like a woman to pull a stunt like that. When all else fails, they become pregnant. He chose not to believe it without calling her a liar to her face.

"Throwing away five years of us is not easy for me," Marla said.

He said nothing immediately, getting used to the idea of a baby. Being a father wasn't the worst thing that could happen. But he convinced himself that she was playing her final card. The ace of desperation. All these years of birth control, and now she slips?

"I'll send for you, Marla, I promise."

"If you leave, Evan, I never want to see you again."

"Don't you understand? It's difficult for me to stay here. I feel smothered. I'll leave first, then you could apply to eastern law schools. It's easier to get established in New York with one mouth to feed, instead of two—"

"Three!"

"Okay, three then—"

"If you leave, Evan, I won't have this baby."

"Why not?"

"I won't be a single parent."

"You won't be single, I'll be in—"

"New York, I know. That makes me single, doesn't it? It's no big deal. I have a career to consider, anyway."

"I don't want you to get rid of it. We should have it."

"We?"

Arriving in New York, having surrendered to wanderlust, he vowed to start off anew. He was no longer into women. Rather, he would confront and celebrate his sexual, emotional leanings toward men. If he'd learned nothing else growing up in racist, homophobic South Gate, that was the lesson Michael and Marla had taught him.

He'd been hustling as a waiter in Chock Full o' Nuts for nearly six weeks, same place where he drank his first cup of New York dishwater coffee, when he was befriended by a co-worker who introduced himself as a struggling actor. At the end of their early-evening shift, the co-worker said he had passes to an offbeat, off-off-Broadway play in the East Village, directed by a friend of his. Evan wanted desperately to see Broadway. *Equus. The Wiz. For Colored Girls Who Have Considered Suicide When the Rainbow Is Enuf.* Unable to afford it, he settled for the free passes, and for what he assumed to be the "less prestigious" off-off Broadway, which, in his ignorance, he likened to the unpolished promise of a college play. Was he in for a surprise.

Once he got past the wordy, imprecise, silly-sounding title, *Neon Shadows on the Blue Meringue,* the unaesthetic decor, and the dankness of the dark theater, he relaxed. What a marvelous piece of work. He couldn't fathom why a theatrical production as critically acclaimed as this was not being exposed to wider, mainstream audiences. It was his first lesson in the politics and variables of commercial entertainment versus art. The first act had been inspiring, audacious, resonant. During intermission, sipping unfiltered apple juice with the co-worker friend, he couldn't wait until the second act.

The most compelling element onstage, though, didn't revolve around the playwright's words, the director's blocking, the stage setting, or lighting. It was the beautiful, black supporting actor. And if Evan, seated in the first row, wasn't mistaken, the handsome actor's eyes were blue. Sky blue. He and Michael could've passed for brothers. Except, the actor's splendor and radiance far surpassed Michael's, rendering him dull by contrast. Hell, he had blue eyes to boot! When the production was over, and the cast joined hands onstage, taking several bows and curtain calls, he toyed with the idea of going backstage. But he decided against it, planning to see the play again and again ... alone.

First Impressions

WASN'T LIKE SKYLAR hadn't noticed him.

Thursday nights, every week without fail, he'd be out there front row center, grinning with a familiarity and intimacy that annoyed Skylar, especially during the one scene he had to himself. Delivering lines of inner monologue, engulfed in a dark stage, bathed in a cone of blinding, white light, he refused to meet the eyes of the blond stranger, who did everything within the parameters of subtlety to get his attention. Only a matter of time, he knew, before the stranger mustered the gall to visit backstage.

"Really loved your performance tonight."

"Thanks."

"I mean it. You're outstanding. You should have the lead."

"Thanks, again."

"I've seen better performances, even ... like last Thursday."

"Oh?"

"Skylar ... isn't it? Am I pronouncing it—"

"Skylar Whyte."

"Pleased to meet you ... Skylar Whyte."

Pause.

"Don't you want to know mine?"

"Do I have to?"

"Evan. Evan Cabot."

"Okay."

"Don't I know you from someplace?"

"I hope not."

"Notice I sit in the same seat every week?"

"How could I not?"

"You have beautiful eyes. Contacts?"

"You wearing contacts?"

"Why so hostile?"

"You're misreading fatigue for hostility."

"Any cast parties tonight?"

"I'll be partying in my bed."

"Now, that's an idea."

Second pause.

"I'd like to see you sometime."

"You see me now. Look, I'm really not in the mood."

"No problem; I understand. Nice meeting you anyway, Skylar."

"Same here, uh..."

"Evan."

"Yeah, right."

Impudence laced with cockiness had made Evan blow it.

He was a pretty white boy. But he knew it. Skylar got the impression that this was a man who couldn't even spell rejection. Used to having his own way. Who could resist this six-foot, well-proportioned, drop-dead beauty of German, maybe Scandinavian extraction when he flashed that winning smile of his? Skylar could. Though he found him physically magnetic, he was offended by the blond hair. The WASPish temerity he radiated. Like Skylar would drop everything for an impromptu fuck. Who the hell did he think he was approaching, anyway? I've picked my teeth with prettier white boys than you, he thought, wickedly.

The following Thursday, the front-row-center seat was occupied by someone else. It was a couple of years before they met again.

Skylar was portraying Private First Class Melvin Peterson in *A Soldier's Play* at Theatre Four with the Negro Ensemble Company.

One night, he was leaving the theater in high spirits. This was usually the case, since he portrayed the murderer who offed Sergeant Waters, the loathsome, pivotal character, who basked in self-hatred, a victim of his own superiority complex. The sergeant and Daddy, to Skylar, were alter egos. Tweedledee and Tweedledum. Even looked alike. It enabled him emotionally, spiritually, to place his father in the role of the petulant sergeant, a device for channeling unspent venom. Like killing Daddy night after night onstage to deafening applause, curtain calls, and rave reviews exploding with hyperbole.

When Skylar turned the corner, there he was.

His arms were full of what appeared to be a dozen roses.

"Remember me?" Evan said. He was dressed like a Columbia graduate student, faded, tattered jeans, thick white socks bunched and sliding down into scruffy penny loafers, a paisley vest over a tight white t-shirt, firm pectoral muscles jutting forward, nipples taut. Skylar caught a whiff of a light, powdery-scented cologne he couldn't identify.

"How could I forget you?" Skylar replied.

"I didn't want to embarrass you backstage ... so I waited for you out here. Hope that's okay."

"How thoughtful. So," Skylar said, sizing Evan up with a sweeping glance, "you've resumed your game of cat-and-mouse, following me around ... no, don't tell me, you're an avid fan of Charles Fuller's work."

"Actually, I am," Evan said, an edge of self-satisfaction in his tone. "I've seen *Zooman* and *The Brownsville Raid.*"

"Hmm," Skylar said, impressed, without letting on. "You an actor?"

"I don't know; I'd like to be."

"You are, or you aren't?"

"Maybe you can help me discover if I have the bug."

They had dinner at Evan's invitation and expense. Furtively, Skylar closely watched Evan's athletic, liquid, masculine movements, the wisp of hair falling in his eye, the nervous twitch in his hollow cheeks. He also had the prettiest, tightest ass Skylar had ever seen on a white boy.

"So," Evan said, snapping a bread stick in half with his teeth. They were hardly seated at their table. "Surprised that I'm so familiar with Charles Fuller's work?" His face was stretched in a smile that screamed one-upmanship.

Skylar couldn't decide whether to lie or not. "Yes ... yes, I am surprised."

"Because I'm a white boy, right?"

"Of course not," Skylar lied this time, noticing the angular shadows of Evan's face in this particular lighting. "Just that a lot of people don't know his work, that's all."

Evan rose slightly out of his seat and leaned forward, as if he were about to share a secret. "I probably know more about your culture than you think."

"My culture — meaning American, right?"

"Don't be funny."

Skylar couldn't squeeze in a word as Evan rambled off a litany of his passions surrounding the African-American cultural experience, uncannily avoiding the word *black*. If he was bent on impressing Skylar, he'd succeeded. As if he were using the dinner opportunity to engage Skylar, his captive audience, with a tap dance. An audition. That's what it was. Evan was revealing himself as an approval junkie. If that was the case, Skylar thought, he was more of an actor than he knew.

Skylar had never met a white guy like this. For someone who seemed quintessentially all-American-white-bread, he certainly knew more than Skylar had expected. Most white boys Skylar met were just that: white boys. They couldn't care less about the music of Nina Simone or Miles Davis, or the little-known works being staged at the Negro Ensemble Company in the East Village. Evan seemed to be a different man from the one Skylar had met backstage about two years ago. Now he appeared incandescent with a boyish vulnerability. His nervousness and anxiety, the tripping over words and blushing and losing his train of thought, the shy yet hungry spark gleaming in his eyes, charmed Skylar more than he wished to be.

Evan talked about growing up in South Gate, California, which bordered Watts. The lands of Us and Them. From the time he was old enough to tell the difference, he noticed the imposed separateness of the two communities. And yet, against the grain of his parents, relatives, friends, and community-at-large, he nurtured an overwhelming magnetism toward Them.

While his friends were listening to the Beach Boys and Jan and Dean, he was playing everything that came out of the Motor City, which caused his friends to wonder aloud why he was so "transformed" by nigger music. "Where I'm from, the entire community blamed all their problems on black people," Evan said. "I don't understand why, but I was never physically attracted to whites. Kind of like my blond, Nordic attributes propel me, subconsciously, toward the opposite end of the spectrum. I really don't know. I don't care. I just know what I like. Where'd you get blue eyes?"

"Same place you got your brown ones," Skylar said.

"But, you can't be black. What are you?"

"Don't be ridiculous," Skylar replied, annoyed.

"I'd trade you mine for those blue eyes any day. You know what? I think I'll call you Sky Blue."

"Call me anything," Skylar said. "Just call me, period."

Evan made a point of monopolizing Skylar's dance card. This week, Betty Carter tickets at the Village Vanguard. Next week, Dance Theatre of Harlem performing *Firebird* at Lincoln Center. Week after, Gil Scott-Heron at the Bottom Line. Pretty hip white boy, Skylar thought, enjoying being seen in public with him, with eyes of admiration, envy, even scorn, staring them down.

And the lovemaking.

So savage, Skylar developed a habit of clicking on the television. Not that they were watching. It just helped drown out their moans and grunts of incoherent passion. Skylar surprised himself by placing his mouth upon, and darting his tongue into, crevices and cavities and creases he'd never dared dream of. Usually a rest period followed. With their bodies pressed together by perspiration, they discussed their backgrounds, families, hopes, dreams, fears, things they wanted out of life. Holding hands, the flames of candles making their shadows flicker on the wall, the erratic vocal phrasings of Laura Nyro in the background, Skylar talked about his hard childhood.

"What about your mother?" Evan asked. "Are you close to her?"

"Very much so," Skylar said.

"I'm close to my mom, too."

They'd go at it again. Then they'd nestle into each other, limbs and appendages locking, forming valleys and labyrinths, arms and legs wrapped and stretched around one another like Velcro monkeys. Evan hardly slept. Rather, he'd watch Skylar snore, twitch, his chest rising in a steady, peaceful rhythm. And there were times when he had to waken a restless Skylar from an obviously disturbed sleep.

"What! ... What happened?" Skylar would say, awakening, as if alerted by radar to an approaching peril. He'd bolt upright, forehead shiny with sweat.

"It's nothing, Sky Blue," Evan would say, cradling Skylar in his arms. "You just had a nightmare. Go back to sleep—"

"But—"

"Sshhh," Evan would whisper. "Go back to sleep. I'm here. I won't leave you."

Evan was the prescribed panacea for his romantic ills.

It had been a bitch sifting through the myriad eligible New York City bachelors to come up with one. Bars were out of the question. Jive, game-playing men primping and profiling against the wall. Manipulating the shadows to hit them just so. Too cute to speak. Too fabulous to breathe. And he had tried nearly everything. Introductions through mutual friends. Blind dates. Parties. Skylar invariably picked the face in the crowd he liked, who turned out to be straight, spoken for, or both. After deciding upon his pick of the evening, he'd find someone who personally knew the unsuspecting target of his affections. Responses were always one of three.

Oh, Sky, he's So-and-So's lover.

Or, I hear he's not into black guys.

And the ultimate caveat: Not him, Sky. He likes them in skirts. To which Skylar invariably replied, "What a waste."

Investigating the alternative of personal ads, he answered a few. His efforts were not without apprehension and a stinging sense of self-abasement. He'd considered personals to be the viable alternative for the nondescript, overweight, unattractive gay men for whom Skylar felt sympathy. Was one thing to be gay. Quite another to be gay and ugly. Especially in a society that penalized both. Even pretty women married ugly men. He picked up his phone and dialed a few.

There was Tom. White/blue eyes/155 lbs./5'11" from Bayonne. Too lame.

And Malcolm. Black/brown eyes/135 lbs./5'4" from Brownsville. Too short.

And there was Angel. Puerto Rican/brown eyes/150 lbs./6'2" from Spanish Harlem, who prided himself on his uncut nine inches. Too tall, too skinny, too fem.

While likeable, they were for Skylar, far too mediocre, hardly stimulating enough. He wanted a mate with drive, ambition, aggression. Someone who could light a match under his ass and keep the flame burning. Angel, the Puerto Rican, had been impressed to meet the actor he recognized from a television commercial some years back. Skylar had wished he could've found Angel as engaging. But physical, spiritual, emotional attraction was a decision his heart made for him. He soon realized the personals weren't the best way to search for a mate. Women, in general — black women, in particular — thought they had it rough landing one. They didn't know the half of it. But Evan, during their second meeting, rescued him from an aimless yearning.

He fit the bill.

And then some.

In time, their bliss came to an end.

Whatever feeling Evan had had for the black experience seemed to be waning.

Or perhaps, it had been merely surface, cosmetic.

To Skylar, he seemed indifferent to the trials and tribulations facing black people. When the black male children were being murdered in Atlanta, Evan accused Skylar of paying far too much attention to tragedies of that gruesome nature. Said he shouldn't bother himself with taking on the world's problems.

"South Africa will continue its legacy of apartheid whether Skylar likes it or not," Evan said. "Why trouble yourself? Be happy it's not you, living the hell of Cape Town and Soweto."

And during the American Embassy hostage crisis in Iran, Evan metamorphosed, with fluttering wings, into a bigoted, flag-waving, die-hard patriot. The very prototype Skylar abhorred. He tried educating Evan on the history of the American/Iranian "alliance," describing the Shah as traitor/hero.

"This hostage crisis," Skylar said, "didn't happen overnight, you know." But Evan persisted with his epithets toward the Ayatollah Khomeini. Skylar remained steadfast in his belief that the Ayatollah was not a madman, as a lot of Americans would have him believe. Westerners couldn't begin to understand Mid-Eastern, Moslem mentality. Too often, they viewed too much through Western eyes, arriving at unfounded, harsh judgments.

Then came the day the black American hostages were released early, the Iranians describing them as fellow oppressed people, crushed beneath the thumb of colonialism and imperialism. Skylar cut out the newspaper clipping — it wasn't quite front-page head-lines — and tacked it on the refrigerator. Evan was unmoved. And acted as if no one had been freed until the others, the white hostages, were released. These marked the beginning of sociopolitical disparities that drove a wedge between them. At the height of his anger, Skylar likened Evan's attraction to blacks to that of the master leering at the slave.

"You think you're special," Skylar claimed, "because you're into black art and culture that hasn't crossed over — things that the average white person never even hears about. And you think that makes you extraordinary."

"Sky," Evan retorted, "you're talking to someone who was branded a 'nigger lover.' I went through all kinds of shit to be around black people. You just don't know! My parents accused me of suffering from jungle fever!"

Their ray of hope — or arbitrator — came along in the form of the gay organization Checkerboard Squares. They'd heard it was geared toward the promotion of relationships, intimate and otherwise, between black and white men, boasting an assortment of workshops, rap groups, consciousness-raising sessions. Skylar loved the idea. It was heaven-sent.

That was before they attended the first meeting.

The blacks and whites broke into segregated groups. In Skylar's group, they discussed their specific problems as black gay men in a largely white and/or heterosexual milieu.

"The gay community and mainstream society are a two-headed dragon," one member said, his lips thick and moist, dreadlocks bouncing on his forehead, as his head jerked with disdain. "White faggots don't like niggers any more than white America!"

"When white people see me," another charged, pushing up the tortoiseshell glasses that had slid down his nose, "they don't see a gay man. They see a black man."

"I heard that."

"What about the bars?" said another. He surprised Skylar when he spoke: he'd been quiet all evening. "I'm sick and tired of being carded when they know good and goddamn well I ain't a day under forty!"

"Quiet quotas, chile," someone whispered, followed by small bursts of nervous giggles.

"They dance off our music, even dance like us. But not with us."

"How come, of all the pictures of beautiful men hanging on the walls in these clubs, there's never — and I mean, never! — one fucking picture of a black man?"

"It would kill 'em to think anybody was beautiful but them."

Skylar never learned of the issues discussed among the white contingent during their rap session. When he asked, Evan replied with silence.

By the time the groups were reunited to air grievances, Skylar knew he was five minutes from walking out the door. They just didn't seem to understand the special problems and alienation experienced by black gay men. Or didn't care to. Impervious to third-world gripes.

"I always thought," a white guy said, "that all black guys liked any white guy they could get."

What! Skylar thought, unsure he'd heard this man correctly. Then that explains why there's so many ugly white men here tonight, he thought. They can't get men like Evan — the best-looking white guy present — so they "settle" for blacks who, Skylar assumed, would sell their mamas to entertain their whim.

Then a black member spoke up.

"I'm fed up with white men's myths and fantasies about black male libido and penis size."

"I am not the cure for jungle fever," another black guy said.

"Why is it," a white member asked cautiously, "that we get blamed for everything that goes wrong with you people? I didn't own slaves, my grandparents didn't own slaves, and I'm tired of being held responsible for that!"

"Somebody's got to be responsible. That's the problem with white America: you never want to be responsible for your bullshit!"

At Skylar's insistence, he and Evan left the emotionally charged meeting. Neither of them said much to the other, entertaining their own private thoughts, staring catatonically through the subway windows, studying their reflections in the graffiti-marred glass. There was so much Skylar wanted to say. To bridge the widening gap neither cared to fill. Skylar sighed, having nowhere else to turn, except possibly to a therapist.

It was a sobering verity to Skylar that a subculture which prided itself on difference, divided itself on matters of race and sex. Leaving Skylar to believe for the moment that no matter how he dealt with them, disguised or dressed them up, what social context he placed them in — that white folks were white folks were white folks...

_I_ Have a Dream

"SCHAEFFER IS THE ONE BEER to have, when you're having more than one!"

"No it ain't," Althea mumbled to the black-and-white images strutting across the television screen. "I prefer Rheingold, myself."

"Woman!" Howard said, lying across the sofa in a t-shirt, cut-offs, and socks. "How many times do I have to tell you, there's no such word as 'ain't.' You want to talk like an ignorant nigger, go right ahead. Just don't do it around my kids. I won't tell you again!"

From across the room, suffocating in the late-August heat, wiping beady sweat with the back of his hand, Skylar exchanged sidelong glances with Althea.

"Daddy," Skylar said. "Mama knows how to talk. She just uses words that—"

"What?!" Howard said. "Are you contradicting me—"

"No, Daddy. I just—"

"Don't interrupt me! Can't you hear me talking?! The next time you..."

Howard was distracted by a roar from the crowd on the television screen. What looked to Skylar like a billion trillion colored people surrounded the reflecting pool of the Washington Monument. The program so far — gospel by Mahalia Jackson, speeches by James Baldwin, Harry Belafonte, folksongs by Peter, Paul and Mary — was pretty boring. He wanted desperately to turn the channel. Maybe _The Mickey Mouse Club_ or _Leave It to Beaver_ was on. And they were missing it because Daddy wanted to watch a bunch of colored people marching on the nation's capital.

"You see that, Skylar?" Howard said. "Because of your big mouth and that dim-witted harridan of a mother of yours, I've missed something important. Goddammit! A man can't even have peace and quiet in his own house!" Howard jumped up from the sofa, strapped on his sandals, pulled a short-sleeve shirt over his sweat-stained t-shirt.

"I'm going to the store for some beer, and when I get back, I don't want to hear a peep out of either one of you. Goddamn woman talking to TV commercials, for chrissakes!" Howard mumbled, walking through the door, and slamming it behind him.

Althea sat in the chair, shaking her head, fanning herself, swatting flies with the newspaper. Skylar watched her curiously.

"Is he my real father?"

"Of course, he's your real father."

"Why do you let him talk to you like that? Why do you take that stuff from him?"

"One day, you'll understand."

"But he called you a dim-witted harridan."

"I don't even know what that is. And probably, your daddy don't know, either."

"We can look it up in the dictionary."

Before she could respond, Skylar dashed from the room, returned, carrying the thick book, set it down, parted the pages at H.

"Here it is," Skylar said. "Har-ri-dan."

"Harry what?"

Skylar spelled it for her, then read Webster's definition.

"Mama, you're no harridan. You shouldn't let him call you that."

"Baby, he calls me a lot of things. And a lot of them, shoot, I don't know what he's talking about anyway."

At Skylar's urging, they looked up other words Howard dropped around the house, words he had deliberately used, knowing they would fly above everyone else's head. Words like "doxy," "tawdry," "gauche," "callow" — words he frequently used to describe his wife. The more definitions they uncovered, the more interested Althea became.

"My teacher says that words hold the power to unlock and free the mind of ignorance," Skylar said. "We learn about fifteen new words a week in vocabulary, and if you want, Mama, you could learn the words too. I'll teach them to you as soon as I get home from school, before Daddy comes home from work."

"What a sweet thing to do," Althea said, pressing Skylar's head against her sweaty bosom. "You know, sometimes, I have a dream — it's kind of like a daydream — of getting my high school diploma and a college degree. Just to show your father that anything he can do, I can do, too. Then I could throw those big words around like he does."

They heard Howard's key turn the lock. Skylar closed the book and disappeared from the room. Althea continued to fan herself and swat flies, her eyes focused on the screen.

In the basement, Skylar acted out *The Mickey Mouse Club* roll call, inserting his name between Karen and Cubby. Bored and uninspired because he had no real Mouseketeer ears — since Daddy hadn't kept his promise of taking them to Disneyland in California — he thought of other distractions to escape the heat. And to get away from his father, who was home from work on a two-week vacation. Skylar wanted to practice the Spanish accent he had picked up from Puerto Rican kids at school. He had to keep it quiet, though. About five months ago, he'd gotten in trouble for the same thing.

"It's not like Skylar," his teacher had said to Althea. "He's one of my more ideal students: a teacher's dream. Straight A's. Always does his homework on time in a neat, legible penmanship. He's never absent or tardy. He speaks only when spoken to, and never talks out of turn. He's considerate and kind to his classmates. Always knows the correct answers, his hand raised, no matter what question I ask. I even used to tease Skylar that his arm would fall off one day from raising it so much.

"But lately, Skylar doesn't seem to be himself — literally. Each day of the week, he speaks in class with foreign accents and I don't know where he's picking them up from. At first, I thought it was cute, amusing even. But it got out of control. One day, he speaks in an English accent, which he claims he learned from *Oliver Twist*. Next day, he's a Puerto Rican. Day after that, a German. And so on. He speaks like that throughout the entire day, and when I ask him why he's doing it, he says he doesn't know what I'm talking about. Well!" the teacher said, flustered, removing her cat eyeglasses that dangled around her neck on a black string.

Althea appreciated the teacher's high praise and concern, but she wondered when the woman would finally come up for air. "It got to the point, I can't get him to speak to me or the class in his natural accent. You can imagine what that does to distract the others, especially since he's one of the class role models. Would you please speak with him? Could you find out why he's doing this?"

"Why are you speaking in foreign accents in class, when you never do it at home?" Althea asked Skylar, when he got home that afternoon.

"I do it at home," Skylar said. "You just never hear me because I'm downstairs in the basement."

"But why?"

"Because I'm going to be an actor. Actors can be anybody else they want to be. They don't have to be who they really are. Remember? You told me that."

"Why do you want to be somebody else?"

"I don't want to be Skylar Whyte all the time—"

"Why?"

"Skylar Whyte's always in trouble at home. Daddy always yells at Skylar. Skylar's always getting a whipping for something. And if I'm not Skylar Whyte, then I won't be in trouble anymore. So, I like to be somebody else sometimes."

He had noticed the tear crawling down Althea's cheek. "Don't cry, Mama. I'm still Skylar. I can be anybody I want. And when Skylar's in trouble, I change into somebody else, that's all."

Remembering how sad he had made his mother, he decided, there in the basement, not to practice accents.

Each night before going to bed, he'd recite the Lord's Prayer. Then he'd ask God to remove his father from their household; from their lives. Daddy is bad. Mama is good. And if God is good, he reasoned, He will answer my prayer. When his father wasn't removed, he struck up a bargain with God. If the Lord would get rid of his father, Skylar would forget about becoming an actor. But God had to keep His half of the bargain first.

When that didn't happen, he made up an imaginary person in his head, Mister Hero, who would come to his and Althea's rescue if only Skylar thought about it hard enough. When he was awakened in the midst of the night by another of Mama and Daddy's fights, Skylar dispatched Mister Hero to the rescue. It never worked.

Skylar had a dream.

Mister Hero would appear to him in his dreams and take Daddy away, up, up, up, into the purple sky with the tangerine clouds, as Skylar and Althea rejoiced. Mister Hero then scooped the two of them up on his horse and rode off into the scarlet sunset.

The zombie movies he watched gave Skylar the idea of what he was about to attempt in the basement. Voodoo, as he understood it, involved dolls and pins. He didn't have a doll, so he pulled a pair of his father's pants and a shirt from the laundry basket, and began stuffing the outfit with other clothes and oily rags — actually, with anything he could find.

He smelled the aroma of food penetrating the cracks of the kitchen floor, filling the basement. During summer vacation from school, it was difficult keeping up with the days of the week. But the smell of Mama's meals each day was a way of identifying them. Friday was fish day, usually fried porgies and whitings. Saturday, beans and franks. Mama called it her day of rest from the kitchen. Sunday was pot roast or ham. Monday, leftovers. Tuesday, boiled chicken and noodles. Sniffing the odors of lima beans, ham hocks, and rice told him it was Wednesday. He hated lima beans, and didn't look forward to dinner that night.

He was just about finished with the dummy. Everything was complete, except it didn't have a head. Skylar searched the basement but found nothing. He took a brown paper bag, his box of Crayolas, and drew his father's likeness on the bag. He darkened the eyebrows, colored the eyes green and menacing. With a white crayon, he drew two fangs. Then, he stuffed the bag with rags, and secured it inside the shirt collar with safety pins. He sat the dummy upright in a chair. For a moment, he studied his creation, his Frankenstein.

"What are you looking at?" Skylar said to the dummy. "What? Who do you think you're talking to like that?"

He slapped the dummy once. Twice. It felt too good. He started slapping it around. He kicked its legs. Punched the head so hard, he tore it off.

"Would you stop all that goddamn ruckus down there!" Daddy yelled at him.

Skylar heard them arguing upstairs. Daddy was accusing Mama of having done something else. Skylar stopped beating up the dummy and listened. He couldn't hear all of what they said, just catching a word here and there. They were using a word he'd never heard before. Bortion. That's what it sounded like they were saying. Bortion. He thought, I'll have to look that one up in the dictionary.

He heard his mother getting slapped. Then he heard her slap his father back. The ceiling began to thump. They were banging against the walls. A plate or glass crashed on the floor. Frustrated by the scuffling, the tearing of clothing, the swearing and cussing, his inability to rescue Mama, he frantically charged his dummy with a curtain rod. Repeatedly, he stabbed the dummy in the stomach, the heart, the groin. Trying to drown out the noise upstairs, he raised the curtain rod over his head, striking the dummy, beating it to shreds, hoping, magically, to have some real effect on the man upstairs in the kitchen slapping his Mama around. The way he'd seen it done in the zombie movies.

Suddenly, upstairs was quiet. Footsteps stomped across the ceiling. The basement door swung open.

"Skylar, bring your black ass up here, since you can't be quiet!" Daddy called down to him. As Skylar reached the top of the staircase, Kendall came rushing through the front door in his blue-and-gold Pop Warner football uniform.

"Dinner ready yet?" Kendall asked.

"No," Althea said, pressing an ice pack against the side of her face. "Go back outside and play. I'll call you when dinner's ready."

"Skylar," Howard said. "I'm giving you two minutes to plant your black ass in that chair. And don't you breathe."

"I don't want to watch television," Skylar said. "Can I go outside and play, too?"

"No!" Howard said, concealing the side of his face where Althea had scratched him. "Watch that television and learn something, boy!"

Skylar giggled inside at the scratches on his father's face. The voodoo dummy had worked after all ... well, a little. Now, Daddy would have to go to work with the scratches on his face. Having eavesdropped on Mama's conversations with her sisters, he knew Daddy would lie to the men at work about a "shaving accident."

"Like those people at work is stupid enough to believe his razor left those marks," he had heard Althea say to Aunt Gloria Jean before they broke up laughing.

"Are you all right?" Kendall asked his father, who nodded. Kendall turned, and ran back outside into the streets, closing the door behind him. As Howard headed for the staircase, Althea stuck her thumb in her nostril and wiggled her fingers at Howard's back.

Skylar didn't understand what it meant. But it must've been her way of getting even. Being forced to watch a television program he didn't want to see, Skylar mimicked her by pressing his thumb inside his nostril and wiggling his fingers at Daddy, thinking Althea would find it cute and amusing. She slapped him across the face.

"Don't you ever disrespect your father like that in this house!"

"I was just doing what you just did," Skylar protested.

"Do as I say," Althea said, pointing a scolding finger. "Not as I do!"

When she left the room, Skylar sat there, rubbing the side of his face, staring at a stupid television show he wanted to turn off. He watched the man known as the Reverend Dr. Martin Luther King, Jr., deliver a speech before the immense marble statue of Abraham Lincoln. He'd never seen so many people in one place at one time, not even during baseball games at Yankee or Shea Stadium. He started dozing off from the heat and boredom, as Dr. King, in the emotion-packed, wavering voice of a southern preacher, claimed, "I have a dream that this nation will rise up and live out the true meaning of its creed. We hold these truths to be self-evident: that all men are created equal. I have a dream that one day, black men and white men, Jews and Gentiles, Protestants and Catholics..."

Althea: The Mother

FUNNY, WHAT YOU REMEMBER. Even stranger are the things you forget.

I can hardly remember what happened and what was said five minutes ago, the television movie I watched last night and liked so much, the color dress my superior wore yesterday, although I complimented her several times. It's even difficult, sometimes, to remember which year I married Howard, or what I was doing the moment I heard President Kennedy had been shot, something everybody supposedly recalls. But I do remember the births of my children.

Like most mothers, I recall the days of the week my sons were born on, the weather, the time, the conditions, the position of the sun in the sky, if there'd been any sun at all, Howard's hastiness and nervousness, even some of the terrible things I said or screamed at Howard, and the redheaded nurse who ignored me while I was in labor. Skylar was a difficult pregnancy, and an even more difficult birth. There were times I had to remember I was pregnant with Kendall who, after three good pushes, fell out of me so effortlessly at the end of nine months I didn't even know it was over until the doctor slapped his bottom and he started to cry.

Though I know I've done the best with what I had to work with, I feel guilty about how things turned out. Not a whole lot I can do about it. But the guilt is there just the same, as a reminder that I'm not as good and effective a mother as I'd like to think I am. Mothers experience more guilt than fathers. Maybe I'm wrong about that, and men just don't reveal themselves and agonize over it the way women do. Because I'm certain that, if only in his quiet way, Howard must feel some guilt over Skylar and Kendall. Whether he realizes it or not, he really abused them both.

I never understood why Howard pulled such an insensitive, cruel stunt, buying a pink party dress for Skylar, having him open it in front of every child in the neighborhood, then blaming Skylar for being called a faggot in the streets. There were many things Howard did and said that caused me to think about the person I had married, but after Skylar's birthday party and the dress, I knew I had a sick man on my hands, a man who needed professional help. And what could I do about it? It was like standing below an avalanche, and you can't get out of the way. If you live through it, hopefully you'll be a stronger, better person for it, full of survival stories, and profiles of courage. Though courage had nothing to do with it. After all, I married the man for better or worse. I couldn't abandon him because of things I didn't know about him before we were married, nor did I have the guts to tell him to get help.

In those days, women didn't leave their men. Even if I did leave him, as Skylar, and my brother, Aubrey, advised me to do more times than I care to count, I would've been a social outcast, a bitch, criticized by and alienated from other women. Some folks wouldn't have understood, like Gloria Jean and my other sisters, who thought I had it so damn good. I didn't talk about my problems much. And now that I've stayed with him, gone through the highs and lows — mostly lows — and will continue to do so until Howard's last breath, which could be any day now, what does that make me?

Poor Kendall. As peacefully as he pushed himself out of my womb and into the world, he came in fighting. He woke up fighting. Went to bed fighting. Maybe subconsciously he knew there would be plenty to fight for later in life and he was just starting a little early. He fought for this, he fought for that, if somebody looked at him too long, if something was said to him in a tone of voice he didn't like. He fought when kids called his brother a faggot. Skylar never seemed to care what the kids called him. At least he never let on if he did. But Kendall cared. Maybe too much. Skylar's homosexuality — Jesus, I can't believe I can finally say it without flinching — seemed to bother everybody except Skylar. He always seemed as comfortable with it as he was with his dark brown skin, his black hair, his blue eyes. Of course, I didn't want to believe it, to accept the fact that my son was a homosexual. There's not a mother who does. But I believe God prepares you for things that will be difficult to accept, and unchangeable.

In my case, it was my baby brother, Aubrey. I think God gave Aubrey to us so that we might learn a little more about men who love other men. My family learned that homosexuals really aren't that different from other men, or anybody else, for that matter, except that they like each other sexually and emotionally. It's pretty natural, if you think about it. Now, I don't mean to sound like I'm an expert, or that I know all there is to know about homosexuals. But through Aubrey, I learned more than I'd ever known, that's for sure. We all did: Mama, Daddy, Gloria Jean, LaVern, Evelyn, Margie, Loretta, James — especially James.

In some way, it prepared me for Skylar. Though I've never told Skylar, and I probably should, I'm not bothered by what he is. Well, maybe a little. Only to the extent that I know he'll never give me grandchildren. But that's my own selfishness and has nothing to do with him. Most mothers want to be made grandmothers, especially by their children who've made such successful, prosperous lives for themselves, and in turn have made their parents proud.

I wonder what Skylar thinks I think about his being gay. To some extent, he and Evan seem to have a better relationship than many married folks I've known over the years. Evan is good-looking, successful, rich, and Lord knows he loves Skylar. That's one of the first things I saw in him. That's what maternalism does to you. It makes you closely scrutinize your child's mate, man or woman, to see if they will love and care for your child almost as well as you did. I hope Evan and Skylar can work out their problems, because they've been together too long not to. Everybody needs somebody to love as they get older. Since Skylar doesn't have children, he has to have somebody, somebody other than me, his brother, and his family. I don't want him to grow old by himself.

Matter of fact, I even like Evan for Skylar, who tends to be emotional, high-strung, opinionated, yet a pushover, which he gets from me. Evan provides the proper balance for him, I think, someone who won't allow himself to be mowed down by Skylar's iron will, but who can stand up and challenge him. That's what I think Skylar really thrives on: challenge. He eats it for breakfast. And if being gay had anything to do with Skylar's success, and the fact that he was always a good student, and a good son, who never gave his parents any real problems, then a whole lot of men should be gay.

It dawned on me one day. I was thinking about my brother, Aubrey, and his success as a theatrical costume designer — something no one else in the family attempted. I considered Skylar, who, again, accomplished his dream of becoming a famous actor. Then I thought about Evan, and it clicked. Maybe three gay men aren't very many for generalizing on homosexuals, but it seemed to me that they're usually bright, sensitive, talented, self-motivated, focused, and successful. Not such bad things to be, if you think about it. If it could change Kendall's predicament, I'd prefer he'd be gay, too.

If Kendall ever had a chance at happiness, it must have been with Tonja, his high school sweetheart. Tonja was a lovely girl, the kind most white folks don't expect to be born and raised in Harlem. She was pretty, sweet, considerate, smart, going places in life, and she loved Kendall deeply. I had checked her out too, while she was dating Kendall back then. Nobody, outside myself, loved Kendall more. But he was off to a bad start, the monster Howard had turned him into, and what happened as a result is not totally Kendall's fault.

Like everything else, Kendall abused whatever was best for him, and Tonja was no different. He'd become just like his daddy, screaming, shouting, throwing tantrums, beating up on Tonja when he couldn't have his way. After a while, Tonja came to her senses, got somebody else who would treat her better and give her a better life. Though she's happy with her husband and two children over in New Jersey, I hear she still loves Kendall, her first love.

"She'll be visiting with the kids on Thanksgiving," her mother said, last time I saw her at the produce stand.

"Will she?" I said. "Would you ask her to stop by? I'd love to see her and meet her family. She was always like the daughter I never had."

But she never stopped by. And frankly, I couldn't blame her.

When my boys were old enough to take care of themselves, I went back to school and found a job. With Skylar's help, I was on the road to self-improvement. I had just started working when I got sick one day and they sent me home. Upstairs, the bathroom door was closed, which I found strange, since nobody should've been home. Though Howard had become a drunk by then, he still went to work every day. I knocked on the door and there was no answer. I turned the knob and opened it. What I saw I'll never forget.

"Kendall James Whyte!" I yelled. "What the hell are you doing to yourself, boy?"

"Mama, would you please close the door," he said, calmly. Imagine that? He was shooting up drugs in my house and telling me to close the door, as if he were sitting on the toilet, reading a newspaper. Yes, Lord, I remember thinking, that's Howard's son.

"If you don't take that damn needle out of your arm right this minute, I'll throw that shit down the toilet!"

"It won't stop me, Mama. I've got more." Just like him. Mr. Smart-mouth, Mr. I-got-an-answer-for-everything.

"How long you been doing this?"

"Longer than I remember."

When I told Howard, he didn't budge. I didn't understand his reaction then, but I think I do now. Probably, Howard felt responsible for Kendall's drug abuse, having driven him to it in more ways than one. Besides, as an alcoholic maybe he felt a kinship with his son. Maybe he was too drunk to care. I don't know.

And just when you start getting comfortable with things you can't change, such as a gay son, and another son who's a junkie, then AIDS comes out of nowhere. When I first starting hearing about it, I stayed awake nights wondering if Skylar would be its next victim. I worried about Kendall sharing needles, and possibly exchanging blood. Though they both seemed to be healthy, I still had to ask for my own peace of mind.

"Skylar," I had said. "Are you being safe?"

"What do you mean, Mama—"

"You know what I mean."

"Yes, Mama, very much so. I've had the same sexual partner for the last several years. Evan and I both tested negative."

"Negative, what? You don't have AIDS?"

"We don't have the HIV virus. I'm sure we'll be fine."

"And what about you, Kendall?" I said. "Don't you think AIDS is the best reason yet to stop using heroin?"

"No, Mama."

"Why not?"

"I don't share my needles with anybody, that's why."

"I don't believe that," I said.

"Believe what you want," Kendall said. "If I had been sharing needles, I'd be dead by now."

I guess he was right, so I left well-enough alone. Still, I worry.

I wonder what prompted me to go back to work when I hadn't seen the inside of an office since I was a teenager. I guess it was a combination of things. I needed to get out of the house. I needed to do something with all my idle time, after my boys didn't need me. And, I'm sure, I was trying to prove something to my husband, who thought I had the brain of an amoeba. Skylar had been such an inspiration, teaching me new words as he learned them. His teacher was right. Words do have power. And the more I learned, the less ignorant I felt. I never felt good about not having finished high school. I felt even worse about it when my mother-in-law asked me about my education in front of her family, who made fun of me. There's nothing like being made to feel stupid. Rather than cry over it, I did something about it.

I knew so many new words by the time I enrolled in the accredited high school evening classes that I was, in some ways, ahead of my classmates, some of whom were about my age. It was difficult going back to school, reestablishing study habits, discipline, and being told what to do by someone younger than me. But it was fun, too. For the first time in my life, I actually paid attention to my books and teachers. I really learned history. I really learned how to use correct English. I really had fun learning to type all over again. I found that education is not always meant for the young. Sometimes, you have to be older, wiser, and more mature, to appreciate the gift you're receiving. I regretted having wasted my education as a young girl, taking most things for granted, learning as much as I thought I needed to know. And when I got my diploma and marched down the aisle and across the stage in a cap and gown, you could've sworn I was receiving an honorary doctorate from Oxford.

The really difficult part came when I decided to go back to work.

Now, that's some scary business when you're approaching middle age and life seems like it's almost over, and yet it's just beginning. I had been checking out ads in the *New York Times*, the *Amsterdam News*, the *Village Voice*, even. With a pencil, I circled the openings I found interesting, sipping my morning cup of Maxwell House coffee, the house so silent I could hear the building settle, the stairs creak. Though my husband was working, my boys in school, as they'd always been, the feeling was different. I knew there was something else I had to do with my time, before I went stir-crazy. As my eyes rolled across the want ads, I began to wonder if my high school diploma was really enough. Now that I had one, employers were looking for college graduates. Jesus, had things changed since I grew up! A high school diploma was plenty in my day, there were so many uneducated folks. High school was one thing. But college, quite frankly, scared me.

Day in, day out, I walked the dirty pavements of New York City in winter, spring, summer, and fall, searching for the job that had my name on it. Most times, I didn't have much money. I couldn't tell Howard what I was doing. He would've given me less, to keep me at home. I used to starve between interviews, toying with the possibility of buying that egg-salad or tuna-fish sandwich I saw in Horn and Hardart, knowing I still had to get back uptown. And I wasn't above walking back to Harlem either, except I'd been walking around all day, from Chambers Street where they had started to build the twin towers, all the way up past Rockefeller Center, and everywhere in between. When I walked into an office and filled out an application, I was intimidated by the young, pretty girls applying for the same jobs. They were just coming out of school. I was just coming out of nearly twenty years of motherhood.

"Just fill this out," the receptionist said, shoving the application in my face with one hand, writing something with the other, never looking up to see who she was talking to. "And give it back to me when you're finished. Someone will call your name to be interviewed, okay?" she said a little too automatically, as if she were trying to get rid of me. But then I couldn't blame her. She must've said the same thing to a hundred people a day.

"What should I put here?" I asked, pointing my pencil to the section on the application called "Work History." Goes to show how naive I was.

"What do you mean?" the receptionist said, annoyed. I could tell I was getting on her nerves. "Haven't you worked before?"

"Yes and no."

"Which is it?"

"Well, I ain't—I mean, I haven't worked since I was a teenager."

"Then what have you been doing?"

"I've been a housewife, raising two boys."

"Well then, put that down."

I sat down and did as I was told, watching the young, pretty, spry girls go through their applications like clockwork. Not knowing whether or not to lie about my age, my work experience, my education, I felt at a loss. I couldn't compete with them. They glared at me as if I was taking the job away from them. Who would hire middle-aged me, when they could have that lovely young girl over there with the legs up to her neck? This is all wrong, I kept thinking. What the hell am I doing here? What am I trying to prove? All I could think about was having to hand-wash the dress I was wearing, the one good dress I could use for job interviews. I hadn't bought a new dress in years. And as I thought about that, it gave me more reason to get a job, to buy things for myself.

"So tell me, Althea," the grave-looking, balding man with the bushy eyebrows said to me, his shiny head bowed, glancing at me over his half-glasses, as his finger slid from one section of the application to the next. I smiled, but he never smiled back.

"How much experience do you have being a secretary?"

He quickly turned the application over, as though the information he'd requested was written there, and flipped the page back over, obviously impatient. I was wasting his time.

"By the looks of this, you have no experience at all ... with anything."

"That's correct, sir," I replied, getting nervous, wishing he would smile just once, the son of a bitch. Didn't he know how difficult it had been for me, already? "But I have a good typing speed, and I learn quick — I mean quickly. So, if you'd give me a chance—"

"Look, lady, uh, Althea," he said, glancing at the application, tapping his stubby fingers on the desk. "I need someone with experience. That's what the ad says: experience."

I know, I wanted to say. I can read.

"You don't have that," he said. "And until you do, I can't use you."

It wasn't until I got up to leave that the bastard finally smiled.

Somebody, I don't remember who, told me about another agency. It must've been the woman I met at one of my job interviews who was also a mother my age. She had taken time off from work to have her children, then she returned to work. The agency she recommended tested me for typing speed, shorthand, vocabulary, grammar, spelling, and math. Though I was nervous, the girl who interviewed me, a girl half my age, said I had done very well.

"I'm going to send you out to a really good position in midtown," she said, her blonde hair streaked with auburn, her crazy-colored fingernails too long, her fuchsia lipstick too loud, her gum-chewing unladylike. And she has a job, I couldn't help thinking. "This place is a management-applied computer-programming outfit. They have a temporary clerk position in personnel that could become full-time, if they like you."

I didn't know what the hell she was talking about. She'd used the words "computer" and "programming" in the same sentence. The word "computer" didn't even exist, as far as I knew, until a few years ago. But I looked at her as if I woke up every morning thinking about computers and programming.

"If they hire you permanently, the starting salary is seven-fifty a month, with two weeks paid vacation, medical insurance benefits, Christmas bonus, and a ninety-day probationary period. The hours are 8:30 to 4:30."

Seven hundred fifty dollars a month, I knew, was no money. But I'd had no money of my own for so long, it sounded like I was going to be rich. Two weeks paid vacation, and paid medical expenses ... my head swelled like a helium-filled balloon.

"You are to interview with a Mrs. Manson. Remember, the job is temp. But if they like you after ninety days, they'll ask you to stay on. It's a great job, with great opportunities for growth. Whaddaya say?"

"What's the address?"

Everything about the job sounded good, except the last part. I didn't want to be interviewed by a woman, and I wasn't sure why. Could've been my conditioning that women were bitches to work for. But weren't men bitches, too? Wasn't I married to one?

When I arrived, Mrs. Manson couldn't see me, because she was in a meeting. After I took the tests, a man interviewed me instead. He was handsome, tall, easygoing, black, and he smiled a lot — all of which put me at ease.

"Good afternoon, Althea," he said, extending his hand, closing the door behind me. "My name is George Wilson. Please have a seat."

I sat in the chair he indicated, crossed my ankles, placed my pocketbook on my lap just so, my expression serious, business-minded, broken up by a courteous smile and chuckle now and then.

"So, you're looking for a job," he said, sitting down, the chair squeaking under his weight. "It's hard, isn't it?"

"Yes ... yes, it is," I said, appreciating his acknowledgment of my trials. No one else had. "It's not easy."

"What were you doing between now and the last time you worked?"

"Well," I said, feeling comfortable about telling him the truth, which I would've done anyway. "I got married and had two boys."

"So, it's not like you haven't been busy," he said. Again, I was glad that he realized that what I had been doing, although I didn't get paid for it, was a great deal of thankless work. I liked this man immediately.

"Actually, in this position, you would've been working for me, and for others here in the office, you know, typing, filing, answering phones, stuff like that. But I'm transferring into another department, so I won't be here, in personnel, that is."

"I see."

"How long have you been married?" I wondered why he asked that question. It could've been personal or professional. It was hard to tell.

"I've been married about eighteen years."

"You're kidding me."

"Why would I do that?"

"You could be a newlywed."

"I don't believe a word of it, but it's kind of you to say so, anyway. And you?" I said, trying to be a little informal, noticing the portraits of what must have been his children. There was no picture of a wife. No wedding band on his finger.

"My wife died some years ago," he said, with a sadness that touched me. A man who missed his wife. "And I never remarried."

"So, there's other people being considered for this job?" I asked, steering the conversation back to the reason I had come, without trying to appear rude. "And you'll call me in a couple of weeks, right?"

"You really want this job, don't you?" he said.

"As a matter of fact, I do."

"You probably want it more than the parade of young, mindless girls who've been in and out of here. If you want the job, it's yours—"

"Really!" I said, not meaning to shout, or cut him off. He was actually choosing me over youth. He sure knew how to flatter a middle-aged woman.

"I got a feeling about you," he said, reclining in the swivel chair.

"What kind of feeling?"

"You're going to do very well here. You're really hungry and eager to work. I know what that's like. I only have one regret."

"What's that?"

"That you won't be working for me."

I wasn't sure how to take that. There was a look in his eye that seemed to be a little less than professional. Then again, maybe it was me, something I thought I saw, something I wanted to see, something I needed to see. Whatever the case, it felt wonderful to have a man pay me compliments, and talk to me and smile at me like I was in the same room, breathing the same air as he was. As I shook Mr. Wilson's hand, for reasons I wouldn't totally understand until much later, I, too, regretted that I wouldn't be working for him.

Withdrawal Pains

EVAN SITS ALONE AT A CORNER TABLE in Peretti's, poring over a script.

Through the window, he watches pedestrians clog the sidewalks of Columbus Avenue. A few people are gawking at him. Being recognized in this setting makes him uncomfortable. He doesn't know why he picked this spot to have lunch. He could've gone somewhere more private. But since he left Skylar several weeks ago, he hasn't been himself.

Again, he tries focusing on his character's lines. Distraction won't let him. Though he told Skylar he'd be in touch, he hasn't been. Tried calling a couple of times, dialing the number, not knowing what to expect when the line clicked. First time, the answering machine beeped on. While the outgoing message played and he listened to his own voice, he considered whether or not to leave an incriminating record of his intentions. More pride than nerve. Second time he called, later that same day, Kendall answered. Shit! he thought. Sky's not letting his brother crash there again, is he?

Kendall never knew the source of the hang-up.

Between appetizer and entree, tossing a crisp twenty on the table for the waiter's troubles, Evan steps outside into the clash of urban sounds. Hails himself a taxi. Doesn't know where he's going. But needs to get away from here. From it. Whatever it is.

He's never been unfaithful to Skylar, never had any reason to be, even through the worst times, but his eyes have been known to wander occasionally. It's only natural, and anyone who denies that to their spouse is full of it. For the first time ever, he refers to Skylar as his ex. Technically, they're broken up, separated, trial-divorced, in limbo, tentative, on hold, whatever he chooses to call it. Yet, having an affair with Mario makes him feel like he's cheating on Skylar.

He was uneasy about living alone — more specifically, living without Skylar. That was a lot of emptiness to fill. At the health spa, he worked off frustration and stress through flat, incline, and decline bench presses, arm curls, military presses, flies, leg extensions, leg curls, squats, lunges, toe raises, push-downs, pull-downs, Lifecycle. That day, he was feeling touchy about being stared at and sized up, with people gawking at him, whispering about him, furtively pointing at him.

And Evan wasn't the only celebrity working out there that afternoon, either. Normally, this never bothered him, but that day, it ate away at him. He was contemptuous of, and bored with, the Jack La Lanne pretty boys, the Lonely Hearts Antisocial Club, who were always there, no matter what hour of the morning or afternoon or evening Evan went. It was as if they lived there, in their male-Victoria-Principal gym drag of matching sweatbands, bandanas, socks, and spandex, and their spanking-new Nikes and Reeboks that looked too clean and pretty to touch the ground. All of their heads were stuffed with the earphones of cassette players. Weight-lifting belts choked their waists. Their hands were covered in Velcro-fastened, fingerless leather gloves. Their aloofness, coldness, and vanity were so repulsive that it rendered their sculpted pecs, abs, biceps, triceps, quadriceps, and deltoids all but meaningless. Were these people really that pathetic, or was he just in a funky mood? Disgusted with the exhibitionists, parading and flexing in the free-weights area, he retreated to his locker and changed for the shower and steam room, thinking, People, get a life!

Evan was pleased there was only one other person in the steam room. He loved the steam room, his reward after a major, ball-breaking workout. The warmth of it was womblike. On uncrowded days like this, he'd lie down across the tiled tier, curl into a fetal position, the hissing of the steam as soothing to him as a newborn's mother cooing in its ear. His nostrils sucked in the pungent, herbal scent of eucalyptus leaves that someone was considerate enough to place over the hot stones. The sheet of steam was so thick, so foggy, he could barely make out the other person who on this day, sat across from him, a towel around the man's waist, his arms folded, head tilted back, pressed against the wall, eyes shut, clouds of mist concealing, then revealing him, like a shot from a decadent Fellini film.

The guy was black, and from what Evan could make out, pretty too, in his early twenties, with calves as round and rigid as cantaloupes. Evan never cruised on the gym floor, the steam room, the showers, or anywhere else. But this guy was cute, innocent-looking. Innocence made Evan hard. The gorgeous boy cleared his throat, let out a cough, uncrossed his arms, raised his head, stretched, yawned, opened his eyes, tightened the towel around his waist, stepped down from the upper tier, and as he pushed through the door, shot Evan a quick yet resonant glance. God, Evan thought. If looks could fuck.

He let go of his attraction, his horniness, the moment the steam room door opened and closed, and thought no more about it.

He had steamed himself, showered, toweled, put on lotion, dressed, blow-dried and combed his hair, sprayed on a little Drakkar Noir, and left the gym, when he stopped by the health-food surplus store to pick up protein powder and amino acid pills. Standing near the aisle of low-cholesterol mayonnaise, reading a box of bran cereal, was Mr. Steam Room himself.

"Do you have any more protein powder?" Evan said to the clerk, approaching the counter.

"If you didn't see any on the shelf, we're out."

Evan hated that response when he was looking for an item the store had run out of, though the clerk had just stated the simple truth. What else should the clerk have said? Evan was leaving the store, as was Mr. Steam Room, when they bumped into each other headed out the door.

"Excuse me," Evan said.

"Go right ahead," he said, allowing Evan to pass. Jesus, Evan thought, this boy is cute. "How're you doing?" They stepped onto the sidewalk.

"Great," Evan said, lying. The boy's eyes held his, and he couldn't turn away. "What's up?" Evan didn't know what else to say, hoping the boy couldn't tell how hot he was for him.

"I know where you can get some protein powder."

"Do you?"

"Cheap, too."

Evan knew this was not a cool thing to do. He could find protein powder anywhere, but he flagged down a cab and climbed in after...

"What's your name?"

"Mario."

"Evan."

"I know."

"So, where were you going? Before you saw me, I mean?"

"Nowhere."

"Live in New York?"

"Yeah, but I just got here."

"From where?"

"Paris and Milan."

"Visiting?"

"Working."

"As what?"

"A model. But," Mario said, turning his head sharply to see something through the rear window, "I'm looking for a place to stay."

"For how long?"

"Couple of days."

"I have an extra room." Evan couldn't believe he'd said that. Was Mario that pretty? Or Evan that horny? Could he have been that lonely, that stupid? "I came to New York as a model, with nowhere to stay. I know what it's like," Evan said, in his most altruistic tone of voice, fantasizing all the things he wanted to do to Mario once he got him home and naked. The fact that Mario knew who he was, without acting star-struck, turned Evan on.

If Mario hadn't been there, Evan might have gone home.

So, Mario wasn't as politically conscious as Skylar. Airheads never are.

"Who's Nelson Mandela?" Mario had asked, watching the evening news.

"You don't know who Nelson Mandela is?"

"No. Why should I? I don't get into all that political, black stuff," Mario said, disdainfully. "I just want to look fabulous and stay in shape and work major assignments. That asking too much?"

Mario, a black man, isn't a gadfly perched upon the ass of a racist America, carrying the weight of history upon his shoulders, belly-aching about racial injustices. This comes to Evan, in part, as a relief. But neither does he have Skylar's biting intelligence, his discerning eye. After five days, Evan's fed up with Mario's self-indulgence — his working relentlessly on his physique at the gym, vexing himself with what outfit to wear to what occasion, at what hour of the day, panic-stricken because the mirror tells him he's gained two pounds, unwilling to be impulsively, wantonly sexual with Evan for fear of mussing his hair or wrinkling his outfit. I. Me. Myself. His three best friends. And Skylar accused Evan of such narcissism. He never should've let Mario move in with him. But the fear of living alone was overwhelming. Mom was known to say, You don't miss the water till the well runs dry.

Evan's thirsty as hell.

By the time he had gotten the nerve to slip backstage following the curtain on *Neon Shadows on the Blue Meringue*, Evan had felt a heightened expectancy about his attraction to Skylar, physically, intellectually, artistically. He had found the engaging, stunning, black actor with the blue eyes to be terse, challenging, elusive. Evan fancied a good chase.

As he confessed his leanings toward the black American experience, he noticed Skylar's eyes lighting up. How could Skylar resist him? Not many people could. But Skylar had since twisted everything around. Accused him of being a "dinge queen." He could've turned around and called Skylar a "snow queen." But he knew it wasn't so. Skylar charged that Evan was too cocky. Revoltingly vain. Assumed he had earned the right to say words like nigger because he was fucking one.

Skylar was wrong. Evan's not sharing his sociopolitical viewpoints on the missing children in Atlanta or the black American hostages being freed from the American Embassy in Iran fell short of a sound argument. If he didn't agree with Skylar's view of the world, it branded him a racist, a bigot, a sexist, a flag-waving patriot. Like patriot was a dirty word. He thought himself to be a multitude of adjectives. Racist wasn't one of them.

"What do you know about racism, Evan? Huh? Please tell me!" Skylar had shouted one night, livid. He clumsily pulled up a chair to sit in, as he awaited Evan's reply, folding his arms, breathing heavily, tapping his foot. "I'm waiting."

"What do you want me to say, Skylar? No, I'm not black, but I can still tell that things have changed—"

"Changed? The only thing that's changed is the new way racism is fed to me. I can't explain it, except to say that when you grow up in a world that despises you for your skin color, you develop an innate detector of people's hatred toward you, even when you can't see it."

"How?"

"You don't know what to look for, Evan. Things change and remain the same. People always think racism means burning a cross on my lawn, or calling me a nigger. There are more sophisticated ways, is all I'm saying—"

"And all I'm saying is, I don't agree—"

"Like you would know! You, of all people. White. Male. And blond!"

Skylar criticizes him because Evan won't allow himself to be moved by the oppression ravaging South Africa. Evan considers himself unequipped, and therefore unwilling, to take on the world's problems. He wonders why he should be penalized for "looking the other way" when the Poles underwent their trials in Warsaw and the Chinese students were slaughtered in Tiananmen Square. Doesn't make him any less of a human being, necessarily. He has one life. A life he wants to share with Skylar. Unwilling to sacrifice it for global ills.

Racism, as far as Evan can tell, has ceased to be as prevalent as it was in the '60s. Social conditions really have improved. And, no matter what anybody does, the world will never be Utopia, he thinks, refusing to accept the legacy of his forefathers as slave owners. It's not his sin to atone for. Between nurturing a career, and banging out the dents of his relationship, who could find the time? His own world is out of control. Some people can't fart and chew gum at the same time. Can't Skylar just love him without distraction? In spite of an imperfect world?

Skylar did make one point. Whether he agreed or not, Evan never forgot it.

According to Skylar, white America doesn't know its black brethren. His people have known white America better than it knows itself, beginning with slavery. The behavior of the masters and mistresses was anything but discreet. They shamelessly conducted all their business, economic, personal, marital, in the presence of their slaves, before whom they were no more embarrassed than if they'd revealed their secrets before the plantation's mules. From history, the press, politics, literature, music, especially television, and movies, blacks have had no choice but to know everything about whites. The sooner white America took the time to know black America, the better. Since whites are the power structure, they don't deem it necessary or important to acknowledge anything outside themselves. "As Americans" — Evan recalls the mocking tone Skylar used — "we have no other choice. We're undivorceable from each other," Skylar had said. "Inseparable as civilization and culture. Our blood and histories have mingled for centuries."

Maybe he's envious of Skylar.

His blue eyes. His reputation as stage and film actor. Evan would die for those sky blue eyes. And a career that's taken seriously. He feels the blue eyes belong to him rather than to a black person. But he didn't mean to insult Skylar by suggesting he couldn't possibly be black because of them. As if he and Skylar have each other's eyes. A freakish act of nature. What really bothers him is the syrupy-sweet relationship Skylar shares with his mother. He's closer to her than anyone. Including Evan. It forced him to lie to Skylar about the warped relationship he shares with his own mom, whom he hardly calls, never writes, barely claims.

There had been times when Evan hated coming home to find what he considered a lazy Skylar sprawled across the sofa.

"Home again?" Evan had said, hanging up his coat in the hall closet.

"What's that supposed to mean?" Skylar had asked, his grinding jaws halting, taking a much-needed break from the family-size bag of potato chips, the crunching of which, Evan swore, he'd heard before opening the door.

"Doesn't mean anything," Evan said, counting backward from ten.

"Yes it does," Skylar said, shoving aside the bag of potato chips, sitting up on the couch. Eight, seven, six ... Evan thought. "Why can't you just say what you mean? I swear," Skylar said, "white boys are so fucking repressed." Three, two, one, zero...

"Why don't you get off your fucking lazy, black ass, and go to work?"

"Work? What work? Have you seen the scripts I'm getting?"

"That's your problem, Skylar, one of many. You can't always play astronauts and monarchs. It's okay to play street types, and rapists, now and then. It helps you to stretch—"

"Stretch, my ass. That's all I ever play are street types. Most of these scripts have black characters talking like imbeciles!"

"I play parts like that, Skylar. I'm not complaining. It's not just black people—"

"You know it's different for me, Evan. You're the power structure. Politically, you can afford to portray who you want. I can't, because too many stupid fucking white people believe all blacks are like that—"

"I think you're just making excuses—"

"Excuses for what, Evan?"

"You're just lazy. Why work, when I can take care of your ass, right?"

"Fuck you, Evan!"

"Thank you, Skylar, and fuck you, too!"

"Shithead!"

"Scumbag!"

And Skylar's envious of him, he has reason to believe.

He resents Evan's commercial success in a career for which he's had minimal training, having paid virtually no dues. Evan's fortune as a model after arriving in New York — for *GQ*, *Women's Wear Daily*, *Esquire* — was moderate. It paid the rent. But he envisioned his name on movie house marquees. And during a promotional party given in Skylar's behalf, he got his chance.

They had been standing around, making show-biz small talk, when a director approached him.

"As a physical type, you're perfect for a role I'm casting. I hadn't found the right mixture of elements," he said, "until I saw you."

Evan jumped at the opportunity. It had fallen into his lap so easily. Like a floozy he could have his way with. Skylar only feigned happiness for him, Evan thought. He could tell by the lopsided smile on Skylar's face, the absence of congratulations. Evan could understand that, for all the sacrifice and God-given talent he poured into his craft, Skylar had never gotten a job that easily.

While Evan empathized with that, it didn't get in the way of his own ambition.

When they discussed it, a few weeks after the New York premiere, Skylar damn near likened Evan's being cast to nepotism.

"I'm not impressed with your beefcake walk-through," Skylar admitted, "nor the unheard-of fee demanded by your agent, nor the subsequent offers being made."

"Was I that bad?"

"Let's just say your stumbling debut was derivative and insipid. And it lacked elan."

Evan had wished the argument was more open to debate. That Skylar was simply envious, perhaps professionally threatened. But he knew every word of it was true. All the critics had said so. His lover was sounding just like them. Maybe Skylar was borrowing adjectives verbatim from their columns.

It hurt Evan more than he let Skylar know.

Would it have been different with Marla?

He thinks about her frequently. Questions nag him, pull and tug at him. Does she hate him? Did she ever become an attorney? Did she marry? Is she still living in L.A.? Did she really abort their child? She probably did. If not, she probably would've found Evan once he became rich and famous. He can't help wondering how their baby might have looked. Gorgeous, he knows. But would it have had Marla's high cheekbones and full lips, Evan's cleft chin and blond hair?

He wishes he could have a baby, with Skylar.

The taxi idles at a red light on Hudson Street near the Holland Tunnel. Having picked up some roasted chestnuts from a street vendor, Evan thumbs lazily through a copy of *Interview* and turns the page to a glamorous, full-length, black-and-white photograph of Skylar Whyte, lips teasingly parted, hair slicked back, exuding attitude, shadows of venetian blinds cutting diagonally across his face, azure eyes translucent as neon.

Evan wonders if Skylar's seeing anyone else. If he's moved anybody in, besides Kendall, to take Evan's place. If he's white, or black, or Asian, or Latino. He misses his man. The one Skylar used to be. His droll, refreshing perspective on life. His ability to help Evan dissect characters he was portraying. Glancing at the script in his lap, the shadows of sleepy buildings casting a passing darkness over the backseat, he knows his ex-lover would zero in on this character's motivation with razor-edged precision. Not Bergman, nor Fellini could pinpoint the character's pulse with a more deft finger.

Too bad there's no Court of Love to appeal to, no judge and jury to hear his case.

Your Honor; ladies and gentlemen of the jury. You have before you an open-and-shut case of a love that's become unfinished business. The man I love, the man I adore, the man for whom I'd give my life, punishes and blames me for bigotry, racism, sexism, patriotism, and every other ism in the world...

Has the jury reached a verdict?

Yes, we have, Your Honor. We, the jury, find the defendant, Skylar Edward Whyte, guilty of a love that's unfinished business, in the first degree.

I, therefore, sentence you, Mr. Whyte, to a lifetime of making it up to your partner-in-life, your spouse, Evan Cabot, and to finish the relationship you've started. Case dismissed!

The judge's gavel pounds in his ear, as he watches a motley bunch of hardhats at a construction site near the West Side Highway harass a cluster of gay men crossing Christopher Street.

Dusk lowers over the city like stage curtains. He directs the cabbie to take him home. Exhausted by a random tour of a city he knows all too well, filled with a vague ennui, he wonders if Skylar's at home. He plays with the impulse of stopping by unannounced, on the premise of needing coaching with the script.

He wonders if Skylar's still having those bad dreams.

hespian

JESUS SAVES FROM HELLo Dolly Revivals!

He couldn't have been more than seven years old when he was first told actors don't portray themselves, that they play characters. Watching Mickey Rooney's dog get killed in *Boys Town*, Skylar started crying.

"What the hell are you crying about?" his father said, leaning over. "Only sissies cry."

"Leave the boy alone," Althea said. "Be glad he feel enough to cry at all. Better than some people I know."

"Lookit," Skylar said, pointing. "His dog's dead." Howard and Althea chuckled.

"Baby," Althea said, "it's only make-believe. The dog ain't dead, he's just playacting."

"You mean, he's not really dead?" Skylar asked, wiping his eyes with balled fists.

"Of course not, baby," Althea replied. "Even the dog's play-acting. When the cameras stopped rolling, he got up and went on about his business."

So that's it! Skylar thought. No wonder actors he'd seen get killed in one movie, were alive in another. He had been confused, questioning the permanency of death. The premise of dramatic acting was an attractive beckoning for the child obsessed with escapism. He could be killed, yet get up and make another movie — plus, he didn't have to be himself. The duality of it for him was doubly seductive.

Invariably, Skylar was cast by teachers in the leading roles in school plays. He had perfect diction, they said, with a memory like an elephant's. Skylar didn't understand the elephant comparison. Mama always came to the plays and applauded his performances, as did Nanna and Poppa, Aunt LaVern, Aunt Gloria Jean, and sometimes Uncle Aubrey, when he was in town. Daddy never came.

During afternoons at home with Mama, Skylar would recite Walt Whitman and Langston Hughes poems he'd learned at school. He'd act out scenes he remembered from movies, his arms poised melodramatically in the air, clutching his heart, his throat, twirling his skinny body onto the floor, sticking his legs straight up and out, bringing them down, his head snapping to the side, Mama's lipstick smeared on his face like dried blood. Sometimes, she applauded. Other times, she stepped over and around him, sweeping and mopping, mumbling to herself, like something else was on her mind. She'd say, "That's nice, baby." But he craved more than "nice," like the way Nanna indulged his five- and ten-minute performances, spoiling him as a reward, with Skylar taking bows, running into the bathroom to flush the toilet — as a youngster, it was the closest he could come to simulating thunderous applause — and taking his curtain calls, as Nanna shouted, "Bravo!"

"Colored people don't become movie stars!" Daddy had said. Skylar had started to believe it, until Uncle Aubrey took him to see *Stormy Weather*, the movie that changed his life. Sitting in the dank darkness of the East Village's Bijou Theatre, he learned his father was a liar. Uncle Aubrey had challenged Daddy and proved him wrong. Skylar had seen an entire movie filled with nothing but colored stars. And he had watched Sidney Poitier prancing up to the podium, as black as he pleased, to receive his Best Actor Oscar for *Lilies of the Field* — during Civil Rights time, mind you. Mr. Poitier was as blue-black as they come. Blacker than Skylar. It gave him hope.

He studied at Columbia where, in student demonstrations, he protested everything from Vietnam to the imprisonment of Angela Davis. By graduation, most of his friends in the performing arts had "sold out." They had enrolled in law and medical schools, ensuring themselves "practical, financially secure" careers. He'd stuck to his dreams, the only one to do so, proud to say he was becoming an actor. Hollywood, Broadway, or bust.

Wasn't like blacks couldn't work in film, it was just twice, even thrice, as difficult. Drama teachers and coaches had told him he was promising, as did agents he read for. When he auditioned for his first cattle call and was rejected, it made him work that much harder, each rejection forming a sinewy layer around a heart unwilling to take no for an answer. He learned quickly not to take rejections personally ... at least, most of the time.

First professional job he got was a television commercial. Those days, the directors pulled no punches about the "black in the back." Regardless of his height, his handsome face, he was the black spot hidden in the back row, a victim of poor lighting, having to convince people, when the commercial was aired, that it was really him. In other commercial jobs, directors shuffled the formation of the group for different shots, but in the final cut, he still ended up in the back.

Competition doubled when he auditioned for black parts. Entering the director's office or the soundstage, he'd glance at the countless black actors, mumbling sotto voce, familiarizing themselves with the script. Taking inventory of his competitors, contrasting shades of beautiful ebony men, he'd think, Hmm, hmm, hmm. God must be black! Though it mattered, he wasn't entirely disappointed by the rejection, knowing at least one of the brothers would be cast. One more of them would be working, a victory for struggling black actors everywhere.

There were times when Daddy's disparaging warnings made plenty of sense. It was a nasty, cutthroat business out there in Rejection City. Yet there was nothing else he wanted to do. Night after night, propelled by his own pennilessness, he'd stop by his parents' house for dinner.

"I see you're not having too much luck with that acting nonsense," Daddy had said, inebriated, stuffing his mouth with bread, sounding like a thick-tongued idiot.

Daddy was so drunk most of the time, drooling, peeing on himself, babbling nonsensically, he was hardly aware of who was in the room. Sometimes, he didn't know his own name. But when Skylar dropped by, Daddy seemed to sober up, finding just enough coherence to bad-mouth Skylar who, because of this, didn't want to be there. It was a question of starvation, not pride.

"You should've listened to me, boy," Daddy had said, his fork raised, about to place it in his mouth. A few grains of rice fell in his lap and he searched for them, as the remainder of his food slipped from the fork onto the floor. "You're wasting your damn time. For the rest of your life, you'll be banging your head against a brick wall, because nobody's going to give you a job. If my son, the hardhead, had listened to his daddy's advice, instead of precious, little Uncle Aubrey, and gotten a degree in accounting, he wouldn't be in this position today. But no, you're too goddamn hardheaded, like your mama here. You'd rather listen to that uncle of yours."

"Yeah, sure," Skylar had said. "Get an accounting degree like you, and be like you, huh?"

All day long he was hitting the pavement, catching subways uptown, downtown, midtown, his pride and stamina seeping with each drop of sweat pouring off his face, finding hope with each audition, then his hope shot down, and coming home and being reminded of it by someone who couldn't tell how many fingers Skylar was holding before his face. He suppressed his rage, reminding himself to store away the feelings and sensations he was having seated at the dining room table with his father, and to use them in his work.

That's what acting was for him. A landfill. A dump. A release. A therapeutic, cathartic purging of all the shit bottled up inside him, past, present, bad, good. Acting was more than craft, profession, skill. It was a way of life. Of survival. The blood in his veins. He believed that having grown up under his father's roof had done more to channel that fuel than all his idols put together.

He recognized his perpetual hunger to please someone — Daddy, Mama, teachers, casting and film directors, colleagues, critics, the public. He hungered to validate his purpose on earth, his self-worth. He was an approval junkie with a vacant, bottomless need for love, for holding the audience breathless in his hands so that he could do with them as he pleased, and be applauded night after night. Such power dizzied him.

Through dedication, growth, perseverance — most of all, perseverance — he finally got his break in a film by a major American director.

You're stuck with that face, those ruins of a body, and you have no fashion sense. And you're trying to convince me that you're not gay?!

Two lines. That's all it was. But he rehearsed those two lines with the same tenacity with which he studied an entire script. He read them a thousand different ways. He would work these two lines for all they were worth.

Nearly every review he'd read of that film mentioned a scene-stealing, rising talent, whose presence on the American cinematic scene was a force destined to be compared to the debuts of Brando, Hoffman, DeNiro, an actor whose brilliance ... well, something along those lines. The telephones rang, offers were made — hardly major roles, but work nonetheless. He was earning a salary sufficient to pay his bills, with a little left over, which in itself was success. He knew plenty of New York actors who couldn't claim that.

He moved into a bigger and better apartment on Ludlow, south of Houston, pre-Soho. He invested his earnings in furniture, a stereo, and decent clothes, which he didn't have many of.

Althea went with him to pick out his new sofa, a six-part, L-shaped sectional that swallowed the parlor in his one-bedroom walk-up. It gave the illusion that the living room was completely furnished. When people visited his apartment, they fell in love with the sofa. Some made offers. He refused. After purchasing the basic necessities, he began banking his money.

Then the work stopped coming, just like that. Living on his savings and residuals, he found himself regressing. After the savings dried up, residuals no longer appeared in the mailbox. One day he had money, next day, he didn't. "Nigger rich," Mama called it.

A playwright friend of his came to propose a possible acting job, and fell in love with the sofa. He made an offer that Skylar accepted, though he didn't want to part with even one piece of furniture. Even more, he abhorred having to scrounge for rent money, eating his meals at Mama's, asking friends for loans. Reluctantly, he sold one of the pieces to the playwright, assuming that in time he would buy it back. What began as a temporary measure of survival ended with him giving in to a nasty temptation. He took out ads, and hustled off the remaining sections: $250 apiece or better offer. One by one, they disappeared. And then there were none.

One night, arriving home after a second meeting with the playwright, who now owned at least half of the sofa set, he found an empty apartment. He'd long ago given up the hope of buying the sofa back. The sales were final. Now his apartment looked as if he'd been robbed, the hardwood floors bare and empty as the day he'd moved in. Had he not been keeping count, he might've called the police to report a breaking and entry. Bad blossomed to worse. He got sick and tired of crawling back to his parents for a meal, though Mama insisted.

Shopping in the supermarket one day, Skylar brainstormed. Spam. He'd eaten it as a kid, especially with Nanna and Poppa. He innovated more ways to eat Spam than Nanna. Cheap and easy, he started calling it his Spam diet. He even considered writing the company about his recipe ideas. He improvised ways of stretching Kool-Aid, too. With little sugar on hand, he made it by the glass. Spam and Kool-Aid. They brought him through rough times. Fried Spam, baked Spam, raw Spam, SLT sandwiches. He thought of writing a Spam cookbook but didn't have the energy to compile it. Even years after he'd become a solid commercial success, he kept a can of Spam in the kitchen cabinet. In case his ego got bigger than his salary, there was always the reminder.

Skylar and his superintendent got along fine, talking mostly about jazz, as his super was a bebop freak. Sometimes, they shared a joint, a bowl of hashish, and listened to Coltrane's "Giant Steps," as long as the rent was on time. When it was late, and for a time it was, even for months, Skylar learned to evade the super, keeping absolutely still when the loud knocks fell on his door. The super had grown tired of next-week-when-my-check-comes promises. Skylar disliked standing in the doorway, shamed, embarrassed, hungry, frustrated, without a dollar to offer for rent.

He didn't like having to be quiet so the super wouldn't know he was home, tiptoeing around the apartment in stockinged feet like a thief. Had to grab his telephone on the first ring — when it wasn't disconnected — so the super didn't hear it. Always snatching his mail out of the box before he was seen, Skylar was a rodent outwitting the trap. He couldn't even play his stereo, which he'd played all the time. When he managed to sneak out each day to look for work, he feared returning home to find the door padlocked. It was as depressing a thought as having to pay for everything with pennies, to the grocer's chagrin. "Money is money," Skylar told the check-out clerk, who stood impatiently, sighing heavily.

JESUS SAVES FROM HELLo Dolly Revivals!

He laughed out loud at the graffiti obviously spray-painted by two authors, in two colors, at different times, laughing because he felt good. There was reason to feel good. He had a job.

Although he was exasperated with the dearth of good, substantial Hollywood work, he jumped at the stage opportunity to play Bernardo, leader of the Sharks in *West Side Story*. If *Stormy Weather* had steered him toward his life's ambition, assuring him that he could be an actor, the movie version of *West Side Story* had said to him that he *must* be an actor. It had all those rough, tough, dirty-faced, blade-toting punks, strolling down their impoverished turf, snapping their fingers to the beat of Bernstein's score. And when it looked as if they were going to jump off the screen into Skylar's popcorn, they broke, instead, into Jerome Robbins's choreography, *tour jete-ing* like nobody's business.

Having seen the movie repeatedly as a child, he had sided with the Jets, the white gang. Like the rest of the audience, he wanted to see the destruction of the Sharks, the Puerto Rican gang. Now rehearsing the role of Bernardo day after day, hour after hour, he realized how he'd been manipulated by the story, which on closer examination of the film's subtext, he resented. White was good. Swarthy with accents was bad. But the way they had danced and sung down the broad, filthy streets of New York's West Side had compelled him to pursue his passion.

He played Bernardo to superlative reviews because, he thought, the soul of Bernardo was his own. He understood the outcast on white turf. He had made that mistake by unknowingly entering the Irish and Italian neighborhoods of New York, where he wasn't welcome. Nothing new. He always felt out of sync with society. He was black and homosexual in a largely white, heterosexual world. Their heroes were never his heroes. While the nation rallied around Bush and Reagan, veritable folk heroes in their eyes, he was inspired by Jesse Jackson and David Dinkins. When the world fell in love with Mary Lou Retton, he adored Joyce Joyner-Kersey and Flo Jo. When they put Bruce Springsteen and Madonna on pedestals, his ears were tuned to Prince and Janet Jackson.

If he had to do it over again, he wouldn't change a thing. He loved being male. And black. And gay. And a New Yorker.

There were film traditions he longed to challenge.

More than he cared to see it, Caucasian heterosexuality was constantly being shoved in his face, rammed down his throat. There were such things as gay and lesbian and Latino and Asian and

American Indian and black love, as well. Lesbians were far more tolerated than was love between two men. When it came to black romance, it was hopeless. There had been times he insisted on having a romantic interest written into the script, with love scenes between himself and a black woman. Hollywood had created a tradition of repressing black male sexuality. The mentality of antebellum slavery maintained a stronghold on contemporary white America. Everyone, it seemed, feared their husbands, wives, sons, daughters, brothers, sisters, fathers, and mothers becoming attracted to black sex symbols. In D.W. Griffith's racist portrait of *Birth of a Nation,* black men were depicted as nonsexual entities. Not much had changed since then. In his professional, political way, Skylar "created" opportunities to challenge these cinematic stereotypes.

Uncle Aubrey had been right.

"My nephew has the makings of an outstanding thespian," Uncle Aubrey had said. "Given time, discipline, hard work, and paying dues."

Skylar didn't understand the word, but pretended to, deciding to look up the meaning the first opportunity he got. But whatever thespian meant must've been good. He could tell by the wrinkles of pride in his uncle's expression. Sadly, Uncle Aubrey was no longer alive when the big day finally came.

The phone had rung nearly ten times before Skylar decided to answer it. He thought it would be Justin, a former college roommate, who was having love problems and was becoming a pain in the ass.

"Skylar, guess what?"

"Who's this?" Skylar said, though he knew who it was. He hated when his agent called him up without announcing himself or exchanging salutations. Skylar had told him about that a couple of times, at least.

"You've been nominated!"

"What?! For what? As what?"

"Best Actor, by the Academy!"

"No!"

"Yes!"

"You're shitting me!"

"No I'm not—"

"Is this a joke?" Skylar said, panting, unable to catch his breath. " Cause if it is, it's a bad one."

"Just turn on the news. Bye!"

There were so many people he wanted to tell — Daddy, most of all. He almost ran to the house to deliver the news. He found his father home alone, drunk, and Skylar played it as nonchalantly as possible, sweat pouring down his face.

"What brings you by?" Daddy said. "Another free meal?"

"Oh, nothing in particular," Skylar said, pretending aloofness, clearing his throat. "I just dropped by to tell you I've been nominated by the Academy for an Oscar."

"Nominated for what, boy?"

"Best Actor."

"By whom?"

"My peers: the Academy of Motion Pictures Arts and Sciences, that's who."

"Oh. Do me a favor and pass me the *TV Guide*, would you?"

Skylar had guessed his father's response beforehand. He had prepared himself for this. But asking him to pass the *TV Guide*...

He fantasized writing a book, his memoirs, a family expose: *Daddy Dearest*. He visualized the movie adaptation, casting himself in the real-life role, as the son. Ossie Davis would play the father. Ruby Dee, the mother. Fade in. Long shot: black American family having Christmas Eve dinner. The time: 1962. The place: Harlem, New York City. Take One. Cut to closeup. Quiet on the set...

When Cover Gets Blown

TEARS INCHED DOWN Althea's cheeks.

She was holding the shredded remains of what appeared to be a dummy. She didn't know what to make of it at first. Doing the wash in the basement, she had accidentally stumbled upon a pair of Howard's pants stuffed with rags and old clothes. Fastened to the pants with safety pins was one of Howard's shirts, also stuffed. She assumed Skylar had been playing one of his imaginary games again. Then she noticed puncture marks caused by the bent curtain rod lying beside it, as if someone had been trying to beat the dummy beyond recognition. She didn't understand. Not until she discovered the severed paper-bag head. The eyes were green, the fangs white. She gasped out loud, catching herself, remembering there was no one in the house but her.

Then it hit her. She recalled the fight she and Howard had had about two weeks before when he found out about her abortion. While they fought, she remembered hearing Skylar downstairs making uncharacteristic noises. That sound, that particular humid, summer day, as if he was striking something, was one she'd never heard before. That child must be in some pain, she thought, shaking her head at the dummy, wiping her eyes with her palms. She had forgotten she was supposed to be adding fabric softener to the rinse cycle.

Upstairs. She knew it was going to be one of those days. Just when Howard had gone back to work after a two-week vacation, the boys back at school, and she thought she'd finally have a moment's peace.

It started with the telephone call.

"Hello," Althea said.

"Is Howard there?"

Althea could've been wrong, but her mother had taught her proper telephone manners. Never call someone's house without announcing who you are, before asking to speak to the person you're calling. She had a mind to hang up on this fool, let her call back and start over. Even if it was her mother-in-law.

"No, he just left five minutes ago, Mrs. Whyte. And yes, I'm just fine, thank you for asking."

"Don't be sarcastic with me—"

"Lady, you called my house—"

"I will ask how you're doing, if you'd just give me a minute. There's more important matters on my mind right now than asking how you're doing..."

Bitch, Althea thought. She heard the woman softly weeping, blowing her nose, and imagined her mother-in-law was pulling a sympathy stunt. It wasn't working.

"Excuse me," Mrs. Whyte said, sniffling, blowing her nose, which Althea also found rude. "My husband passed this morning, and..."

"I'm sorry to hear that. I can imagine how you feel—"

"No, you can't. You've never been widowed, have you?"

"Can I have Howard call you?" Althea said, her tone impatient, two seconds away from hanging up on this, this...

"It's an emergency, yes, what do you think? Tell him the family's gathering at my house here in Jersey City. We expect to see him and Kendall at about five o'clock." She hung up.

That was no request, Althea thought. That was an order. And what about me and Skylar? Ain't we family? She had a mind to call her back and tell her to go fuck herself. If Mrs. Whyte hadn't been grieving the loss of her husband, Althea might have done that.

She was distracted by a Martha and the Vandellas song playing on the radio. She'd heard on the news that the song was being pulled from nationwide air-play because of some nonsense about secret messages in the lyrics for Negroes to incite race riots. She knew that if the woman sang "dancing" in the streets, then that's exactly what she meant. She clicked off the radio, and contemplated how she would break the bad news to Howard.

■

Althea waited for the receptionist to finish what she was doing. Again, she cleared her throat. The receptionist flipped back her blonde mane and looked up. She acted surprised to see Althea standing there.

"Sorry, miss," the receptionist said. "But we have no job openings at this time."

"I'm not looking for a job," Althea said, glancing around the office.

"Then how may I be of help?"

"I'm Mrs. Whyte, and I'm here to see my husband, Howard. He's a CPA here."

"Are you sure?" the receptionist said.

"Of course I'm sure."

"We don't have any CPAs by the name of Howard."

"Sure you do. He's been working here well over ten years. How long've you worked here?"

"I'm new, but believe me, I know the names of all the CPAs by heart. Why don't you have a seat, and I'll locate him for you, okay?"

Althea sat down, and clasped her hands ladylike, when she wanted to place them around the blonde's throat. She was in no mood to be played with.

Moments later, a middle-aged white man appeared. He forced a smile, shook Althea's hand.

"I'm Mr. Benson," he said. "How can I help you?"

Althea sucked her tongue. "I've already told this lady, I'm looking for Howard Whyte, my husband. He's a CPA here."

"Excuse me." He peered downward at her. "We have a Howard Whyte who's a bookkeeper, not a CPA."

"There must be some mistake."

"I'm afraid there isn't, but I'll get him for you. Please wait." He exchanged a glance with the receptionist.

What the hell's going on? she thought. If she had smoked, she'd've pulled out a pack of cigarettes and lit one.

Howard appeared, his face flushed like she'd never seen it.

"What're you doing here?" he asked in a polite, almost cheerful tone, touching her shoulder. She turned her head in the direction of his touch, gazing at his hand, as if she'd never seen it before. Then she got on with her urgent business.

"Your mother called." Her voice wavered. She motioned for him to sit. She couldn't look him in the eye. "Your father died this morning. Heart attack. I didn't know how or when to tell you—"

"Why didn't you just call?"

"Call? Because you told me not to."

"I'll be home at lunchtime." He got up and started walking away. She caught him by the back of his shirt.

"They told me you're not a CPA," she whispered. "Are you a bookkeeper?"

"I'll explain when I get home," he whispered back, and smiled. He hadn't smiled at her in years.

She wandered aimlessly through the city on the subway, unaware of where she was going, not caring where she ended up.

It all made sense, somehow. He'd lied about his relationship with his parents, and she'd believed those lies — until, that is, she witnessed their behavior toward him in the presence of his brothers and sister. Howard hadn't even told Althea the man was his stepfather. It slipped out of someone else's mouth that Howard was a Whyte by adoption, not birth. She'd always wondered about his relationship with his parents. His father ignored him. His mother was merely pleasant with him. Most times, she spoke to him the way Howard spoke to Althea and Skylar. Howard kissed the old woman's ass to get along with her.

Nine years. That's how long it had been. She thought she had married a CPA. He had thrown those letters around in the way he threw his dirty clothes on the floor for her to pick up. Why had he lied? He'd led her and her children to believe he was a certified public accountant. She didn't need a high school diploma to know the difference between a CPA and bookkeeper. Did he really think she did? What else is he lying about? Is Howard L. Whyte, Jr. his real name?

It dawned on her that his brothers were all successful professionals. Two were lawyers, one was a doctor. His sister was married to a gynecologist. Maybe he was trying to be on their level. But, Lord Jesus, he didn't have to lie about it. She would've married him anyway.

He had been the finest, prettiest colored man she'd ever seen.

The Elks parade had just about run its length, marching down St. Nicholas Avenue. The maintenance men, with long-handled brooms, were sweeping up the evidence. She and her girlfriend were giggling at the group of fellows standing across the street.

"He's looking at you, Thea," her girlfriend giggled. "I'm sure of it."

"Which one, girl?"

"The one with the pretty eyes and the good hair. Look at how he looks at you."

Howard broke away from the group, crossed the street, hands in his pockets, head cast downward.

"Hi," he said.

"Hello," Althea replied, then looked away bashfully, giggling with her girlfriend.

"Howard," he said, and shook her hand.

"Nice to meet you," she said.

"Do you have a name?"

"Yes."

"What is it?"

"Thea."

"What?"

"It's short for Althea," her girlfriend chimed in.

"Oh, I see," he said, grinning, his eyes glowing in the sun like jade. "Would you like to go for a stroll in the park?"

"Sure." Althea turned to her friend. "Excuse me for a moment. I'll be right back."

"Ready?" he said, offering an elbow.

"Could we just stop by the corner luncheonette?" Althea asked him. "I have to use the ladies' room." Actually, she wanted to let out the scream building inside her. When she met him back on the sidewalk, he took her hand. Trees rustled, the grass and dead leaves crunched beneath their feet, the lake in the distance was rippling, lapping, framing the city's steel, jagged landscape in its reflection. They sat on the grass and Howard threw three pebbles into the lake.

"Where are you from?" he said, breaking the silence.

"Harlem."

"Really? I don't normally hang around Harlem but some of my buddies dragged me over here from Jersey. But if I knew I was destined to meet the girl of my dreams, I would've come without them. Will you show me Harlem?"

"Sure."

"I don't have a lot of time. I'm a senior at Rutgers, getting my degree in accounting. After that, I'll be preparing for the state exam to get my CPA certification."

Althea was impressed, though she wasn't sure what a CPA was or did. Where she came from, folks didn't talk like him. He was so perfect-looking, it made her feel inadequate. She wondered why he was attracted to her, him with his curly locks falling over his forehead, his smile, the dimples in his cheeks.

He took her to dinner, then to a movie, and wrapped his arm around her shoulder. She nestled her head on his shoulder, not watching the movie, but inhaling his cologne. He said all the right things, things women wanted to hear during courtship in 1950. He made all the right moves — more importantly, he didn't make the wrong ones. Most guys she had met had their hands up her dress and inside her blouse before she could tell them her name. Not this man. He had class. He was worldly, with a verbal fluency she didn't know existed. He touched her in all the right places, physically and emotionally, without taking advantage.

"Would you like to have a drink?" he suggested, after the movie. Here it comes, she thought. Just when I think he's a perfect gentleman, he's planning to get me drunk so he can have his way. But he didn't. He took her home in a taxi, made a point of exchanging phone numbers, planted a good-night kiss on her lips, and walked her to her door.

"I'll call you in two days. I'm busy with first week of classes, and I can't call you any sooner."

She knew it was the last time she'd see him. A man that gorgeous probably gave that line to every girl who threw herself at him. She tried not to think about it, not wanting to set herself up for the letdown.

Two days later, he phoned.

"Would you like to go with me to an outdoor baroque concert?"

She didn't know what the hell he was talking about. But she'd be damned if she wasn't going to get all dressed up to find out.

■

"Lady ... lady ... this is the end of the line."

Althea opened her eyes. The conductor loomed above her, shaking her by the shoulder.

"Pardon?" she said, becoming alert, clearing her throat.

"You'll have to get off here," he said. "This is the end of the line, ma'am."

"Where am I?"

"Sheepshead Bay."

"What?! You mean to tell me I've gone all the way to Brooklyn?"

"I'm afraid so, ma'am."

"Could you please tell me what train to catch back home? I'm lost. I'm looking for Harlem."

ul-de-Sac

SLAMMING THE DOOR BEHIND HIM, Kendall plops himself on Skylar's sofa, kicks off his Reeboks, crosses his legs on the coffee table. He's ticked off because a check he's been waiting for at his parents' house hasn't come in the mail. A few weeks back, he did some odd jobs through a temporary employment service, Johnny On The Spot, cleaning toilets and urinals at Madison Square Garden. He suspects Mama has intercepted his check — back payments. He has left her a nasty note to that effect.

Broke, he wonders how he's going to get high. He has considered dealing smack on the streets for Kenny Boy, a neighborhood heroin supplier. But selling dope last time almost got him killed. He had sold nothing. He had shot all the merchandise into his arm. After which, he was forced to chill out, lay low until the headhunters exhausted their search for him in the streets. He became dependent upon other junkies to cop his drugs for him, as humiliating an act as asking a starving man to bring him a plate of food. Luckily, the dealer who issued the contract on him died mysteriously from a shot of battery acid. Thank God, he remembers thinking. But he isn't fool enough to think lightning can strike twice.

He's as fed up with Mama as she is with him. She swears she's hot shit because she got a job. She never paid Kendall as much attention as she pays her job. She's always loved Skylar more than him. No secret Skylar's always been her favorite. Kendall would like to have it out with Mama, get it over and out of the way. It's her fault he's in this predicament. He refuses to give in to her demands to turn himself in to a rehab. There's nothing wrong with him. He just likes getting high. For Daddy it had been whiskey and God. Skylar has his acting. Mama has her job. Kendall loves smack. How and why should he expect them to understand that smack's the best feeling in the world. Better than sex.

He clicks on the television. Notre Dame's Fighting Irish are slaughtering Iowa's Hawkeyes. Kendall's eyes are transfixed on the halfback's remarkable interception, scoring an incredible fifty-yard touchdown. Wishing it were him, Kendall pictures himself as the game's MVP. Ah, the taste of victory and collegiate stardom, the glory that escaped him. As long as he lives, he'll never forgive Coach Pettiford's harsh, irrevocable decision. Even now, more than a decade after it all happened, Kendall hopes the man is dead, that his wife ended up selling her ass on the street, that his children have grown up to be retarded, deformed, Mongoloid idiot faggots.

"What did you call me, Whyte?!" Coach Pettiford had screamed at him. "Go ahead, say it again!"

"I already did—"

"Say it again, Whyte. I want the whole team to hear what you called me! I want witnesses after I finish frying your ass!"

"I called you a motherfucker—"

"Say it louder, Whyte! I can't hear you!"

"Motherfucker!"

"Okay, that's it. You're chucked from the team!" Coach Pettiford yelled, spit flying in Kendall's face, Coach's face so red, Kendall thought it would burst. "You have a bad attitude, Whyte!"

"You can't do that," Kendall was pleading, trailing behind the large man who acted as if Kendall wasn't there. "You've gotta let me play. This is my senior year."

Coach didn't want to hear it.

"I've had it up to here with you, Whyte!" Coach Pettiford screamed. "You fight your own teammates when you should be fighting the opponent. You don't know how to take instruction, or participate in group activity. You're not a team player. You want stardom by your own definition and means. You want to be a one-man high school football team. And you lack discipline, the ability to function as a spoke instead of trying to be the whole goddamn wheel!"

"But you're gonna blow my scholarship—"

"I don't give a shit! You should've thought about that a long time ago, boy!"

"Well," Kendall said, his face and hopes utterly collapsed. "What if I have my father come talk to you?"

The coach said nothing. After a long, deadly silence, he turned toward Kendall, without looking at him directly.

"Turn in your uniform, Whyte," he said, softer this time, his voice cracking. Coach sounded as if he were crying. Kendall thought he saw him wipe a tear from his eye. "I'll give number thirty-three jersey to a more deserving athlete. There's nothing you or your father can do. I've been thinking about this for the last two years. It's a goddamn shame, really. You're so talented, I kept making excuses for you, letting you slide. No more. My decision is final. End of story."

"But when you talk with my father—"

"No. I don't want to talk to your father. I'm talking to you. Now, you go back and tell him what I said. You're finished, Whyte, washed up. Understand English?"

Kendall told Daddy, watching the tear crawl down Daddy's cheek. He'd never seen his father cry. It was the liquor, Kendall guessed. Kendall cried too. They leaned on each other's shoulders, wetting each other's shirts with tears.

"I promise I won't let this happen to you, Kendall. We've groomed you from the days of Pop Warner, with dreams of getting you a scholarship to a school like Notre Dame, then the pros. Coach Pettiford is tampering with destiny. Don't worry. I'll talk to him. Tomorrow, first thing."

"Thanks, Daddy," Kendall said, cautious about what he had to say next. "Daddy, just make sure you're sober when you talk to him, okay? Not one drink. If he smells liquor on your breath, it's over. Don't go in there as the Alphabet Man, okay?"

Mama was sitting on the living room sofa, pretending she wasn't listening, sucking up every word he and Daddy said, unconcerned and apathetic as ever. Sky was at Columbia by then. Though he wasn't living on campus, he was rarely home. There was no one else to turn to. Kendall and Tonja hadn't been getting along too well. She didn't understand him anymore. He found no comfort in his friends. Jealousy, Kendall thought. Getting rid of him would afford his teammates rare opportunities to display their mediocre talents. He had heard them giggling and snickering and slapping five when Coach chucked him from the team.

Althea, Skylar, and Kendall had been watching television when Howard came home. He slammed the door, which startled them, then stood, his back against the door, his body faltering like a toddler taking his first step.

"Hi, Daddy," Kendall had said. As usual, he was the only one to greet Daddy, who then attempted to make his way to the living room. Kendall got up from the sofa he was lying on and assisted Howard. Tonight, Howard's body seemed to be in the shape of a C, the house filling with the stench of liquor and vomit with his every breath. Every night he came home drunk, his body shaped, contorted, like a letter in the alphabet. Kendall struggled with removing Daddy's jacket, as Daddy mumbled gibberish, and Mama and Skylar didn't lift a finger to help.

"You see that?!" Skylar said to Mama, gesturing toward the TV. "I told you she was the killer."

"No, I don't think so," Mama replied. "I still think it's the brother-in-law."

Freeing Howard from his jacket, Kendall sat him on the couch, laid him down, and flopped his long legs up. He removed Daddy's shoes, and placed a pillow under his head. Kendall hung up the jacket, then lifted Daddy's feet and sat at the end of the couch, with Daddy's stockinged feet in his lap. Howard continued to babble, and began punching and swinging in the air.

"It's all right, Daddy," Kendall said, reaching over to catch Daddy's swinging fists. "You're home now. You're safe. Nobody's going to hurt you."

"Would you keep quiet," Skylar said. "We can't hear the TV."

Kendall started to say something nasty to Skylar, but changed his mind. Ever since Skylar had gotten older, and taller, he challenged Daddy with more frequency, and said things he wouldn't have dared say if Daddy hadn't been drunk, and defeated. Since Mama had found out that Daddy had been lying about being a CPA, Daddy had become weaker, Skylar stronger. Once, Daddy was about to strike Skylar, who blocked the blow with his hand, held his father's fist in his grip, and twisted his arm.

"If you ever try to strike me or my mother again, I'll kill you," Skylar had said. "Just because you're no CPA after all, don't take it out on us. You fake."

He pushed Daddy on the couch, and walked away. Kendall nearly kicked Skylar's ass for disrespecting their father, but Kendall let it go, since he was too high to defend anybody.

Skylar got on his nerves, chasing the dream of a movie star, like he was a white boy or something. Skylar had all the luck. All the wonderful things happened to him. Nothing ever turned out right for Kendall.

All through elementary and high school, Kendall had lived in Skylar's shadow. Teachers were forever comparing them. Skylar this. Skylar that. Skylar was an exemplary student. Why hadn't any of it rubbed off on Kendall who, they said, acted as if the world owed him something. "I'm not my brother," he'd told them. "And I don't want to be like him, either." He was Kendall — cool, laid-back, NFL glory and stardom written all over him. Not the articulate, theatrically inclined straight-A student who never stepped on anybody's toes. They were brothers, but different. The teachers had to deal with Kendall for who and what he was.

"Who and what you are ain't much," Mama had said. "Certainly nothing to brag about. And the sooner you learn the earth doesn't revolve around you, and the sun don't rise and set in your ass, the better off you'll be."

She was always putting him down, cutting him in half, unimpressed by anything he achieved, on or off the field.

"God helps those who help themselves," Mama said. "He only takes care of babies and fools. And as far as I know, you're neither."

Daddy had started snoring, his toes twitching in Kendall's lap, when an Alka Seltzer commercial came on, and Mama and Skylar started sniffing the air. Mama glanced around her chair, and Skylar was checking the bottoms of his shoes. Kendall knew what it was, and where it was coming from, since he sat closest to it.

"I smell shit," Mama said.

"Me, too," Skylar said.

"Is that ... did your father shit on himself again?" Mama said, getting up from the chair, walking toward the couch where the smell got stronger. "Jesus, Lord!" she said, holding her nose. "I'm not cleaning him up this time. I'm tired of cleaning up that man's shit. Next time I'm at the market, I'm going to buy him some Pampers."

"I'm not cleaning him up, either," Skylar said. "He can drown in it for all I care."

"This is your father you're talking about," Kendall said, fed up with Skylar's disrespect. It made him want to kick Skylar's ass.

"No, he's not," Skylar said. "He's your father. You're the only child he ever had."

"You should clean him up," Kendall said. "You never do it—"

"That's right," Skylar said. "And I'm never going to, either."

"Put him on the floor," Mama said, "before he messes up the couch, like the last time."

"Skylar," Kendall said, ignoring Mama. "I said you should clean him up. It's your turn."

"Don't hold your breath," Skylar said.

"I should kick your butt, you know that?" Kendall said, shoving Daddy's ankles from his lap. He got up, walked over to Skylar's chair, and stood over him.

"You try it, Kendall, and I'll—"

"Okay, you two," Mama said. "That's enough!"

"I'm sick and tired of you," Kendall said to Skylar. "He's your father, and you treat him like dirt—"

"No different than he's ever treated me—"

"You never gave him a chance to be a father. You're such a mama's boy—"

"And you're such a spoiled brat, I should kick your butt—"

"C'mon, Skylar. I've been wanting to kick your ass for the longest time—"

"Watch your mouth, Kendall!" Mama said.

"And I wouldn't mind stomping you a few times, myself," Skylar said. "I want you so bad, I can taste it—"

"You've never been a son to him," Kendall said, pointing at Daddy.

"And you've never been one to Mama. So, we're even—"

"Okay, you two. I won't tell you again!" Mama said. Daddy stirred on the couch, turned over, and continued snoring.

"You jet black, tar baby motherfucker!" Kendall said.

"Kendall!" Mama shouted. "What did you just say—"

"You high-yellow-ass punk!" Skylar said. "What an appropriate complexion for you. You're a coward, just like your drunken-ass father!"

Kendall swung at Skylar, who dodged, then jumped up from the chair. Mama slid between them and held Skylar back.

"Let him go, Mama," Kendall said, the three of them pushing, shoving, the brothers reaching for one another, Althea keeping them apart. "Fucking faggot—"

"This faggot will whip your ass!"

"You probably hit like a bitch! You must, when you take it up the ass—"

"I'm gonna put my foot in yours in a minute—"

"You're just mad because you're a tar baby faggot. Dick sucker!"

"Kendall!" Mama said.

"See, that's what I mean," Kendall said. "You never say anything to Skylar."

"You're the one who's mad," Skylar said. "Nobody wants your yellow ass and green eyes anymore. Black is in, and you're just jealous the tables have turned! You little druggie!"

Kendall had considered pulling Skylar by his thick Afro, getting him into a headlock, and beating his pretty face like a drum. Skylar would definitely pull Kendall's hair back, scratch him, and bite him, like girls tended to do.

Mama pushed Skylar back into his chair and shoved Kendall toward the couch. Kendall bent over, picked up his father's stinking body, and carried him, with much difficulty, up the staircase. In the bathroom, he clicked on the light, laid Daddy on the floor, and filled the tub with hot water. Kendall unbuttoned Daddy's shirt, the tails of which were stained. He unzipped the pants, wet from urine, bunched them up, and tossed them beside the shirt. Carefully, he removed Daddy's Fruit of the Looms, the odor so strong Kendall's eyes burned.

He placed the underwear in the toilet, and flushed it, holding onto the briefs. He turned off the hot water in the tub, and lowered Daddy's limp body in it, cursing under his breath, the old man so drunk, so unconscious, he would've drowned if Kendall hadn't been there. Kendall rinsed the stained clothing in the toilet, balled them up, and placed them inside a plastic bag. The bathroom stank, as he wiped Daddy's buttocks, inner thighs, and legs with a washcloth.

He was furious with Skylar, who was probably right about the "black-yellow" issue.

With the arrival of the Black Revolution of the '60s and '70s, Kendall found himself falling out of favor with his own race. He discovered black was where it was at. Yellow was no longer mellow. It was the celebratory epoch of blackness. Black Is Beautiful! The blacker the better. Those darker-complected, who had been out of favor with white society—and, in some cases, with their own black society — were now considered superior prototypes. Skylar had fallen appropriately, comfortably in place. He was dark, his hair kinky, bushy, making for a dynamite 'fro. Kendall was no longer "privileged" because of his butterscotch skin, green eyes, and wavy hair.

Sisters were hunting down darker brothers, those with six-inch 'fros, like Skylar's. Kendall's Afro wasn't as thick as Skylar's, his hair not as coarse. He couldn't dye his complexion, for which he had once considered himself lucky. He joined militant black organizations, clothed himself in dashikis, African beads, dark glasses, and buttons that said Black Power. He read *Soul on Ice*, *The Fire Next Time*, and anything authored by Nikki Giovanni. Tonja, his steady girlfriend of two years, had even left him for a darker brother.

When he met her in his sophomore year, she had loved his wavy hair, his green eyes. He'd watch her same time, every day, passing by the statue of DeWitt Clinton outside the auditorium. She used to watch Kendall, too, he knew, though she never looked at him directly. He could tell by the way she smiled as she passed him. One day, she dropped her books — even years later, she'd swear it was an accident — and Kendall picked them up.

"Thanks," he had said.

"For what?" she asked, stooping, giving him eye contact.

"For dropping your books here."

"I didn't do it on purpose."

"Sure you didn't. What's your name?"

"Tonja."

"I'm Kendall."

"I know."

"How do you know?"

"You're a football star. Everybody knows you."

Kendall liked the sound of that. She was light-skinned, hazel-eyed, with hair that bounced on her shoulders as she walked. He never dated girls darker than he was.

"You're the best halfback Clinton High's ever had," Tonja had said, after they'd been dating several months. Kendall liked that she praised him and paid him a lot of attention.

"How do you know?" he'd asked. "What do you know about football?"

"Nothing, actually. I just know you're the best there is, and I'm lucky to be your girlfriend."

This was the girl he wanted to marry, and make pretty, light-skinned, light-eyed babies with.

But when they were seniors, Tonja got caught up in that white broads' Women's Lib crap, too, like Mama. He had had to slap her around a few times. Knock some sense into her. Sometimes, she was a stubborn bitch to deal with. Cold as penguin lips.

"You're too ornery, inconsiderate, unyielding," she'd said, a bright, college-bound girl who liked to show off her vocabulary.

So he had a few bad habits. But he was the man. He was in charge. Tonja acted as if their relationship was fifty-fifty. Like they were equal. Kendall reasoned, bottom line, if she couldn't kick his ass, how could she be boss? How in hell did she expect to share in half the power? Feminism. That was a white broad's trip. Black women had no business messing with that stuff. Women. He understood them far less than they did him.

"If we're not at my house, with your feet propped up on my coffee table," Tonja complained, "we never go anywhere. But it's different with your friends. You have all the time in the world for them. You spend more time with them than me. You never surprise me with anything."

Bitch, bitch, bitch, Kendall thought, listening to her gripes.

"But I'm here with you now, ain't I?" he said. "Be happy for that. There's a whole lotta girls out there who want me if you don't. There's no law that says I have to be with you right now, right this minute."

That's what confused him about this feminist shit. They acted like they didn't need men, and wanted to be treated equally. But then they'd start a fight with you when you didn't take them out or pick up the tab. Back and forth he and Tonja volleyed complaints, wrongdoings, shortcomings, emotional injustices. He started to tell her, at the height of his frustration, that already he was fucking several other sisters, who would pay him to fuck them. Be cool, or be by yourself, he started to say. But he "let" her win the argument. He promised her they would go to the Ice Capades the following week.

The following week came. Kendall didn't.

"I waited for a phone call, at least," Tonja said. "I thought something had happened to you. This is a case in point of your inconsiderate nature. You don't even feel bad about standing me up!"

She was getting on Kendall's nerves. His eyes were closed and his head rattled from the drugs inside him. If she didn't shut up, she was going to blow his high.

"That's another thing," Tonja said. "I don't want to go out with somebody who shoots drugs. I've asked you before to stop and you won't."

"You want me to lie? I like drugs. And I won't stop doing them for nobody. Not even you, Tonja."

"Is that all I mean to you, Kendall?"

"Tonja, I just got kicked off the football team!" he screamed. "Cut me some fucking slack! Can't we think about me for a change?"

"We always think about you."

"Get outta my face."

"Okay then, Kendall. It's quits."

"I tell you when it's quits. You're seeing Gavin, ain't you? That tar baby motherfucker. You like him because he's darker than me, don't you?"

"Kendall, please."

He grabbed her by the arm, and jerked her. She slapped him; his ears rang. He pounded her with his fists and ripped her blouse.

"You son of a bitch!" Tonja shouted. "Yeah, I'm fucking him! At least Gavin treats me like a person. Your ass has been on trial. And you have failed my test, miserably!"

Her father rushed out of the house, grabbed Kendall by the collar, and threw him down three steps, onto the sidewalk.

"You yalla motherfucker! If you ever lay a hand on my daughter again, I'll cut your balls off and frame them over my mantelpiece!"

Notre Dame's Fighting Irish cease to hold his attention. The gastric rumblings in his stomach scream for a fix. He's desperate to get back to paradise, the Shangri-la called Poppyland, the only place in the world where he feels at home, tranquil. The white witch is his only sympathizer, the only thing that understands him, helps him to feel halfway decent about himself.

Perspiration gathers on his forehead. He feels queasy, panicky, shuddering from hot and cold flashes. Skylar no longer leaves cash lying around. He begins eyeing bankable objects in his brother's townhouse, something he can trade with the Jewish pawnbroker downtown. The stereo, television, and VCR are too bulky. Last thing he needs is the neighbors witnessing a black man in dreadlocks carrying a television out of the building.

He jumps up from the sofa. In Skylar's bedroom, he rummages through a jewelry box. A Cartier watch ticks softly among the gold cufflinks, rings, chains, medallions. He wonders if Junebug, the shooting gallery owner, his supplier nowadays, is in pocket. He's in no mood to tangle with those crazy-ass Puerto Ricans on Avenue B. Having pulled a fast one on them last time, he'll steer clear of that neighborhood, fearing for his life.

Closing the door behind him, he reminds himself to call Morris Steinberg and inquire about the status of his personal injury lawsuit. The lawyer has informed him they're close to settlement. Kendall hadn't really hurt himself by slipping and falling in front of that posh, midtown restaurant. He was toasted out of his bird on smack, too stoned to feel anything, and his attorney knows it. "Back injuries are difficult to contest in a court of law," Steinberg assures him, knowing there isn't a thing wrong with Kendall's back. Kendall hopes this settlement comes through. The attorney says it will. But then, attorneys have told him that before. This is his fourth litigation attempt after intentionally injuring himself on someone's property — none of which have produced a single penny.

"It's the sickest way of earning a living I've ever heard of," Mama had said. "You should be ashamed of yourself. I didn't raise you to be that damn pitiful."

Before the Fall

HOWARD WAS RELISHING his first day back at work after a two-week vacation. Goodness gracious. How did Althea put up with it every day? Two weeks of the kids constantly fighting each other, running in and out of the house, slamming the door every ten seconds, the noise of radios, cars, open fire hydrants gushing rusty water on the bodies of screaming children, the ice cream truck's three-times-a-day visits, as it rolled down the street to the tinkly tune of "Three Blind Mice" — all this and he felt ready for a vacation from a vacation.

It was good to have the guys at work to return to. During the ten-thirty break, they were huddled around the water cooler teasing Bob, who'd gotten engaged over the weekend.

"When's the big day?"

"You sure you've thought about this?"

"Have you tested the merchandise?"

"Always test the merchandise first!"

"Get it while it's young, tender, and tight—"

"'Cause it's gonna get real old, real quick."

"Marriage ain't all roses, you know."

"Ain't that the truth?!"

"Don't believe us, ask Howard!"

They turned their attention to Howard, pointing and laughing at the scratches on his face.

"I'm taking bets," Al of Hackensack said, "that Howard's wife raked him this time with a fork. Anybody want some action?"

"Her aim's getting better every time," Marty joked.

"Better watch out, Whyte," Buddy said. Howard had never liked Buddy. "Next time it'll be your eye."

"Honestly," Howard said, chuckling. "I was shaving."

"With what?" Al said. "Cat claws?"

They howled and screamed. They hadn't seen or heard Mr. Benson calling Howard over to the side. When Howard looked up and saw him, he could tell that something was wrong.

Benson fondled objects on his desk, unable to meet Howard's gaze.

"Whyte," he said. "Your wife's here to see you."

"My wife?"

"She says she's your wife."

Howard started to rise, and was halfway out of the chair, when Benson leaned forward, the chair creaking.

"Before you go, Whyte, I'm just curious. Your wife insisted that you're a CPA with the company. Why would she think that?"

"You know how it is with women. Tell them you're a truck driver, they tell their girlfriends you're a neurosurgeon."

He'd been thrust, against his will, into fierce competition with his brothers from the word Go. His mother made sure his brothers received the finest of everything. His parents didn't seem to care what he did with his life, as long as he got himself together after college and moved out of the house. His brothers were being prepped by their parents to study law and medicine. It was Howard's decision to get a college degree, not his parents'. He chose to move out of their house for college and set up a new home in New Brunswick. Law and medicine held no genuine interest for him. Numbers were far more alluring.

As an accounting major with a year left before graduation, he felt confident about passing the CPA exam.

Then he met Althea Hutchinson.

She looked up to him, respected him; the way she clung to him when they danced, it was like she needed him. It was meant for him to be there that day, that hour, on that street corner on St. Nicholas Avenue. Watching her from across the street, he had reduced her to a Sunday afternoon motel reservation. But she proved to be different from other girls he'd dated. They didn't care about his aspirations. They looked up to him for his looks.

He spent nights at Rutgers distracted from his studies by his thoughts of Althea. He didn't want to risk losing her. Living in another city, another state, across the river, there was no telling who else was pursuing her during the long periods between his semester breaks.

When his mother and the rest of the family disapproved of Althea, he knew he was doing the right thing. He didn't like the man his mother had married, either. The best revenge against his family was to taint their bloodline with the darkest woman he could find.

He dropped out of college, considering it a recess from his studies. He had every intention of completing his degree; he had only one semester to go. He could've told Althea that, except he was ashamed to admit that he had temporarily dropped out of school to marry her. So excited about marrying a CPA — she'd told everybody — he thought she might've dumped him, called him a fake, laughed in his face.

Then came the children. First Skylar, and Kendall right behind. They bought a house. He found a job with a good firm and planned to return to school at night, if necessary, so that he could be promoted to the position he'd been preparing for. The company promised to finance his studies. With his brains and dedication, he'd do very well, making him the first Negro CPA in the company's fifty-year history.

But somehow, somewhere, he got lost. Everything happened so quickly. He hadn't anticipated that his responsibilities as a husband and father would widen the gap between him and the one semester he had still to complete.

■

It was almost four o'clock by the time Althea sauntered into the house. He had to be at his mother's by five and he was late.

"Where have you been?"

"I caught the wrong train to Sheepshead Bay."

Here's a woman born, raised, and living in New York City, he thought, and now she doesn't know what train to catch back home. He suspected she had visited a divorce lawyer. He thought he might return home from work one day and find them gone.

Sitting at the kitchen table when Althea walked in, he was already on his third whiskey. He'd only meant to have one.

Sunday morning, he took a long, aimless walk through the neighborhood, and ended up at Ebenezer Baptist Church. There music and sermon spilled out into the street and, like hands that wrapped around him, pulled him inside. The parishioners were smiling, grinning at him, as if they knew him, knew everything about him, had been expecting him.

He found an empty spot in the crowded pews, planted himself there, in an atmosphere that he was not a part of. Loud, throaty voices shouted and sang and screamed and cried and testified, and tambourines shook and popped, and feet stomped, and hands clapped, and walls rocked. Whatever spirits and forces were moving these people would not move him. Could not move him. He refused to let go. He kept the power, the spirit, at bay, protecting himself from letting go, from losing it, terrified of never getting it back...

"Is there anyone here this morning who wants to come to Jesus?"

If he had a dollar for every time he'd heard that phrase ... What was so different about it that morning? Was it the way the pastor said it? The way the congregation responded to his call? Was it written so visibly on his face, that the blue-haired old lady beside him with the safety pin holding her dress together, and the young man who sang the loudest and smiled the widest and thanked Jesus the most, knew why he was there? Knew why he had somehow understood, all along, if only on a subconscious level, that when he took his random walk to get away from his family, whose eyes he could no longer look into, that he'd end up here?

He never remembered actually standing, leaving the pew, stepping over people's toes. But suddenly the blue-haired old lady and the young man were walking him toward the altar, each grasping an elbow, the old woman humming, her eyes closed, the young man singing, crying, praising God. And yet, the force that carried him had nothing to do with either of them, or himself. He fell to his knees at the altar, looked up at the minister, who gazed back down at him, as omnipotent as God Himself. His expression was neither judgmental nor skeptical, but relieved, as he touched Howard on his forehead, the cold hand warming upon contact.

"Just let go, son," the pastor whispered, a man younger than he was. "Jesus will catch you. Come to Him as a child."

It was the first time he'd cried in over thirty years.

When he got home, he got himself a clean glass, pulled a bottle of Seagram's Seven from the cabinet, ginger ale from the refrigerator, crushed ice from the freezer, and sat at the kitchen table. For a moment, he arm-wrestled temptation, drumming his fingers on the table, knowing if he took one drink, he'd never stop. He read the label in its entirety, unscrewed the cap, sniffed the contents, sighed, and poured a glass. He poured himself a second, a third, then a fourth, promising himself to stop at the fifth, or when he could no longer read the label, or if he passed out.

He woke up Monday morning for work, hung over, his face pressed against the living room floor.

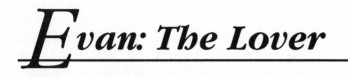

Evan: The Lover

I'M REALLY SORRY I called Skylar a nigger.

I hope he accepts my apology. I've never used that word before, at least not as an epithet. It just popped out, Skylar got me so angry. Nigger really isn't synonymous with black people. Anybody can be a nigger. The way to dull the stinging effect of it is for black people to stop getting upset when they hear it. Like Skylar. By getting angry, he empowers me and my use of it. He can take that power away. I must admit, though, I'm beginning to understand his criticisms of me. I do love black people, their passion, their exoticism, their colorfulness, but maybe I don't look beyond that. I probably felt more compassion for their struggle while watching the Watts riot on television with my dad. It's nothing intentional, I'm just an apolitical animal. There are things, problems in the world, that I don't allow myself to see.

I don't know. I'm fishing here. But knowing Skylar has brought it to my attention, given me something to examine about myself. That's just like Skylar. Life with him is anything but dull. He's the most provocative person I know, and anyone who knows him, whose life is touched by him, is lucky, blessed, because he has so much life and love and feeling and energy to give. Skylar experiences more passion watching a well-made television commercial than most people will ever feel over a loved one. He makes you know you're alive. He's the most extraordinary person I've known, and my life has undoubtedly been influenced by him. He forces me to constantly reevaluate my values, my life, my purpose, my prejudices, my feelings. He's like a drill sergeant who never lets you rest. He never lets you fall asleep, because there's too much life to live, too many things to consider.

And when Skylar loves you, you know you're loved. I've never known anyone more openly affectionate and loving with me, anywhere, in front of anybody. Sometimes, I have to remember he was that way for a long time. I often wondered if he'd get tired of paying me so much attention. And he knew exactly when to shut it off, he's so intuitive. The last time I saw him affectionate was the night I left. I could tell he wanted to stop me from leaving. And I wanted to be stopped. But everything had gotten so crazy. I'd never seen him violent and it frightened me. Was it because he's black and from Harlem? On a conscious level, I don't think so. Why am I not sure? This bothers me, this ambivalence. I'm not sure about anything anymore. Despite what he says, I don't think Skylar is either. Boy, do I miss him.

Does he miss me? It hurts to think about it, because he hasn't made an effort to contact me, though he could if he wanted to. I keep telling myself he's busy working, spending time with his family at the hospital. But then, it was my idea for us to separate from each other. So, what am I crying about? Love really confuses me. It makes me feel conflicting emotions simultaneously. It has to be the most irrational emotion there is. Theoretically, I want to get back together with Skylar. But I know that's impossible. I don't know how we could pick up and continue through this. Maybe there's no fuel left. We've outgrown each other, and we're forcing it, out of familiarity, loyalty, habit. We've been through a lot together and I can't be with him or without him. Skylar, technically, is my first love. I loved Michael before him, I think I did, but that was one-sided. Mario's staying here reminds me of Skylar. It doesn't help me forget him.

If we get back together, we'll be so smitten with each other for a while, from having missed each other — if he misses me at all — then we'll be back to where we were, like so many times before. Something will happen in the news, Skylar will get upset about it, I'll try to calm him down because I don't like watching him develop an ulcer about something he can't control, and then he'll accuse me of apathy, racism, this-ism, that-ism, and we'll end up outscreaming each other.

I've begun examining the types of black men I'm attracted to, something else Skylar brought to my attention. When I consider him, Mario, or Michael, I realize I'm hot for black men who aren't dark — although Skylar's the darkest I've been with — black men who look like white men, with so-called Caucasoid features, and who don't have large lips and wide noses. Now that I think of it, it makes me ashamed. But why should it? People like what they like, right? It probably has a lot to do with Madison Avenue telling us what our ideals of beauty are. All people of color are considered physically beautiful the more Western their features are. And yet, I've known white guys who are also exclusively into black men, yet they would never date Skylar. He's too "white" looking for them, in terms of his small nose, high cheekbones, square jawline, thin lips. They like black guys who look like ghetto, prisoner types, rags tied around their heads, sucking on toothpicks, thick-lipped, and all.

"Hello?"

"Hi, Evan!"

"Well, long time no hear. What's up, Matthew?"

"I'm great! I hear you are, too."

"I'm okay."

"What's been going on, Cabot?"

"Not much."

"Not much? New phone number, new address. Tell me, is this a trial separation or a divorce?"

I was wondering how long it would take him to get to that. The real reason he's calling.

"No, we're getting back together. We just need space right now."

"Well, while you're 'spacing,' how about if we come over for a drink Saturday night?"

"Who's 'we'?"

"Brian, Gerard, and myself — oh, I might bring a date, if that's all right."

"Sure, come on over."

"It would be great to see you, Evan. No one ever does when you're married."

"Don't start that shit, Matt. You could've seen me then, you just didn't want to—"

"Now, that's not true."

"Bullshit, it's not." I pause a moment. I'm getting angry with Matthew. I haven't talked with my good friend in months. I shouldn't be arguing with him. "I guess you spoke with Brian. He told you?"

"Told me what?" Matthew says.

"Oh, come on."

"Actually, Evan, I haven't seen Brian for weeks."

Brian is the only person I've told about me and Skylar. Matthew must have talked to him.

"Are you dating?"

"Not really," I reply, tempted to tell him about Mario, though we're not really dating. It's more like roommating and fucking.

"You should be—"

"So what time?" I say. "Saturday night, I mean."

"Eight-ish?"

"Great!"

Though I hate to admit it, that's something else Skylar's right about. He's told me about his inner detection of racism in people. He knew Matthew, Brian, and Gerard were racist, and he'd barely met them. Should I have friends like this? We should be able to have friends who don't think exactly as we do. But some things are more tolerable than others, I suppose. I don't think I'd hang around people and consider them friends if they hated gay people and wanted to see AIDS wipe us out. So why should it be any different for race?

The doorbell rings, and I cross the living room to push the intercom button and buzz them in, fastening a cufflink.

They walk in, Brian, Gerard, Matthew, Matthew's date, and another man I don't know. I take their coats, sweaters, hats, and throw them on my bed.

"Evan, you must meet Dirk," Matthew says, damn near pushing the kid toward me. It's so obvious why they've brought him.

"Hello," I say, uncomfortable and annoyed about this, as I shake his hand.

"Hi," Dirk says. "Nice place you got here."

"Thanks. What are you drinking?"

"I'll have a glass of wine," Dirk says.

I excuse myself and walk into the kitchen, Matthew and Gerard following behind me. Last night, I asked Mario to find something to do while some old friends of mine visited. Now I'm angry with myself for having done that, though Mario didn't care one way or another.

"What do you think?" Matthew says.

"He's cute, isn't he?" Gerard says.

"Who?" I say. "Matt's date, or the other guy, what's his name?" I know his name.

"Dirk," Matthew says. "Isn't he adorable? He couldn't wait to meet you."

"You guys look perfect together," Gerard says. "He's blond, you're blond. A match made in homo heaven."

"So?" Matthew asks.

"What?" I say, twisting the corkscrew into the bottle.

"What do you think? On a scale of one to ten?"

"Zero!"

"Bullshit!" Matthew says, as if he's personally wounded.

"If you don't think he's gorgeous, you're blind," Gerard says.

"You both know I don't like white guys," I say, uncorking the wine, pouring it into Dirk's glass, bits of cork floating at the top. "You've never said Skylar is gorgeous, and I never called you blind. Excuse me." I walk out of the kitchen into the living room and hand Dirk his drink. I know I've broken Matthew's and Gerard's faces, just mentioning Skylar. I can feel their eyes on me, their shoulders shrugging, eyes rolling to the backs of their heads, looking at each other, shaking their heads with pity, as if I've just refused their cure for what they consider to be my ailment. We sit down in the living room. I sit as far as possible from Dirk, who keeps giving me the eye.

"Guess what Dirk does?" Matthew says, sitting on the couch, leaning into his boyfriend.

"What?" I say, trying to look and sound interested.

"Tell him, Dirk."

"I'm a model," Dirk says.

I never would've guessed. "Skylar's making a new film, you know," I say, before I realize it's out of my mouth.

The room grows quiet. Furtive glances are exchanged. I can't stand it anymore.

"Why do you guys get so quiet when I talk about him?" I ask.

"Who?"

"You know who the hell I'm talking about."

"What was the question again?"

They start laughing, which irritates me more.

"Every time I talk about Skylar, you guys get quiet."

"No, we don't," Matthew says. "I'm sure you're imagining that."

"Am I? Why is it I haven't seen you guys in God knows how long, and now that I'm not with him, you show up at my door?"

"C'mon, Evan. You don't call us either," Brian says.

"That's because you don't accept my lover. Why should I?"

"Evan," Matthew says, patronizingly. "Can't we talk about this some other time? Gerard, Brian, and I are your friends. But Dirk and Greg ... you know."

Matthew is probably right. How does this look in front of total strangers? But I really don't give a shit.

"No," I say. "Let's talk about it now."

"Come on, Evan."

"This is getting boring."

"Is it? Then you can leave. I'm not sure I want you here anyway."

I wish I had a camera to capture their expressions. Matthew is nearly spilling his drink in his boyfriend's lap. "Well!" Matthew says.

"We won't stay where we're not wanted," Gerard says.

They grab their sweaters and coats, and leave as quickly as they came. Dirk lingers behind, his hands in his pockets, looking as if he's interested in the Romare Bearden art on my wall.

"Can I call you sometime?" Dirk asks.

"No, Dirk," I say. "I don't think that's a good idea. Nice meeting you anyway."

"Same here."

"Sorry about ... you know, all this."

"Don't apologize."

"You'd better hurry. They're waiting," I say, closing the door, relieved, satisfied, pleased with myself, wondering how proud Skylar would be of me.

West of the Hudson

SKYLAR HAD BEEN BUNKING with his brother in Kendall's bedroom. Uncle Aubrey, who had come to spend the weekend, had taken Skylar's bedroom. A sudden shake aroused Skylar from his sleep. When he woke, his sleepy eyes saw his frenzied father pulling the blankets off them. Skylar felt an unbearable heat engulfing the bedroom, he first assumed was the late-June humidity. He and Kendall were sweating profusely. Somewhere in the house, he could hear the crackling of flames. Smoke was climbing the staircase, seeping into the room, making him choke. Daddy scooped Kendall up in one arm, Skylar in the other. He could smell fresh whiskey on his father's breath. Drunk, Daddy stumbled and jerked, bumping against the wall, carrying him and his brother to safety. Skylar felt certain that Daddy would trip and they would fall down the staircase.

Skylar was now alert. As Daddy swayed and staggered on the staircase, the roaring of the fire increased. Skylar glimpsed the familiar living room melting beneath the wave of flames into something horrid and unfamiliar. Daddy kicked the front door open with his foot. He placed Skylar and Kendall outside on the sidewalk, barefoot, nearly naked in their BVDs. Althea stood on the curb, her hands locked over her mouth. Terror flickered in her eyes.

"Go get my brother!" Althea was screaming. "Hurry up, Howard! Go get Aubrey!"

Skylar, clutching his mother's bathrobe, watched the lights of neighboring homes and apartments click on in sequence. People were raising their windows, filing out into the street to watch the blaze at 4:18 in the morning. They brought blankets, slippers, pants, shirts. Althea was frantic, pulling at her hair, wiping tears, imploring her husband to see about her brother, who was obviously in a deep, drunken sleep, unaware of the fire burning in the room directly beneath the one where he slept.

"It's too late to go back into the house!" Howard shouted. "The fire has spread to the staircase. I could get trapped. I'll be risking my own life!"

His wife pounded on his chest, trying to push him aside.

"I'll do it myself," she said. "I'm not about to stand here and let my brother burn up. I'll go get him my damn self!"

Howard and Althea struggled, Howard blocking her entry.

"Woman, are you crazy? Well, go on, get burned by yourself!" Howard said, releasing her.

"Hey, Mister, you gonna let your wife go back in there?" said one of the neighbors, standing within earshot. "You should go instead."

As Howard approached the doorway, the fire leaped through the windows, smashing the glass into fragments. The sheer curtains glowed a bright orange. Sirens whined in the distance. By the time the firemen reached the front door with water hoses and hatchets, the fire was spreading rapidly. By now, Althea was hysterical.

"There's someone else inside!" Althea breathlessly explained to the fireman. Before he could ask what room the person was in, Althea fainted, her body sprawled across the concrete.

The firefighters broke several windows, only to be confronted with walls of flame. Skylar heard them shout something about entering through the roof: it was far too dangerous to go through the front door. He didn't recall much else of what happened. But he never forgot the ambulance pulling up, the siren screaming in his ear, the revolving red light bouncing off the dark houses, the paramedics, dressed in white, rolling his uncle's charred body on a stretcher into the idling vehicle.

Jersey City wasn't all it was pumped up to be. Living temporarily with his paternal grandmother on Stevens Avenue, near Garfield, while their house was being repaired, Skylar failed to understand what his father had been boasting about. Sure, it was a nice house, impressively furnished, with plenty of room to accommodate them. But the block Grandma Whyte lived on was no different from theirs in Harlem. There were tenements, winos, B-boys, rowdy drunks, who shot each other up on Friday nights in the taverns. Daddy had always painted his native neighborhood in a suburban light with grass, meadows, rolling hills. As far as Skylar could tell, Jersey City dirt was as thick, if not thicker, than what they'd left behind in Harlem. Maybe the community was once the picture of middle America, with white neighbors and manicured lawns. But not anymore. He'd heard Daddy call this White Flight.

"What's that for?" Grandma asked Skylar when he kissed her on the cheek.

"I'm just kissing you," he said, confused.

"Why?"

"'Cause you're my grandma."

"What makes you think you have any reason to kiss me? Do you normally go around kissing folks?"

Out of boredom, Skylar eavesdropped on conversations between Grandma and Daddy. Mostly, they talked about politics, colored folks, or both.

"...Garvey never did much for colored folks except stir up trouble and commit fraud," Grandma said. "Good thing they deported his big-eyed, black behind back to Jamaica where he belonged, old ugly nigger. Now take W.E.B. Du Bois, for example. That was a man with a vision. The NAACP is still alive and well today."

"Lena Horne is on television tonight with Tony Bennett, Mother," Howard said, flipping through the *TV Guide*. "That's one gorgeous colored woman—"

"Sure is. Better-looking than that Dinah Washington or Nina Simone, with their big lips and big eyes."

"Lena's more than just a pretty face, too. She was down there in Washington when King marched—"

"I'm glad she was. Better that white folks see her and Harry Belafonte than people like Dick Gregory, James Baldwin, or Nat King Cole. Now they are some African-looking things I sure don't want representing me."

Skylar was forbidden from doing this, prohibited from touching that. Games he usually played in the basement at home were out of the question. Grandma had a basement but he wasn't permitted to play in it. He could go outside, but he had to stay in front where Grandma could see him.

When Howard went to work, Grandma and Althea repeatedly fought about the boys' discipline.

"I'm tired of you running my children," Althea said. "Especially Skylar, who you seem to pick on, as if I'm not here. Like your word is final. These are my kids. I birthed them. I tell them what to do."

"And this is my house," Grandma said. "If you don't like it, you could pack your things, what little you brought, and catch the subway back to Harlem. Suits me just fine. That's your problem, gal. You don't know how to take criticism."

"And I don't think you're in any position to criticize or pontificate," Althea said, using the word she learned from Skylar.

"Skylar doesn't know how to behave himself like my other grandchildren. They're lovely, obedient kids who do as they're told. They never answer back or contradict me."

"What you really mean, is that your golden yellow grandchildren are good; tar baby Skylar is bad."

Exhausted by the constant bickering with her daughter-in-law, Grandma would wait in silence, her rocking chair creaking, until Howard got home from work. She'd tell her son, in detail, about Althea's "recalcitrant" nature. Knowing Daddy would take Grandma's side, Skylar would sneak out through the front door. Standing on the porch, facing Garfield Avenue, he could see Bayside Park bordering on the cemetery that stretched up the river, the Statue of Liberty holding her torch in New York harbor, her tarnished, weathered green back facing him, the Empire State Building towering with supreme distinction over the skyscrapers across the Hudson. He longed to have his house repaired. New York was so close, he could reach out and touch it.

■

He began having nightmares.

Surrealistically replaying the events of that harrowing June night, he'd wake up screaming when the paramedic pulled the sheet off his dead uncle's face. Kendall complained. Skylar was causing him to lose sleep. Tossing, turning, talking nonsense, kicking Kendall. Althea would rush into their bedroom and take Skylar in her arms.

After several nights of waking to her son's screams, Althea said, "Everything's all right, baby. You're safe with Mama. Tell me about the dream."

"No! I can't!"

"If I knew, I could make it go away. Come on and tell Mama."

"I don't remember much, except the house is on fire, and Mama, you float like a ghost into my room and float out. Next thing I know,

I'm outside on the sidewalk. I don't know how I got there. Then all of a sudden, two people from the ambulance roll out a stretcher. One of them pulls back the sheet, and Uncle Aubrey..."

"What? Uncle Aubrey what?" Althea asked, clinging to his every word.

"He was dead."

"But, your uncle's not dead. He's in the hospital getting better every day. You know your Uncle Aubrey wouldn't die and leave you, baby." Tears began creeping down her cheeks. She tried hiding them, pretending something was in her eyes. When she left, returning to the adjoining guest room where she slept with Daddy, she was quietly weeping. Nearly every night, Skylar had heard Mama through the bedroom wall. Sometimes she was weeping. Other times, Daddy was begging her for sex.

There was nothing to do in Jersey. Weren't many children around to play with, nobody his own age, no basement where he could practice acting. The one boy he'd befriended, he was forbidden to play with. One afternoon for lunch, he'd brought the youngster home to meet his family.

"Are you hungry?!" Grandma said to the boy.

"Yes, ma'am. Can I have a peanut-butter-and-jelly sammich?"

"'Sammich'?" Grandma repeated, wincing. "The word is 'sandwich.'" She told Howard about it when he came home. Skylar was told never to bring the boy back, or be caught playing with him.

Grandma and Daddy usually sat and talked, watching the CBS Evening News with Walter Cronkite, and Andy of Mayberry together, acting as if Mama wasn't there. Grandma made sure Daddy had a plate of food as soon as he walked through the door after work.

"Let me tell you about that negligent wife of yours, and her indolent ways," Grandma said, setting Howard's dinner before him on the table. "If I didn't start dinner, waiting all day on her, your dinner wouldn't be ready when you got home. She can't do anything right, Howard, without my supervision."

Skylar could see Mama was just as weary with the living situation as he was. She had done everything in her power to accommodate the old woman, cleaning her house, washing and ironing, cooking most of the meals.

But when Daddy's brothers and sister came to visit with their spouses and children, Grandma nearly ignored Howard, making even Skylar feel embarrassed and ashamed for his father.

"Despite the progress of the Race, the NAACP notwithstanding, colored people have always hated each other's guts."

"I know. Negroes are the most divided people on the face of the earth. They spend too much time opposing each other on differences, rather than uniting on common goals and issues."

"There's a whole lot they could learn from Jews."

"Why are you all saying, 'they'?" Howard said. "Aren't we—"

"Keep quiet, Howard," Grandma said. "Listen to your brothers and learn something. They know what they're talking about. They have advanced degrees, and they don't drink up their salaries."

After several beers, Grandma started mourning her late husband, as the smell of barbecued chicken and ribs filled the backyard, black smoke rising from the pit. Skylar's aunts and uncles — who, Mama said, never visited Grandma except on holidays — silently ignored her. No one attempted to console her, not even her daughter. No one except Howard.

"Why didn't you become an attorney or doctor, like your brothers? You've ended up a pitiful drunk instead. Your brothers are all living high and well, and look at the predicament you're in with your wife and two boys living in Harlem, of all places."

Skylar wondered how she could jump from missing her late husband to chiding her son for not getting a law or medical degree.

"This beer is running right through me," Grandma said, heading for the bathroom. Howard guided her to the stairs. "Leave me be," she insisted. "I'm no invalid. I can find the bathroom myself, as I've been doing for almost thirty years without your help, thank you."

That week, Althea had to travel into the city to meet with insurance underwriters and check the status of their home repair. Skylar and Kendall remained in Jersey, though Skylar pleaded to go with her. He didn't want to see the house, but he wanted to get away from Grandma for a while.

If theatrical performances delighted Nanna, he thought he could win Grandma over as well with a recitation from a Langston Hughes poem he knew by heart. As he uttered the first lines, Grandma's eyes were glued to the soap opera.

"Sit down here with me and keep your lips shut."

During a commercial break, she reached forward, turned down the volume, and faced him.

"What really happened to cause that fire?"

"I don't know," Skylar said. "I just remember waking up, Daddy pulling us out of bed, and him rushing and carrying me and Kendall down the stairs, that's all—"

"I know all that. How did it get started?"

"I don't know."

"Then why are you having nightmares about it?"

"I don't know. Because it scared me."

"I'd be willing to bet that that alky father of yours fell asleep with a cigarette in his mouth."

Skylar said nothing. He had his own secret thoughts about the origin of the blaze. He wasn't about to confide them to her. She'd be the last person he'd tell.

Each day, he found himself wishing for Nanna. He ached for her smiles, her sweet disposition, her rewards of rice pudding. He missed her hugs, her kisses, the aroma of food on her neck. Every day, he begged Mama to take him to visit Nanna, who was separated from him by the Hudson River. Nanna liked to laugh. Grandma grunted and complained. Nanna planted small surprises — cupcakes, nickels, red licorice — in places where she knew he'd find them. Grandma slapped his hand when he reached inside her refrigerator.

"This is not your home," Grandma said. "You have to ask for things, like you have some manners. Didn't that mother of yours teach you any manners? Nothing in my house belongs to you."

He loathed the old lady. He hardly knew her, and what he did know of her, he liked even less. He prayed their house would be repaired ahead of schedule. And when Althea returned from her four-hour trip into the city, which to Skylar seemed like four days, it appeared he'd been granted his wish.

Mama came home smiling. First time he'd seen her smile since before the fire. Anxious about her brother's condition, she visited him at the hospital every chance she got. She burst through the door grinning, her arms opened wide, embracing him and Kendall. She kissed them repeatedly on the foreheads and cheeks.

"We'll be back home before you know it."

Skylar felt it didn't matter to Kendall.

"You like staying with Grandma, don't you?" Skylar had asked Kendall the week before.

"It doesn't matter," Kendall replied. "I kind of like being in a strange neighborhood, making new friends in Jersey."

That evening, about the time Howard arrived home from work, Althea received a telephone call.

"I wanted to be the one to call you, Thea," her mother explained, her voice cracking.

"What's wrong, Mama?" Althea said, her stomach tightening. "Aubrey all right? ... Is he? ... Mama?"

"The Lord done took your brother this afternoon about three-thirty," her mother said, sniffling. "I wanted to wait awhile before telling you. I know, better than anybody, how close he was to you ... and Skylar."

*F*riday Night, 1969

"ARE YOU HAVING PROBLEMS meeting girls?" Howard said to Skylar in a drunken slur. "Maybe you're approaching it all wrong. What do you usually say to a girl when you first meet her?"

"The first thing I ask, Daddy, is if she has any brothers."

Howard seemed to sober up. Althea dropped the glass she was drying, shards scattering across the kitchen floor.

"What'd you say?" Althea asked.

Skylar walked away, headed toward the staircase. Howard ran after him, grabbed him by the back of his pants. Skylar broke his father's grip.

"What's the problem?! Huh?!" Skylar shouted. "For sixteen years, you've been calling me a sissy, a faggot, a creampuff! Why're you so goddamned surprised?!"

"Skylar, now," Althea said, rushing into the living room where they stood, wiping her hands on the dish towel. "Don't you take the Lord's name in vain. You're not that damn angry!"

Howard pushed at Skylar, his drunken, rubbery body unsteady.

"What's this shit?" Howard said, the sour liquor on his breath making Skylar turn his head. "You've told me a lot of things in your day, boy, but you can't be telling me you take it up the ass ... Look at me when I'm talking to you!"

"I would look at you! Except you smell like a distillery! All gay men don't take it up the ass! That makes about as much sense as all black people being lazy and shiftless!" He turned to Althea. "Mama, please tell me the truth. You've never lied to me in my life, so tell me the truth. He's not my real father, is he?" he said, poking Howard in the chest. "There's no way he could be my real father! Tell me; I won't hold it against you!"

Howard swung at him but Skylar dodged, and came back with a crashing left hook to the jaw. Howard tilted backward, landed on the floor, disheveled and stunned. Skylar stood over him.

"I told you the next time you tried that you'd be sorry."

Althea threw herself between them, pushing Skylar aside, helping Howard off the floor. Skylar walked away, and headed for the staircase.

"Get out of my house, you faggot!" Howard yelled. "Don't you ever come back again! You can live on the streets for all I care!"

"That's your whole problem," Skylar said, coolly. "You've never cared, period!"

He was supposed to be joining friends for the Roberta Flack concert at the Fillmore East. Now he didn't know what to do with himself, though he knew he was in no mood for anyone's concert. He felt dangerously hyper, so charged and flustered that he could hardly speak. Malice and anger and violent thoughts raged inside him. Fathers and sons. Sons and fathers. He walked several blocks in an attempt to cool off.

He stopped at a telephone booth and called Sugar and Gypsy, two part-time transvestites he knew who also lived uptown. They agreed to meet at the subway at eight-thirty.

When Sugar and Gypsy arrived, he hardly recognized them. He'd never seen them as men. They were carrying duffel bags, their eyebrows plucked, fingernails painted.

"Why aren't you in drag?"

"We will be," Sugar said.

"Watch us," Gypsy said, and winked.

They descended into the murky subway, and waited for the express at the far end of the platform. Upon boarding, they moved to the last car, which was empty. As the train pulled out of the station, zooming down Manhattan island, Sugar and Gypsy unzipped their duffel bags.

"We need your help."

In the privacy of the last car, Sugar and Gypsy slipped into shabby L'eggs panty hose, tawdry dresses, slingback toe-out spike heels that they called come-fuck-me pumps, along with wigs, anklets, G-strings, girdles, stuffed brassieres. Skylar helped zip them up, straighten out the wigs, patch up stocking runs with clear nail polish. Using the subway windows as mirrors, they applied Revlon, Maybelline, and Coty to their eyes, lips, and silicone cheekbones. By the time the train reached Grand Central Station, and commuters packed in, standing room only, Sugar and Gypsy were two floozy-looking women.

∎

The Village was humid and sticky, and spilled over with summer tourists. A long line of them stretched from Trude Heller's at Ninth Street, along the Avenue of the Americas, turning into Eighth Street. Beyond the Bon Soir at the corner of MacDougal, Skylar could see his friends openly kissing one another, flaunting their sexuality, harassing the busload of out-of-towners. While Skylar's friends fondled each other, the tourists snapped photographs with 35-millimeter cameras and flashbulbs. He had to laugh. Coming to the Village with Sugar and Gypsy made for a more jovial mood. Challenging his father, acknowledging his sexual orientation once and for all, running away from home, made him feel like a man.

At the corner, his cronies greeted one another, slapping each other with the gay high-five handshake, snapping fingers, air-kissing both cheeks.

"Hey, Miss Thing!"

"All right, girlfriend."

"Work it, baby. You look fab!"

"Oooooh, Miss Thing, you're truly looking tired, girl. You give us nothing!"

"That's okay, Miss Two, 'cause you give us less!"

Several of them, shirts tied to bare midriffs, jumped a fierce game of double-dutch rope.

"Two-four-six-a-ten-a-two-four-six..."

Leaning against parked cars in front of Orange Julius, catching a breath of fresh air outside Bon Soir, the stuffy, claustrophobic hole-in-the-wall, a trio harmonized Smokey Robinson's "Ooo, Baby, Baby" a cappella. Skylar joined in the chorus, lending a hand with the do-wops and the la-las. Straight boys patrolled on foot up and down the street. Furtively, they huddled with each other, laughing, snickering, pointing. One of them jumped into the double-dutch rope, and pushed Gilbert, Skylar's friend, against the iron railing outside Capezio. Gilbert turned, regrouped, and slugged the straight boy in the face as his friends jumped Gilbert. They, in turn, were jumped by Skylar and his friends, Bon Soir patrons, and anybody else in the mood for a Friday night ass-kicking. A police siren sounded from the direction of Washington

Square. The straight boys broke loose and ran toward Mercer Street, knocking down passersby in their zigzag paths.

"Yeah, motherfuckers!" Gilbert yelled, clenching a fist in the air. "You better go on over to the Electric Circus! You don't belong over here! This is our turf! Come back and you'll get your asses kicked again!"

1:00 a.m. Skylar was strolling back toward the BS from Nathan's. With Gypsy and Miss Bambi, another drag queen, they had gotten a late-night snack of frogs' legs and french fries. They walked around the corner, sat in the doorway next to Capezio. As they finished their snack, licking their fingers of ketchup and spicy frogs' leg sauce, Miss Bambi pulled out a glassine bag and a nail file. She broke the tape, held the bag in the light, plucked it with her middle finger until the white powder settled. Dipping the file into the bag, she poised it beneath Skylar's nostril.

"What is it?" Skylar asked, though he knew.

"Courage," Miss Bambi replied, deadpan.

He sniffed it. Took a second hit in the other nostril. He'd never touched the stuff before. Had never wanted to. It was running rampant in his neighborhood and school. Kendall, he knew, had experienced heroin; "Doo-jee," Kendall called it. He'd been getting high for about a year. Once, he offered Skylar a blow, which he flatly refused. But sitting on the MacDougal Street doorstep with Sugar and Miss Bambi, he felt, anything goes. He needed something, liquor, chemicals, anything, to distract his mind from striking his father, and replaying it over and over in his head, ashamed, yet vindicated.

The bitter taste of the heroin-and-quinine cut dripped like a faucet leak down the back of his throat. It tasted rancid. He sipped his soda as a chaser. Cleaned his nostrils of the caked powder that hadn't dissolved. When he stood up to throw his trash into the receptacle that reminded him to Keep New York City Clean, an instant rush of enveloping warmth flowed through his body, making him feel dreamlike, euphoric.

Without warning, Skylar just blurted it out. He told his friends about his father, what had gone down in the house before he left.

"I've decided to run away from home. I need a place to stay."

"You could stay with me, chile," Miss Bambi assured him. "I keep a room at the Earle Hotel down the street."

Skylar smiled, knowing his friends wouldn't let him down. He closed his eyes, leaned his head back against the door frame.

"I told my parents I'm gay," Skylar said, his voice dropping from the smack. "I probably shouldn't have done it the way I did, but what the fuck! My father was getting on my nerves. I know I hurt my mother. But she couldn't have been all that shocked. 'Mothers always know their children better than anybody,' Mama always says. So, there's no reason for her to act surprised—"

Suddenly, people shot around MacDougal from Eighth Street, out of nowhere. Excited, panting, they could barely speak.

"Stonewall's being raided!"

"Gay boys are in the street fighting the police back!"

"Come on! We need all the people we can find!"

Folks stampeded out of Bon Soir. Skylar, Sugar, and Miss Bambi rushed with them, cascading through the heavy traffic sweeping north on the Avenue of the Americas, drivers swerving, leaning on their horns.

When they reached Stonewall, a few blocks away, gay men were striking back at the police. Hordes of squad cars and paddy wagons idled in the street. Angered patrons hurled rocks and bottles at the crowd of policemen. Threats and warnings blared from bullhorns. Glass shattered, heads were cracked with billy clubs. Revolving patrol car lights flashed and bounced off the buildings. Dispatch radios hissed with static. Skylar and his friends threw bottles, garbage cans, milk crates, anything they could get their hands on. Skylar noticed the police weren't using firearms the way they had during the Summer of '64 race riots. He guessed they assumed they didn't need guns to subdue a bunch of queers. This reminded him of Fag Day at Clinton High. An officer on horseback, a poor imitation of John Wayne, began firing shots into the air. The horse reared, then came crashing back down to the pavement. When Skylar heard the gunshots, it was time to go. He grabbed Sugar and Miss Bambi by the arms, ducking down the alley leading into narrow Gay Street. Last thing he saw was the army of police receding, as the rioters shouted in unison, "Out of the closet and into the streets! Out of the closet and into the streets!"

Saturday morning sun shone down on them from over Brooklyn. On a bench in Washington Square Park, Skylar, Sugar, and Miss

Bambi marveled at the previous night's riot. They felt proud, they agreed, of having fought the N.Y.P.D.

"I got busted at Stonewall once," Miss Bambi said. "They threw my ass in that squad car so quick, girlfriend, my wig fell off."

"Really?" Skylar said. "Then what happened?"

"Nothing," Miss Bambi said.

"Didn't they take you to the station and book you?" Sugar asked.

"Nuh-uh, Miss Thing, chile," Miss Bambi said. "I ate my way out of that one."

Skylar and Sugar laughed.

"You know," Miss Bambi continued, "all last night, I didn't turn one damn trick. Friday's my best night, especially during summer, with the tourists. If I wasn't forced to throw bottles and garbage cans at Stonewall, I could've been working. What's a girl to do?" she said, sighing, without a trace of laughter. "Oh-oh. Though I see it's not too late."

Sugar and Skylar turned to see what she was staring at: a middle-aged man wandering aimlessly near the arc at Fifth Avenue.

"Okay, look," Miss Bambi said, excitedly. "I'll walk up to him like I'm a real woman. They never know the fuckin' difference anyway, and most times, they don't give a shit. I'll distract the john by sweet-talking him, like I'm gonna take him to my hotel room. Skylar, you come up behind him, snatch his wallet, and meet me over near NYU. Sugar, you keep watch. Make sure Mary and Alice" — their pet names for police — "ain't nowhere to be seen."

"Uh-uh," Skylar said. "I don't know nothin' 'bout birthin' no babies."

"Sky, if you wanna be a true runaway, honey, callin' yourself roughin' it in the Village, you gotta learn survival," Miss Bambi said, her tone impatient. "Unless you got a steady job somewhere, you'll truly be peddlin' much ass on the street or boostin' from department stores or rippin' off johns, take your pick, girlfriend. Remember, Miss Thing, I said you could stay with me but I won't support yo' ass. As I recall, me an' you ain't even fuckin'. Now, where was I? ... oh yeah. After we hit this mother, we all do a mad Bangla-dash up Fifth, okay?"

Skylar agreed to be lookout, nothing more. He strolled around the park nonchalantly, hands in his pockets, whistling tunelessly, glancing up and down the street. He watched Miss Bambi approach the unsuspecting man, Sugar sneaking up from behind. He could see the man grinning, stroking Miss Bambi's copper hair. Quietly and unobtrusively, Sugar knelt down behind the man on her knees. Miss Bambi pushed the man, who fell backward over Sugar. Miss Bambi reached into his pockets, grabbed his wallet. Skylar couldn't believe he was an accomplice to this. The man struggled for his wallet, he and Miss Bambi engaging in a tug-of-war. Miss Bambi reached into her shoulder bag. Skylar couldn't make out what was in her hand. It looked to him as if she were punching the man in the stomach. Finally, the man let go, holding his stomach, and doubled over.

"You fucking nigger bitch!"

Miss Bambi and Sugar joined Skylar under the arc and broke into a dash up Fifth Avenue.

"What happened?" Skylar asked. "What did you do to him?"

"I had to stick the motherfucker!" Miss Bambi said.

Skylar thought she was bluffing until he saw the fresh blood dripping off her stiletto.

"Why'd you hurt him?" Skylar asked. "Is he dead?"

"Why?" Miss Bambi asked. "Why you so fuckin' concerned? Miss Thing, fuck him! They been doin' it to us for years! Serves their asses right! Especially after Stonewall last night!"

"You still didn't have to stick him."

"And, Miss Thing, I don't have to let you stay with me either, do I?" Miss Bambi shook a curl out of her eye, and the wig moved. "Now, y'all listen. In case somebody saw it, we should split up and meet at Bosco's."

"I thought I was staying with you at the Earle," Skylar said.

"Not now, fool! What's wrong witchu, girlfriend? You want us to get popped? We'll come back this afternoon."

Miss Bambi pulled the thick wad of twenties from the billfold and tossed the wallet into a trash can. At the corner of Eleventh Street, they split up. Miss Bambi repeated that they would reunite at Bosco's, an after-hours gay bar in Harlem.

By the time Skylar boarded the subway alone, glancing suspiciously over his shoulder, he'd decided the night had been far more than he'd bargained for. Fighting with straight boys, snorting heroin, battling police at the Stonewall, contributing to a mugging and stabbing, fleeing Washington Square for his life, convinced him that running away from home was not the answer. He couldn't see himself committing lewd acts to eat. Instead of getting off the subway at Bosco's, he went home. He strolled up the subway stairs into the blinding Saturday morning sunlight, the same subway stairs he'd descended around eight-thirty the night before.

Kendall: The Brother

KENDALLJAMESWHYTE!KendallJamesWhyte!KendallJamesWhyte!

Mama called me that so much, for a while I thought they were all my first name, and that Kendall was a shortened version. From the time I could talk, I stayed in trouble with Mama.

Growing up in a divided home is a strange experience. Mama and Daddy seemed to be in competition over how they raised us, like Skylar was Mama's only child and I was Daddy's. I'm sure Daddy did what he thought was right — at least I'd like to think so. I hate to think of myself as the lamb Daddy sacrificed so he could make a point, whatever the fuck that point was. I'm not sure. I've never really known why I was his favorite. On the surface, you could say it was because I'm the lighter-skinned child, and Daddy's so fucking color-conscious, like the rest of his sorry-ass family. But it goes beyond that. It must. How could anyone treat Skylar the way he did? My brother has always been a better person than me. No shit. And that made it more difficult to be a bastard to Skylar, as Daddy wanted me to be.

Growing up under the roof of a tyrannical parent who treats you like gold ... I was probably as afraid of Daddy as Skylar was. Yet knowing that his anger would almost never be directed at me made life easy, even if it gave me a distorted view of the real world. As a child, I considered myself lucky. I was light-skinned, green-eyed, wavy-haired, and spoiled. I had it made. Now when I think about how my father ruined me, it almost makes me despise him and feel sorry for him at the same time. I never hated Mama, but growing up, I don't think I liked her very much. She was trying, as much as she could, to avoid my turning out this way. I guess that's what she was doing. She saw how Daddy was creating a monster out of me and tried to stop it. I thought she was giving me a hard time, saving her sweetness for Skylar, who, I guess, was her only child, in a way. If I were a parent with a kid like me, I'd probably keep my foot in his ass. When I think about my pugnacious attitude, something a teacher once called me, and the opportunities I lost, I wish Mama had been able to take control of me. Then maybe, I wouldn't be fucked up today.

I really love Mama, though I don't think I've ever told her. I probably haven't showed it much, either. I should. It could be her in that hospital, instead of Daddy, who I don't really hate, but I'm so angry with him, I can't get past it. I try to blame Mama for my life, when in truth, I know it's not her fault. I could've grown up to be a lot worse — which is nearly impossible for me to imagine — if it hadn't been for her. No longer do I believe that she favored Skylar. It was just a matter of him being the good, obedient kid who listened to her, and made her proud. She could do absolutely nothing with me. And I think any parent who is forbidden from disciplining their own child is affected by that shit somehow.

I love Skylar to death, I swear to God, and always have. When I was a kid, I would pretend to Daddy that I didn't like my brother as much as I did. That was probably the beginning of my understanding that something was fucked up in my house. Daddy never came out and said for me to hate Skylar, but he never encouraged me to love him, either, that's for goddamn sure. What the fuck did Skylar ever do to him? I used to wonder as I got older. Skylar, to a point, seemed to kiss his ass to get along with him. The more he puckered up his lips, the farther away Daddy moved his narrow ass out of Skylar's reach.

I felt sorry for him, yet I was glad as hell it wasn't me. Of the two of us, I'll bet I was more frightened of our father. I was just better at concealing it. I've never been more proud of anybody or anything than Skylar. When it looked like I was turning out to be a fuckin' loser, I channeled my hopes through Skylar, and in some way, lived and still live through him. Ain't it some strange-ass shit that our father gave everything he had to fulfill my dream? And still, Skylar went on to accomplish his goals by himself, so to speak. If that ain't some indication of serious character and determination, I don't know what the fuck is.

When I lived with Skylar and Evan, in the beginning, before I got jealous of my brother's relationship with his lover, I did everything

I could to please Skylar. I did the dishes, washed clothes, took clothes to the cleaners, mopped floors, washed windows, made beds, changed sheets, folded laundry, reshelved counters, emptied garbage, did some grocery shopping, anything I could think of. And he'd never asked me to do a damn thing. Skylar, whose career had gone through the roof, had too much else to take care of, so I did what I could. I felt like I was serving my brother, assuming it was my duty to care for him, and take care of the little details that he shouldn't have to be bothered with.

It's kind of like football. When I carried the ball, it was the responsibility of every other teammate to get me down the field and over the goal line as easily as possible. If Coach Pettiford knew the things I did for my brother, he'd understand that I'm more of a team player than he gave me credit for. And when Skylar came home, saw what I'd done, and thanked me with a big smile on his face, I felt like I had helped him carry that ball. It became one of my few sources of self-esteem. I shit you not.

Now Evan? I could take or leave that white boy. I've never really liked his ass, and don't to this day, but I do think he's good to my brother and takes care of him. And I guess I began to fuck up while I was living with them, because Evan threatened my place with my brother — or at least I thought so. Skylar paid him so much attention, it was difficult getting used to it. I had never had to share my brother before Evan. I even thought I'd be glad if they split up, which they since have. But I'm not happy about it. Skylar doesn't think I know Evan left. Mama slipped and said something. I guess Skylar didn't tell me because he didn't want me to think I could stay with him indefinitely. I must admit though, the house is a bit empty and quiet without Evan running around, going through his neurotic, white-boy changes.

I've never really liked faggots — I mean, gay people. I can't understand how men could be attracted to one another, or two women fuckin'. I've heard it often enough, and Skylar has told me it's not a decision you make, but somehow I do think it involves a decision, on some level.

"Did you decide to be straight?" Skylar had asked me.

"No. I'm naturally—"

"See?"

"What?"

"It came to you naturally. You just said so yourself. Well, Kendall, it's no different for me."

"Bullshit!"

"Hey, Kendall, think about it. I'm already black, right? What makes you think I want to give society another reason to hate me without knowing who, and not what, I am?"

"I never thought about it that way."

"Maybe you should."

I have thought about it. I still don't feel comfortable about fa—gay people, but I make an exception for my brother, I'm sure. I don't understand why they have to make themselves known, and conduct protests in the street, or march in parades during Gay Pride Week. Who the fuck cares? I mean, if that's your thing, so be it. But I don't need it shoved down my throat just because somebody likes to get butt-fucked. Well, I shouldn't say that. Skylar has told me a million times, all gay men don't get fucked. He's said it so much, I believe he's one of them which, though I know it's weird, makes him less gay than, say, Evan, who probably does take it up the ass.

Skylar even explained to me the parallels between homophobia and racism. While I can appreciate that, I still can't help how I feel about being around other naked men. It's got to be one of the most fuckin' uncomfortable feelings in the world. If I see a man's johnson get hard, and nobody's in the room but me and him, shit, I panic like a motherfucker, like most straight men, I'm sure. I'm not trying to take away gay people's rights, don't get me wrong. I just don't want them to parade their shit around me, is all I'm saying. Be what you want to be, as long as it's behind closed doors and I don't have to see it. As for that bisexual bullshit, the same goes for those dudes, too. You either suck dick or you don't.

"Skylar."

"What?"

"You better watch out, man. Be careful."

"About what?"

"AIDS."

"I know."

"You know what?"

"To be careful."

"Good."

"Why're you so worried about me?"

"'Cause you're my brother. And I don't want you to catch no fuckin' AIDS."

"Like you won't?"

It was the first time I'd thought about it that way. I guess I was still considering it a gay disease at the time. Secretly, I got tested. After waiting about ten days, assuming my concern was in vain, since I never took it up the ass, never sucked dick in my life, the results came back positive. I'm HIV-positive. But I'll never tell anyone that — especially Mama and Skylar. Not until then did I start using my own needles.

■

Finally! I can't fuckin' believe it!

Just like Steinberg promised, the settlement has come through. I just left his office. Steinberg had me sign the appropriate papers, a million of them motherfuckers. Then he took his percentage, and even cashed the check for me, since I don't have a bank account. I could make a new beginning with a few thousand dollars. It could be the break I need. I'm walking down Broadway, on my way to the subway, grinning my ass off. Hey, what the fuck! I can take a taxi, can't I? I'm so used to riding the subway and walking, I've forgotten what it's like to flag down a cab. And I better do it now, while it's daylight, while one of these racist fuckers will still stop for me. Black people can't get cabs in New York City no more, especially black men, especially at night.

"Taxi!" I yell, and whistle. I'm in such a good mood, man. I always am when I'm on my way to get high. But I'm going to give Mama some money, save some, maybe give it to Skylar, who'll hold it for me — oh, shit! I have to replace Skylar's watch, too.

"Avenue B," I instruct the cabbie. "No, fuck that. Take me to 116th."

When I see him getting ready to protest, I flash a fifty-dollar bill at him, slip it through the plastic door in the divider, and it shuts that white boy the fuck up.

I can't make up my mind. I shouldn't go to Avenue B, the Puerto Rican turf, where I pulled a slick one on them a few weeks ago. If they see me, they'll probably break my kneecaps with a bat. Fuck that. Let me go on up where the brothers are. Both neighborhoods are treacherous, but somehow I feel safer uptown.

I get out of the cab, pay him, the fuckin' punk, and make my way toward the shooting gallery.

I walk up the stairs and knock on the door. No one answers. This is weird. I knock again. And again. The locks snap open, the bolts unlock, the door cracks. The dude standing behind it I've never seen before.

"Junebug ain't here, man," he whispers.

"Where is he?"

"He got popped, man. This place is hot, so you better stay away for a while."

"But what about—"

He slams the door shut before I can finish. I walk back down the stairs. Shit! When I ain't got no fuckin' money, Junebug's always around, always in pocket. Now I got plenty of cash money, and it's all about, Who do I have to fuck to spend my money with them?

I pass two brothers on the street who I've never seen before.

"Yo, man," one of them says to me. "You just left Junebug's, man?"

"Yeah," I say, wondering who the fuck they are, though I know they ain't the pohlice.

"We know where something else is," the other one says, a frog-eyed motherfucker.

"You do?" I say. "Uptown?"

"Yeah. Up on 135th. We headed that way. You could hang with us."

We begin walking north on Lenox Avenue.

"Wait," I say. "Let's catch that gypsy cab."

We climb in and climb out at 135th Street. I pay the cabbie with another fifty. That's all that seems to be in this envelope Steinberg gave me, which I have stuffed in my pocket. The two brothers, whose names I don't even know, have seen the money I have. They turn around and look at each other. Nice fuckin' going, Kendall. I haven't had no real money in so long, I've forgotten how to act with it, especially around strangers, especially around strangers who are fuckin' junkies.

I follow them to a second-floor apartment. They knock on the door.

"Who is it?" a woman's voice says from the other side.

"It's me," one of them says.

"You alone?" the woman says.

"No. I got two people with me."

The door cracks open, just enough to transact the deal.

"What y'all want?"

"Give us three balloons—"

"No," I say. "Make that ten."

The brothers look at each other. The woman passes the balloons through the crack, and we pass the money, theirs in singles, mine in fifties.

"Can we do it here?" I ask.

"Hell, no," she says. "This ain't no fuckin' gallery, man."

"We know a place," one of the brothers says.

"Good," I say. "Let's go."

They take me to an abandoned building. I've been in many. But not this one. We walk through the front door, which looks as if it's about to crumble any minute. We step over piles of garbage, broken glass, wood, dog shit, used Pampers, bricks, you fuckin' name it. We walk toward the back of the hallway where there's a steady drip of water falling through the ceiling. A beer can moves. I turn and watch a rat flee into what used to be somebody's first-floor apartment, where the faucet still works. We use it to cook up the dope.

Being greedy, I cook up not one, but two bags, watching the steam rise from the cooker, my stomach bubbling with anticipation. Squatting on the raggedy-ass floor, I tie up my arm with my belt.

"Yo, blood," one of them says. I hardly hear him. I'm too into what I'm doing. "We don't have no works."

"Could we borrow yours?"

"No, man," I say. "That ain't too fuckin' healthy, you know."

"We know. We'll sterilize them after you, if that's okay."

"Hey, man," I say. "I warned you. After that, you can keep them. I don't want them back."

I get a hit. The blood slowly rises in the dropper, mixing and swirling with the liquefied dope, like a fuckin' lava lamp. I loosen the belt around my arm. Press the nipple and boot the blood back into my veins. My face becomes itchy, my mouth dry, and I can feel it sagging at the corners. The two men become four, their voices fading, and my head feels hot. I pull the needle out of my vein, try to stand up, which is nearly impossible, since this rush is seriously kicking my ass, and I feel the dropper slip from my hand and hear it hit the floor...

When I come to, I'm in a hospital.

I'm still pretty fucked up and try to lift my head. They have me hooked up to all kinds of intravenous shit, which reminds me of Daddy.

"What the fuck happened?" I ask the nurse, who's checking my chart, pretending she doesn't hear me. "Did you hear me?"

"You don't know what happened?" she says, without facing me. "You overdosed, sir."

"How long have I been here?" I say, getting excited.

"Don't get yourself worked up," she says. "Take it easy."

"Where's my money?"

"What money?" she asks, her eyebrows raising.

"I had almost four thousand dollars in my pocket! What the fuck you mean, what money?!"

"Sir, when you were admitted, we found no money on you. Just your identification and a few subway tokens. Now get some rest."

Where's My Forty Acres and My Mule?

"OKAY, NOW WHERE WERE WE?" Brett What's-His-Face is saying, flipping back notebook pages with his thumb. "Ahoy, let's see, here we are. Two or three sessions ago, you were going to discuss dedicating the Golden Globe to the memory of your Uncle Aubrey."

"You sure?" Skylar says. "I thought we covered him three sessions ago—"

"Well, not exactly. You said, and I quote, 'The seed to act was always inside me, and my uncle cultivated it,' unquote. Tell me about that."

"What's to tell? I think my uncle was a frustrated performer and—"

"Excuse me," Brett says, thumbing back a few more pages. "Please hold your thought. But I understand you're having difficulty completing a scene which involves fire. I'm told it's holding up production—"

"It's not holding up production. We're working around that scene, leaving it for last, that's all—"

"Okay, I got my wires crossed. You afraid of fire?"

"As much as anybody, I guess. Just that when I was about, oh, nine or ten or so, our house caught fire in the middle of the night. It's the single most traumatic event in my life. To wake up with the house on fire is quite a jarring experience—"

"Was anyone injured?"

"Yes."

"Who?"

"Uncle Aubrey."

"Tell me about it. Is it painful—"

"I just told you it was the single most traumatic event in my life. Yes, it's very painful. There wasn't enough time to get him out of the house. When my father tried to rescue him, the fire was out of control," Skylar says, his voice wavering, a tear crawling down his cheek. "Could you switch that off for a moment?"

Brett obliges him, and signals for the photographer to back off. The three of them sit quietly a moment. Brett lights a Marlboro, offers one to Skylar, who refuses.

"So," Brett says, flicking an ash to the October wind. "Suffice it to say that the filming of this scene resurrects unpleasant memories. Is that correct?"

"Yes, very much so. When I'm supposed to charge through the flames to rescue my father in the film, I don't see my father. I see ... Uncle Aubrey, I guess, lying there helpless."

"But you don't think that, as an actor, the experience might help you to — how can I explain it? Break through, or face the tragedy and exorcise yourself of it, overcome it, so to speak?"

"That's an interesting thought, but easier said than done, I'm afraid ... Anyway, that's the abridged version, which is pretty much, in a nutshell, why I dedicated my first major acting award to him."

"Speaking of awards, how did you feel about not winning the Oscar earlier this year? Were you surprised, hurt, disappointed?"

"Actually," Skylar says, sniffling, "I feel that I did win, we all did. I know that sounds cliched and corny, but it's true. From the time the nominations were made public in February, everyone expected the sentimental favorite to win."

"As in, he didn't deserve to win, except for him having been around Hollywood since our parents were infants?"

"No, not at all. I think he gave an outstanding performance, probably the performance of his career. He was quite deserving, actually. I mean, there I was, one-fifth of a loaded category of some of our finest, seasoned, veteran actors. Dark-horse nominee or not, there's nothing disappointing about that. Besides, the awards aren't what's important, the work is. But having my shot at the big one was nice. It was a kick."

"Were you pleased with your work?"

"In the film, you mean?"

"Yes."

"Yes ... I was. What we did together was pretty impressive, I think. But I don't view it in terms of my work. I think an actor gets into trouble when he or she views a film as 'my' work. I think it's everybody's work from the director to the gaffer, the best boy."

"Anybody you'd like to work with in the future? Say, Streep, DeNiro, Nicholson, or any particular directors?" Brett says, his face going blank.

"I'd like to work with all of the above, so if you're reading this, guys ... But then, how probable is that, you know, my working with Streep or DeNiro? And, why do you throw at me only the names of white actors?"

"Okay then, what black actors would you like to—"

"I'd love to work with Danny Glover, and let's see, there's C.C.H. Pounder, Rosalind Cash, and uh, what's his name, Morgan Freeman. These are fine, working actors, too."

"Do you feel now, with an Oscar nomination, a Golden Globe award, that you're in a position to call the shots?"

"I wouldn't say that. You see, my approach to Hollywood has always been one of knowing there was undoubtedly a place for me in it somewhere. I'm a born performer. Hollywood had to deal with me whether they liked it or not. And I'm pleased they liked it, don't get me wrong. But it's kind of like showing up at the back lot plantation, demanding, 'Where's my forty acres and my mule?'" Skylar says, laughing, his head falling back. Brett doesn't flinch. "Honestly, I don't believe I was born to do anything else. I grew up on movies and television in the '60s, the most exhilarating decade in my lifetime, so far. I've never known life without them, a true TV baby. I knew one day I'd get what I felt was already promised me—"

"In a fatalistic sense."

"Absolutely."

"What, specifically, made you feel that you'd one day take Hollywood by storm?"

"I didn't say I took it by storm. But *Stormy Weather* gave me the fuel I needed. It gave me belief in the possibilities. One is always hearing that blacks can't become movie stars, which they can't. But they can be actors and they do work. *Stormy Weather* taught me that, for which, again, I thank Uncle Aubrey."

"Why do you think there are no black power brokers in this industry?" One eyebrow arches, and Skylar wonders why.

"Racism, I guess. I tend to agree with William Faulkner, who said, and I'm paraphrasing, that essentially blacks have accomplished such overwhelming progress with no opportunity, that if given one, maybe we'd just take over. According to Faulkner, we could very well threaten the white man's economy, etcetera, etcetera."

"You believe that?"

"Look at sports. Who would've thought what was going to happen years down the line after an unknown black ball player was recruited by the Brooklyn Dodgers. We've damn near taken over sports. And I don't say that arrogantly. What do you think the Lakers-Celtics rivalry is about? Look what we've done in the music industry, as well. Consider this: had there been no slavery in this country, America probably would have no original music forms. Jazz is an original American music form, but more specifically, it's a black American musical heritage. Same with rock and roll. It belongs to blacks. But you can't tell that to an audience at a Springsteen or Stones concert. Elvis was nothing more than the great white hope. The true kings of rock and roll are Little Richard, Chuck Berry, Sam Cooke—"

"But we all know that—"

"No, we don't all know that—"

"I want to get back to something you said. In terms of jazz, where would you place the contribution of uh, say, a Benny Goodman or Glenn Miller or ... Gershwin even?"

"I'm not taking anything away from them, you see. Just that the baby had already been born. Their 'contribution,' as you say, had mostly to do with dressing it. Look at bebop. Bird, and Dizzy, and Coltrane, they got tired of white boys stealing licks and getting the credit for it."

"And you think that could possibly happen to Hollywood?"

"Who knows? Anything's possible. There's thousands of hungry performers out there. We're talking ravenous. Artistic hunger is nothing to tamper with."

"In an age saturated with survivals and remakes, is there any project you'd like to do — I mean, something which has already been done?"

"The classics notwithstanding — and, mind you, I consider *A Raisin in the Sun* to be as much a classic as *Twelfth Night* — I don't really know. Someone said, 'Nostalgia is the enemy of history because it tends to focus on happy times.' I find that to be very true. Nostalgia, these days, is big business. I'm more about moving on, fast-forward progress, tackling the problems that face us today. While I would love to play Othello or, um, uh ... Walter Lee Younger from *Raisin*, I'd rather play Nelson Mandela or a character in an August Wilson piece, or something like that. You know what I mean?"

"You still live in New York. Why?"

"Keeps my feet on the ground. This turning point in my career is crucial. I can't lose sight of focus. Aside from being the most fascinating city in the world, it's home. I'm a New Yorker to the marrow, born and raised here. Hollywood, L.A., are not my kinds of towns. I only work there."

"Are you presently in a relationship? Married? Kids?"

"I'm married to my career. I don't have time for relationships right now."

"You're roommates with Evan Cabot, isn't that right?"

"No, it isn't."

"C'mon, I won't make any cheap insinuations—"

"You can't. We don't live together. We're just good friends."

∎

Just yesterday, after picking up a gallon of milk, a dozen eggs, and a loaf of bread at the supermarket, Skylar was leaving the store when the tabloids caught his eye. Evan's picture, an unflattering one at that, was cover story. The headlines were calling him a ladies' man. Having broken one engagement with a soap opera star, with whom he was photographed leaving a New York restaurant, he was, according to the rag, now romantically entangled with someone else. A woman, a white woman, of all things. Skylar laughed.

Perhaps he had been too hard on Evan, knowing Evan lived for his approval. For too long, Skylar had been cast against white boys in fierce competition. Everything they wanted, he wanted. And he felt handicapped to begin with, competing, striving, surviving a structure designed specifically for white men to succeed. He had to be twice, thrice as good as they. In sports, academics, especially at Columbia, and then as an actor, his black-American-survival conditioning wasn't as easy to turn off. Yes, Evan was his lover. But Skylar also viewed him as a professional threat.

He realizes he expected too much from Evan. In the weeks of their separation, he's concluded that his being black and socially, politically conscious simply overwhelmed Evan. What could he expect from his marginally talented, pretty, blond boyfriend from South Gate, California? Whatever it was, it had been too much.

While he's sexually starved, Skylar refuses to have anyone else, or even masturbate. Nothing can tame his libido like his ex-lover. Picking up strangers would leave him empty.

"And I don't even know where he is," Skylar said to the air, walking home from the supermarket, getting caught in a thunderstorm.

And then suddenly, there was Evan a half block away. His back turned, he didn't see Skylar behind him. He was wearing the unconstructed overcoat Skylar gave him last Christmas, his collar upturned. Skylar wanted to surprise him, yet was terrified of Evan's rejection, or apathy.

Skylar started toward him, the rain coming harder, distorting his vision. He stopped. An exceptionally attractive black man appeared. He'd been inside the store where Evan was standing. The black guy said something to Evan, who replied, his lips barely moving, as if he were disgusted. Skylar wished he could hear what was being said. The black guy laughed, popped something in his mouth, thrust an arm around Evan. Then Evan stepped into the street, covering his face against the slanting drops, and flagged a yellow Checker. He held the door while his friend boarded the taxi. How gallant, Skylar thought. He never did that for me. Evan got in, collected the bulk of his sagging coat, closed the door behind him. The taxi sped off into the stream of traffic, the tires hissing over the wet asphalt. Skylar stood there, getting soaked, his spirit crushed. He watched a weathered scarlet leaf floating toward the sewer. He shivered from the cold, likening his heart to the scarlet leaf.

"I think that's a wrap," Brett says, rewinding the tape, popping the cassette out of the machine, dispersing Skylar's daydream.

"You mean, that's it?" Skylar says, yawning, stretching his arms. "We're finished?"

"After about seven or eight sessions of good transcript, I think we are. Let me say, I've enjoyed it immensely."

"Thanks for your patience."

"Well, Skylar, what can I say? It's been real." Brett stands, shakes Skylar's hand. "I wish more of my subjects could keep me awake like you. I think you'll be pleased with the cover piece," Brett says, reaching into his pocket.

"Let's hope so," Skylar says, walking away. "Nice meeting you, too."

Brett stops him, pulls a business card from his wallet, presses it into Skylar's palm.

"You'll pardon my unprofessionalism," Brett says. "But I'd like to get together sometime, maybe for dinner or something, whatever ... that is, if you don't mind."

Skylar says nothing, tucking the card in his back pocket.

"You give good interview," Brett says, winking, lighting another cigarette.

One Night, I Awoke

IS IT TRUE BLONDES have more fun?

"Can't be true," Althea said to Uncle Aubrey, mirth in her voice. "I ain't blonde, but I'm married to Howard L. Whyte, Jr., and lookit all the damn fun I'm having!"

She and Uncle Aubrey laughed so hard, she began choking on her sip of beer. Listening from his upstairs bedroom, Skylar heard Uncle Aubrey patting Mama on the back. The choking and coughing mixed with spurts of giggles told Skylar his mother was having a good time. She even sounded a bit tipsy, and Mama never drank that much. He was rummaging through what Mama called his "rat's nest" of a bedroom, searching for something he wanted to show his uncle. He found it. His *Meet the Beatles* album was stuck underneath a pile of *Encyclopedia Brittanicas*. Daddy must've hidden it there since he complained when Skylar played it. He pulled it from beneath the heavy books, wiped the dust off with his sleeve, clicked off the bedroom light, and started downstairs. Mama was whispering to Uncle Aubrey. Skylar paused on the staircase to listen.

"...around here, and I'm sure you noticed," Mama said, "that Howard ain't here with us tonight."

"Noticed? That's why it's so damn quiet," Uncle Aubrey said. "Not that I miss him. Where is the s.o.b.?"

"He's probably down at the Crosstown Tavern, getting drunk. I don't care what he does, as long as he brings my child home in one piece."

"Why is he always drunk nowadays? I've never seen my beloved brother-in-law drunk until recently."

"He stays drunk these days. I guess it's the only way he can look me in the eye ever since ... I found out..."

"Found out what?" Uncle Aubrey whispered so loudly, Skylar didn't have to eavesdrop. "Another woman, huh? That son of a bitch!"

"No," Mama said. "I wish it was that simple. I had to go to his office about a year ago come September to tell him his father had died of a heart attack — the man wasn't even his real father, by the way. The receptionist said she didn't know what the hell I was talking about when I asked for my husband, a CPA with the company. I thought the woman was kidding, giving me a hard time. But then I spoke to Howard's boss, who said Howard wasn't nobody's CPA with nobody's company—"

"What is he?"

"A bookkeeper."

"What!" Uncle Aubrey gasped. "Just stop, girl!"

"Ain't that nothin'?" Mama said. "And all this time he's walking around here like Godzilla, lying his ass off."

"Do the kids know?"

"No, I haven't told them. What's the point?"

"This is incredible, Thea! I can't believe—"

"Shh," Mama said, lowering her voice. "I wonder what's taking Skylar so long upstairs. I don't want him to hear this ... Skylar!" she yelled.

Skylar stood frozen on the dark staircase, tiptoed backward, retracing his steps, slammed his bedroom door loud enough for them to hear.

"Yes, Mama, I'm coming!"

When he got downstairs, he noticed that half the Jack Daniel's was gone, and his uncle's eyes were bloodshot. He showed him the record.

"I've been a Beatles fan since they came on *The Ed Sullivan Show* in January," Skylar said. "Daddy hates them and I'm forbidden to play it when he's home." He showed his uncle the latest 45 single they'd just released, "P.S. I Love You."

"What are their names?" Uncle Aubrey asked, grinning.

"This is John, Paul, George, and that's Ringo at the bottom," Skylar said, pointing. "They come from Liverpool, England, and John's the only one married."

"I hear their songs on the radio," Uncle Aubrey said. "But I haven't heard the whole album. Won't you play it?"

"Can I, Mama?"

"I don't care. But after I watch my favorite TV show." She walked to the television and clicked it on.

They watched a drama about a boy Skylar's age who became the town hero. While his family slept during the middle of the night, a fire started in the house. The boy was the first to smell the smoke downstairs. He alerted his parents, who panicked. In their haste, they'd forgotten the boy's younger brother sleeping in the attic. While the parents phoned the deputy sheriff and firefighters, the boy climbed the stairs, picked up his brother, and carried him outside to safety. His parents were overjoyed with his deed, impressed with his bravery. Everybody found out, including the sheriff, the firemen, the newspaper reporters, even the mayor. That week, a parade was held in the small town, honoring the hero for saving his younger brother from a burning house.

To the beat of "I Wanna Hold Your Hand," Skylar taught his uncle the latest dance steps, and flashed before him one Beatle card after another.

"Skylar," Mama said. "Now you just calm down a bit. You're smothering your uncle. He's gonna be here tomorrow, honey. You ain't gotta show him everything in one night."

"It's okay, Thea," Uncle Aubrey said. "I don't get to see my nephew much. Skylar's just excited to see me, that's all. Tomorrow," he said to Skylar, "we'll go to the record store and buy anything you want."

"Anything?" Skylar asked.

"Anything!" Uncle Aubrey said, pouring himself another shot of Jack Daniel's. "Besides, I want to get "Walk On By" by this new singer named Dionne Warwick. Have you heard it, Thea?"

Howard walked in the front door. Uncle Aubrey jumped up to greet Kendall, who had started for his open arms. But Kendall stopped, glanced at Daddy. Instead of an embrace, Kendall stuck out his hand for a shake. Uncle Aubrey shook his hand.

"You too big to give your uncle a great big hug?"

Kendall's gaze dropped to the floor. Daddy pulled Kendall away, and led him toward the staircase. "Go change into your pajamas," Daddy said. He looked at Skylar, his body unsteady. "You, too."

"Can I stay up since Uncle Aubrey's here? I don't get to see him much—"

"Be grateful," Daddy said, "you get to see him at all."

Skylar looked to his mother for support. She said nothing.

"Let the boy stay up for another half hour," Uncle Aubrey said.

"What did I say?" Daddy said. "I'm his father, not you. What I say goes! And ... what the hell...?" Daddy stomped across the living room floor toward the hi-fi. He snatched the tonearm off the Beatles record.

"That wasn't necessary, Howard," Mama said. "You don't have to ruin the boy's record. He bought it with his own allowance."

"I told him not to play that trash around me."

Skylar ran to his uncle and hid behind him.

"And I told you to get your black ass upstairs!" Daddy said again to Skylar. "Right now!"

Skylar started toward the staircase. He began climbing, slowly, reluctantly, but stopped midway when he heard the two men arguing.

"What're you trying to prove?" Daddy said. "I believe I asked you before not to contradict me in front of my kids. You got one more time to pull that shit and it's you and me, punk!"

"I may be many things," Uncle Aubrey said, "most of which you don't approve, but I'm no punk! I've kicked much ass in my day, including yours, so don't be fooled by who I sleep with, okay?"

"You hear that?" Daddy said to Mama. "Listen to him. That's your brother, Althea. Got the nerve to be proud of being a freak. Now, I've heard it all."

Howard marched across the room, plopped himself in the easy chair.

"You had a bit much to drink," Mama said to Daddy. "Maybe you should be going to bed, too."

"A man can't rest in his own home when you've got somebody like him around. Filling that boy's head up with movie star nonsense. Come home and find my house invaded by the Beatles, those punks. Only screaming girls listen to that, not boys, not real men. God knows what else he's trying to turn Skylar into."

"Now wait a goddamn minute here," Uncle Aubrey said. Skylar's view of Uncle Aubrey from the middle of the staircase was from the waist down. His body was as wobbly as Daddy's.

"Howard," he said, lowering his voice. "I know you don't like me, you never have. Matter of fact, you don't like anybody in my family — and I do mean anybody, including my sister here. And why you ever married her is a bigger mystery to me than the Shroud of Turin. Be that as it may, I want you to know I don't like your ass either. And I've tried, believe me, I have. But you won't let me. And guess what? I'm not trying anymore. We got three things in common, you and I: Thea, Skylar, and Kendall. Beyond that, you know what I've always liked about you? Not a goddamn thing—"

"Would you two please stop!" Mama said, sandwiching herself between them.

"You're always taking sides with that sissy!" Daddy yelled. "When he's filling your son's head with that movie star crap, you never have anything to say. I'm your husband, you should be my ally, not my adversary."

"Sure, sure!" Uncle Aubrey said, pushing Althea out of the way. "So he can grow up and be a CPA like his father? God forbid he should grow up and be a liar. Telling folks he's a CPA when he's not. Is that your idea of aspiration? ... Huh? ... Answer me, Mister C-P-A!"

Daddy got quiet. He seemed to shrink. He stared at Mama in disbelief. She was looking at Uncle Aubrey, her mouth agape.

"You told him that?" Daddy said, quietly. They were four of the most quiet words Skylar had ever heard Daddy utter. Mama said nothing. She bowed her head. Turned to walk away. Daddy grabbed her, pushed her across the room where she fell and bumped her head. Uncle Aubrey jumped on Daddy and they scuffled on the floor. Skylar ran downstairs and helped Uncle Aubrey subdue his father. Kendall ran down the stairs behind him, kicking and punching his brother and uncle.

"Get out of my house!" Daddy said, his nose bloody, lip swollen. "And don't ever come back! You've worn out your welcome here!"

"Says who?" Uncle Aubrey laughed, panting and wheezing, examining his blood-stained knuckles.

"He's staying here with us tonight," Mama said.

"No he isn't," Daddy said.

"Yes he is," Mama said. "This is my house, too, and that's my baby brother. Besides, he's too drunk to go home by himself."

"Please yourselves," Daddy said, picking himself off the floor, as Kendall cried, helping Daddy get up. "Don't be surprised if I try to kill you niggers one day!" Daddy said, stumbling up the staircase.

"It's okay," Uncle Aubrey said to Mama. "I'll go sleep at Mama's."

"No you won't," Mama insisted. "You'll stay here with us. Who does he think he is, kicking my brother out? You'll sleep in Skylar's room, like you always do."

In the upstairs foyer, Althea led her brother to Skylar's bedroom. Stopping at Kendall's room, she tucked him and Skylar in bed, kissed them on the forehead.

"Don't forget to say your prayers," she said.

Uncle Aubrey's eyes scanned the walls covered with Jim Brown, Mickey Mantle, and Jackie Robinson posters, New York Mets and Yankees buttons, collegiate football pennants, boxing gloves hanging on a nail, dart boards. In Skylar's bedroom, he studied the black-and-white posters of current girl groups: The Supremes. The Shangri-las. The Ronettes.

"These boys are different as night and day," Uncle Aubrey said, scratching his head, glancing upward at the pasted smile of Diana Ross, her frail arms poised dramatically over Mary and Flo.

"Yeah," Althea said over her shoulder, changing the bed sheets. "These are all Skylar's girlfriends. As you can see, he likes all kinds: colored, white, and in-between."

"Nah!" Uncle Aubrey scoffed. "He likes them all right, but it's not the way you think, Thea ... believe me."

When Althea left him, her brother was sitting on the edge of the bed stripped down to his pants. His shoes, socks stuffed inside them, rested beside his feet, his shirt hung on the doorknob. She kissed him good night, hugged him tightly, and turned to leave.

"I'm sorry, Thea," he whispered.

"About what?"

"All this mess. I didn't mean to tell Howard I knew. I didn't know it was a secret—"

"Don't even worry about it."

"By the way, you were right."

"About what?" she asked, her hand clutching the doorknob.

"Clairol blondes don't have nearly as much fun as you, that's for damn sure." They laughed, trying to stifle their laughter.

"You're so crazy," Althea said. "Get some sleep. You're drunk as a skunk. I'll see you in the morning." She switched off the light, closed the door, and whispered, "Pleasant dreams..."

Almost midnight. Skylar couldn't sleep. Kendall was not easy to bunk with. When Skylar slept in a strange bed, he always found it difficult.

He was ecstatic about Uncle Aubrey spending the night. Looking forward to the morning, Skylar rolled on his back, arms folded behind his head, and stared at the ceiling, listening to the mosquitoes buzz in the darkness, Kendall's breathing rising and falling. Skylar thought of breakfast next morning with Uncle Aubrey, their trip downtown to the record store to buy records — anything he wanted.

So, Daddy wasn't a CPA, after all. What did that mean? Would they have to sell their house? Would Daddy suddenly stop bringing home paychecks? Did he really have a job? Would Skylar still be getting an allowance? Earlier that evening when he had asked to go with Daddy to the tavern, Daddy refused to take him along. He took Kendall instead.

Skylar thought about the television program where the boy had been celebrated for saving his younger brother.

The basement was unusually warm that June night. Skylar felt it would make an ideal place. Other than the washer and dryer, most of the junk could've been thrown away. Mama was always promising to haul it off to the Salvation Army one day, anyway. Skylar thought he could set it, a little one, stay wide awake, and as soon as he smelled smoke, he'd alert his parents and uncle and save his brother — no, it had to be done another way. Rescue Kendall first. Then alert his parents and uncle to the danger in the basement. That way, he'd be the hero for sure. Then Daddy would love him. There would still be time to save the house, which wouldn't have burned much.

He found a box of stick matches and one of Kendall's faded football jerseys. He struck the stick match on the concrete floor, considering, as it burned, whether he should carry out his staged rescue attempt. He wondered if anybody had heard him tiptoe downstairs. Kendall was fast asleep when he climbed out of bed.

He'd heard Uncle Aubrey's snores through the adjoining wall. Daddy's snoring filled the entire second floor, as was always the case when he was drunk. And if Mama had heard Skylar, she'd have asked what he was doing up in the middle of the night. "Ouch!" The flame moved along the stick so quickly, it burned his hand.

He struck another. Dropped it on top of the jersey lying on the concrete floor. The fabric started burning, slowly. As the flame caught, he ran, quietly as he could, upstairs. The house was completely dark. The bottle of Jack Daniel's rested on the coffee table. The lamp and end table lay toppled over from the struggle. He saw the family portrait lying on the floor — the picture from Daddy's company's Labor Day picnic, with Mama holding him, and Daddy holding Kendall. In his mind's eye and ear, Skylar saw and heard the color photograph tear down the middle, leaving Daddy and Kendall to one side, he and Mama to the other. He heard the kitchen clock ticking. Funny, he thought, he'd never heard it before. It read close to 12:15 a.m. He groped his way through the darkness, walked slowly, quietly up the stairs, climbed back into bed with his brother, and against his will and plan, fell asleep. Next thing he knew, he was being awakened by Daddy in the middle of the night.

Howard: The Father

I'VE ALWAYS HATED my mother.

Growing up, I wouldn't allow myself to feel such a thing. A child wants to love his mother, no matter how badly that child is treated. Nowadays, we're always hearing about child abuse. Organizations have been established to deal exclusively with this growing problem. Where the hell were these organizations and enlightened social workers when I was growing up? I've often wondered if there was anyone, besides my stepfather, who saw that I was abused. I don't remember anybody else in our lives actually, until Mother remarried. I remember almost nothing but abuse from her. I can't recall her ever doting on me, or smothering me with affection, if in fact that ever happened, and I imagine it did.

My first conscious memory as a child has to be Halloween. I remember the frightening costumes, thinking those were real witches and skeletons passing by us on the street. I remember the wind howling, the leaves falling in such bunches that our feet made crunching noises as we stepped over them. I recall my fear, and my wanting to be carried. Mother seemed to be gracious and accommodating then. She spoke to me in a kind voice, one I'd almost never again hear after that day. She smiled a lot, rubbed my head. I guess that can pass for affection, can't it?

I can see Mother picking me up to carry me, my nose pressed against her perfumed neck, her hair tickling my nose. I can still feel my legs wrapped around her, my feet dangling, meeting at the base of her spine, my bottom resting on her stomach, which felt to me like a ball. And God knows I'll never forget the pained expression on her face when she felt dizzy and sat on the stoop, water leaking from somewhere — I wasn't sure where — and dripping down the stairs as Mother pressed her thighs together. That's the day I lost her. I left my mother there, in Jersey City, on that neighbor's stoop, on Hallow's Eve, grieving and panicked over a miscarriage, unaware of what the hell was happening to her. And I never saw her again.

I think it's doubly tough when you have no father. Like mothers, I think all children want a father, too. Regardless of what they say, children want both parents, and why should they be denied that? Listen to *me*. After the way I raised Skylar. But I know now, through the knowledge that's available, abuse is something handed down, like a legacy. I've heard television reports and watched documentaries explaining how child abusers have themselves been abused, emotionally, psychologically, sexually. Thus a cycle is set in motion.

I used to hate my father, too. I hated him for abandoning me. I hated him for not wanting me enough. Mother always said she forbade his visiting me. But if he had wanted to come badly enough, he wouldn't have let that stop him. I know I wouldn't. Although I knew him during the formative years of my life, I remember little, if anything, about him. Mother acted as if he had died. She never mentioned him. Never showed me pictures of him. Never told me I had a different father from my siblings until, it seemed, she could hurt me with it.

"Where do you think you're going, Howard?"

"I'm going with Daddy, and Raymond, and—"

"No, you're not."

"Why? You just said we could go out with Daddy when he—"

"That's right. But I didn't mean you, silly. He's not your father."

What a way to find out. From physical appearances, it wasn't apparent that I was a half brother. And I think my brothers, who were never close to me, could have been close, had they not been coached by Mother and ... that man. In subtle ways, they were discouraged from treating me as an equal. It's devastating to be part of a larger family yet feel like an only child, an only child in reverse, that is. Normally, the only child is showered, sometimes smothered with love. The only child usually has his parents' undivided attention. But my only-childhood was far more isolated, neglected, abandoned.

What had I done that Mother and her husband were so repelled by me? I think I can understand his dislike; hell, I wasn't his. But I've never been able to figure her out, other than I didn't fit neatly into the family portrait she was sketching for herself. Stepchild. That word holds a lot of meaning for me. A meaning I epitomized.

When I became a young man, believing I had somehow mirac-
ulously survived my family, I turned around and did to my wife
and children what my family had done to me. I don't know if I was
reacting to losing another important woman in my life to another
male, or what. The memories are too fuzzy. There's no justifying
what I did, I know, and I'm not asking for anyone's sympathy. But
at the time, there had to be a reason, no matter how twisted it was.
I did have the best intentions, though. When I married Althea, it
was because I loved her, and because I knew she loved me. But even
more importantly, she respected me, and looked up to me as if I
were somebody. I needed that so desperately, I probably would've
married the first woman who gave it to me. Marrying her meant life
would be different. Since I didn't fit into the Whyte household of
my childhood, I would create a Whyte household into which I
would fit. If I was in control, then things would be designed, so to
speak, to fit my liking. That's what I tried to do. I felt Althea would
always love and respect me, and show it. That was something I
could depend on, like money in the bank. She was Mother all over
again.

Then Skylar was born, and it seemed that Althea's love to me
had been divided. I was being forced to share it. I was depriving
Skylar of his mother because I still needed one, had never had one.
It's been said that most men marry their mothers, or turn their
wives into mothers. Same was true of me, and in many ways. I was
jealous of Skylar because he was soaking up sun rays meant to shine
on me. I was jealous because he had a wonderful, attentive, giving,
loving mother.

To this day, I think Althea talked back to television commercials
because she didn't dare say certain things to me. Sometimes, she
was brave enough to speak her mind. But I'm sure the things she
really wanted to say were locked up inside her. So, she'd lash out
against television commercials, of all things. For Skylar's sake, I'm
glad she was there. If not, Skylar would probably be worse off than
Kendall. I wonder how he survived me. As sensitive as he is, he's
just as resilient, with a strength and a sense of himself I could only
wish to have. Perhaps that made me jealous of him, as well.

Skylar certainly made me proud. He was, undoubtedly, the
model child any parent would be happy to claim. Every A he got
on a test, the citywide spelling bee competitions he won, the debate

teams where he served as captain — all these things made me glad he was mine. But I couldn't get past my hatred and insecurity to embrace it — or him.

I'm glad I'm dying. It's long overdue. Since my family found out I was a fraud, and the night of the fire, I have not wanted to live. I couldn't face myself, couldn't stand myself, stuck inside my skin, thinking my thoughts, looking through my eyes, tasting with my tongue, being looked at by my family through different eyes. It was more painful and humiliating than I can find the words for. Whiskey was the only thing to silence that raging pain. I could never stay drunk long enough. I still had to earn a living, but I drank every moment I could. First, liquid lunches; then I started drinking before work. I kept a pint hidden in my desk at the office. I drank before and after I went to church. And I'd never been much on booze before that.

Though I've never said it to her, I'm glad Althea has improved herself. God knows she deserves better than I've given her. It also assures me that she'll be okay when I'm gone. She doesn't need anyone to support her. Though I could never say it to her, I hope she finds someone else to love her while there's time. She's still beautiful, with a great-looking body for a middle-aged woman with two adult sons, and doesn't have a line in her face. She deserves to be loved. She'd never have an affair behind my back, not even while I'm lying up in this hospital half-dead. She just wouldn't. Hopefully, she will when I'm gone.

I wish Kendall had come by to see me more often. But I can't blame him. He probably hates me, too, with good reason. And I can't get angry about his feelings. I have myself to blame. I can only hope that he gets off drugs before it's too late, cleans himself up, and starts anew. As a young man, he owes himself that. He's as bright and articulate as Skylar, though most people wouldn't assume that because he's a heroin addict. But he's still my son, raised in my house, and that, in itself, makes him bright, articulate, and knowledgeable.

I'm ecstatic Skylar dropped by today. I was able to unload years and years of excess baggage off my chest, which I hope was good for both of us. I know it was for me. Now I can die in peace. Before you can make amends with your Maker, you must begin with your earthly family. Skylar's always been compassionate, open, forgiving, and it moves me to tears to think that he still wants to be friends, to let go of the past. Just too bad I'm dying now. I feel such relief that we talked about the fire. Now we know the truth. Hopefully, we'll both be better off for it. We held hands this afternoon, probably for the first time since he was a little boy. We embraced, even cried together. It was the single most meaningful moment of my life. And I thank God for it.

I'm afraid to meet God.

I shiver at the thought, terrified of His judgment. It's the only discouraging thing about death. I first sought God because there was nowhere else to turn. Between Him and whiskey, I found the hook to hang my guilt on. I figured that humbling myself would move Him to judge me less severely, that by visiting Him in church every Sunday, I had already begun my life sentence of repentance, that by the time I met Him face-to-face, which could be any day now, any hour, any minute, any second, my term would be half-served, the remaining punishment to be reconsidered and determined, with perhaps time off for good behavior. So when I meet Him, and gaze back into His eyes of burning coals, and feel the scorching winds of His breath, and tremble from the roar of His voice, I can only hope for His understanding, that He'll forgive every bad thing I ever said or did to Althea, Skylar, Kendall ... and Aubrey.

I was so insanely jealous of that man, it provoked my most violent impulse, drunk or sober. He was everything I wasn't, everything I aspired to be: educated, traveled, sophisticated, well dressed, passionate about his career, loving and living every moment of his life. When he was around, I felt inferior. I shrank at the sight of his impeccable clothes, the sound of his fluency in foreign languages, the scent of freedom he radiated, mixed with his expensive cologne. On top of which, he so totally controlled Skylar, that I wanted to ... well, maybe not kill him, exactly, but I entertained my most violent, murky thoughts when he visited. His shadow dwarfed the big shot I was trying to be. No matter what I said, he made me look stupid and inconsequential in front of my family. Like he was Althea's revenge, her roundabout way of getting even with me.

The night he found out the truth about me, I felt naked before him. I'll never forget what he said, and the vituperative way he said it. I wanted to kill him, for him to die for merely being privy to the knowledge.

I hope I see Aubrey where I'm going. Maybe he'll forgive me, too. Maybe we can be friends on the other side, in the next life. It would be nice to be family for once, the brothers-in-law we never were.

I don't know how much longer I can stand these tubes stuck in my nostrils and my veins, these doctors and nurses prodding me with cold, metal instruments, playing and experimenting with my naked body underneath this hospital gown. Lying here day after day, I might as well be paralyzed. Television has become my sole connection with reality, with the world outside this hospital. At night, when the lights are out and the hospital is quiet, I swear I can hear and feel my liver disintegrate, swishing and splashing around in the years of whiskey that have kept it afloat. Cirrhosis of the liver is supposedly, among other things, a hardening of the liver. But I can swear mine is kept soft and mushy from more than a decade of Seagram's Seven, falling apart bit by bit, layer by layer, tissue by tissue, like a roll of toilet paper sitting in a tub of water.

Maybe it's all in my mind, but when you're dying, you feel your body falling apart, like an old toy that's winding down, the springs popping, the wheels rusting. The only things I smell anymore are my own rancid, liquorless breath, and death. I can't describe what death smells like. I can't even say I've smelled it before these past few weeks. But when you smell it, you know, unmistakably, what it is. And death can be seen, too. At least once a day, I see him sitting in the corner, the dark shawl pulled so far over his face that i can't make out his features, can't tell if he's black or white, man or woman. He waits patiently, a hooded shadow, foot tapping out the remaining moments of my life, like an hourglass dripping sand. He waits patiently.

If only, in my life, I could have been so patient...

I'm having a dream.

My body is no longer in pain. My joints are no longer stiff, achy, inflexible. I feel good and there's not a drop of liquor in my bloodstream. I am standing, tall, erect, sturdy, my body youthful, as on the day I met Althea. My mind is free, liquid, uncluttered. Breathing comes easily, evenly, without the congestion, the wheezing. My

eyesight is clear, single-visioned. No longer do I see two of everything. My skin tightens, no longer sagging, wrinkling. The mucus
in my nose and eyelids is dissolving. I feel an intense warmth wrap
around me. It's relaxing and puts me at ease. My muscles and
nerves untighten, they seem to sigh, unraveling, unfolding, untangling themselves. My ears are deafened by the blaring of trumpets,
the sweet sound of brass falling from the horns' bells like the
pouring of honey. Though the melody is beyond identification, the
blaring of these trumpets resemble a fanfare and yet something
else, something more beautiful, more melodic, a melody only the
inner ear can hear, something beyond articulation, like what
Gabriel's horn is supposed to sound like.

There's a white radiance I can reach out and touch, yet it seems
light-years away from me. It starts out like the dot that clouds your
eye when a camera flashes. The white dot throbs, vibrates, and
grows in intensity. As it gets larger, it calls my name without saying
a word, and I walk toward it, into it, illuminated by it, the bright-
ness blinding me until I can no longer see, like during an eclipse.
The light intensifies, as if I'm standing within reach of the sun, and
the trumpets blare sweet, concordant, brassy sounds, and I walk
and keep walking, nearly running, for it is too late to turn back
now...

New Beginnings

SITTING AT HER DESK, daydreaming by the thirtieth-story window, Althea's eyes lazily watch the sun beginning its arc above the skyscrapers, the dazzling Art Deco spire of the Chrysler Building, the Queensboro Bridge hovering above Roosevelt Island, the sluggishness of the East River. Her thoughts are scattered, as she thinks about Howard dying in one hospital, Kendall recovering from an overdose in another. She doodles on a notepad, staring out her window. She has a short memorandum to write and distribute, but she can't get motivated today. She swivels in her chair, and turns toward the IBM Personal Computer III screen that's staring back at her, empty, the green cursor blinking. There's a knock on her door.

"Yes?"

"Excuse me, Althea, but what am I supposed to do with these?" asks Karla, one of the new girls Althea hired.

"First you should photocopy them, log them in the black binder notebook and distribute them to the staff, okay?"

"Gotcha."

She likes Karla, a sweet, personable, hardworking girl, who reminds Althea of herself when she started.

On Althea's first day at work, she was doing a million and one things at once. Bob Rosonoff needed a letter typed, a job Althea had started. Then Mary Hobkins asked her to make copies and collate them. Althea jumped up from her desk, Bob's unfinished letter stuck in the roller, and ran to the photocopy room. She waited patiently while a co-worker made two-sided copies.

"Hi," Althea said, trying to be friendly.

"Hi," the woman said.

"I'm Althea Whyte," she said, extending her hand. "I'm new here."

"Yes, I saw you earlier this morning. Welcome aboard; my name's Theresa Gordon. Nice to meet you."

"Nice to meet you, too," Althea said, proudly feeling like a member of the corporate work force.

"I'm in a different department than you," Theresa said. "But sometimes our work will overlap, so we'll see a lot of each other."

"Good."

Theresa was finishing her copies. She pulled sheets of paper from the automatic collator, stacked them, and removed the original. "This is a great machine. It does everything but bring your morning coffee. It never breaks down. Bye." Theresa left the copy room.

Althea examined the humongous machine, not sure which button to push first, there were so many. After reading the directions, she placed the original on the glass and pressed the "On" button. Nothing happened. She reread the instructions and did it again.

"You have to punch in your personal I.D. number, then the client number," said a handsome young man with a ponytail, standing in the doorway. "Hi, I'm Donnie," he said, shaking her hand. "This machine won't work until you punch in a number. Didn't anybody give you one?"

"Yes," Althea said. "I think so." She couldn't remember. She'd been given so much information since she'd arrived, she didn't know which was which.

"See?" Donnie said. He punched in a four-digit number and the machine turned on. He made his copies. As Althea was about to place her original in the machine, he punched out his number and the machine turned off.

"You can't use my number," Donnie said.

"Why not?"

"Because the numbers are for billing purposes. This way, the appropriate people get billed for what's theirs."

"I see," Althea said, though she really didn't. What was the big deal about making a few more copies on his client's I.D. number?

She left the copy room, headed back to her desk, and found her number. The phone rang and she grabbed for it, knocking over the cup of coffee, which soaked nearly everything on the desk.

"Jesus, Lord," she said, clicking her tongue, hoping nobody was watching her, feeling like Lucille Ball. "Hello!" she said into the mouthpiece, then remembered she was at work. "Good morning, Human Resources."

"I want to speak to Mr. Aronson!"

"Sure, one moment," she said. She put the call on hold, and buzzed Mr. Aronson's office, which didn't answer. She buzzed again, thinking, Please pick up the phone. Please make my job easier. She buzzed and buzzed until it became apparent he wasn't there, or wasn't answering. She pushed the blinking button on the telephone. "I'm sorry, he's not available, sir. May I take a message for him—"

"Look, this is Mr. Liefer! You tell Aronson I'm sick of leaving messages!" The man screamed so loudly in her ear, she held the telephone away from her face.

"Okay, sir. I'll be sure to give him the message."

"You better! Bunch of fucking idiots over at that office!" he said and hung up.

You have a nice day too, she thought, grinning, writing down the message, which fell from her hand into the coffee. She grabbed the tissue box from the corner of her desk and started blotting the coffee, remembering why she'd come back to her desk. The phone rang again.

"Hello — I mean, good morning, Human Resources."

"Good morning," a woman's voice said. Thank God it's a woman, Althea thought, who sounds friendly. "May I speak with Mr. Jason?"

"Sure, one moment, please." Althea pressed the hold button, and buzzed Mr. Jason. "I have a call for you."

"Who is it?"

"I don't know. I forgot to ask."

"Well, ask. Never put my calls through without screening them."

"Okay," Althea said, thinking, Why can't you just take the call and find out who it is? She depressed the blinking button. "Excuse me, ma'am. Who may I ask is calling?"

"This is his wife."

"Okay, ma'am. One moment, please."

She tried to depress the hold button, but instead, hit another extension and lost the call. Oh, Lord! What am I going to do, now? She buzzed Mr. Jason, still sponging up the coffee, tossing the brown, soggy tissues into the wastebasket.

"Yes?"

"I'm sorry, sir. But it was your wife."

"Well, why didn't you say so?"

"Well, sir, I didn't know ... I'm new here."

"Okay, whatever. Put her through. What're you waiting for?"

"I can't, sir."

"What do you mean, you can't? You just told me she was on the line."

"I lost the call—"

"How the hell did you manage to do that?"

"I pressed the wrong—"

"Jesus H. Christ!" He hung up.

I know it's Monday morning, she was thinking, but these folks are going to have to be a little more patient with me.

"Psssst!" someone whispered from the door. "Did you leave something on the copy machine?"

"Oh, yes!" Althea said, slapping her forehead. "I forgot all about it." She got up from the desk and was nearly out the door when she remembered her identification number. She turned quickly, bumped into one of the secretaries holding a Styrofoam cup of coffee in her hand, which spilled a few drops on the woman's bright yellow dress.

"I'm so sorry," Althea said. The woman turned red and seemed on the verge of bawling out Althea. "Please, let me clean your dress for you." She grabbed another tissue from her desk, held it under the faucet of the Sparkletts water cooler, and began scrubbing the woman's dress. The woman sighed, sucked her tongue, rolled her eyes. Althea was panicking because the stains wouldn't come out. "I'll be more than happy to pay your cleaner's bill—"

"Don't worry about it," the woman said, walking away in the midst of Althea's scrubbing. Althea headed back to the copy room. She pushed in her number, the "On" lit up red, and the machine clicked and hummed. She placed her original on the glass, closed the cover, and pushed "5," then "0." After the fourth copy, the machine stopped, and instructions lit up to consult the manual or the key operator. Althea didn't know what to do. She didn't know why this was all happening to her on the first day of her first job in almost twenty years. She consulted the manual attached to the machine, unable to figure out what it was saying, though gazing confidently down at it as if she understood every word. The line for the copy machine was growing. When she glanced over her shoulder, five people stood waiting.

"What happened?" a secretary asked.

"I don't know," Althea said. "It just stopped working. Just like that."

"This machine's a pain in the ass," the secretary said. "Did you drop any paper clips inside?"

"No, I don't think so."

"This machine is more sensitive than me, I swear," the secretary said. She did something, Althea didn't know what, and the machine clicked back on. Althea made her copies, thanked the woman, and got out of there. When she got back to her desk, Bob Rosonoff was standing nearby.

"Did you finish my letter?"

"No," Althea said, embarrassed. "I was making copies and the machine broke down. I'll have it in a minute."

"No rush," he said.

Bless your heart, she thought. She set the copies aside, sat in her chair, and turned to the typewriter.

"I need this A.S.A.P."

Althea turned around, facing another gentleman she hadn't met. "You need what?"

"I need this ASAP."

Althea looked at the cassette tape he was thrusting in her face. She'd never heard a cassette called that before.

"Excuse me, sir," she said. "But I'm new here. What's an ASAP?"

"You really are new," he said, laughing. "A.S.A.P. means, as soon as possible."

"Oh!" Althea said, laughing, relieved they were speaking the same language. "I can have it for you by noon."

"Are you sure? It's both sides."

"Yeah, I can do it," Althea said, wondering what she'd just gotten herself into. Maybe it was too much to get done before noon. She finished typing Mr. Rosonoff's letter and started the tape. The dictation gave her the date, the addressee, and the address. That much she understood.

"New paragraph," the dictation said. "Re: Medical and Dental Insurance Benefits—"

"What?" Althea said, hitting the rewind with her foot.

"Re: Medical—"

Who the hell is Ray? she thought. Jesus Lord, I'm not going to last. I just know it. It's only ten-thirty and I've done nothing but make a mess of everything I touch. She rewound it again.

"Excuse me, Althea," Mr. Aronson said, suddenly in front of her desk. "Could you please get me a cup of coffee?"

"Sure," she said. Anything to get away from these screaming phones and Ray. In the lunchroom, she poured a cup, then remembered that she'd forgotten to ask him how he drank it. Black? Sugar? Cream? Decaf? She spotted another woman about her age, reading the *Daily News* on the table near the vending machine.

"Excuse me," Althea said. "But who's Ray?"

"Pardon?" the woman said.

"Well," Althea whispered, too embarrassed to let anyone overhear that she didn't know her job. "I'm doing a tape for—"

"You mean, transcribing—"

"Yes. And," Althea chuckled, "he's talking about this guy named Ray. Who's Ray?"

The woman laughed. "Oh that's funny," she said. "You're new, aren't you?"

"How can you tell?"

"Listen. He's saying, 'Re.' It's short for 'Regarding.' You just type, R-e, colon."

"Oh, I get it," Althea said, shamed by her ignorance.

"That's pretty good, though," the woman said, laughing. "I'll have to tell the girls that one."

It ain't that damn funny, Althea thought, leaving the lunchroom. She took the coffee to Mr. Aronson, placed it on his desk, and turned to leave.

"Did a Mr. Liefer call me this morning?"

"Yes, he did."

"Why didn't I get a message?"

Althea gasped. In her mind, she saw the written message drowned in coffee on her desk. She'd forgotten to write another one. She started to explain.

"It's okay. Just make sure I get his messages, or I'll never hear the end of it."

She was transcribing the tape, getting a feel for it, enjoying it, allowing a few words to play as she pressed the pedal with her foot, typing them as she heard them. This wasn't so bad, at all. She'd been working a good twenty minutes without one interruption.

"...shall not exceed thirty days," the dictation said. "Open paren, three zero, close paren," the dictation said.

And just when she thought she was getting the hang of it.

Sitting alone at the table in the lunchroom, flipping mindlessly through an *Essence* magazine, she thought it was only a matter of time before they told her they didn't want her anymore. Things had certainly changed since she last worked. It was now much more sophisticated, complicated, hectic, computerized. She felt she could do it, once she got used to it, but she didn't know how long their patience would last. Her head spun, she felt dizzy, she didn't want to eat, and hadn't eaten a thing all day, not even breakfast. A tension headache was beginning at the back of her head, and it was barely twelve-thirty. She had four more hours to go.

It would have been better had one of the other ladies talked to her. They smiled, nodded their heads, and some introduced themselves. But no one invited her to join their group and she felt left out, noticing how cliquish the groups were. In time, she'd discover she didn't fit into any of the cliques, which suited her just fine, once she realized all they did was gossip and talk about each other and everybody else like dogs. She wondered, sitting in the lunchroom, who among them knew she was incompetent, who would spread around the gossip about her. She was convinced every woman in that lunchroom, young, old, black, white, Latino, and Filipino, knew about her entire morning, and the only reason they were not laughing about it and making light of it was because she was there. A part of her didn't want to get up, for fear of them whispering and pointing behind her back. And if she left before they did, they'd talk about her for sure.

"Having a Murphy's Law kind of day, are you?"

She didn't want to look up. Here was yet another term she'd never heard of, and she was at lunch. Who the hell is Murphy? she wanted to ask. And what's his law?

"Oh hi," she said, pleased to be gazing into a friendly face. "What's your name again?"

"George. George Wilson," he said. "Mind if I join you?"

"No, not at all. Please do," Althea said, closing her *Essence* magazine and shoving it aside.

"You're having a Murphy's Law kind of day, are you?"

"I'm sorry, but what does that mean?"

He laughed, and Althea did, too. "Murphy's Law means anything that can go wrong, will go wrong."

"Yes, that sounds like my morning, all right."

"Don't worry, hang in there. You're tough."

"I sure am. But I don't know if I'll last."

"You will," George said.

"Where're you working now?" Althea said.

"I'm upstairs on the thirty-first floor. You should come up and visit sometime."

"Maybe I will."

"Look, Althea," he said, his expression suddenly serious. She didn't know what he was about to say. "I realize you don't know me and ... well, would you like to go to lunch sometime?"

Yes, yes, yes! Althea thought, gazing at this tall, handsome man who was gently pursuing her, as she had suspected when he interviewed and hired her last week. Maybe he meant a friendly, platonic lunch. Maybe he even meant they could go dutch. But a widowed man asking a woman to lunch?

"I'm sorry," Althea said. "But I shouldn't."

"Why?"

"I'm married."

"I see," George said. "Well, at least I asked. I mean, I knew you were married, but I didn't know if you were separated or..."

"Thanks for asking," Althea said. Suddenly, the day seemed right. All the mistakes she'd committed that morning had now been corrected. This was the first man she knew of since Howard who took an interest in her, making her feel like a woman with needs. Lord, was she sorry she had to refuse him.

"What about these other ladies?" Althea said. "Man like you shouldn't have no problem finding somebody—"

"When I got my eye on one, that's the one I want," George said, rising. "And nobody else."

"I'll see you around," Althea said, struggling with the temptation of the lunch request and the invitation to visit him on the thirty-first floor.

"You take care. Have any problems, come and see me," he said, smiling, patting her shoulder as he left.

She hadn't noticed until she turned around that the women at neighboring tables, women about her age, were giving her dirty looks.

She is considering going home.

She can't get a thing done — it's one of those days when all she does is think about her family. Her supervisor has recommended that she take the rest of the day off. Doodling, her eyes crawl across the poster tacked on the back of her door: WHEN GOD MADE MAN, SHE WAS ONLY KIDDING. The poster reminds her of Howard, who considered it offensive, even blasphemous.

There's a knock on the door.

"Yes?" she says.

George peeks in. "May I come in?"

"Of course, George," Althea says, smiling. "Have a seat."

George sits down and the two stare at each other for what seems like minutes.

"How's your family doing?" George asks.

"Good, I guess. The same." She wonders if he really means Howard, the only obstacle wedged between her and him.

"How's yours?" Althea asks, genuinely. She'd met his children at a holiday barbecue George invited her to a few years after she'd met him. She found his sons, daughters, and grandchildren to be as charming and likable as George.

"Everybody's fine. But," George says, looking out the window at the Queensboro Bridge, "they often ask about you. They wonder when you're coming back."

"I will one day, George. I will."

They sit a few more moments without speaking. George clears his throat.

"Have you eaten?"

"No, I sure haven't," Althea says, and laughs.

"What's so funny?"

"You. You're so cute. You just won't take no for an answer—"

"But I thought you said no just because you're married?"

"I did."

"And that we could be friends—"

"Right—"

"Platonic friends—"

"That's what I said."

"Well, Althea, damn. This is a platonic invitation for a platonic lunch, at which we'll do platonic things and talk about platonic subjects. Maybe I'll even order a platonic hamburger. Whaddaya say?"

Althea is laughing so hard, she can't answer him. She really likes George, and has every reason to believe he'd make a wonderful companion. Can't be any worse than Howard. What's she going to do? She's been stalling him for over ten years, and he's still hanging around. If there were no ring on her finger, she would've jumped at the opportunity a long time ago. There are times she has shameful thoughts of Howard expiring while George is still interested. She often refuses his invitations, not afraid of what George might do or say, but afraid of what she might do or say.

"You're sure this is platonic?" She can't resist it.

"Hell, we can even go dutch, if that makes you feel any better."

"Okay, let me get my jacket and handbag," Althea says, rising from her chair. "I'll meet you in the lobby."

"Great!"

"But I've got to be back here by—"

The telephone rings. She removes one of her clip-on earrings, shakes her hair back, and picks up the receiver.

"Althea Whyte's office. May I help you?"

"Yes, Mrs. Whyte," a woman's voice says. "This is Dr. Erdrich at Columbia Presbyterian. We spoke earlier this morning."

"Yes?" Althea says, her pulse racing, as she sits back down.

"Everything all right?" George asks, noticing the grave expression on her face.

She waves him away with her hand.

"We're sorry to bother you, Mrs. Whyte," the woman says. "But we're calling you about your husband ... We don't expect him to last the night..."

E*pitaphs & Other Lies*

RESPLENDENT IN WHITE CREASED robes, the choir glides ceremonially down the aisles. In a rhythmic two-step, they march, swaying together to one side, then to the other, the organist fingering the keyboards, striking gospel chords fraught with emotion. Heads erect with pomp and circumstance, they file onto the empty platform behind the altar. The closed gray-green casket rests among the foliage and fragrant splendor of floral wreaths and blankets. Sculpted, ceramic faces of saints impassively watch the quiet pageantry, fixed smiles chiseled into their faces. Women in white nurse uniforms and white gloves line the walls, their expressions solemn. With the aisles now empty, the choir assembled behind the pulpit breaks into thunderous song, the organist becoming animated, the parishioners rocking, the presiding clergy seated, bobbing his head, tapping his foot to the beat.

Skylar glances around the church. Seated in the front row, sandwiched between his mother and brother, he feels the mourners' eyes crawling over them. In standard widow black, a veil covering her face, Althea sits erect, her sullen gaze transfixed on the altar. Dreadlocks tied behind his neck in a ponytail, Kendall stares at his clasped hands, his head raising and lowering, coughing, clearing his throat, covering his mouth with a clenched fist. Skylar takes Althea's black-gloved hand, squeezes, and releases it.

Having finished the song, the choir sits, in unison. The presiding pastor, the Reverend Rufus P. Wilkinson, rises and walks slowly to the pulpit. Bidding a good morning to his congregation, widow, sons, family, and friends of the deceased, he produces a pair of half-glasses from inside his frock. Rising and spreading over the sounds of faint coughs, throat clearing, and a restless, whiny toddler, his voice is a soft but resonant monotone.

"Death, as we know it here on earth," Reverend Wilkinson says, "is not the last word. Jesus said, 'He who believeth in me, shall have everlasting life.' Brother Howard Whyte here was a believer," he says, shifting his gaze toward the casket. "I knew him well, from the first day he walked through the doors of Ebenezer Baptist, lost and frightened, from the time he walked down that aisle," he says, pointing, "found his way to this altar, and gave his life to Jesus. And believe me, brothers and sisters, he was, indeed, a child of God."

Skylar loosens his necktie, unfastens the shirt button crushing his Adam's apple, and taps his foot on the carpeted floor. His eye is caught by the large crucifix suspended above the pastor's head. The Savior's head is cocked to one side, crowned in barbwire, hands and feet bloodily impaled upon the cross. His eyes reflect anguish, agony. Painted drops of blood trickle down his forehead.

Pastor Wilkinson sits. A choir vocalist rises, walks with folded hands toward the microphone. She nods to the organist who does some fancy footwork on the multitude of pedals beneath him. Breaking into Clara Ward's "How I Got Over," the choir and congregation frantically clap their hands to the thumping rhythm, the organist's head bouncing, his fingers sliding, R&B-like, down the keyboards. The pastor wiggles his hand in the air, his eyelids shut. An elderly woman bolts from her seat, popping her tambourine like a gypsy. Her frail body convulses with the Holy Ghost, gray hair coming undone, bobby pins and barrettes falling in the carpeted aisle. Parishioners shout, "Amen!" "Thank you, Jesus!" and "Take your time!" cooling themselves with cardboard fans from Parkinson's Funeral Home.

Returning to the pulpit for the next order of business on the program, Pastor Wilkinson stands and faces his congregation.

"Please open your Bibles to the New Testament, Book of John, chapter six, verse twelve." Reverend Wilkinson's eyes jump back and forth from the pages beneath him to the sea of faces. "I want to call your attention to Jesus feeding the multitudes, the miracle of the fishes. The Savior takes the loaves of bread, distributes them among his disciples, and feeds five thousand hungry people. 'When they were filled,'" he reads, removing his half-glasses, leaning on the wooden pulpit, his arms embracing its square corners, glaring down at his parishioners, spit flying from his moist lips, "he said unto his disciples, 'Gather up the fragments that remain, that nothing be lost.' I want y'all to think about that this morning."

Skylar becomes alert. Intently, he listens to the pastor, ears hanging on every word. He waits for him to continue, to expound on the verse that has struck a chord within him. Pulling a handkerchief from his pocket to wipe his face and mouth, the pastor continues, his volume rising a notch.

"Most times, when family and friends lose a loved one, we want to throw in the towel of Life. Oh, yes! Whenever we lose a dear one, we are overcome by loss and self-pity. Sometimes," he says, pausing dramatically, jerking his head to punctuate each word, "sometimes ... brothers and sisters ... we even get ANGRY about the deceased leaving us without prior notice. But I tell you ... my brothers and sisters ... God waits for no man. When it's time to go ... it's time. And rather than dwell on our hardships ... our grief ... our sense of loss ... we should focus instead ... on what we have left of that loved one ... what they have left behind. We have children ... we have wives ... we have husbands ... we have families ... we have friends ... and I'm here to tell you ... we must make the best of what we have ... and move right along. The life God gives us ... is nothing to waste. We, my brothers and sisters, are the fragments that remain here on God's good earth. We must carry on as God expects us to..."

The pastor wipes the sweat crawling down his temples, the saliva around his lips. He shouts louder now in a singsong voice, a thunderous volume bringing the congregation with him, filling them with his exuberance.

"JESUS-AH SAID-AH ... GATHER UP-AH ... THE FRAGMENTS THAT REMAIN-AH ... THAT NOTHING ... NOTHING BE LOST! CAN I HEAR Y'ALL SAY AMEN?"

"Amen!"

"Y'all ain't prayin' with me this mornin'. CAN I HEAR Y'ALL SAY AMEN?"

"AMEN!"

"I WANT Y'ALL TO PRAY WITH ME THIS MORNIN'!"

"I know you right, Rev!"

"Well!"

"Take your time, Rev! Take your time!"

Skylar explodes emotionally. The pastor's boisterous call and response is stirring, piercing, life-affirming. He starts to cry, tears splashing on the legs of his black suit. Through his tears, he can hardly see the choir as it bursts into "Oh, Mary, Don't You Weep."

The choir and congregation simmer down. Pastor Wilkinson addresses his flock in general, and the immediate family of the deceased in particular, as he delivers the eulogy.

"Brother Howard was a credit to his race, the human race, a true man of God," the pastor says quietly, his voice hoarse and cracking from screaming only moments before. "He was a member of Ebenezer Baptist for nearly twenty years, a fine, hardworking, decent, God-fearing man dedicated to his lovely wife, Althea; a devoted father to his sons, Skylar and Kendall. Heaven smiles upon his passage through the holy gates. Their gain is our loss. Over the years, during weekly talks after service, Brother Howard had discussed with me the many years of his hard work as a certified public accountant, the first black with his company, praise Jesus; how he put his elder son through college; how instrumental and supportive he'd been to a son who wanted a career in the movies. And this is the first time that I've had the privilege of meeting Brother Howard's lovely family. Praise God! It's unfortunate to be meeting you under these circumstances, but I feel I've known you a long time. We welcome you to Ebenezer Baptist."

Skylar looks at Althea, who returns his glance. Again, he squeezes her hand, appalled by the preacher's well-meant, benevolent words.

When Skylar had last seen Daddy alive, not quite a week before, he'd been perturbed to find Marshall, the boy with leukemia from the adjoining room, sitting at the foot of Daddy's bed.

"Is it okay if Marshall leaves for a short while?"

Skylar didn't want another visit interrupted and upstaged by the brat. Skylar didn't want him showing off his crayon drawings, shoving them in the old man's face, to the old man's delight, while Skylar tried to talk with him in privacy. Besides, the kid never said anything to Skylar anyway, even when Skylar said hello to him.

"Marshall," Daddy said, "you think you could come back later on, so I can talk with my son?"

Skylar felt suddenly embarrassed over his petty request, reduced by his jealousy of the child, wishing he'd kept his mouth shut. For several minutes, he just sat on the edge of the bed and watched the television monitor.

"So, how's my son, the movie star?" Daddy said, his disheveled head nestled upon double pillows, the remote in his hand.

"You know, Daddy," Skylar said, "you were right. You used to tell me black people don't become movie stars. And you know what? They don't. There's no such thing as a black movie star."

"Looking at you," Daddy said, "you couldn't convince me of that. Making movies, doing big-shot interviews, getting nominated for the Academy Award ... Jesus Christ, boy! ... I know I've never told you, son, but you've done ... well, you've done extremely well for yourself."

Skylar couldn't believe his ears.

For a half hour, they watched television. Skylar didn't know what else to say. Apparently, neither did Daddy. Skylar sat, dazed, recovering from the sudden, unanticipated praise which sent his head whirling. He was physically exhausted. Brett What's-His-Face's final installment of the *Rolling Stone* interview had all but zapped him completely. He craved the company of someone that night, someone to talk to. He didn't want to be alone. He remembered Brett's business card in his back pocket, the card he'd meant to throw away. Sitting at his father's bedside, he considered calling Brett, taking him up on his dinner invitation. He'd have to stress the "dinner only," so there was no misunderstanding. Brett was attractive, but he wasn't Evan Cabot.

Falling asleep, chin pressing against his collarbone, Skylar decided he should leave.

"I'll be back first chance I get, whenever my shooting schedule allows."

For several empty moments, the two men faced each other in silence. Skylar turned to walk away. His hand was on the doorknob, the door halfway open.

"The fire wasn't your fault...," Daddy said.

Skylar stopped, frozen, his muscles taut. His head turned, a slow sweeping movement, toward his emaciated father whose eyes pleaded, it seemed, for forgiveness. Skylar walked over, sat at his bedside. Again, the silence was long and disturbing, his father gazing away from him and the television monitor.

"I, um ... well, I, uh ... I didn't mean to hurt anybody," Daddy said, swallowing, biting his lip. "I just ... I don't know ... I just got out of control somehow. The night your Uncle Aubrey and I had that fight, I wanted to end it all. The rage inside me was not one I could contain anymore. I was so godforsaken miserable, I wanted to die. I wanted to take my family with me. Hell, I was drunk, but I knew exactly what I was doing even though it was ... well, like a dream...

"When everyone was asleep, I got up to use the bathroom. I felt like I wanted another drink. My throat was parched as hell, so I went downstairs. I didn't even remember your uncle was staying with us until I saw the bottle of Jack Daniel's and the overturned furniture. I thought I heard noises in the basement. Huh, thinking about it now, the noise was probably in my head. But when I got downstairs, I saw a partially burned football jersey on the floor," he said, his voice thin, raspy, a ghost of its former thunderous self. "It looked like somebody had tried to start a fire, but apparently it had gone out. That's what gave me the idea, I guess. Then, I came back upstairs, struck a match, and set it on something, I don't even remember what. The fire caught and spread so quickly, I sobered up. It was no longer like a dream. I knew what was happening was real. Naturally, my instinct was to save my family. Suddenly, I didn't want to die. I didn't want my family to die. And as soon as the fire began raging, I got your mother to safety first. Then I got you and Kendall. By that time, it was too dangerous to go back in the house. I didn't mean to kill your uncle, Skylar, I swear, you've got to believe me..."

Skylar absorbed the revelation, emotions vacillating between exuberance and pity. He wanted to say something, anything, but the words wouldn't come. He wondered, fleetingly, if the shock which had overcome him was registered on his face.

"I didn't understand the burned jersey at first, or who had done it, but, instinctively, I knew. I interpreted it as jealousy of your brother. Then once we moved in with Grandma Whyte, and you started having nightmares, I was sure. One night, I overheard you say something incriminating in your sleep. I didn't mean to allow you to suffer all these years ... I just couldn't face what I had done. Who would've believed me? Your Uncle Aubrey wasn't a bad man. But I was so jealous of him, Skylar ... I mean, you looked up to him like he was your father, not me. It was a taste of my own medicine, the way I treated you all these years, I know that now, but I couldn't swallow it. He had more influence over you than I..."

Overwhelmed, Daddy started crying. It was the first time Skylar had ever seen his father weep. He too, began crying. The two men sat together, sniffling, blowing their noses into Kleenexes.

"Could you ever forgive me, Skylar? ... not just for the fire but for everything? If you can't find it in your heart ... I'll understand."

Skylar kissed his father on the forehead. They embraced for the first time in Skylar's memory.

■

Skylar went to bed earlier than usual. It had been a couple of days since his last hospital visit which had since become a comforting, healing obsession. He slept peacefully. The mystery had finally been unraveled. For years he had failed to understand what had happened. He had started the fire in the basement. When the house caught, the fire raged at the opposite end, the basement untouched, except for smoke damage. He still bore the blame, carrying it with him throughout his life. He assumed, in his ten-year-old mind, that the fire, somehow, had rerouted itself. His memory of it at the time, of the specific events, the precise details, was vague, fuzzy, most of it blocked out.

Turning over on his side, he became peculiarly aware of a presence. He knew Kendall wasn't home; he hadn't seen him in days. He was startled by the translucent configuration, a sort of hazy, filtery outline against the darkness. Daddy smiled at him. He was not the emaciated, decaying man lying in Columbia Presbyterian. He was youthful, virile, every hair on his head neatly combed and shiny. He said nothing. Just watched Skylar, grinning childishly. The vague outlines of the apparition began fading. It happened in all of five seconds. One moment he was there, the next, gone.

When Skylar awoke the next morning, it was the first thing to pop into his thoughts. Usually his first thoughts of the day involved Evan. He wondered if it had been a dream, a portent, if he'd actually seen what he thought he saw. Lying pensively in bed a few moments longer than usual before he showered, he turned it over in his mind, perplexed. His thoughts were interrupted by the ringing telephone. He started to let it ring. It was barely six o'clock in the morning, hardly daylight. Instead, he picked it up.

"Skylar, honey, it's Mama. Did I wake you?"

"No, Mama. I have to get up anyway. What's up?"

"It's your father..."

"Your husband has a smile on his face," the mortician explained to Althea. "I'll do whatever I can, using my knowledge and skill, my years of experience. But since the rigor mortis set in before the body arrived, I'll have to manipulate the muscles, so I'm making no promises."

"Promise me this," Althea said. "You'll leave the smile as it is. You can dress him, shave him, and comb his hair as you wish, but don't tamper with the smile. I don't care what anybody thinks."

Skylar is recalling his final conversation with Daddy, wishing he were alive.

He walks up the aisle in the slow procession behind the coffin and its pallbearers as they file outside toward the idling hearse. Parishioners stare at him recognizing him, despite the dark glasses. Through puffy eyes, he spots, among the black faces, a flicker of something white, something blond. Evan stands in the middle of the pew, pushing past the people in his way, excusing himself. Evan reaches out his hands. Skylar embraces him, tears rolling down his cheeks.

At the graveside, everyone is gone except the immediate family. Strong October winds rush through the flapping trees, scarlet and gold leaves dancing, skipping, hopping, forming a sweeping trail, blowing down the hillside. The sun is bright, blaring. Geometrically lined white tombstones cast shadows to the west. Birds fly from branch to branch, chirping to one another from neighboring trees. The four of them stand: Kendall, Althea, Skylar, Evan, staring reverently into the oblong hole. They join hands for a long while, the chain broken when Althea slowly bends over and picks a rosebud from a floral blanket. She inhales the fragrance, nods her head, indicating she's ready to leave. In single file, they move toward the waiting limousine. Sitting on the fender, the chauffeur stubs out a cigarette beneath his heel. He smiles, tips his cap, and opens the doors as the family approaches.

 kylar: The Son

MY HAPPIEST MEMORY OF Daddy is the trip we made to Coney Island.

After the funeral, I'm sitting in my old bedroom at my parents' house, staring at the Coney Island pennant on the wall, and then I remember. I'm not sure which summer it was, but I think it was right before I entered the sixth grade. But what I do remember—

"Skylar!" Mama calls from downstairs, sitting at the kitchen table with Evan, and Kendall, drinking coffee.

"Yes, Mama?"

"Coffee's ready!"

"Okay, I'll be right down!"

I stand, walk into the hallway, start down the first step when I get the urge to slide down the bannister, the way Kendall and I used to do as kids. I raise my pant legs a bit, climb on it like a horse, the smooth wood feeling like an old friend, and slide down to the bottom of the stairs...

...into Daddy's arms, as he waited to catch me at the bottom of the staircase. After I slid, Kendall came down right behind me.

Only moments before, we had been fast asleep. It could have been no later than five-thirty, six o'clock in the morning. It was still dark outside. Then we heard Daddy stomping down the foyer, passing the bathroom, throwing open first Kendall's bedroom door, then mine, shouting "Rise and shine! Last one in the Atlantic Ocean is a rotten egg!"

Little did we know, Mama had been downstairs about an hour already, making bologna, liverwurst, salami, and ham-and-cheese sandwiches, with Wonder Bread, Miracle Whip, and lettuce, just the way we liked them. Night before, after we'd gone to bed, she had fried chicken, baked an upside-down cake, a peach cobbler, and boiled potatoes and eggs for potato salad. After Kendall and I brushed our teeth, washed up, and put on our clothes, we slid down the bannister into Daddy's arms, and rushed into the living room where blankets lay folded, and a beverage cooler sat on top of picnic baskets.

"How are my two favorite boys this morning?" Daddy said.

"Great!" Kendall and I said, both wary. I couldn't help wondering what had put Daddy in such a mood, but neither was I asking. I wanted to enjoy it for as long as it lasted.

"You boys hungry?" Mama said. "Come on and eat these cornflakes before they get soggy."

"Where are we going, Mama?" Kendall said, wiping sleep from his eyes. Even though we usually got up early to watch cartoons, it had never been this early.

"Baby," Mama said, "we're going to Coney Island."

"We are?! Oh, boy, can I ride the bumper cars?" Kendall said.

"I want to go on the Cyclone," I said, knowing I was scared to death of that roller coaster, but I said it anyway. "Am I big enough, Mama? Can I?"

"Y'all can do all that, and more," Mama said. "But eat your breakfast first."

"And I'm going to take you on the Wonder Wheel, my dear," Daddy said to Mama, kissing her on the cheek.

"Not in this life, you ain't," Mama said.

"Why not?" Daddy said.

"That's just too high up for words," Mama said.

By the time Daddy's smoke gray Buick was leaving Manhattan, and we were speeding across the suspension bridge that hummed, Daddy had started singing "Does Your Chewing Gum Lose Its Flavor on the Bedpost Overnight?," a silly, but popular song they used to play on the radio.

"Come on!" Daddy said. "Join in! You know the words!"

And there we were laughing, singing, smiling, and driving, as if we did it every day of our lives. People in neighboring cars in the lanes on either side of us thought we were either crazy, or just a happy family who always sang in the car. As I sang, consciously freezing the moment in time, preserving it in my mind, I wondered how far this was going, if someone would pinch me and wake me from this dream.

"What do you call this bridge?" I asked Daddy, my chin resting on the edge of the front seat, looking in the rearview mirror as it reflected Daddy's eyes.

"This is the Brooklyn Bridge, Skylar," Daddy said. "It was built in 1884, I believe, and the engineer's name was Roebling, a German, who died before the bridge was completed. Isn't that something?"

"Yes," I said, though the additional information was of little interest to me.

The drive seemed to take forever. But then, there it was, the unmistakable landmark of Coney Island: the infamous parachute jump. Even when I was a kid, it had already been closed down for several years, because of accidents, I was told. We walked along the boardwalk, carrying our blankets, the beverage cooler, and picnic baskets, Mama in her pastel-colored, low-cut summer print dress, sunglasses, and sandals, toenails painted cherry red, her hair blowing in the wind, looking like a movie star, Kendall and I in matching shorts, t-shirts, and sneakers without socks, and Daddy with his big straw hat, his shirt unbuttoned, blue Bermuda shorts, sandals and socks, blankets in one arm, the cooler in the other, a cigarette dangling from the corner of his lips. We found a place on the beach, sat down, and Kendall and I started blowing up the multicolored beach ball, the surrounding bathers staring at us, probably because we were the only Negro family on the beach — and, I thought, we were pretty to look at.

After Kendall and I changed into our swimming trunks, Daddy picked us up, one son locked in each arm, and charged the breaking waves, which nearly scared me to death. He held us suspended, as what looked to me like tidal waves rose and rushed us with a roar, Daddy dipping us just enough to get us wet. Kendall and I screamed and giggled. One at a time, he placed us on his shoulders and walked around in the ocean.

After we tired of the water, and had eaten lunch, we strolled around the amusement park, begging Mama and Daddy for cotton candy, and begging them to play the game of breaking dishes in Hell's Kitchen, and to go on every ride we saw, and to munch on Nathan's crinkle-cut french fries and Sabrett hot dogs, and wear the feathered hats that read, "Coney Island," in silver-and-gold sparkles. Before we knew it, darkness had fallen, the entire park was lit, and we were headed back home to Harlem from Brooklyn, Daddy humming some song I'd never heard, Kendall and I falling asleep in the backseat, Mama covering us with blankets.

When we got home, exhausted, spent, but satisfied, Kendall and I headed directly up the stairs to our bedrooms without being told, we were so worn out...

■

"Skylar, what are you doing in there?" Mama yells from the kitchen, having heard me hit the floor.

"Nothing, Mama," I reply.

"Didn't sound like nothing," she says to me, then whispers to Evan, "He's still nine years old."

"I was just sliding down the bannister," I say, picking myself up from the floor. I walk into the kitchen and sit at the table beside Evan. He looks so handsome, so stunning in his suit. I've never seen him in a suit and tie before. I'm pleased he attended my father's funeral, especially since I hadn't asked him. I hadn't even talked to him.

Evan's right. He says I'm angry, and I can't argue with that. But racism makes me angry. Homophobia makes me angry. Bigotry and sexism and sheer stupidity make me angry.

The world I live in is so full of unjustified, arbitrary hatred, it's making me paranoid. When I walk down any street in America, I usually assume that most white people I see — the construction worker, the commuter businessman, the secretary in stockings and Adidas, carrying her shoes in a handbag — are either racist, homophobic, or both, unless proven otherwise. It's something I'm not proud of, but I must be honest. I've had enough racist and homophobic things happen to me, it's difficult not to think it.

And I'm not looking for a racist under every bed. I know there are genuinely good, upstanding white people who don't have a racist or homophobic bone in their bodies. But when I consider places like Chicago, Boston, Bensonhurst, Howard Beach, I'm reminded of what I already know: blacks bear the brunt of everyone's contempt. Racists should come back in another life, if there is such a thing, and embody that which they are prejudiced against. White racists should come back for second lives as black people and homophobes come back as gay people. If it's true that we live several lives to perfect our experience and the human condition, that would be a foolproof way of eradicating bigotry. I even meet people who will tell you racism no longer exists. I invite them to walk through America in my black skin.

Sure, there are black racists, as well. But I believe there are three brands of racism: aggressive, like Skinheads, neo-Nazis, and the KKK; passive, like most people who subconsciously buy into the racist mentality without questioning it; and reactionary, which describes most black racists. Blacks as a people have never impressed me as being aggressively racist. Their hatred is bred of stimuli, and this is the response. I'm not making excuses, I'm only trying to put it in perspective, so that people will stop dealing with the symptom, and examine the disease. Blacks did not invent American racism as much as they are victims of it.

The gay community only minimally represents me. Some of the most bigoted people I've met are gay. While the gay liberation and pride movement has its important function in society, it's the result of millions of white, male, often blond and blue-eyed people who never before had to deal with bigotry, feeling appalled that they could be denied a civil right — or denied anything in this country.

Blacks taught this country how to protest. After Martin Luther King marched on Washington for civil rights, every other group, women, gays, Vietnam veterans, and pro-abortionists, followed suit. Now it's standard procedure. Like most black gay men, I stand on the periphery of the gay community, something Evan can't understand. I don't see myself represented in Gay Pride Week, during the parades, in the bars, in the press, and if I could get a film role for every white man who's not into black men or Latino men or Asian men...

"Why?" I asked a friend of mine.

"Because there are cultural differences to overcome—"

"What?" I couldn't believe my ears.

"Yes, it's true. I just feel I have more in common with white men who've had the same experiences I've had."

"I can't believe people still think that way," I said, outraged without showing it.

"Also, lots of black guys aren't circumcised, and I don't like uncircumcised men—"

"I agree, there are some. But most black men are circumcised, don't you think?"

"Not from what I see."

"You're not looking."

"Well, anyway, that's why I don't date black guys."

"Why don't you just say it?"

"Say what?"

"C'mon, you're just making excuses. At least be honest. You don't find black guys attractive—"

"That's not true. I think you are."

"But you wouldn't fuck me, would you?"

I'm also bored with the promiscuity that's synonymous with the gay lifestyle. Why don't we promote and encourage monogamous, long-term relationships? No emphasis is ever placed on that. I know boys will be boys, but that gets old after a while. It's enough to make you want to be a lesbian, to be among a subculture that does value commitment.

I got so much shit all my life from black males — and females — who just don't accept homosexuals as a reality of the black community.

"That's a white thing," someone once told me.

Sitting in the kitchen with Evan, Mama, and Kendall, I'm wishing Daddy were here with us. Yet I'm grateful to be with the three most important people in my life, three people I love deeply. What will Mama's life be like now? It's hard to imagine her without Daddy, so it will be interesting to watch what she does with her remaining years. Whatever she does, I hope it includes George.

"I'm going to join a rehab," Kendall says suddenly, sitting at the table, peering into his lap, as if he's ashamed of what he's just said.

"You are?" I say.

"That's wonderful," Mama says. "Why all of a sudden?"

"It's not that sudden," Kendall says. "I've been thinking about it but ... after ODing last week, I made up my mind. I was left for dead. Those guys I was with could've killed me and ... I don't know, I guess it just scared me. I don't want to die. I want to live—"

"Oh, Kendall," Mama says, wrapping her arms around him, kissing him on the forehead and both cheeks and the lips. "Thank the Lord. If there's anything I can do—"

"Me, too," I say.

Over the years, I've often been asked the same question when people realize I have a brother.

"So, Skylar, what does your brother do?" they say, smiling, expecting me to say he's an attorney, a doctor, a college professor, or all three. There was a time, admittedly, when I was ashamed of my brother. Then I realized that what he is has nothing to do with me; it's totally on him.

"He's a drug addict," I reply, to which they are either appalled and embarrassed, or they laugh, assuming I am being flip.

Upstairs in my bedroom, Evan and I are lying across my bed, which is so small, I can't believe I actually slept in this thing. My head is in Evan's lap, and he strokes my hair and face, tracing my lips with his finger, an arm folded behind his head.

"What are you thinking about?" Evan asks me.

"Nothing," I say. "What are you thinking about?"

"Us."

"Actually, I was, too." I pause, hoping he'll continue, but he doesn't. "Do you think we can get back together?"

"You want me to be honest?"

"Of course."

"No ... I don't ... think so."

"I don't, either, I guess ... but you never know."

"That's right. Anything's possible. I'd like to."

"So would I. But we'll see."

"Skylar?"

"Hmmm?"

"Can I spend the weekend with you?"

"Yes, Evan. I'd like that."

"Good. After we've spent some more time with your mom, could we leave in a couple of hours or so, so we can be alone? That okay?"

"No," I say, getting up from the bed, smoothing out my hair and the wrinkles in my clothes. "Let's leave right now."

Second Wind

SOMEONE'S KNOCKING on the door.

Skylar wakes up, glances at the clock, which reads eleven-thirty in the morning, then at the empty space beside him, remembering Evan got up early to run errands. The knocking persists. He stumbles out of bed, pulls pajamas over his naked body, and puts on a bathrobe, tying the belt around his waist.

"I'm coming!"

He opens the door. An attractive, well-dressed black woman about his age, stands in the vestibule with an adolescent boy, who stands nearly as tall as she.

"Can I help you?" Skylar says.

"Yes," the woman says. "We're sorry to wake you."

"That's okay. I was getting up anyway."

"We're looking for Evan Cabot," she says. "Does he live here?"

"Well," Skylar says, hedging, unsure of what to say, who this woman is, and what she wants with Evan. "No, he doesn't live here anymore. But ... he'll be here later on this afternoon. Can I give him a message?"

"Would you give him this?" she says. She digs into her handbag and produces a card which she places in Skylar's hand. Marla K. Watson, Attorney-at-Law, the card says. "We're old friends from way back. From California, actually. Pardon my manners. I'm Marla, and this is my son, Khalil." Skylar shakes hands with them.

"Pleased to meet you both. I'm Skylar."

Skylar thinks the child looks familiar. Skylar has seen his face somewhere before. But how? When? Where? Under what circumstances?

"I'm the woman who's been calling," she says.

"Oh, yes," Skylar says, recognizing the voice.

"Sorry I sounded so mysterious, not leaving a message, or anything."

"That's okay. Won't you come in?"

"No, we really should be going. But could you tell Evan there's someone who's been wanting to meet him. And ... we don't want anything from him."

"Sure, I'll tell him..."

It hits Skylar! The boy's cherubic, caramel face is framed by thick, curly blondish hair which cascades into brassy locks over his forehead. The face is unmistakable. He's what Evan must have looked like at that age, down to the cleft chin.

"Bye now," Marla says, holding Khalil's hand, walking down the hall toward the elevator. "By the way, I love your movies!" she says.

"Thanks!" Skylar says, closing the door.

He can't believe what he's just seen. Why hasn't Evan ever told him? How could he keep something like that from Skylar all these years? Pangs of jealousy shoot through Skylar. He's never thought about Evan's past life, his past lovers, men or women, naively assuming that he has been Evan's one-and-only relationship, ever. That beautiful mulatto boy who just stood in his doorway should be his and Evan's.

"I want to be closer to my parents," Evan says, lying in bed with Skylar later that night, massaging Skylar's shoulders.

"Where'd that come from?" Skylar asks.

"You've inspired me to do that ... before, you know, one of them dies."

"Have I?" Skylar says. "How?"

"The relationship you have with your mom — I don't know, I just don't get along well with my parents and ... I'd like to change some of—"

"I thought you said you were close to your mother?"

"I lied."

"I see. No wonder you never call her."

"I'd also like you to meet them."

"Even though we're not living together anymore—"

"Doesn't matter. I lived with you for several years. I want them to meet the special, significant other, you know, who was in my life—"

"Was?"

"Well, you know."

"Not really."

"What do you mean?"

Skylar sits up, leans against the bedpost, and looks Evan in the eyes. He pulls out the business card and hands it to Evan.

"What?!" Evan says. "Where'd you get this?"

"She stopped by today—"

"Really?"

"Why didn't you tell me?"

"About what? Her? What's to tell?"

"Why didn't you tell me you have a son?"

"A son? Get out of here, Skylar. You're bullshitting me—"

"No, I'm not. Why didn't you tell me?"

"Because I didn't know, myself. Did she tell you that?"

"She didn't have to. The boy was with her and he looks like your twin."

"Oh shit!" Evan says. "I'd better call her. Was she mad?"

"No. She even said she doesn't want anything from you. She just said someone wants to meet you."

There is a lingering silence.

"How does that make you feel, Skylar?"

"Well ... it was weird ... at first. Then I felt ... jealous, I suppose. What do you want me to say?"

"I can't believe this. After all these years and she never told me."

∎

In Skylar's dream, Mama sits on a checkered blanket in the deserted Coney Island sand. Her hair blows in the salty wind, the edges of her summer print dress flapping in the sea breeze. Beside the picnic basket is a transistor radio. WABC's Cousin Brucie is gabbing like a drumroll, spinning Bobby Darrin's "Mack the Knife."

Kendall and Daddy, in bathing trunks, play a netless volleyball. Jauntily, Daddy skips over to the blanket, sand kicking up at his heels. Bending down, he steals a bite from Mama's Blimpie while her head is turned. She catches him in the act, chases him around the blanket, grabs him by the trunks. They fall, tumbling in a locked embrace, the two of them laughing deliriously. The tumbling stops, Daddy on top of her, kissing her passionately. She allows him, then pushes him away, panting, out of breath.

"Howard, the children...," she says, shaking sand out of her hair. Kendall laughs, pointing at Mama and Daddy, kicking the beach ball.

Suddenly, Skylar is watching his family from high up on the parachute jump. Looming in the distance is the Cyclone roller coaster. The ferris wheel, stationary except for the empty cars swinging and creaking in the wind, is below him, next to the boardwalk and an empty, immobile, soundless merry-go-round. They have Coney Island all to themselves.

"Jump!" Daddy yells to Skylar, his hands cupped around his mouth. "I'll catch you!"

Skylar is terrified. A flock of seagulls and pigeons light on his feet, cooing wildly. Rushing, crashing waves of the Atlantic Ocean fill his ears, receding with bubbly white foam, the rumbling of the waves making the parachute jump creak and sway. His nostrils inhale the misty sea air. Summer winds blow, his tongue licking the salt in the atmosphere.

"Jump, Skylar!" Daddy yells again.

Mama waves at Skylar, shading the sun from her eyes with her hand, her toes dug into the sand. A gust of wind catches and carries him. He sails downward, without a parachute, his body dropping down ... down ... down ... down ... into Daddy's cradled arms. They cheer; Mama jumps up to applaud, Kendall rushes to him, and wraps his arms around Skylar. Daddy smiles at him, rocking him, Skylar's head pressed against his hairy chest.

"See," Daddy says. "I broke the fall. I wouldn't let anything hurt you. Let's try it again!"

He and Daddy go up and hold hands on the parachute jump platform. Mama stands below, ready to catch them. Daddy taps Skylar on the shoulder.

"Son, do you want to fly away instead?"

Skylar nods. "But what about Mama and Kendall? Can they fly away with us, too?"

Mama and Kendall appear on the platform.

"Everybody hold hands!" Daddy says. "Don't let go. If you do, you'll break the spell. Ready? On the count of three. One ... two ... three!"

They sail into the air, holding hands, Skylar, Kendall, Mama, and Daddy, seagulls and pigeons screeching and cooing, flapping their wings at the take-off. Over the beachfront, they glide, balanced by the wind, over the ocean, into the misty yonder...